THE STONES OF SILENCE

COCHRANE'S COMPANY, BOOK ONE

PETER GRANT

SEDGEFIELD PRESS

This book is dedicated
to my friend and fellow author,
LARRY CORREIA,
who encouraged me to get started
on my own writing career,
and supported my fledgling efforts
with enthusiasm. Thanks, buddy!

CONTENTS

1

INTRUDERS

MYCENAE SYSTEM

"There it is!" The console operator's voice was hushed as she bent over her radar screen.

"Bearing? Range?" the skipper demanded.

"Bearing 020:005, range fifty thousand." She frowned. "They're idjits t' leave 'spensive hardware swanning around out here wi'out protection. They're 'bout to lose a small fortune!"

The older man shrugged as he adjusted the controls to aim directly at their target. "A fortune for us, p'rhaps, but pocket change to them. Besides, they can't afford to spend too much on local security yet. Until they get title to this system, free an' clear, it might be money down the drain; so, they're takin' a chance wi'out it. That's about to bite 'em in the ass, but if it was us, we might take that chance, too. I dessay they figure it's worth th' risk t' get a head start."

"We're gonna take their head start away from them," the console operator retorted. "They might've gotten away with it 'gainst low-tech smugglers or pirates, but not 'gainst fleet-grade hardware like ours."

"Watch out with that military talk, even in here! Remember, as far as anyone else knows, we're *s'posed* to be just pirates 'r smugglers. If word gets out who we really are, they'll hear it on Rousay sooner or later, an' then there'll be hell to pay."

She snorted. "It's only you and I in here, Chief! Who else is gonna hear a word we say?"

"Dammit, May, use y'r blasted head! If you watch your mouth all the time, you don't have to worry 'bout whether it's safe to talk. If Security heard you, they'd pound all over you – and on me, too, f'r lettin' you babble! What if they snuck a recorder in here, t' listen for that kind o' loose talk?"

She frowned, then sighed. "I s'pose you're right. Sorry, boss. I guess we'd better run our own security scan, to catch any recorders 'fore we dock with the ship."

"You got that right!" The man fumed silently for a moment, then added, "Tell the boys to suit up. Let's grab us a satellite."

He directed the cargo shuttle into position alongside the satellite, hanging in geostationary orbit over the virgin planet below. Four spacers emerged from the shuttle's open doors, clinging to the handholds of a maintenance sled as it sped across the few hundred meters separating the shuttle from its new neighbor. Their expert hands and tools made short work of the connections holding the solar power arrays to the satellite. One by one, the external components were towed across to the shuttle and into its cavernous cargo bay, where they were secured.

When the pilot was satisfied, he directed the shuttle in a series of slow, carefully judged maneuvers toward the denuded satellite. Her massive cargo doors gaped even wider as she enfolded it, seeming almost to suck it into her maw like a giant shark eating a smaller fish, whole and entire. The spacers used the cargo bay's tractor and pressor beams to position it over a set of cradles, then tied it down with nets of plasfiber webbing. At last one of them reported over the radio, "She's secure, boss."

"Good work. Everything and everyone inside?"

"Yes, boss."

"*Dumbass!* What about the maintenance sled?"

"*Aw, shit!*" Chagrin was audible in the junior NCO's voice. "Sorry, boss. Hold on – we'll get it."

The Chief Petty Officer pilot watched as the spacers used a tractor beam to snare the drifting sled, pulling it inside the cargo doors and securing it. "Everyone back into the crew quarters," he warned. "Soon as you're in, I'll close the cargo doors, then we'll go hunt the other two birds." A series of muttered acknowledgments from his crew answered him.

As the cargo shuttle moved away, passing around the equator of the planet toward the second of the constellation of three survey satellites, the cessation of signals from the first satellite alerted a monitoring station on the planet's biggest moon that something had gone awry. It powered up additional sensors around the moon's equator. They recorded the emissions from the cargo shuttle's gravitic drive as it scooped up the other two satellites in the array, then tracked it back to the larger ship from which it had come. Other signals sped from the monitoring station to sensors on the moons of two other planets, hundreds of millions of kilometers away. They were sent over laser tight-beam channels, that could not be detected or intercepted except in a direct line between the transmitting and receiving stations. The distant sensors were already monitoring the binary star system in general. Now they, too, began paying closer attention to developments around the fourth planet from the major star.

That accomplished, the carefully camouflaged monitoring station adjusted another tight-beam dish, aiming it at a communications satellite beyond the system boundary, over a billion kilometers from the star around which it orbited. It sent an update, and kept the channel open. There would be more signals soon.

THE CARGO SHUTTLE reversed slowly into the docking bay of its mother ship, pulled gently by tractor beams, nudged hither and yon by pressor beams, lining up precisely with the rails of its assigned airlock. The rails slid into their waiting tracks and locked down, then a concertina airlock extended from the ship's hull and mated with the collar around the shuttle's crew compartment hatch. A light above it flickered from red to green, indicating that pressures had been equalized and the airlock was now safe to use.

Chief Petty Officer Lawson shut down the cargo shuttle's systems, then followed his crew into the docking bay foyer. He dismissed them to their quarters with a word of thanks, then hurried up the high-speed walkway in the center of the main passage, heading for the Operations Center. He drew himself to attention before the Command console.

"We got 'em all, sir. No problems."

Commander Lamprey looked up alertly. "There were just the three satellites? No others keeping a sneaky eye on things?"

"Not in orbit 'round this planet, sir, or any o' its moons. We took a real careful look with our radar. I dunno 'bout the other planets in the system, o' course."

"Of course, but I don't expect to find any there. Surveillance satellites are very expensive. I doubt NOE could afford to spend that kind of money up front, with no guarantee of a return." He thought for a moment. "Very well, Chief. Carry on."

"Aye aye, sir."

As the senior NCO turned on his heel and left the OpCen, Lamprey turned to his Executive Officer. "What d'ye think, Aidan?"

Lieutenant-Commander Macaskill shrugged. "I agree with you, sir. I don't see how NOE could afford to plant surveillance satellites elsewhere. Another thing, sir. We crept into this system under silent running, taking weeks for the transit, so they wouldn't detect our arrival; but if they've got nothing apart from the three satellites we've just captured, they won't notice our departure."

"You're right." Lamprey rose to his feet. "Tell the Navigator to plot a direct course for home, and get us to the system boundary at maximum cruise. No sense in hanging around. Let's get our loot back to base, where the experts can look at it."

"Aye aye, sir."

THE MONITORING STATION recorded the gravitic drive signature of the larger ship as it turned and headed for the system boundary, accelerating at a rate no merchant freighter could match. It listened as the other sensors reported in from their distant locations, and merged their input to arrive at the ship's precise course and speed. It sent regular updates to the far distant communications satellite as the visiting vessel sped away, culminating in the unmistakable gravitic emission signature of a hyper-jump as soon as it had crossed the system boundary.

The artificial intelligence system running the monitoring station consulted the timetable it had downloaded when it was installed. The next visit from its owners should take place within two weeks. It prepared a full report on what it had observed, and uploaded it; then it put itself and the sensors around the system into standby mode, awaiting further instructions.

The sensors and robotic vehicles on the planet below, whether flying or crawling, continued with their assigned missions. They could no longer pass the data they gathered to the orbiting satellites, but they could store months of it in their own memory circuits. Sooner or later, someone would be along to milk them of all that they'd learned.

CALLANISH

Three weeks later, a string of curses blighted the atmosphere in a conference room on a planet many light-years distant. The four listeners seated around the table winced as the speaker gave vent to his frustrations.

"Is it possible Commander Lamprey's technicians were mistaken?" one of them inquired in a carefully neutral voice.

"No, dammit! That's the first thing I had Maconachie check. There's no doubt about it. The satellites' memory storage banks were scrubbed clean every day, by design, after sending all their data to a monitoring station somewhere nearby, probably on one of Mycenae Primus Four's moons. Next time we visit there, we'll have to look for it – but I've no doubt it'll be well concealed. Those bastards at NOE have some good people advising them."

"So, we still don't know what, if anything, they've found on Primus Four?" another asked.

"No, we don't. That's where they've concentrated their initial survey, so there must be something worthwhile there, but what it is, we don't know – yet."

"And the other sites in the system?" a third listener queried.

"None of them have orbiting satellites to collect data, so we reckon they're lower priority than Primus Four."

A long silence fell, as the group considered their options.

"Is it worth sending *Colomb* back to look for the monitoring station?" the first questioner asked at last.

"She's leaving for Goheung next week. She'll spend six months in the orbital dockyard there while they upgrade her systems, revamp her workshops and install new gear. She'll be the next best thing to a brand-new ship by the time she gets back."

"It'll take NOE that long to build and deploy new satellites, so we can send her to snatch them when she gets back," another observed. "Still, that might be risky if they suspect what we're up to."

The group's leader looked at him angrily. "Not once in a generation does an opportunity like this come along. I'm willing to chance NOE's anger if we can skim off the cream before they find out what we're doing. With that in our bank account, we'll have the last laugh!"

"But... what if they upgrade their system security before we can do that?"

"*With what?* It'll cost them billions to do it properly, and they don't have that much yet. They haven't raised enough from investors. Rousay's government won't let them use its warships to secure Mycenae – they don't have enough of them. We're delaying their application for exclusive rights every way we can, but they've got the gelt to grease the right palms at the United Planets. Sooner or later, they'll get it, and that'll bring in more investors. With their money, NOE will sew up the Mycenae system tighter than a rat's arsehole; but before then, we'll have located the richest deposits – with their help, the stupid fools! – and grabbed as much as we can. We'll be gone before they can afford proper system security."

"And if they find out what we're up to?"

"Then we'll spit in their eye and dare them to do something about it! Our government will back us. They're already having wet dreams at the thought of all the tax revenue they'll milk us for, and they know Rousay won't go to war for NOE. That's why they allowed us to use *Colomb* last time, and they'll let us use her again, if need be, when she gets back. As a warship, even an auxiliary, she carries more clout than just another merchant freighter. She can browbeat any civilian security setup, if she has to – and that's all NOE can possibly afford out there for at least the next year or two."

"So, we aren't going to send one of our freighters to look for that monitoring station?"

"No. Let's wait until NOE's installed new satellites, then we can snatch them and the monitoring station at the same time. I want to cost them as much money as we possibly can. If we can bankrupt the bastards, so much the better!" The speaker suddenly looked more cheerful. "In fact, we'll sell the first three satellites at Medusa, or another planet that won't ask too many questions. Survey birds are very expensive. Even at stolen-goods prices, we should get enough for them to buy a couple of fast freighters. We'll need them to carry what we're going to steal from Mycenae under NOE's nose, as soon as their own surveys show us where to send our thieves!"

For the first time since the meeting began, his audience laughed.

2

DILEMMA

ROUSAY

Cochrane took advantage of the elevator ride to straighten his uniform jacket, tug the sleeves of his shirt out through its cuffs to just the right length, and make sure his mirror-polished shoes had not been scuffed during the security check. He was ready and waiting by the time the elevator reached the top floor. He walked to the security desk.

"I'm Captain Andrew Cochrane. I have an appointment with Mr. Marwick at eleven."

The security officer checked his log. "You're listed, sir. I'll have Dando escort you to his suite."

Dando proved to be a younger guard, looking rather like one of the many recruits Cochrane had helped shape and form into spacers over the years. He scurried down the corridor ahead of him, looking back over his shoulder to make sure the Captain was keeping pace, and led him into the open door of a spacious corner suite.

"Captain Cochrane to see Mr. Marwick," he announced officiously.

"Very well. Return to your duties."

The secretary's response was haughty and unfeeling, Cochrane noted, as the young man nodded jerkily and backed out. She was doubtless a First Families descendant, just like her boss, although surely the offspring of a rather lower-ranking ancestor than his. She didn't bother to look up at the visitor, but kept on with her work, making it clear without words that she was his social superior, despite his senior rank and her nominally lower position.

"Take a seat, Captain. Mr. Marwick is slightly delayed. He'll be along shortly."

He didn't thank her. She wouldn't have cared whether he did or not, anyway. He sat down silently in a corner, from where he could observe all those passing in the corridor outside through the open suite door.

The sound of voices heralded the appearance of a small group from the elevator foyer. The secretary looked up from her desk, suddenly alert, and stood. The visitor took his cue from her, also coming to his feet as three men and two women entered the anteroom.

"Good afternoon, Mr. Marwick," she said, pasting a bright smile onto her face.

"Hello, Marti," the oldest man said, his voice a low, weary growl. He glanced at the man in the corner. "Captain Cochrane?" He didn't offer his hand as he ran his eyes over the tall, ascetic-looking visitor.

"Yes, Mr. Marwick."

"Our previous meeting ran over time." He shook his head, obviously irritated. "Those of us in business may say that 'time is money', but as far as Ministers of State are concerned, it's not *their* money, so they don't feel any pressing need to be punctual." He indicated the woman standing next to him. "This is Marissa Stone, another member of our Board of Directors. She'll be joining us this morning."

"Ms. Stone," the Captain acknowledged with a nod.

The older man turned to the others in his group. "Very well. You all know what to do. Keep me informed."

"Yes, Mr. Marwick." "Yes, sir." "I will, sir." A chorus of muttered responses came from them as they turned and left the room.

"Join us, Captain." Marwick gestured to the door of his office. "Marti, coffee for three." He didn't ask whether Cochrane wanted any, or something else, but that was no surprise to the visitor.

He followed both directors into Marwick's inner sanctum. It was luxuriously carpeted and furnished, with a large, ornate desk made of what looked like real wood, beautifully grained, lustrously gleaming. The desk alone would be worth enough to buy a decent-sized mansion. Four original oil paintings of Earth's Orkney Islands hung on the walls. A quick mental estimate suggested that the combined value of everything in this room would be sufficient to put down a deposit on a brand-new interstellar freighter. The place positively reeked of money. Cochrane smiled to himself. *That's good,* he thought, *because I intend a lot of it to come my way, if this works out.*

A robotic serving cart rolled through the door behind them, clearly summoned by the secretary. It served coffee at the round conference table in the corner, then whisked out again as they sat down.

As soon as the door had closed, Marwick began. "Your report was very comprehensive, Captain, but your conclusions and recommendations raised more than a few eyebrows."

"I'm sure they did," Cochrane replied with a slight smile, trying to project an aura of self-assuredness. These people would have little respect for him in terms of their social structure. He had to jolt them into realizing that he was, in fact, essential to them. His report had been the first step.

"Mine were among them," Marissa Stone added. "You do

realize you're talking about a response that, if a planet did it, would amount to an act of war?"

"Yes, Ms. Stone. Since you've already been the victims of such an act, you have two options. One is to roll over and accept it, thereby guaranteeing that more will follow. The other is to administer a short, sharp lesson, to demonstrate to those behind it that they went too far. You need to draw a line. If they cross it again, they must be made to understand they'll have to pay a price for it – one they may not be able to afford."

"Yes, but we've only paid a price in monetary terms. You're talking about making them pay in blood, if necessary." Her voice was sharp, almost querulous.

"Blood and money, Ms. Stone. Both are the realities of this sort of situation. I presume you've never had to deal with that before?"

She shook her head. "I went to Neue Helvetica for my graduate studies, then came home to work my way up through the ranks of the New Hebrides Corporation. I've traveled to more than a dozen planets, but only on business."

"In that time, how many competitors did you 'defeat' in business terms, costing them money or even driving them out of business?"

"I suppose it must have been scores of them, although only a few closed their doors. We've taken over several competitors." She preened slightly. "It was one of those 'defeats', as you call it – I suppose a 'victory' from my perspective – that led to my being appointed a Director of the New Orkney Enterprise."

"Then I don't need to tell you what 'cut-throat competition' means, Ms. Stone. However, in the non-corporate world, 'cut-throat' can be literal as well as figurative. That's what whoever stole your satellites is trying to do to you. They want to make it too expensive for you to continue surveying the Mycenae system. They know you can't commit unlimited resources without the guarantee of a return on your investment. You won't have that unless and until the United Planets recognizes Rousay's claim to colonize the system. If they stop you surveying until then, assuming it happens –"

"It'll happen," Marwick grunted. "It may take a couple of years, thanks to interference from competitors who are mounting fake counter-claims, but it'll happen. Count on it."

Cochrane knew Marwick's assurance must mean that a lot of money was changing hands under the table, to make sure things went according to plan. He nodded. "Very well, sir. *When* that happens, you'll still have to complete all the surveying you were trying to do ahead of time. The cumulative delay means it'll take you three to five years from now to even begin earning a return on your investment. Given the size of that investment, and your need to sell debentures to finance it, you're going to be out of pocket by anywhere from ten to twenty billion Neue Helvetica francs by the time you see any income at all from Mycenae. By the way, if I may ask, why did you denominate this project in francs, instead of Rousay kronor?"

The woman shrugged. "It's as you said. We'll need to raise hundreds of billions through debentures over the life of the project. Investors understand Neue Helvetica francs. It's one of the three currencies most frequently used in interstellar trade, along with Bismarck Cluster marks and Lancastrian Commonwealth credits. The kronor's a minor currency compared to them."

"Do you think you'll be able to raise that much, ma'am?"

"We expect to spend up to a trillion francs to fully develop this project over the next two decades or so. On the other hand, we expect to take out of Mycenae anywhere between ten and twenty trillion francs over the same period. With that sort of return, yes, we believe we'll attract more than enough investors."

"But you'll have to produce good initial returns, to persuade them to invest more."

"Precisely."

"And you won't earn those returns for several years, if your surveying is long delayed."

"You have it in a nutshell, Captain," Marwick acknowledged. "We have to deal with these intruders, whoever they are, before we do anything else. We were reluctant to commit a large sum of money to security at this stage, but your report has convinced us that we have to do *something,* or risk losing everything."

Cochrane paused for a moment, searching for the right words. These people had to be impressed with how serious the threat really was. At last he said, "Mr. Marwick, I don't think you've fully understood the implications of my report. Your security risks are only just beginning. Even if you deal with your immediate problem, sums like those you've just mentioned so casually are going to have every low-life, smuggler, pirate and criminal in the galaxy frothing at the mouth. You've got to be willing to be hard, tough and ruthless, right from the start.

"The instant such people think they might be able to get away with something, they'll be after you with foot, horse and artillery, to use an ancient military expression from Earth. Just one successful raid, on just one of your precious metal shipments, will set up a pirate ship's crew for life. If just one smuggler manages to skim off even one-tenth of one percent of your mineral shipments, he'll be able to retire in luxury after just a few years. He'll inspire dozens, maybe even hundreds, of others to follow his example. You can't just deal with the present problem, then sit back and relax. You've got to push security *hard,* from now until the end of the project. If you don't, then, as you said, you're going to lose it all."

Marissa shook her head. "I don't see how we can possibly set up a system-wide security force for Mycenae at this stage. We won't earn enough revenues to pay for that for some years yet."

"Not necessarily at once, ma'am; but your business opponents, and half the low-lifes in the galaxy, are already planning to take Mycenae away from you. If you aren't already working to stop them, they're going to succeed. You'll be late to the game, and you'll never catch up."

She glanced at Marwick. "Alasdair?"

The senior director nodded heavily. "I fear he's right. So, Captain, what do we need to do right now, and what will it cost us?" His tone had changed now. It was no longer one of the elite of Rousay talking to a flunky far his junior. It was now a businessman talking to a subordinate who had an important contribution to make; still somewhat superior, but also attentive.

"You're the experts in how to run an interplanetary business, Mr. Marwick. I won't try to tell you how to do that. My expertise is in space warfare, securing a star system against intrusion, and dealing with pirates and smugglers."

Marissa nodded. "You made an enviable name for yourself for all three things in the Benbecula system. In fact, I understand that it was your efficiency, plus your refusal to allow a senior Government minister to get away with his crimes, that led to the end of your military career there."

Cochrane inclined his head. His voice was cold as ice. "I should point out that I had a personal stake in the matter. One of the Minister's minions seduced my wife, leading to her divorcing me. In the process, I uncovered what the Minister was up to – massive graft, smuggling, interference in shipping markets, the lot. He and several of his people are now serving extended sentences at a prison mining project in the Uist system."

His audience winced visibly. Cochrane had done the socially unforgivable. He had ensured that *their* sort, descendants of the New Orkney Cluster's Founding Families, were now no better than slave laborers in an asteroid mining project, without benefit of most of the safety precautions and systems that were common in commercial ventures. It was dangerous work, often fatally so.

"Unfortunately," Cochrane continued, "a number of other Ministers felt... uncomfortable... that a senior officer had refused to recognize what they regarded as the perks and privileges of their station in life. That led to pressure on my superiors to get rid of me. I saved them the trouble by resigning my commission."

Marwick stirred uncomfortably. "Yes... well..." He cleared his throat. "You've done well since then, as a free-lance consultant in the New Orkney Cluster on space security issues. That's how you came to our attention, when you broke up that interplanetary smuggling gang in Cubbie. That was good work."

By which you mean, I stopped criminals robbing people like you of their rightful rake-off, Cochrane thought with cynical amusement; but he was careful to keep his voice unemotional and impassive. "Thank you. It was also bloody work, I'm afraid. They were making a lot of money, smuggling drugs in and transuranics out. They didn't give up without a fight."

"You hired your own security team to deal with them, didn't you?"

"Yes. The local authorities didn't want to disrupt their relationship with asteroid mining and orbital worker trades unions, which would have happened had their own security forces done the job. By bringing in an outside team to take down all the suspects at once, then get out under an apparent cloud of official disfavor, we were able to end the problem, while persuading the unions that the politicians had really been on their side all along." He mentally added, *Got to keep the plebs in their place, you know. Carrot and stick, and all that sort of thing.*

"That's what we heard," Marissa commented. "Their Prime Minister speaks very highly of you, in private, of course."

Cochrane hid a smile. The fact that he'd uncovered the Prime Minister's family's involvement in the problem, and agreed to cover it up again in exchange for a *very* handsome off-the-record, tax-free cash bonus on his project fee, was neither here nor there. A man had to be realistic, after all – but these two didn't need to know that.

"There are several things you need to do right now," he began. "Most of them are outside my purview, such as internal security, personnel screening, and so on. They need immediate attention, too, but not from me. What I can offer you is space security, in planetary orbit, in the asteroid belt, and, in due course, conveying high-value output from Mycenae to its destination. Those are my specialties. Ultimately, you'll need to establish your own system defense force to protect Mycenae from intrusion. It'll have to be a big one, because Mycenae's a binary star system with over twenty planets and two asteroid belts. There are plenty of places for criminals to hide, and to establish bases from which they can mount their operations. You'll need a dozen heavy patrol craft to do that, or eight corvettes, plus a full supporting infrastructure."

"But forces like that cost tens of billions to establish and operate," Marwick objected. "We can't afford that until Mycenae is generating enough profit to support it."

"Then you need a cheaper alternative; a private security service, funded with seed money but largely supporting itself at the expense of your enemies, until your project is earning enough to justify a more conventional solution."

The silence around the table was palpable. At last Marissa said slowly, "You're talking about funding security for Mycenae out of what you capture from those raiding us, aren't you?"

"That, and their other assets, yes, Ms. Stone. Those assets may not be in the Mycenae system at all, but I'm sure they'll be... accessible... to someone willing to do what it takes to go after them."

"But isn't that committing a crime, to prevent a crime being committed? Stealing from others, to stop them stealing from us?"

"What laws apply in Mycenae, ma'am? Who would define it as a crime there? The system has no government, no laws, and no courts."

"What about disposing of what you take?" Marwick asked. "Selling stolen property is a crime everywhere."

"Yes, sir, but who defines 'stolen'? If it comes from an uninhabited system that's not yet under anyone's jurisdiction, and

thus has no legal system, is taking such property technically
'theft' at all? If we need to deal with criminals on their own planets, that may involve acts that would be classified as crimes there,
but Rousay need take no official notice. Its writ doesn't run
outside this system. None of the laws governing the New Orkney
Enterprise would have been broken.

"That leads me to another very important point, sir. You, as
Directors, are legally responsible – and liable – for every decision
the New Orkney Enterprise takes, and everything it does. You
need to be able to plausibly deny any knowledge of any illegal
activity of any nature whatsoever. If it ever comes to a trial, you'll
be deposed under a truth-tester, by court order if necessary. Right
from the start, you need to insulate yourselves from whatever
needs to be done to establish and maintain security in the
Mycenae system. You don't need – you don't *want* – to know
whether it's legal or illegal. That goes double for the period
before Rousay is awarded colony rights there by the United Planets. Given that separation, you can't be found guilty of anything
that may happen there."

There was a long silence. Both Directors were clearly
thinking hard, and Marissa Stone was looking at him in a way
that Cochrane recognized. Clearly, his hard-boiled approach and
reputation as a killer were attracting more than just her business
interest.

At last she said, "If the Board hires you to take care of our
initial security needs in the Mycenae system, it'll have to issue
clear and specific policy directives as to what's expected of you."

"Yes, Ms. Stone, but they'll have to be very carefully worded.
You'll set out your requirements, of course, but in such a way that
you tell me *what* to do – not *how* to do it. That's the critical thing.
You can include verbiage about 'using all legal and legitimate
means', or words to that effect, to cover yourselves: but the laws
governing that are those of Rousay. They won't apply in Mycenae
unless and until this planet is awarded colonial power status

there. Even after that, until someone is appointed with the authority to enforce Rousay's laws in that system, they'll be moot."

"Which will give you several years to take care of business in your own fashion," Marwick observed dryly.

"Yes, sir. What's more, you'll need to authorize me to fund our operations from, shall we say, the 'exploitation of resources recovered' in the Mycenae system. That's sufficiently vague and non-committal that you can deny anything incriminating, but it still gives me a semblance of legal cover."

"Very well. So far, this has all been theoretical. I accept that we'll eventually need to fund a proper system defense force, plus its operating expenses, but the longer we can avoid that, the better. What do we need to spend right now? Give me a number."

Cochrane paused for a moment to gather his thoughts. "You've just lost three hundred and thirty million francs worth of satellites, right, sir?"

"Yes. That's what their replacements are going to cost us, at any rate."

"If you enter into a security contract with me, sir, please don't finalize the order until I've told you what additional features I'll need built into them. I'll also need to make several expensive purchases up front, including weapons systems, for which I'll need end user certificates. Are you familiar with them?"

"No. I've never been involved in arms purchases."

"It's a diplomatic document, provided by the purchasing planet to the planet of manufacture. It certifies that the weapons will be used on or by that planet, and not by anyone else. There are some planets that will sell military hardware to anyone for cash, and not ask awkward questions about possibly forged documentation, but they don't necessarily make everything I'll need. If you can arrange for Rousay to provide a couple of dozen blank end user certificates, that'll make things much simpler. They'll state that my security company is licensed to operate armed vessels; therefore, Rousay certifies any weapons it purchases – leave the details and the supplier blank – will be used for approved purposes under the supervision of its government." He smiled wryly. "That supervision had better be theoretical rather than practical, for our purposes, of course, sir."

"Of course. I daresay we can arrange that."

"Good. That being the case, here's what I'll need."

Beneath the table, Cochrane crossed the fingers of his left hand. This was make-or-break time. If he succeeded in persuading these hard-nosed business people, he had a real chance to forge a future he'd long been pondering for himself and his closest colleagues. If not...

"I'll set up a shell company to provide a commercial cover for this operation. I'll need two hundred and fifty million francs up front, in cash, in its bank account on Neue Helvetica," he began. He ignored the hiss of indrawn breath from his listeners as he went on, "That's to prevent anything being traced back to you, in the event of the wrong sort of questions being asked. You can describe it on your books as an 'investment', rather than security expenses, to be secured by a lien against any assets the company buys for use in its duties. If the shell company repays the money – plus, say, ten percent interest per calendar year or part thereof – the lien on its assets is terminated, they are indemnified from any claim by NOE, and its relationship with NOE becomes merely that of a security contractor. That gives you an easy way out if something goes wrong. I can always borrow the buyout money from you, if necessary. It's not as if you won't be getting it straight back!" The two directors laughed.

"The money will be my capital budget," he went on, "to purchase weapons and systems. I'll need a further one hundred million francs every year to fund our operations – salaries, supplies, spare parts, maintenance, and so on. The first year's money will have to be made available immediately, along with the two hundred and fifty million in the capital budget.

"Over and above that, I'll need the medium-term loan of three spaceships. Two will be freighters, each a quarter of a million to half a million gross register tons' capacity. They should be ordinary, unremarkable ships, the kind you'll find anywhere in the galaxy. You can take them from your own commercial fleet, or dry-lease them from companies elsewhere. They'll carry supplies, serve as depot ships in the Mycenae system in due course, and do anything and everything else I need. At least one, preferably both, should have personnel pods in a couple of holds to expand their accommodation facilities. I'll also need a fast courier vessel. We'll draw up formal lease agreements for all three ships, to provide arms-length deniability. I'll provide crews for them, and pay their routine operating expenses. They've got to be in good condition with reliable, trustworthy systems, not worn-out old barges. You'll get the ships back in two to three years.

"I'll also need to borrow some big-budget equipment from the armed forces of your member planets for the same period; for example, cutters and cargo shuttles, and a comprehensive ship-board hospital pod. I presume you can apply pressure through politicians to make that happen?" Silent nods from his listeners. They weren't even objecting to the sudden absence of 'sir' or 'ma'am' from his side – a very positive sign.

"I'll need six months to get everything in place, but it'll take you that long to order new satellites and have them built. Thereafter, I'll patrol Mycenae and try to prevent any further attacks on them. I should be able to stop anything except a ship with military-grade systems. If one of those turns up, it'll mean someone's willing to risk an all-out war with you. That'll require a military-grade response, which I won't be able to provide on so small a budget. If that happens, it'll be up to you to decide how to handle it. I'll also stop smugglers and pirates from setting up bases in or near your operations, to make your lives hell when you begin to exploit the system. I'll use anything I capture from them – the 'resources recovered' that I mentioned earlier – to fund my ongoing operations. If I capture enough, you won't have to pay my annual operating budget.

"I suggest you contract with me for five years. Termination may only be for non-performance – I need that security if I'm to buy high-cost items like armed vessels, and offer stable employment to good people. If, after five years, I've been able to secure Mycenae to your satisfaction, we can extend the contract. If not, you can form your own System Patrol Service at that point."

Another long silence.

Marissa said thoughtfully, "You're effectively asking us to pay to replace our satellites twice over, up front, but with the expectation that we won't have to do so again."

"Yes, unless you face a military opponent, which I won't be able to handle." *At least, not at first,* he thought to himself, but he was careful not to say so aloud.

"And the alternative to hiring you on those terms, is to spend twenty to thirty times as much, right now, to buy, equip, staff and deploy our own system security force," Marwick observed.

"Yes, sir."

Marwick glanced at the woman beside him. "I know the Board won't be happy, particularly at the lack of control over how Captain Cochrane spends the money; but I don't think any more cost-effective solution is on the horizon."

Marissa shrugged. "Control's all well and good, but as the Captain's pointed out, there's a lot to be said for plausible deniability, too. Besides, his reputation precedes him. If we can trust anyone not to cut and run with the money, I daresay it's him." She licked her lips as she looked at him, almost like a predator spotting a tasty meal.

"I promise you, that's the last thing on my mind," Cochrane assured her. "If the underworld hears that someone's on the run with that kind of money, they'll all be looking for him. Also, if I did steal your money, I'm sure you'd offer a rich reward for its recovery. Either way, my life expectancy would be short, interesting and painful.

"There are two final points. The first is information. I need to know where your enemies are likely to concentrate their efforts; in other words, which places will be most profitable for them to look. Therefore, I need to know what you've found so far in Mycenae." He saw his listeners' faces stiffen, and added, "You don't have to tell me in detail, of course; I'm not in the mining business. However, others are, and they'll know what to look for. If I can be there waiting for them when they do, I can swat them down before they get started. Otherwise, I'll have to hunt for them through trillions of cubic kilometers of deserted space. It'll be like looking for the proverbial needle in a haystack. It'll take a lot longer, and probably be much less successful."

The two directors relaxed. "That makes sense, I suppose," Marwick agreed. "And your second point?"

"You've got to give me *carte blanche* in the way I operate. That's got to be explicitly agreed. Your instructions need to be worded generally, not specifically. There can be no interference, no second-guessing, no nagging, no observers on board my ships to make sure I'm following company procedures. You're asking me to provide steak-and-potatoes security on a bread-and-cheese budget. I can do that, but only by using methods that are, shall we say, far removed from normal corporate operations. They certainly won't be politically correct, and they may be legally dubious at best. That's why you're hiring me to do them for you, without attribution, rather than doing it yourselves. I'll take the heat, but you've got to stay out of the kitchen, if I can put it like that.

"Consider, for example, what I had to do in Cubbie. A lot of people died there – more than were arrested, in fact. I daresay I'll have to kill some in Mycenae before we're through, because that kind of money attracts criminals like honey attracts flies. That's why I'll need to operate at arm's length from the New Orkney Enterprise. It's as much for your sake as it is for mine."

Marissa Stone's eyes were wide as she looked at him. *Is she getting turned on by that?* he wondered. *She wouldn't be the first person to find the prospect of violent death sexually exciting. I should play up to that. It may get her on my side, and keep her there. I could use a friend at court, so to speak... but I mustn't let it get out of hand. If I give in to her, I'll be just another man to be used, then discarded. I've got to walk a fine line here.*

Marwick rose from the table. "Very well, Captain. Your initial report certainly impressed the Board. We'll convey to them, informally, what we've just discussed. I think you can expect to hear something within a week to ten days."

Cochrane and Marissa stood as well. "Thank you, Mr. Marwick," he replied politely. "You know how to reach me."

"I'd like to ask you some more questions, Captain," Marissa put in. "If you'll come with me, we can leave Mr. Marwick to get on with his work."

"I'm at your disposal, ma'am."

She licked her lips again. "Thank you. This way, please."

She led him down the corridor to her office, smaller than Marwick's, but almost as luxuriously furnished. She closed the door behind them, and walked over to the window, looking out over the city far below.

"So you've had experience of dealing with criminals... the hard way?" she said musingly.

"I have," he agreed, stepping up to the window beside her, standing deliberately close to her. She didn't object. "You might say that hardness is a way of life with me."

"And how did you... deal with them, Captain?" Her breath was coming a little faster, he noted with satisfaction. *Oh, you're turned on, all right. I just have to play the part for you, and you'll be eating out of my hand.*

"There are many ways," he said softly, a purr of mingled satisfaction and menace in his tone. "I've always found that a thrust in the right place, at the right time, can be very effective."

"A... a thrust?" She gazed at him, the pupils of her eyes widening into dark pools.

"Yes." He reached slowly into his jacket and took out a black, deadly-looking polymer spear-pointed dagger. "I've used this to... penetrate... many defenses. I've used other things, too."

Her eyes locked on the short, perfectly proportioned blade. He slid a finger up and down it, and her lips parted, tongue protruding slightly in awestruck fascination... then he returned it to its sheath inside his jacket. Her shoulders slumped slightly as she exhaled, a long, slow sigh.

He kept his voice steady, unruffled. "Now, Ms. Stone, what did you want to discuss?"

3
_____

THE TEAM

ROUSAY

Cochrane looked up from his cup of coffee as a knock
sounded at the door. He began to rise, but Murray beat
him to it. "I'll get it, sir."

"Thanks, Jock."

They watched as the tall Scot opened the door. A petite brunette
woman stepped through it, looking to be in her mid-forties, her
body clearly well-muscled under civilian work clothes. She seemed
a little out of place in the plush setting of a mid-ranked hotel conference room, and the more formal attire of those waiting inside.

"Sorry I'm late, boss," she said cheerfully as she took a satchel
from over her shoulder and dropped it in a corner. It clanked
loudly.

"I see you're still carrying half the Engineering Department
around with you," Cochrane observed with a smile.

"Och, it's just a few things that might be needful here and
there." She headed for the sideboard, where a coffee machine
burbled gently to itself. The remains of two trays of breakfast

sandwiches and pastries showed that the others had already helped themselves. She followed their example with gusto, loading a plate with two sandwiches and two pastries before bringing it and a mug of black coffee to the table to join them.

"Still dieting, too, I see," the other woman at the table said with a cheeky wink.

"Och, Doctor, you know a girl's got to look after her figure. What would my muscles do without fuel to stop them wasting away?" The others laughed again.

Cochrane waited until she'd seated herself, then said, "All right. We're all here now. For the benefit of those of you who don't know everybody, let me make brief introductions. Our new arrival is Sue McBride. She was the best Warrant Officer Engineer I ever served with. She got out at the same time I did. She's now running her own maintenance business for local asteroid miners."

Sue grinned through a mouthful of food, spraying a few crumbs as she said, "The independents want someone reliable and low-cost to keep their prospecting boats running, because they don't have a big company paying the bills for them. I can keep my prices low because most of them pay in cash, or a bit of gold or platinum they've sneaked off the refinery ship. The taxman never gets to hear about that, of course. Keeps my overheads down." More quiet chuckles.

Cochrane added, "She's also just completed an engineering degree, so she's got the smarts to back up her very extensive practical experience. Next, most of you know Dr. Elizabeth Masters. She spent eight years as a Fleet Surgeon before returning to private practice. It seems she misses the fun and games of those years."

"Nice to have you with us, Doc," a tall, burly, red-bearded man said. His facial hair contrasted incongruously with his clean-shaven and highly polished pate.

"I couldn't resist seeing your beard again, Dave," she retorted, to further amusement.

Cochrane smiled too. "Commander Dave Cousins skippered two vessels under my overall command, a patrol craft and a depot ship. He's a specialist in combat systems and tactics. He left the service two years ago." He looked at the next person. "Lieutenant-Commander Caitlin Ross is an intelligence officer. Most of you have never met her, or even heard of her, but I've had occasion to work with her. She's good. She'll leave active service at the end of this month. Next to her is Senior Chief Petty Officer Tom Argyll. He was the Chief of the Ship in my last command, and left the service last year. He's probably the best senior NCO I've ever served with."

"You're just sayin' that to flatter me, sir," Argyll said with a wink.

"Of course," Cochrane said gravely. They grinned at each other. "Next to the Senior Chief is one of only two civilians among us, Lachlan McLachlan. He's a shipping specialist in his family's cargo line. He probably knows more about freight and freighter availability and movements, shipyards, and ships for sale, than anyone within a hundred light years from here. He may not be military, but he's trustworthy. I've seen him demonstrate that on more than one occasion.

"Next is Jock Murray. He's an electronics specialist. He rose to Warrant Officer in the Fleet before striking out on his own in the asteroid mining business. He now runs his own contracting firm, providing prospectors and mining boats to the bigger companies, and doing a lot of electronics maintenance that costs too much for them to do in-house. There's not many who know circuits and chips at his level. I swear he can design and diagnose them in his sleep."

Murray grinned. "Not quite, sir, but I do my best."

"Last but not least, we have Henry Martin. Henry's a criminal."

There was a rustle of surprise around the table as the others looked at him. "I hasten to add, he's not your average crook. He never touches drugs, prostitution, slavery or any of the nastier vices out there. He's strictly into theft, particularly high-value shipments and well-protected cargoes. He and I butted heads a few times, and honors are about even between us. I came to respect him as a principled man in his own way, strange though that may sound. He helped me clean up Cubbie, because some of what the bad boys there were doing stuck in his craw. I've invited him here today because we're going to need someone with his skills, and I can offer him an opportunity to 'go straight' with a nice fat nest-egg."

"I thought you were mad when you approached me," Martin admitted, "but you convinced me to hear you out. If I like the rest of what I hear today, we'll see what we can do working together, instead of against each other."

"With your beauty and my brains, we'll go far," Cochrane solemnly promised him. The others laughed aloud.

"All right, with the introductions over, let me tell you why I invited all of you here this morning. I know you've all been looking, in your own way, for a chance to grab the brass ring; an opportunity to make enough money to get the hell out of the New Orkney Cluster, and make new lives in a more promising part of the galaxy. We've all had enough of the First Families. They allow us to be moderately successful, but if we get too big for our boots, they move in and cut us down to size." Growls of angry agreement came from the others.

"The brass ring may have come along, if we all work together to make it happen. I took a consulting job for the New Orkney Enterprise. Based on what I learned, I made them an offer, and they've accepted it." He described the agreement he'd worked out with NOE. "A lawyer's already setting up a front company on Neue Helvetica, and the money's on its way there too – three hundred and fifty million of that planet's francs, or just over a billion Rousay kronor." There was a swift intake of breath as his listeners absorbed the number.

"If you agree to join me, those of us around this table will be the core leadership team, and in due time the board of directors, for Eufala Corporation – that's the name of our company. Each of us will either run one or more areas of our day-to-day operations, or be our lead specialist in their field. You'll also help me find the people, equipment and systems we'll need to do our job. If you prefer to look at it in military terms, I'll be the admiral, and you'll be my staff officers."

Cousins raised his hand. "What does 'Eufala' mean, sir? I don't know the word."

Cochrane grinned. "I don't either, really." Everyone chuckled. "I came across it in a book I read last year. It was the name of some minor town in a country-within-a-country called Florida, back on Earth, way back when. The writer set a murder mystery there. I've no idea if the town was real or not. The name stuck in my mind, so I decided to use it.

"Anyway, back to business. If we get this right, we can make enough money to set ourselves up as a security company in another system, one so well equipped and so experienced that minor planets and alliances will fall over themselves to hire us. Mercenary companies for planetary operations are all over the place, but there are very few offering space operations, because of the difficulty and cost of buying and operating warships. We're going to finance them by grabbing all we can out of Mycenae, as quickly as we can."

"But that means we'll all be thieves, not just Henry here," Dr. Masters objected.

"Technically, no, we won't. Remember what I said about the terms of my agreement with NOE? They've specifically authorized me to keep and use anything I seize from intruders in the Mycenae system. They've even worded it in such a way that I can arguably take resources from the system for my own use. They didn't intend that, of course, but if it comes to a court case, I think my interpretation of that clause will stand up."

"Not if it's a New Orkney Cluster court," Cousins pointed out gloomily. "They don't care about what the law or the contract says – only what the First Families want."

"True. That's why my contract specifies that any legal dispute will be subject to arbitration or legal action under Neue Helvetica law, in a court on that planet."

"That was damned crafty of you! And they signed it without havering?"

"They did. It gives us a lot of room for maneuver. I'm hoping we'll get enough out of Mycenae to buy the warships we'll need to become a credible space security operation. I'd like us to end up as well-equipped and powerful as the system defense force of a middle-grade planet, if not better."

A rustle of astonishment ran around the table. "But, sir... you're talking about tens of billions of kronor to do that," Cousins pointed out. "Warships aren't cheap. What's more, if we're to secure the Mycenae system against intruders from day one, we don't have any warships of our own. How the devil are we going to operate without them?"

"I have some ideas about that, but I won't share them in this gathering. One of our cardinal principles, at least at first, is going to be compartmentalization. Each of you will only know what you need to handle your own areas of expertise and operations. The rest will be kept out of the loop. You all know the old saying: 'Three can keep a secret, if two of them are dead'?" A murmur of agreement ran around the table. "We've got to be hyper-vigilant about security. Among her other responsibilities, Lieutenant-Commander Ross will be supervising that aspect of our operations. That includes truth-testing everybody who works for Eufala, including ourselves. There will be no exceptions."

"Well, sir, if you reckon you know how to get us what we need at such short notice, I won't quibble. You've proved many times before that you know what you're doing." Cousins sat back.

"Thank you. Now, let's get to the point. I need each of you to commit yourselves to work for me, full-time, harder than you've ever done before. For the next few years, we'll all be overloaded, running at full speed just to keep up with everything on our plates. I'll pay you all good salaries during that time. In due course, after at least five years but not more than ten, you'll have a choice. You can carry on as a Director of our new security operation, with a guaranteed profit share. If you don't want that, or if things don't work out, you'll have a minimum of five million francs, payable anywhere in the settled galaxy, in any currency you wish. I'll set that up within the next month, using an escrow account with a lawyer on Neue Helvetica. Even if our operation folds up, or anything happens to me, all of you will get your money at the end of five years, no matter what. Note that five million is a minimum figure. It might be several times higher than that, if all goes well.

"To earn it, you'll have to do anything and everything I tell you. That will include some things that are against the law in this system, and perhaps in other systems as well. I don't feel any qualms of conscience about that, because they'll be directed against the powers that be in the New Orkney Cluster, particularly the First Families. We've all been screwed over by them, one way or another, often enough that we need feel no loyalty to them. We're going to make them help us to get out from under their thumbs, and set ourselves up in a better part of the galaxy.

"Before we go any further, I need you to commit yourselves. If you back out now, the only condition is that you don't say a word about what we've discussed this morning. I believe I can trust all of you to do that. If my trust is misplaced, and one of you talks out of turn, you should understand there'll be... consequences. Bad ones. That's just the way it is. If you agree to join me, then from now on, you're committed. You'll see this through to the end. There won't be any early quitting clause. It'll be root, hog or die. What do you say?"

Sue McBride spoke up at once, a cheerful grin on her face. "Count me in, boss. You've proved yourself before. If I can ride your coattails to a fortune, I'm in!"

"You won't be riding anybody's coattails. You'll be working your ass off!" Cochrane assured her.

"I'm in, too," Henry Martin said quietly. "There are too many hard men moving in to the criminal scene here, bringing too many drugs, too much of the worst of the worst. If you try to stand against them, they'll kill you. I need a way out. I'll help you."

"I'm in." Commander Cousins' voice was emphatic. "I'm not part of the First Families. I saw several of their young sprogs, with service records shorter and poorer than mine, and lower performance ratings, promoted over my head, just because of their surnames. That's why I quit the service. I reckon I'll do a lot better with you, sir."

"I think you will."

One by one, the others signified their assent. The last to speak was Dr. Masters. She hesitated. "Why did you invite me, sir? I'm just a doctor. I don't have any expertise in operating spaceships or setting up security systems."

"No, you don't, but you're a damn fine doctor and emergency surgeon. I expect we'll face opposition from time to time – smugglers, pirates, perhaps even others who want to do what we'll be doing. Someone's already stolen three of NOE's satellites, remember, and I'm pretty sure they'll be back for more. I want us to have a fully-fledged emergency hospital in the system, properly equipped, stocked and staffed. All of us will sleep easier knowing it's there, particularly those who have families depending on them. I think your role will be essential." A loud chorus of agreement rumbled around the table.

"All right, sir. I can bring in a locum for my practice within a month. I'll try to sell it, but that'll be difficult if I'm not there to supervise it."

"If necessary, Eufala will buy your practice from you at market rates, then re-sell it through a broker. I don't mind if we take a small loss on that. I think you're the best fit for what we need, medically speaking, and I'm willing to pay to get you."

She smiled. "All right, sir. I'm in."

"Good! Thank you all very much. As of right now, you're each on a salary of ten thousand francs per month. It'll be paid in Neue Helvetica, in accounts you'll set up with a bank there. I'll leave you to make your own arrangements as to how much you want to bring here every month or quarter, depending on your local needs."

There was silence for a moment as everyone converted the amount into kronor. Cochrane knew it was substantially higher than any of them were earning at present. Satisfied smiles dawned on most faces.

He rose and went to the sideboard, taking out a tray with a bottle and nine glasses on it. "I think we deserve a drink. I happen to know most of you enjoy a good port, as I do, so I brought along a bottle to toast our future together."

They watched as Cochrane uncorked the bottle and carefully filled the nine glasses half-full. The heady smell of the thick, aromatic wine set more than one pair of nostrils twitching with pleasure. He handed the glasses around the table, then took up his own.

"The first Marquess of Montrose, James Graham, back in the seventeenth century in Scotland on Earth, had a favorite toast. It went like this:

He either fears his fate too much,
Or his deserts are small,
Who dares not put it to the touch
To win or lose it all.

"I think that's a pretty fair summation of what we're all going to do over the next few years. We're going to put it all 'to the touch'. We'll either triumph, and make a new future for ourselves, or find ourselves on the trash heap of the galaxy, because the First Families won't forgive us." He raised his glass. "To win or lose it all!"

"To win or lose it all!" they chorused in response, and drained their glasses.

Cochrane put down his glass. "I'll meet with each of you individually this afternoon, to outline what I want you to do, and where and how to get started. After that, I expect each of you to take the ball and run with it on your own. Work as hard, as fast and as smart as you can, because each of us will be depending on all the others to bring their part. There's no room for passengers or deadweight.

"Now, let's look at the plan in broad outline."

4

FIRST STEPS

ROUSAY

"That doesn't look like it's worth *thirty* kronor, let alone thirty million!"

Sue McBride winced. "Sir, you don't understand. These robotic prospectors often look this beat-up – on the outside, anyway. They spend their working lives in near-absolute-zero temperatures, a total vacuum, and close to zero gravity, fergawdsakes! They've got propulsion units to move around on the surface, anchors, laser drills, core samplers, spectrometers, gravitometers, a pretty advanced assay module, and a bunch of other stuff. Without them, you just couldn't mine asteroids at all."

Cochrane shrugged. "If you say so. You know a whole lot more about it than I do. How do you use these things?"

"You start with a remote survey from your mining boat. If an asteroid shows enough signs of being interesting, you deploy one or two of these to it, then go off to look for another. Over the next few weeks, this will hop around the surface, drill holes, analyze the mineral content, and figure out whether the asteroid's worth your time, based on what you've told it you're looking for. As soon as it's done, it activates its beacon to tell you to come pick it up. You do that, then look at its results. If they're good, you mark that asteroid to be hauled off to the refinery ship. With luck and careful selection, you might get something good one asteroid in five, maybe one in ten. Without that... maybe one in a hundred, or, if you're real unlucky, one in a thousand."

"I see. Well, at thirty million kronor apiece, we simply don't have the money to buy our own – at least, not yet."

"You're going to have to, real soon, boss. To make an asteroid mission worthwhile, you need up to a hundred of these things, in much better shape than this one, plus three or four prospectors with their own boats – and they're upwards of two hundred million kronor apiece, fully equipped. Alternatively, you can buy more expensive prospector bots, with artificial intelligence systems to guide them, and their own miniature gravitic drives to move between asteroids under their own power. They're about twice the price of this one."

He nodded ruefully. "You didn't mention the cost of a mother ship, with her crew, plus the prospectors's salaries and profit share. That, or the more expensive bots, will probably bump everything to a mission cost of about five billion kronor, or one and a half billion Neue Helvetica francs. That's out of the question for us right now."

"But, boss... if it's out of the question, how do you plan to raise the money we need?"

"I think there's a way. Forgive me if I don't go into details. I'm going to have to work very carefully to prepare the ground."

"OK, boss. I trust you."

Cochrane studied the robot for a moment, then said softly, "You know... those bloody great stones have been swimming in space, in as near to absolute zero temperatures as makes no difference, with no air, no life... nothing at all. Silence and darkness is all they've ever known for millennia. Suddenly, out of nowhere, this bipedal race comes along and dumps one of these things on them. If they pass muster, they're hauled off to be reduced to dust and rubble, then put through a raging inferno to separate the ore from the rock. Their silence is gone forever. For the asteroids around them, that don't pass muster, it's back to more millennia of silence. It's a strange thought."

Sue said slowly, reflectively, "The stones of silence. That's almost poetic, boss. I like it."

"I have these odd moments of whimsy sometimes." Cochrane heaved a sigh. "How's your planning for our engineering setup?"

"I've got the basic outlines in place. I'll need to know more about what ships we'll be using before I can finalize them, and start buying equipment to install in our depot ship. A lot of gear is tailored to the sort of vessels it'll be used on."

"Very well. Carry on with that. I may have some good news for you soon."

∾

NEW WESTRAY

"It ain't right, dammit! It just ain't *right!*" Master Chief Petty Officer Mike Wallace shook his head angrily, and drained his tankard of beer.

Seated at the small table with him, Tom Argyll nodded sympathetically, and gestured to a waitress to bring them another round. He glanced idly around the barroom. It was noisy and smoky, a typical spacer's dive. Scantily clad waitresses squeezed between tables and chairs, slapping away prying hands, exchanging coarse remarks with the regulars.

"It never has been right, the way they treat us enlisted spacers," Tom agreed. "Rousay's System Patrol Service was the same. Damned officers made sure a lot of what we recovered from smugglers never got sent to the Prize Court at all. They siphoned off all the good stuff for themselves, then took their half share out of what was left as well."

"*Bastards!* I figured on getting at least twenty thousand out of the last seizure. I waited a year for the Prize Court to rule – and then they gave me only a lousy three thousand! *Three!*"

Tom waited for the waitress to set down their fresh tankards and load the empties onto her tray, then handed her a twenty-kronor note. "Keep the change."

Her eyes widened. He'd tipped her as much as the beers had cost. "Thanks, spacer!" She sashayed off, swaying her hips and rear suggestively at him.

"You got money to throw around, Tom." There was more than a little jealousy in the speaker's voice. "What'd you do? Rob a bank or somethin'?"

"Let's just say I'm in a line of business that pays well – real, *real* well."

"What is it? Is there room for another spacer? I reckon I've had enough of service life, an' I'd sure like to have somethin' more than my pension to live on."

Tom regarded him quizzically. "How far are you prepared to go, Mike?"

The other NCO's voice was suddenly wary. "What do you mean?"

"If you're serious about making a lot of money, you might be able to do that, right now." He reached into his pocket and handed something to Mike under the table. "Careful how you look at that. Don't flash it about."

Mike looked down, cautiously opening his hand, and sucked in his breath as he saw the flash of gold. "Wha... what *is* this?"

"It's a hundred-mark gold piece from the Bismarck Cluster. It's worth about... oh, around two thousand kronor."

"It's heavy, an' real pretty," the older man said enviously. He made to hand it back, but Tom shook his head.

"Keep it, and think about it. If you're interested, and willing to take a chance, there's four hundred and ninety-nine more of them – all with your name on them."

"That's... that's a *million kronor!* Where'd you get your hands on gelt like that?"

"That's not important right now, and it's not in my hands – at least, not here. I just work for the people with the moneybags. The thing is, are you interested?"

"Hell, yeah! What have I gotta do to earn it?"

"You'd better be serious about that, Mike." Tom's voice was deadly earnest. "Once you're committed, you're in – or else. You've got to go through with it. If you don't, you'll pay dearly – not to me, but to the people I work with. They don't play games, and they play for keeps."

"Sounds like they're a dangerous lot. What sort of trouble might this get me into?"

"You bet they're dangerous! As for trouble, if you play your cards right, I don't think you'll be suspected of anything. I won't deny there are risks, but the people I'm working for are the most professional I've ever seen. If anyone can pull this off, they can."

"Pull what off?"

"Come on, Mike. You understand security. Until you commit yourself, I'm not saying anything more. I've got to cover my own ass, too, buddy."

"Yeah, I guess you have." The older man picked up his fresh tankard of beer and half-emptied it in a single swig. "Dammit, if you can make sure I don't suffer for it, I'm in! I've got less than six months left of my final hitch. A Fleet pension ain't great. A million kronor will make my life a lot more comfortable."

"Yeah, and it's tax-free, remember. That makes it worth half as much again. If you don't declare it, and only turn one or two of those coins at a time into kronor, it'll give you a very healthy retirement. It'd better not be here on New Westray, though. If you're seen to have more money than you should, people will ask questions."

"You got that right! I know a nice resort on the coast, over on New Sanday. It's a tourist harbor, with a nice beach on one side for the ladies while their menfolk go out after the big fish. A guy I know owns a bar and a seafood restaurant there. They're nice places – much nicer than this dive. I reckon if I pay him in cash, in gold, I can buy in with him; maybe as a partner in both places, maybe buy the bar and let him run the restaurant. That'll give me something to do in my retirement. My wife likes it there, too, which is a bonus – and on another planet, it'll be light years away from awkward questions here."

"Sounds great to me. If you do that, I'll come by now and then to sample your beer."

"The first one will be on the house, every time, buddy! Now, what do I have to do?"

"Drink up. We're going to take a walk, and have a long talk where no-one can overhear us."

~

MARANO

Caitlin Ross wiped her lips delicately with her napkin, and sighed in repletion. "That may be the best *tournedos de boeuf* I've ever tasted. The truffles and paté seasoned the meat to perfection."

"Our planet may not be a major center of interplanetary cuisine, but Marano does its best to entertain our valued clients," her host assured her, ogling her openly.

She restrained a sudden impulse to slap his leering face in public. "I'm sure it weakens your customers' negotiating ability, if they're too busy digesting to think straight."

Guido Gaspari guffawed. "I fear you have seen through my nefarious plot. However, I assure you, our business will be as fulfilling to your needs as the food was to your appetite." He waved to a waiter, who cleared the table, served coffee, then left them in peace.

Ross waited until they were alone once more. "Signor Gaspari, you're going to have to sharpen your pencil. You quoted us three million per. You know very well that's far above market prices. We can get equivalent units from Medusa for one-point-eight million."

"Not at all! Their hardware is technically inferior, far behind ours. If you buy their mines, you'll never be sure whether or not they'll work."

"That's not what other customers of theirs have said. My principals have undertaken a good deal of research into available alternatives. Your products are well thought of, and admittedly a little – a *little* – more advanced than Medusa's, but no more so than those from several other planets."

"Ah... well, there is the matter of confidentiality, and lack of formalities. We can be rather more discreet than other vendors, thanks to our more relaxed approach to such things."

"Yes, but since my principals can offer a valid, verifiable end user certificate, that's not of such great importance as it might otherwise be. We value confidentiality, but we want value for our money, too."

"But your order is not very large. Only fifty nuclear space mines? Our customers usually order them in multiples of a hundred at a time."

We'd be ordering only a dozen, if we thought we could get away with it, she thought, *but no planet or serious buyer would ever order so few. We've got to make this look convincing.* "We'll do the same in future, if we're satisfied with what we get," she temporized. "This first order is in the nature of a test. My principals will employ the mines as point defense for a single installation. If they prove satisfactory after six months to a year, including testing their stealth characteristics and their ability to adopt a randomly changing pattern, to prevent potential intruders from pinpointing them, you can expect a larger order. If they don't prove satisfactory, then that order will go elsewhere."

"I see." The arms dealer's face sobered. He was all business now. "I have overheads of my own, which I must cover, but I understand the need for flexibility in a situation like this. Shall we say two-point-five million apiece for the first order? That's the best I can do for so small a quantity."

"I don't think you were listening to me, Signor Gaspari. You know what we will have to pay elsewhere."

"But you want them right away, without delay. That means I must draw them from stocks manufactured to meet other orders, which will then have to be made up in a hurry. There is naturally a premium for immediate availability."

I'm willing to bet you have no other orders, she thought cynically to herself. *You're probably getting them from Marano government stocks.* "Perhaps you have a point. Shall we say two million apiece?"

Gaspari looked despairingly up at the ceiling, as if pleading with his guardian angel to provide succor. "You are trying to ruin me! I could not possibly supply them at so low a price. Two-point-four million!"

They went back and forth and around and around for ten minutes. At last he sighed. "Very well. Two-point-two million, payable in cash. Half in advance, the balance as soon as they are loaded aboard your ship."

"Agreed. The Handelsbank of Neue Helvetica has a branch right here on the space station, to expedite transactions such as ours. I'll go there with you tomorrow morning, and have them pay you the first half of the price. After that, we'll supervise the loading of the mines. As soon as they're all aboard and my technical specialist has certified that they're in order, you and I will return to the bank, and I'll have them pay you the balance. I have the end user certificate with me, of course."

"Very well." Gaspari rose from the table, and pulled back her chair as she stood. "You are a tough negotiator. It has been interesting doing business with you. I hope and trust there will be more orders to follow."

"That depends on how well your mines perform, Signor. If they do, we shall probably see each other again."

"I shall look forward to it."

~

ROUSAY

"I wish Caitlin was here to brief you, Captain," Lachlan said with a frown. "Intelligence is her bailiwick, not mine."

"Unfortunately, I had to send her on another very important mission, so we had to rope you in. What have you got for me? Start with the theft of the satellites."

"All right. Our ship found the monitoring station where you'd suspected, on one of Four's moons. They downloaded a copy of the memory module, leaving the original intact. I ran it through Caitlin's analyzer. It shows that there are other sensors on moons around other planets, keeping an eye on the system and feeding back their information to the monitoring station. It's sending everything it gathers to a communications satellite outside the system boundary. I'm guessing NOE sends a ship now and then to download everything from the satellite. It'll tell them who's been in the system, and roughly where they've gone while they were there."

"Do we know where that satellite is?"

"Not exactly, Captain. We know its bearing from the monitoring station, but it's over a billion kilometers out. It's probably also stealthy, because we couldn't pick it up on radar."

"All right. So, the monitoring station will have reported our ship's visit?"

"Yes."

"I expected that. What about sensors in the asteroid belts?"

"There's something odd going on there, Captain. The NOE told you they don't have any sensors or satellites out there; but our ship picked up small gravitic drive signatures and other emissions from three places in Mycenae Primus' asteroid belt. It sent cutters to investigate all three. In each area, it found several dozen prospector robots. They were bigger than usual, independent units with gravitic drives, able to move from asteroid to asteroid under their own power. They appear to be targeting S-type and M-type asteroids – the kind that contain a lot of metal – and analyzing them in detail. They haven't marked many of them for recovery; just a few dozen in each area. They've deployed beacons on them, which can be activated by signal."

"Do we know the signal?"

"The ship brought some of the beacons aboard from each field, and read off their chips before putting them back in place. We know how to make them respond if we want to."

"Good. Do we know what it is about those asteroids that makes them worth marking?"

"They were all on the small side, and a quick gravitometer analysis showed them to be extremely dense. I reckon NOE is looking to raise as much money as it can, as quickly as it can, to fund its operations. If I were in their shoes, I'd be looking for asteroids rich in gold and platinum-group metals, and perhaps rare earth elements. At a guess, that's what these are."

"You make sense," Cochrane said thoughtfully. "I recall reading about one asteroid in the Mannerheim system. It was only about a thousand tons of rock and ore, but it yielded more than four tons of gold and over seven tons of platinum-group metals. Its value to the finder, after refining fees and all the rest, was almost ninety million Lancastrian Commonwealth credits."

"Sounds about right. He'll have gotten a quarter of its value as a free-lancer. The refinery would take a quarter share, the planet owning the asteroid belt would take a quarter, and the rest would go to the company that grubstaked him. That's the way most independent asteroid miners work."

"So, he lost three-quarters of its value, but still made a small fortune? I must remember that. How many asteroids had been marked with beacons, and how big were they?"

"The ship we sent located a total of ninety-seven at the time of its visit. There may be a few more by now. They're all small, five hundred to five thousand tons. That makes sense, of course; they'd be more easily maneuvered for capture. Bigger ones are probably out there, but they'll need space tugs to lay hold of them. Smaller ones can be towed in by a cutter, or loaded into a cargo shuttle; and they'll fit into a ship's holds, where a big one might not."

"I see. Will NOE's sensors have detected our ship looking around the asteroid belt?"

"I don't know, Captain, but I'll be surprised if at least some gravitic drive signature radiation wasn't picked up and logged. However, with those satellites gone, their sensors may not have been able to relay that to the monitoring station. There's another question, too. Were those robotic prospectors NOE's at all, or were they put there by some other outfit?"

"That's a very good question, particularly because NOE's data didn't mention those areas."

"That doesn't mean they weren't NOE's. They may have decided that what they'd found there was so valuable, they didn't want anyone knowing about it – not even you."

"That might be so, even though it would make our security job more difficult. All right, let me think about that. What about the ship that stole those satellites? What records did the monitoring station have of it?"

"It didn't appear on sensors until after the satellites had been loaded aboard a cargo shuttle. It must have come in without using its gravitic drive at all, from a long way outside the system, to avoid being detected."

"That's a common tactic. Go on."

"The shuttle went back to the ship and docked; then the ship activated her drive and headed straight for the system boundary at max cruise. There are two interesting things about that. First, her gravitic drive signature was disguised using a frequency modulator. I've only heard of warships, pirates or smugglers using them. Because of that, we can't read her signature well enough to identify her. Second, she reached a much higher cruise speed than the average freighter. They move at point-zero-eight to point-one Cee. She hit point two Cee on her way to the system boundary."

"A fast freighter could reach that speed and more, but she wouldn't normally be fitted with a frequency modulator. That makes the most likely suspect a military auxiliary; a depot ship, or a repair vessel, or something like it. They're big and heavy, but built to travel faster than merchant vessels of the same size, to keep up with the warships they're supporting. What was her course?"

"That's another interesting thing, Captain. It was on a direct line for Callanish."

Cochrane's eyebrows shot up. *"Callanish?* What the hell?"

"I thought that, too, but then I did some checking. Callanish's System Patrol Service operates a repair ship, called the *Colomb*. It's three hundred thousand tons or thereabouts. It was built a century ago for the Lancastrian Commonwealth Fleet. They sold it fifty-odd years ago, because it had grown too small for their needs. It's passed through several owners and planets since then. It's being refurbished and modernized right now. The hull's still in good shape, of course; after all, there's nothing in space to wear it out. They'll replace or upgrade her systems, workshops and accommodation. She has the usual auxiliary warship systems, including a more powerful gravitic drive to reach higher speeds, and an electronic warfare suite. That can be used to disguise her gravitic drive signature, which would fit what the monitoring station saw in Mycenae."

"Why does Callanish need a ship like that?"

"They use her to maintain their patrol craft – they operate a squadron of them, all old boats – plus the asteroid mining ships in their system. That's another thing, Captain. An asteroid mining consortium based in Callanish is contesting NOE's claim to Mycenae. They've lodged a formal protest at the United Planets, saying they were there first. They've offered no evidence to prove that, and it's my professional opinion that they're lying. They probably want NOE to pay them to go away. NOE isn't about to do that, of course, or they'd have more claimants coming out of the woodwork, all demanding money.

"If the Callanish people wanted to add to NOE's worries, and make a stronger case to be bought off, wouldn't it make sense for them to steal those satellites? I reckon they have enough influence with Callanish's government that they could borrow *Colomb* to do that. She's the only interstellar vessel operated by its System Patrol Service, and she's got all the engineering facilities she'd need to analyze the satellites on the way home. What's more, they could use her warship-grade sensors and systems to get a closer look at parts of the Mycenae system on her way in and out. If they wanted to locate a few spots to send their own prospectors, to skim off the cream before NOE gets its rights finalized and moves in, that would be a good way to start."

"That makes sense. It may affect our plans to do the same thing."

"That's what I thought, Captain."

"When do you think the Callanish people might send in their own prospectors?"

"I don't know. They aren't there yet – at least, when our ship visited there a few weeks ago, there were no ship gravitic drive signatures or other emissions anywhere in the system. I think they still don't know where to look. That may be one of the reasons they wanted those satellites; to learn what NOE had found, so they could steal as much as they could before NOE could exploit it. From what NOE told you, the satellites scrubbed their memory modules every day, as soon as they'd uploaded their data to the monitoring station. I'm guessing the Callanish consortium didn't learn much from them. I reckon they'll either have to mount their own survey mission, like we're doing, or plan to steal the next batch of satellites as soon as they're installed. While they're doing that, they'll probably steal the monitoring station as well, now they know it's there, and download its accumulated data. If I were in their shoes, that would be the simplest and cheapest way to do it."

"How long will *Colomb* be in refit?"

"I don't know, Captain, but I presume at least three or four more months. Even with robotic shipyard construction equipment, and new systems lined up ready to install, you can only work so fast on a complete refurbishment like that." He gave a short laugh. "As a matter of fact, it won't surprise me if the Callanish consortium is paying for her modernization. They'll be the most likely candidates to use her, after all, and I doubt the government there has enough money to pay for an expensive upgrade like that. It'll be a lot cheaper for the consortium to upgrade her than to buy a new repair ship of their own."

Cochrane nodded. "So, the new satellites will be operational just as *Colomb* returns to service. I think... no, we'll have to see how other elements of our operations work out. If they do, we might be able to... never mind."

Lachlan grinned. "Planning a nasty surprise for them, Captain?"

"Something like that."

"I look forward to it. Oh – one more thing. I heard just yesterday that the Callanish consortium has bought two brand-new fast freighters from a shipyard in Goheung. It was building them for another customer that defaulted on payment. The consortium has already paid the arrears, plus the balance owed, by selling some sort of spacecraft at Medusa – details weren't provided. They'll send passage crews to take delivery of the ships in a few months."

"What do you know about the ships?"

"They're a million gross register tons capacity, and can cruise at point two five Cee, about three times as fast as most ships their size. That means their turnaround at planetary stops can be cut in half, or even less. They can also hyper-jump three times in one day, unlike most merchant ships that are limited to twice a day, so they can cover interstellar distances that much faster."

"What sort of passage crew will Callanish send to collect a ship like that?"

"A couple of dozen spacers and engineering hands, plus four or five officers – enough to stand three watches for the delivery trip. They don't need enough to handle cargo as well."

"How will the crews get to Goheung? What's the usual routing from Callanish?"

"They'll take the weekly ferry from Callanish to New Stornoway, the main planet of the New Hebrides Cluster. From there, they'll take the monthly freight run to Durres. The ship carries a personnel pod for passengers, usually spacers or asteroid miners. There's regular service from Durres to Goheung, part of a circular route around a dozen planets."

"I see. Please keep a weather eye on that consortium from now on, as closely as you can. In particular, I want to know when they plan to send their passage crews, and their routing, as far in advance as you can manage it. Oh – one more thing. I need you to dry-lease a freighter for me, about half a million tons capacity. She should not have visited the New Orkney Cluster before, so no-one here will be familiar with her beacon or gravitic drive signature, and there must be no traceable connection between her and us. I want her ready within thirty days, if possible. I'll have a crew for her by then, or soon afterwards. We'll need her for at least six months, with her lease renewable for another three to six months if necessary. She should have two cargo shuttles, plus her normal complement of cutters."

"That'll need a deposit of about half a million francs, plus quarterly payments, Captain."

"I'll cut you a bank draft as soon as you give me the name of the ship's brokers."

As Lachlan watched the Captain leave the room, he pondered, *What's going on in that shrewd, sly head of yours? I don't know whether it's always safe to be around you, Captain, but it's sure as hell interesting!*

HENRY MARTIN STUCK his head warily around the workshop door. "How's it coming, Jock?"

"It'll come a lot faster if you *stop interrupting me,* dammit!"

"Sorry, but I thought you must be hungry by now. You've been at it for ten hours straight. Here, I brought you a tray of sandwiches and a flask of coffee."

"Food? *Coffee?* You're a saint! All is forgiven! Come in, lad!" Jock set his nanotech control console down on the workbench, and hurried toward his visitor as he entered.

Henry watched as the former Warrant Officer wolfed down the first sandwich, seeming to almost inhale it rather than chew, washing it down with gulps of navy-style coffee; black, unsweetened, and thick enough to stand a spoon upright in it. "I don't know how you can drink that stuff," he said with a grimace.

"Och, lad, you've been spoiled by too many artsy-fartsy coffee shops planetside," the Scot joked, picking up the second sandwich. "Fleet coffee puts hair on your chest!"

"And other places besides, I'll bet!" He gestured at the maintenance sleds racked against the wall. "How many have you done so far?"

"Five, and I'm working on the sixth. Have those parts arrived yet?"

"They're on the freighter that just signaled her arrival at the system boundary. She'll be in orbit tomorrow, and the parts will be here a day after that."

Jock's face fell. "Damn! I'll have a day or so with nothing to do until they get here."

"Why not catch up on your sleep? You've been pulling eighteen-hour days for the past week. You could use the rest."

"I suppose maybe I could, at that. Still, I've got to work fast. There's a deadline on these things. They've got to be where they're needed in less than six weeks from now."

"Don't worry. If you build them, I'll get them there. If worse comes to worst, we'll load you and your equipment aboard the ship, and you can finish the job while we're in transit."

"Not bloody likely! As soon as this job is finished, there are others waiting, thanks to Cap'n Cochrane – frequency modulators for all our ships' gravitic drive units, for a start. I wish I could hire a crew to help me, but the Cap'n says that for now, security has to be tighter than a mouse's arsehole. That means I've got to do it all myself."

"Yes, but think of the reward once you've done it."

"That's what keeps me at it. It'll be nice to be rich."

"You said it! I'll leave you to it. I have to get some cradles made."

"*Cradles?* For babies?"

"No, idiot! Steel cradles, to hold ships securely."

"Oh. Like in a dockyard, you mean?"

"Something like that."

"Sounds interesting. Anything to do with what I'm building in here?"

"In a manner of speaking, yes, you might say that."

NEW WESTRAY

Master Chief Petty Officer Michael Wallace returned to his office to find a visitor waiting. He'd met him only once before, and knew him simply as 'Paul'.

"Did you get them signed?" the visitor demanded without preamble.

"I sure did." Wallace handed over an electronic tablet, and watched as Paul brought up a series of screens. He indicated the stylus-signed blocks on the electronic forms. "You're good to go."

"The Commander didn't suspect anything?"

"Why should he? I didn't even put these documents in his queue. They were all uploaded by the executive officer – or, at least, that's what a data trace will show. The boss never reads them. He just dashes off his signature, then goes back to his porno movies. These forms never passed through my hands. Even the tablet isn't mine." He reached into an inside pocket of his uniform jacket and pulled out a wallet filled with data chips, each securely held in its socket. "Here are the blueprints, schematics and manuals you asked for. They're all there."

"Thank you. You've done very well. That being the case, Tom said to give you the next instalment." He handed over a small leather purse, which chinked meaningfully. Wallace opened it to see the gleam of gold coins inside. Grinning, he closed it and handed it back.

"Thank him for me, but tell him it's too risky for me to have this much on me in foreign currency while this is going down. He can hold the money for me until it's all over. I know he's good for it. I'll get it from him off-planet, or have him send it to my wife. She's already left for New Sanday."

"I'll tell him."

～

ROUSAY

Dr. Masters sipped wearily at her cup of tea. *"Oh,* that tastes good! It's just what I needed."

"I figured you would, after the day you've had," Dave Cousins said sympathetically. "Did you manage to sort out the interface with the ship's sanitary systems?"

"Yes, thanks to a couple of engineering techs with big pipe wrenches. Their motto seemed to be, 'If it doesn't fit, get a bigger hammer!' It was primitive, but it worked."

"I had a few techs like that serve under me during my time in the Fleet. Delicate, they aren't, but they tend to get things done."

"That they do! I think the hospital pod will be ready for use within two weeks, if we can get it properly stocked with medication, surgical equipment and supplies. Thank Heaven NOE was able to arrange for us to borrow one. I hate to think what it would cost to buy our own!"

"We couldn't afford it right now, and that's a fact. The personnel pods also cost a lot, although not nearly as much as your hospital pod. We'll have them ready in another four or five days."

"Where do we go from there?"

"I don't know for sure. This ship will wait here until I get back. The Captain has an urgent job for me, and a scratch crew. We're picking up a leased freighter for a special mission. I should be back within a month."

"That sounds very mysterious."

Cousins shrugged. "The Captain's not letting his left hand know what his right hand is doing. That's good security."

"I suppose so. When are you leaving?"

"Tomorrow morning. You'll be in charge here until I get back. Don't worry, there won't be anything special to do. Let the NCO's handle bringing the personnel pods online. They know what they're doing."

"If you say so. Take care, you hear?" There was affection in her voice.

Tom warmed to hear it. "I will. You do the same."

"I'll be the soul of discretion."

"I just bet you will!"

Chuckling, they went their separate ways.

CONSTANTA

Cochrane's host pushed his coffee cup away with a sigh. "That was excellent, thank you, dear."

"It was my pleasure, darling." His wife beamed at their guest, a warm look of immense gratitude. "It's been even more of a pleasure to see you again, Captain."

"And mine to see you, ma'am," Cochrane assured her.

"I'll go and deal with the kitchen. I know you two want to talk business."

They watched her push a trolley out of the dining room. "She seems to have gotten over the trauma very well," Cochrane observed.

"In most ways, she has. It's been five years, of course, and they say that time heals all wounds. Aurelia still sometimes has nightmares, but I wake her and comfort her when they come. I – I don't think we can ever thank you enough for rescuing her from those pirates, Captain. We'll both be forever in your debt."

"It was absolutely my pleasure, Mr. Grigorescu, and for my crew as well. Those scum won't be hijacking any more ships, or ruining any more lives. As for being in my debt... well, if you'll allow me, I have a favor to ask of you and your shipyard."

"Anything! Name it!"

"I need to service and refurbish several vessels that I'm looking for right now. They'll probably be old, outdated ships, with systems that are just about worn out. I hope to find up to six that are worth refurbishing, plus some others to be cannibalized for spare parts. They may be military ships, or civilian, in which case we'll be fitting weapons to them. Please excuse my uncertainty; it's because we're not yet sure what will be available at a price we can afford. I'll have documentation for them, including an end user certificate for any military ships or weapons systems.

"We're setting up a system security service for an asteroid mining project. We don't want it known that we've acquired the ships. We'd rather that came as a nasty surprise to smugglers and pirates in due course. Will it be possible for you to refurbish them, while concealing their nature and identity? The fewer people who know about this, the better."

Grigorescu nodded. "The end user certificate will satisfy Constanta's government that this is a legitimate transaction, which takes care of one problem. It's not as if you're buying weapons here; rather, you're bringing them here temporarily. I think I can persuade our officials to keep it under their hats. A few palms may need to be greased to ensure discretion, if you follow me."

"I do, and the necessary grease will be available. There's another thing. I know work like this isn't cheap."

"No, it isn't. If these ships are in as poor a condition as you say, it might cost tens of millions to refurbish each of them to operating condition, even if we use spares taken from the non-operational craft. You might find it cheaper or more cost-effective to buy newer ships."

"Newer ships aren't in our budget at this stage. I'm trying to obtain the necessary funds, but they won't be available immediately, and I need ships as soon as possible. Would you be prepared to extend credit to me for the shipyard work, for one to two years?"

"Mine is a family-owned shipyard, Captain. We don't have the capital resources of a larger corporation. You'll have to obtain credit from other sources if you want the work done quickly. However, I'm prepared to help in two ways. I'll do the work at cost plus five percent, rather than my usual profit margin. That's a practical way to thank you for all you've done for us. I'll also introduce you to my bank. If you have an end user certificate, and you're able to offer acceptable security for a loan – for example, some of the vessels, the ones you'll use as a source of spare parts – that should get you at least some of the financing you need."

"I understand, and I'm grateful. I know a five percent profit margin is a lot lower than usual in your line of business. If necessary, I'll leave some of the ships here at Constanta as security, or pledge another vessel for that purpose."

"Very well. I'll take you to my bank tomorrow morning. Please bring that end user certificate with you. It'll help prove to them that everything's on the level."

"I shall. One last request. If we refurbish the ships here, may I bring some of my people to work alongside yours in the process? That's the quickest way I know for them to learn the ins and outs of their new vessels, as well as any problems they're likely to encounter in service."

"That will be a pleasure. We don't have much spare accommodation at the shipyard, but I daresay we can rig up something."

So far, so good, Cochrane thought wearily to himself as he undressed in the guest bedroom later that evening. *Now to find out whether we've got the ships and their weapons; then comes the really tricky part.*

5

GRAND LARCENY

NEW WESTRAY

Shift change at New Westray's System Control Center was its usual, casual Saturday evening routine. The weekend saw relatively little orbital traffic, because the System Patrol Service usually gave liberty to its spacers. Those who hadn't gone planetside were patronizing one of the bars or dance halls on the space station housing SysCon and OrbCon. There had been only one merchant freighter in orbit during the past week, and it was now under way toward the system boundary.

"*Flyco*'s headed out, I see," the Chief Petty Officer in charge of the console operators noted as he sat down beside the outgoing NCO of the watch.

"Yeah, she left orbit about five hours ago. She's taking her time. At the rate she's moving, she won't hit the system boundary for another day or so."

"Must be trying to conserve something or other – even if it's only her crew's energy." The two grinned at each other. "What was a big ship like that doing here, anyway? They normally send a much smaller freighter. She didn't offload much, either. Can't see why they'd send a hulking great bugger like that to a minor planet like this."

"Dunno. Maybe her owners didn't have enough cargoes to fill her holds, so they're keeping her busy on shuttle runs to planets like ours until the freight market picks up again."

"That's probably it. All right, let's do this."

The outgoing operator swiftly ran over the information his relief needed to know. "Oh – just so you know, the team preparing the Reserve Fleet for its annual inspection finished their work. There'll be no more traffic out there until the inspectors go out next quarter."

"Sounds good. Less work for our techs this year, with them hiring that outside maintenance team to do the job. They should do that more often."

The new arrival glanced at the three-dimensional Plot display. The icon representing the Reserve Fleet hovered next to Westray Six, a deserted rock-and-ice planet almost halfway between New Westray and the system boundary. The old ships were in parking orbits around it. Each emitted a transponder signature in case of need, but they weren't going anywhere... unless it was to the scrapyard in due course, or to be used as targets.

"They were a lot more thorough than our lot," he continued. "Stores was going nuts! The team insisted on filling all the tanks and loading all the supplies the ships are supposed to have on mobilization. Even the spare parts had to be racked and ready on board. Stores didn't have enough parts to issue for all the ships. Some heads may roll over it."

"Serve the bastards right! All those ships have been in reserve for over a decade. I'll bet someone in Stores reckoned they'll never be needed again, and decided to make a bit of extra pocket money by selling their spares for scrap."

"Likely. All right, I've got it. I relieve you."

"I stand relieved. Who's your Officer of the Watch?"

"That'll be Ensign Spalding."

"An *Ensign?* When did they start letting novices run the Watch? Most Ensigns are so wet behind the ears, you can use them for water slides!"

The other laughed out loud. "That's a good one! Yeah, he's pretty useless, but he spends most of his time watching movies in the OOW's office, so we don't have to worry about him. Besides, nothing ever happens around here, so he won't have anything to do."

"True enough. All right, see you next time."

NWS *SKELWICK* HAD BEEN BUILT MORE than ninety years before, and only upgraded once during her long, hard years of service. That had been forty-two years ago, when New Westray had bought her and her seven sister ships from a much larger, more powerful Fleet, that was replacing them with more modern vessels. They'd shuttled around the New Westray system for thirty years, patrolling to ward off pirates and smugglers who hardly ever appeared – not surprising in a relatively unimportant star system, well off the main trade routes. Twelve years ago, it had been decided that the old patrol squadron was worn out. They'd been shuffled off into the Reserve Fleet, along with their depot ship, joining several other utility craft and small freighters.

The past two weeks had seen an almost unprecedented whirl of activity in the Reserve Fleet. Every ship had been inspected, but the old patrol craft and their depot ship had received particularly thorough attention. Every protective cover had been removed, every system had been powered up and checked, every laser cannon barbette had been trained around its arc of fire, every tank filled with whatever liquid it needed, every store-room stocked in preparation for mobilization. The racks in the engineering section were laden with every spare part that an overworked Stores department could provide on such short notice, and the depot ship's holds were filled with anything left over.

The patrol craft didn't carry missile pods while in reserve, of course, but all the pods stored in the armory holds aboard the depot ship had been circuit-tested as well. A large proportion of the missiles had failed the tests, and an even larger percentage of their warheads; but with such old weapons, poorly maintained, that was only to be expected. It would mean a lot of work for the missile techs later, though.

All this had been accomplished under the uncaring eye of a single supervisor from New Westray's System Patrol Service. He'd been far more interested in eating, sleeping and watching tri-dee entertainment than in following the techs around. They'd encouraged him to enjoy himself. With their enthusiastic support, he'd taken the last few days off to be with his family, ignoring his orders to keep an eye on the civilian maintenance team. They hadn't informed his superiors about his absence. It had made their task a lot easier.

Aboard *Skelwick,* four techs manned their positions in the tiny Operations Center and the engineering section. The maintenance team hadn't left the ships, as officially presumed. Their shuttle had returned to New Westray that morning, but had been empty except for the pilot. He'd fed their access badges through the reader in the docking bay, making it look like they'd returned, then logged himself and them aboard the freighter before it departed. However, that had all been window-dressing. The techs still had work to do.

"I wonder what they'll think when they realize what's happened?" one mused to the other in the OpCen. "It's going to be the biggest consternation and monkeyhouse this system has ever seen!"

His teammate sniggered. "You can say that again! Just let them stay fat, dumb and blind until we're gone, that's all I ask. Once these ships are delivered, we can throw one hell of a party with the money we're earning for this caper. I plan on staying drunk for a week!"

"Not me. I'm going to use my money to buy a part share in an asteroid prospector's boat. You know what those guys earn, if they strike it lucky?"

"Sure, but what if they don't?"

The other shrugged. "You win some, you lose some."

Their conversation was interrupted by a crackling voice, coming over the intercom. "I'm ready with the sled."

The team leader glanced at the time display. "All right. Switchover time is twenty-one-thirty precisely. Synchronize the sled's internal clock with the ship's, and your own timepieces as well. On my mark, it will be twenty-one-hundred precisely. Stand by... stand by... three, two, one, *mark!*"

"Synchronized. I'm on my way. Don't leave without me!"

"No such luck. You may not be good company, but you're better than no company at all."

"Gee, *thanks!* I'll remember those kind words when I cook breakfast for you!"

Chuckling, the two OpCen crew started another check of the old ship's systems. As they did so, one of the Engineering techs slid out into the vacuum of space aboard a maintenance sled. He used its tiny thrusters to position it one hundred meters beneath the center of the keel, making sure it was stationary relative to the ship above it. That would ensure it remained in the same parking orbit for the foreseeable future.

As the deadline approached, the techs abandoned even the pretense of work. One tuned the ship's radios to the frequencies used by OrbCon and SysCon. If those stations detected anything, the first warning of it would be a broadcast ordering local patrols to investigate the Reserve Fleet ships. If that happened, they'd have to get out while the getting was good, and trust to luck that they could evade pursuit.

The team leader poised his finger over the cut-off button for the transponder, just in case the automated handover went wrong, while his teammate counted down, "Five... four... three... two... one... *cutoff!*" As he spoke the last word, the green light on the transponder transmitter panel blinked out. Both men glanced at the emissions display. The transponder indicator there showed green, proving that the correct signal was still being transmitted on the assigned frequency. However, it was now coming from the maintenance sled, one hundred meters below the ship.

They waited long enough for the light speed delay to pass, to reveal anything stirring at the main planet, but nothing was visible in the Plot display. "No signals from SysCon or Orbcon?" the leader breathed quietly, tensely.

"Not a thing. I reckon they didn't notice the switchover."

"They shouldn't have – it was a pretty seamless transition – but you never know... Are all the other transponders also in the green?"

"Yeah." All the Reserve Fleet ships were still showing their transponders in the normal way. A casual observer would never suspect that the patrol craft and the depot ship were no longer emitting any signal at all.

"All right. We move at twenty-three, at five-minute intervals. If you need to use the heads, do it now. You won't have time later."

Behind them, in the docking bay at the stern of the ship, the engineering tech eased himself through the airlock. He racked the propulsion unit he'd used to get back to the ship, took off and stowed his spacesuit, then returned to his station in the drive compartment, whistling cheerfully.

As twenty-three approached, the tension on board ratcheted up once more. One of the engineer techs swung the four reaction thrusters out of their housings and tested their range of motion once more, just in case. The other brought the gravitic drive to standby mode, and made sure the reactor was ready to provide power to it. The two in the OpCen prepared the ship's systems for departure. They kept all active emitters in standby mode, so that their transmissions would not alert local forces that something was wrong. They would rely on passive sensors alone.

"The freighter's right where she's supposed to be," the leader observed. "With luck, we'll rendezvous with her by midnight."

"Just as long as she doesn't hyper-jump out of here without us. I wouldn't like to have to answer unfriendly questions."

"You and me both!"

On the stroke of twenty-three, NWS *Skelwick* activated her gravitic drive at its minimum power setting. She was far outside effective radar range from New Westray, and her emissions signature at low power would not be detected by Syscon's sensors. A more modern installation would have picked it up, but the local authorities had seen no reason to waste money on that sort of upgrade. After all, nothing had ever happened to justify the expense. At five-minute intervals, the other seven patrol craft followed her out of their parking orbits, with the depot ship bringing up the rear. Silently, stealthily, they slipped away toward the oncoming freighter.

Fifteen transponder icons still identified the ships of the Reserve Fleet, if anyone had bothered to count them at that moment. However, only six of them now represented ships. Nine were maintenance sleds, carefully prepared by Jock Murray. The capacitors powering their transponders would last for at least a week, not long enough for them to drift far enough out of position that observers might realize something was wrong. The Reserve Fleet icon blazed undisturbed in SysCon's plot display.

On *Flyco's* bridge, Henry Martin paced to and fro. He'd never been part of a space-based operation before; his previous criminal experience, extensive though it was, had been on planets. It galled him to be cut off from all his usual sources of information. He was utterly dependent on what the crew chose to tell him. He was paying them enough to ensure their cooperation, but even so, he hated the feeling of not being in personal control of the situation.

He whirled on his heel as the communications operator announced suddenly, "Tight-beam detected! Synchronizing." He knew that outside the hull of the giant freighter, a turret would be turning to align a laser beam with the one from the approaching ship. A few seconds passed, then he heard a familiar voice crackle over the speakers.

"One to Mother. We're ten minutes out. The others are following us. Are you ready? Over."

At the command desk, the skipper picked up his microphone. "Mother to One, we're opening our hold doors now. Assume formation as arranged, and we'll reel you in. Over."

"One to Mother, gotcha. Out."

Henry muttered to the skipper, "Are you sure they can't read that on the planet?"

"Not a chance. It's a tight-beam laser. You've got to be right in the path of transmission between stations if you're to pick it up. The planet's way off behind us, and the only patrol they have in the system is on the far side of the star." He sniffed disapprovingly. "It's about the most careless, half-baked patrol system I've ever seen. You could run a *fleet* through this system and they probably wouldn't notice!"

"Don't complain. It's helping us now."

"You got that right!"

One by one, the other ships reported in. Henry knew that they'd be turning slowly, delicately, to come onto the same course as the big freighter; then they'd be closing in on their assigned holds, where the cradles he'd ordered were carefully spaced out and waiting for them.

It took a full eight hours to get the patrol craft aboard. As each drew level with its hold, at a distance of over a kilometer from the freighter, it matched velocities, then used its reaction thrusters to drift very carefully toward the larger ship. The nine-thousand-ton patrol craft looked like minnows compared to the three-million-ton whale-like freighter.

When each patrol vessel got to within a couple of hundred meters of the freighter, tractor and pressor beams licked out from the open holds, measuring, grasping, taking control of the docking maneuver. Moving so slowly it seemed snail-like, each of the patrol craft was drawn into the yawning, cavernous hold awaiting it, and positioned precisely over the cradles. More tractor and pressor beams pulled the ships down into them, locking them in place against the stress of maneuvering. All the while, the bigger vessel ambled toward the system boundary.

By the time the last patrol craft was locked down, Henry was soaked in perspiration, as if he'd run a marathon. He felt mentally and physically exhausted from the strain. The captain, on the other hand, looked fresh as a daisy.

"I told you it would be fine," he pointed out genially. "This isn't the first time we've loaded smaller vessels while under way. It's tricky, but you get used to it."

"That's all very well for you to say, but this is all new to me," Henry retorted. "I've got to hand it to you, though, Frank. You made it look easy."

The speaker crackled again. It was the depot ship. "Nine to Mother. Looks like it all went well. I'll take off now, and see you at Constanta. Over."

The skipper picked up his microphone. "Mother to Nine. Yes, you can head out. Be careful not to let them spot you. Over."

"Nine to Mother. Teach your grandmother!" The bridge crew chuckled to hear the retort. "We'll be careful, boss. You do the same. You haven't paid us yet! Nine out."

As he replaced the microphone, Frank said, "Speaking of payment..."

"Of course." Henry reached into his chest pocket and pulled

out a folded envelope. "Here's the second payment; five million francs, as agreed."

The skipper took out the interplanetary bearer bank draft and inspected it closely, then nodded. "Looks good to me. All right, we'll close the hold doors and get ready to hyper-jump out of here. Don't forget, this is a slow ship compared to smaller freighters, so it'll take us about fifteen days to reach Constanta. The depot ship will take much longer, of course. She'll be in local space for ten to fifteen days, getting far enough away from the planet for her hyper-jump signature to be lost in the background radiation of space. We don't want New Westray to notice her departure, and wonder why only one ship left orbit, but two hyper-jumped out of the system. We'll be long gone by the time she arrives at Constanta."

"That's OK. She's got to rendezvous with another ship on the way there, anyway. The shipyard will start work on the first two patrol craft while we're waiting for her. They're going to have to work like demons to get them ready as fast as possible. I'll give you the third payment once the ships are offloaded at Constanta, then you can go your way."

"Thank you. This job's been just like you promised. A slow trip here, a slow trip to Constanta, but nothing much to worry about in the way of cops or security. Fifteen million francs for two months' easy work. I wish we had more jobs like that!"

"Just don't talk about it. By the way, I'll be grateful if you can keep enough spacers handy to form two passage crews for freighters. We may need them real soon, and without much notice."

Frank grinned broadly. "For clients who pay as well as you, it'll be a pleasure! You know how to reach me."

~

TWO WEEKS LATER, a meeting of the entire Cabinet of New

Westray convened to hear a report from the Minister of Defense. He didn't mince his words, castigating the System Patrol Service from its leadership down to the lowliest spacer in its ranks – but carefully failed to mention that he and his predecessors had turned a blind eye to its relative inactivity for the past two decades or more. It had been an expedient way to save money from the funds authorized in the Defense budget... money that had been diverted into ministerial pockets.

"So, what do you plan to do?" the Prime Minister demanded.

"I'd like to fire every senior officer in the Patrol Service, but you know we can't get away with that. They're all First Families, just as we are, even if they're the dregs among us – people we shunt off into the Patrol to keep them out of business or politics, where the real money is. If we punish them, we'll damage our own image among the populace."

"It's going to get damaged anyway," the Foreign Minister pointed out sourly. "When this gets out, we'll be the laughing-stock of the galaxy! We'll be forever painted as the planet that let someone sneak off with more than half its Reserve Fleet. What's more, we didn't even *notice* it for over a week, until the fake transponders the thieves left behind ran out of power! It doesn't bear thinking about!"

"But... but... what can we do, then?" the Minister of Finance asked querulously. "Can we cover up the loss?"

"We can say that the missing ships were destroyed as targets," the Minister of Defense offered. "That's a common enough use for them, after all. The System Patrol Service can announce that officially. It's not like anyone here's going to argue with them."

"But that means we can't circulate the ships' descriptions to other planets, and ask them to be on the lookout for them, and report them to us if they turn up," the Foreign Minister objected.

"No, we can't – but as you said yourself, we'll be a laughing-stock if this gets out."

"What if the thieves, whoever they are, tell the story?"

"Why should they?" the Prime Minister asked. "They're probably planning to sell the ships on the open market for whatever they'll fetch. I doubt whether any planetary government worthy of the name will buy them. After all, they're so worn-out, it'll cost too much to refurbish them. They'll probably end up at some newly-settled planet in a galactic backwater, one that's looking to spend as little as possible on its System Patrol Service. The thieves won't want to identify them as stolen property, otherwise they'll have a lot more trouble selling them."

"You have a point," the Foreign Minister admitted. "I just wish I could understand why they stole ships as badly worn-out as ours were. Surely, they could have done better somewhere else?"

"I've wondered the same thing," the Defense Minister acknowledged. "I can only presume they wanted warships – any warships – as quickly as possible, and we were the nearest available target. We'll probably never know for sure."

"What about that freighter?" the Minister of Education asked. "Can we trace her?"

"I doubt it. We've learned that the only ship named *Flyco* listed in the United Planets Merchant Vessel Registry is a small tramp freighter in the Norcross system. The ship that called here was several times larger, with a completely different gravitic drive signature. By now she'll have changed her name again, altered her drive signature – she can do that with a military-grade frequency modulator – and disappeared back into the commercial shipping world. There's no point trying to trace her, even if we could afford to sponsor a search throughout the galaxy."

"We can't," the Prime Minister said tersely. "Let's cut our losses. It's not like we've lost much, anyway. Those ships were the next best thing to scrap metal. Let's simply say we disposed of them as targets, and leave it at that. We'll have the Patrol Service publish the announcement where it's least likely to be noticed, and tell our tame editors in the news media to downplay the story. All those in favor?"

Everyone around the table raised his or her hand.

"Very well. Let's put this behind us, and get on with more important things."

CONSTANTA

Cochrane went aboard the depot ship as soon as she pulled into her parking orbit near the shipyard. Sue McBride was waiting in the docking bay to greet him. He shook her hand warmly.

"I'm glad you were able to rendezvous with her as planned. You've had two weeks to look over the missile pods. What's the verdict?"

"Let's go to my cabin, sir. We can talk in private there."

"That sounds ominous," he said, lowering his voice.

"You don't know the half of it!"

When they'd closed the door, she turned to him. "It's bad, sir. I can hardly believe any service would let its missiles deteriorate like this, even if they were old units in reserve."

"All right, give me the details."

She began counting off on her fingers as she spoke. "Each patrol craft can carry one missile pod, holding fifteen main battery and fifteen defensive missiles. There are twenty-five pods aboard this ship, for a total of three hundred seventy-five each of offensive and defensive missiles. My techs and I have been running tests on them ever since we came aboard. At least half of them are unserviceable. I'm not sure how many of them can be salvaged. Even those that passed our circuit tests may not stand up to more detailed inspection when we tear them down. Drive units, micro-reactors, sensor and homing systems... they're all in poor shape.

"It's not just the missiles you have to worry about. Most of the nuclear warheads are bomb-pumped lasers. I reckon four out of five of them are *useless*. The laser rod assemblies weren't properly stored. They just left the warheads on the missiles, rather than take them out, disassemble them, and store them under controlled conditions. If you can find as many as fifty working laser warheads on this ship, I'll be surprised – and even those I wouldn't trust under combat conditions."

Cochrane sighed. "And the other warheads?"

"You've got eighty-four electromagnetic pulse warheads. They're designed to take out a target's electrical and electronic systems, shutting her down so she can't even move under her own power. Most of them seem in reasonably good shape, or they will be once we've stripped them down and checked their chipsets. They'll need new capacitors – most of the old ones won't hold a charge any longer – but fortunately, there's a standard commercial unit that will fit into the cavity designed for them. I think we can return most of them to service. You've also got a couple of dozen high explosive warheads, although I don't know why you'd use them in space. Perhaps they were meant to bombard an asteroid, or damage a ship without destroying it.

"As for the defensive missiles, they're standard thermonuclear blast units, intended to burn out the sensors of incoming missiles. Their warheads aren't in great shape, either, but they're a much simpler design than a bomb-pumped laser. I'd say we can restore up to a quarter of them, with luck. Amazingly enough, this ship's robotic missile and warhead maintenance systems are in good shape – probably because they were never used much! I think New Westray simply didn't bother with routine maintenance. At any rate, we'll be able to work on all the missiles and warheads, which is a blessing. We wouldn't have been able to without that gear."

"I see. Caitlin managed to buy fifty nuclear space mines at Marano. They're much more modern than these missiles, of course. They use the same bomb-pumped laser warheads as Marano's missiles, which is very helpful. I checked the specifications provided by our contact at New Westray. We should be able to shoehorn the Marano warheads into these old missiles, to replace non-functioning ones. I want to keep ten mines. I'll leave forty with you. Take their warheads and wire them into forty thoroughly tested, refurbished missiles, but keep the rest of the mine shells and systems intact – we may rebuild them when we have access to more warheads. You can use a couple of the modified missiles for testing, if you need to. Refurbish as many of New Westray's nuclear warheads as you can, with the emphasis on total reliability. I need at least five fully loaded missile pods, and as many more as possible for use as reloads."

"Five pods? Is that how many of the patrol craft can be modernized?"

"Yes, more's the pity – the shipyard says the other three are so far gone they aren't worth refurbishing. Fortunately, we can replace many of their old-fashioned military systems with modern commercial equivalents. The state of the art has advanced a lot since they were built. Even so, it's going to cost us close to fifty million francs to modernize each ship to even a limited extent."

Sue winced. "That's a heck of a lot of money! Where are you getting it from? I thought our budget was pretty much committed."

"It is. I've taken out a loan from a local bank, with the help of the shipyard. We've got the equivalent of two hundred million francs from them – enough to refurbish four of the patrol craft. The fifth will stay here, awaiting funds to put it through the same process. The remaining three hulls will be held in reserve. We'll cannibalize them for spare parts. What about this depot ship? Did you get a chance to look at her in depth on the way here?"

"I did, sir. I don't think she's worth saving. She's worn out. Too many of her systems keep breaking down. I'd rather transfer the support gear for the patrol craft to one of our freighters, to serve as a temporary depot ship until we can afford something better.

This ship carries four of the same laser cannon as the patrol craft, though, and they all seem to be in working order, along with their fire control system. We can mount them for point defense on one of our other ships."

Cochrane nodded approvingly. "We probably will. They're not as good or as powerful as more modern units, but they're accurate up to about two hundred and fifty thousand kilometers. That's enough to help with missile defense, or target a nearby vessel. We'll leave the depot ship here for now, because I've pledged her as collateral for the loan, along with the patrol craft we won't be modernizing. You'll stay with her at first, along with your technicians, to refurbish the missiles and warheads, and keep an eye on what the shipyard is doing. I've told them I want the first two patrol craft ready within six weeks from now, if possible, and they've promised to do their best. Please try to have missile pods ready for them at that time."

"I reckon I can, sir. What are you going to be doing?"

"I'm waiting for Commander Cousins to get here with a newly leased ship. He's been handling a special mission for me. He should arrive tomorrow or the next day, if all went well. If he's succeeded, I'll park that ship here under your supervision for safekeeping, then ferry him and his crew back to his original freighter in my courier vessel. He'll bring her here. I want to fit her with a missile pod, if you can get a sixth unit working for her, plus those laser cannon you mentioned, then load the first two patrol craft aboard her."

"OK, sir. I'd best get back to work."

Commander Cousins was bone-tired when he showed up at Constanta the next day. His crew wasn't much better. "We should have had twice as many spacers as we did, sir," he complained when Cochrane joined him in his office aboard the leased freighter. "We've been working watch-and-watch for three weeks straight. That's too much, sir."

"It is, and I'm very grateful to you and your people for working so hard. Unfortunately, we have to be very careful who we hire. Caitlin's doing a great job on interviews, background checks and truth-tester analysis, but she and her team are also too few for what we need. After all, we're expanding from nothing to an organization of two-hundred-plus people by the end of six months. Between us all, we know enough good officers and senior NCO's to form our leadership core; and they know enough qualified spacers and junior NCO's to set up our initial cadre. Fortunately, that means we won't have the added headache of training people."

"I guess so, sir. Sorry if I sounded whiny. I'm just plain exhausted."

"I can see that. You'll have a few days aboard my courier boat to relax and catch up on sleep on the way back to your own ship. There are ten cabins available, with two bunks each, so some of your people will have to put mattresses on the deck, or hot-bunk; but we'll fit you all in somehow. How did it go in the Mycenae system?"

"Very well, sir. We recovered one hundred sixteen asteroids in the three areas you identified, all beaconed by the prospector robots. They've been working hard since our first visit."

"One hundred and sixteen?" Cochrane's voice was astonished.

"Yes, sir."

"I... That changes things. I'd hoped for a few, at best a few dozen, but *that* many... d'you realize what this means? We may get enough for them to pay for our ten-year plan in less than half that time!"

"Yes, sir. The news gets better. We ran preliminary assays on the asteroids during the journey here. They're amazingly dense, sir, and seem to have a very high concentration of precious metals or rare earth elements. I'd say those prospector bots were programmed to cherry-pick only the very best, richest, densest asteroids they could find, those offering maximum value. We're lucky we were able to collect them before the people who put the robots there came back for them.

"That brings up something odd, sir. There are three fields of prospector robots out there. All three are using bots from different parts of the galaxy. One field looks to be related to the New Hebrides cluster. The robots are from a supplier there. The second field is probably linked to the New Orkney Cluster, because that's where its prospector bots were made. The third one, though... its robots' data plates are in Cyrillic script."

"*Cyrillic?* Who the hell could that be?"

"I don't know, sir, but the impression I get is that each of those fields was sown with prospector robots by a different person or company. I reckon NOE's probably behind one of them, and the Callanish consortium is behind a second; but there may be a third player involved, and we've no idea who it might be. I'm hoping we can use the Cyrillic data plates to identify where those prospector bots were made. That would give us a starting-point to look further – and we need to. You see, every time we tried to approach those bots, they self-destructed. They blew up. We recovered the data plates from their wreckage. Their computer processors and memories were melted down into slag, as if someone didn't want us reading them."

"That's worrying. If they're just fly-by-night claim jumpers, we can probably handle them; but if a planet or company is that paranoid, perhaps with some military muscle behind them, they could make life difficult for us. Were any of the fields protected by sensors, to monitor anyone who came calling?"

"We didn't see any, but if you or I were doing something like that, we'd sure as hell have deployed sensors, sir. I reckon we'd better assume that they did, too."

"You're right. At least the gravitic drive emissions of your leased ship are different to any of those we'll be using in the

Mycenae system in future. They won't necessarily be able to link her to us. We can't worry about that now, though. We've got too much else on our plate. As soon as you get back to your freighter, bring her here. Have Warrant Officer McBride and her people help the shipyard to install a missile pod and laser cannon, plus their guidance and control systems, then load the first two patrol craft as soon as they're ready."

"Aye aye, sir."

"I'm going to see someone about those asteroids. I'll leave most of them aboard this freighter, and load some of the smallest aboard my courier ship. Her hold isn't very big, but it should be large enough for a few of them, and I'll put another one or two inside her cutter. It won't be usable for general transport while they're on board, but we can hire planetary shuttles for that. I'll want your assay reports on those I take with me, and I want you to have a team conduct more comprehensive assays on those we leave here – as detailed as possible.

"As soon as possible after I get back, you'll head for Mycenae. The new satellites will be installed there in about two months' time, and I want you to be ready when they are."

"Ready for what, sir?"

"You'll see. It's going to be fun."

6

THE DRAGON'S LAIR

BARJAH

Cochrane walked into the ornate foyer, looking around with approval. Clearly, no expense had been spared to create the right impression.

A black-suited *maître d'hôtel* stepped forward to greet him. "Good evening, sir. Welcome to the Royal Golden Dragon restaurant. Do you have a reservation for tonight?"

"My name's Cochrane. I have an appointment with a Mr. Huang."

"You are expected, sir." He clicked his fingers, and a waiter hurried forward. "Take Captain Cochrane to the private suite."

"Yessir! Please come this way, sir."

He ushered him into a luxuriously furnished room. A table for four was set in the center of the floor. Two men came to their feet as he entered, the waiter closing the door silently behind him. They wore formal business suits, looking more comfortable in them than he felt in his own.

"Captain Cochrane? I am Huang Cheng. I am the leader of the Dragon Tong on Barjah. This is my colleague, Hsu Jin. He is the general manager for an asteroid mining operation in this system. As a specialist in what you wanted to discuss, and since his refinery ship will be involved in any business we may do together, I thought it would be best to involve him from the beginning."

"I'm honored to meet you both."

So, the Tong controls asteroid mining in the Barjah system, Cochrane silently thought. *That's interesting – and what's even more interesting is that they aren't concerned about my knowing it. They must have good friends in high places on this planet, and they want me to realize that.*

Handshakes were exchanged, and the three took their seats. Huang pressed a button beneath the edge of the table, and the door opened again as he looked at Cochrane. "Do you know Chinese food, Captain, particularly at gourmet level?"

"I'm afraid not. I haven't had the opportunity to eat any of it except fast food takeaways, and I'm told most of them aren't nearly as Chinese as they claim to be."

The other two laughed. "That is true. Since this restaurant offers the very best Chinese dishes, may I suggest that I order for you? I assure you, you will find it pleasing to your palate."

"By all means, Mr. Huang."

Huang gave rapid instructions in Chinese. The waiter bowed, and scurried off.

"He will be bringing food and drink in and out at intervals. He will sound a gong every time, so that we can stop talking while he is in the room."

"That's thoughtful. Are you sure this restaurant is secure from snoopers?"

Both men laughed. "We own the Royal Golden Dragon, Captain," Huang assured him. "Look for a restaurant with the same name on almost every major planet, and you will find one. It is a convenient way to locate the Dragon Tong, if you should wish to speak with us. It is also, and always, fully law-abiding, offering no excuse for the authorities to look askance on it. That allows us to meet outsiders like yourself in an undisturbed atmosphere."

"I'll remember that, thanks."

They passed a few minutes in pleasantries until the waiter wheeled in a cart bearing bowls of an appetizing thin soup, pouring glasses of an excellent white wine to accompany it. As they enjoyed the first course, Huang got down to business. "I showed Mr. Hsu the assay reports you provided, Captain. He was impressed."

"Astonished might be a better description," Hsu said with a nod. "I've seldom seen asteroids graded as richly as that. Are you sure the assays are accurate?"

"I am. As a matter of fact, I have all five of those asteroids in orbit aboard my courier vessel. If we agree on terms, I'm prepared to leave them with you for processing, without payment, as a sign of good faith. You can see their yield for yourselves once you've refined them. If it lives up to the assays, that will hopefully show that the assays of other asteroids I provide will also be accurate."

"That is true. Your confidence in bringing them here is encouraging."

"We have to trust each other," Cochrane pointed out. "If I thought you would cheat me, I wouldn't be here. I know you're going to drive a hard bargain, but I also know the Dragon Tong's reputation. Once you've agreed to something, you keep your word. I figured we'd best start off on the right foot, to give you a chance to see that my word is good too."

"I wish more of our customers and partners had that attitude," Huang observed. "I know you contacted us through Henry Martin. He is someone we've learned to trust at a lower level, in the limited contacts we've had with him. It's due to that trust that your inquiry was referred up the line to my level in the organization, because you're talking about much more money than lower-level operatives would be trusted to handle."

They paused the conversation while a meat course was brought in, accompanied by several vegetables, sauces and condiments. When the waiter had left once more, the discussion resumed.

"If your assays are correct, even the five small asteroids that you've brought will yield precious metals and rare earth elements to the value of approximately five hundred million Neue Helvetica francs, once they've been refined," Hsu said. "Under normal circumstances, an independent prospector who brought them in would receive one-quarter of that."

"Yes, but I'm not a prospector. Furthermore, these asteroids aren't from this system, so the local government doesn't get a share; and there's no grubstake involved, so that share also falls away. Basically, the value of the asteroids becomes a two-way negotiation between the refinery and their owner."

"And what proportion are you expecting to get, Captain?" Hsu was looking at him keenly, and Cochrane knew that they were approaching the critical point of the discussion.

"That's what I'm here to discuss. You have to make a profit as well, Mr. Hsu; and I need to deal with a partner whose integrity and reliability are beyond question. It's still strange to me, after my former career fighting smugglers and other criminals, to say this about the Tong, but you do have a reputation for honesty among both criminals and law enforcement throughout the galaxy. Everyone who knows you, even if they hate you, admits that the Tong keeps its word, and never betrays its clients unless they betray it. That's worth a great deal to me. Therefore, I'm willing to offer you a third of the proceeds from each asteroid."

Hsu frowned. "That does not adequately offset the costs we must incur, Captain. Let me describe what's involved. To process an asteroid, its rock must be completely broken down. Its minerals are then extracted, usually by smelting, but sometimes – in the case of some rare earth elements, for example, which are very hard to separate from each other – using more complex techniques. The extracted bounty must then be purified. All that is an expensive process. A refinery ship costs well over two billion francs, and its operating expenses are also very great, many times higher than the average spaceship.

"After extraction and refining, the detritus – usually well over ninety percent of the asteroid's original mass – must be gathered up, bonded together either chemically or mechanically for ease of handling, and removed. We usually dump it on a deserted, unused planet, but in this case, because the chemical composition of your asteroids will be different from those in this system, we must ensure than no comparison tests can ever be run, to prevent that being discovered. We shall therefore dump your asteroid residue into Barjah's sun, to be destroyed beyond any possibility of recovery. That means periodic spaceship flights for that purpose – an added expense.

"All those costs add up. For a very high value precious metal asteroid, they may amount to as little as two to three percent of the net value recovered; but few are so profitable. Most yield lower returns, so their processing costs are several times higher as a proportion of those returns. A one-third share will be too small to cover that while making the process worth our while. I therefore propose a fifty percent split. We each get half of the gross value recovered. That will allow us a fair and reasonable profit after refining expenses, and you the same after the costs of prospecting for and gathering up the asteroids, and shipping them to us."

Cochrane thought for a moment. He wouldn't have to bear the prospecting costs, of course, which was a bonus. He might get better terms from a commercial, rather than a criminal enterprise, but he'd have to find one that would ask no awkward questions – an almost impossible task. If he wanted the anonymity that the Dragon Tong would guarantee, which was essential if he hoped to dupe the NOE over the long term, then he would have to pay their price. He nodded reluctantly.

"That's less than I'd hoped to get, but I see your point. I'd like to ask for some money to be paid up front – perhaps one-quarter of the assayed value on delivery to the refinery. The output could then be valued, and the balance of my half of the funds paid into my account when the asteroids have been refined. To earn your trust, I'm prepared to leave the first few asteroids with you without advance payment, so you can assess them for yourself. Does that sound fair?"

Hsu glanced at Huang. Clearly, this was the older man's decision.

Huang stroked his chin thoughtfully. "That may be possible, Captain. We might need to assay a few of each shipment of asteroids you bring, to compare our initial findings to your own reports. How many do you think will be in each shipment?"

"I think twenty to thirty asteroids at a time, all high-yield like the first five, and almost all larger in size."

"And how many shipments do you anticipate?"

"At least five, perhaps eight or nine by the time we're through."

Both men looked at him in astonishment. "But that means tens of billions of francs!" Hsu exclaimed. "Where are they from?"

"I'm not at liberty to say, Mr. Hsu. Just please accept that I have access to them, and I have the means to cherry-pick the richest asteroids out of a very large field. I expect to be able to obtain at least a hundred to a hundred and fifty of them."

There was a long silence as the two men absorbed the magnitude of the numbers involved. Eventually Huang observed, "This promises to be extremely lucrative for both of us, Captain. I propose that we assay one out of every five asteroids you deliver, selected at random by us. We can do that in about forty-eight hours, if you will allow our team access to the freighter that brings them. Once we compare their assay reports to yours, we can be confident that we both know what we're dealing with. At that point, yes, I'm willing to pay you twenty-five percent of the likely yield of the asteroids. We can deposit it into an off-planet bank account of your choice; or we can give you an interplanetary bearer bank draft; or we can deal in hard assets such as gold and platinum-group metals, paid at the prevailing market price in this system. Once refined, we shall take our fifty percent share, and pay the balance of your share to you or your representative."

"That would work," Cochrane confirmed gravely. "When I'm here, I'll ask for my funds in cash and hard assets. In my absence, such as with the balance of my share after each batch of asteroids has been refined, I'll ask you to deposit the funds into an account with the Handelsbank of Neue Helvetica as soon as they're available." He'd already set up a special account to handle such transactions, separate from Eufala's main corporate account.

"We can do that," Huang agreed. "To show good faith on our part as well, I suggest we start with the five asteroids you have brought with you. We'll assay them all – it will be good practice for our team. In forty-eight hours from now, if their reports agree with yours, I shall pay you twenty-five percent of their assessed value. When can we expect the next shipment?"

"I think I can get one to you every two to three months."

Hsu smiled. "That will give us time to arrange a few extra security measures. We don't want Barjah's government learning of this windfall. If they did, they would want to share it, even though it's from outside this system."

"Then, by all means, let's keep them out of the loop," Cochrane agreed. "There's one more thing I'd like to ask for, Mr. Huang. I'm aware that the Tong operates several freight lines, so it knows about merchant freighters. There are also rumors concerning a certain planet that's said to be its home world, and is reportedly very well defended. That being the case, I presume the Tong knows a good deal about the market for warships and auxiliary vessels as well, plus their weapons, systems, sensors and other equipment."

"That... might be so," Huang acknowledged cautiously.

"I'm in the process of establishing a private company that will concentrate on space, rather than planetary security. I need ships to do that; if possible, warships, enough of them to deter casual attack, and even give a larger opponent pause for thought. I'm looking for shipbuilders and weapons dealers who meet five criteria. First, they must be discreet and trustworthy – so much so that the Tong itself would buy from them, if necessary. Second, they must offer high-quality goods with up-to-date technology. Third, they must charge fair and reasonable prices. Fourth, they must be reliable suppliers over the long term, who won't cut me off without spares or reloads at the wrong moment. Fifth, they must be willing to be... let's say, flexible concerning United Planets regulations governing arms supplies to private companies.

"I have the names of certain potential suppliers that I learned during my military career. However, they must be only a small fraction of those out there. Can the Tong recommend individuals and companies who fit those requirements?"

Hsu and Huang glanced at each other. "That is outside my purview," the latter said slowly, "but I can send your questions to those who will be able to provide answers. By the time you come back with more asteroids, I should have some information."

"Thank you. If there's any fee for the Tong's services in that regard, of course I'll pay it."

"We will make enough profit out of our asteroid venture together that I shall recommend no fee should be charged. However, the final decision is not mine to make."

"I understand. Thank you."

"Is that why you're bringing us these asteroids?" Hsu asked with interest. "Will their proceeds be used to buy warships?"

"Yes, and other necessities. There are many expenses in setting up an operation like this."

Huang smiled. "The Tong has many expenses as well." He

raised his glass in a toast. "Let us by all means help each other to pay them!"

THREE DAYS LATER, they met again at the Royal Golden Dragon restaurant, this time for lunch. Huang took the opportunity to order Korean dishes, declaring it high time Cochrane received exposure to the best recipes from all over the Far East on Earth. He was forced to admit that, while spicier than he normally preferred, the food was extremely tasty.

Over dessert, Hsu handed him an envelope. It contained three documents. The first was an interplanetary bearer bank draft, drawn on the Handelsbank of Neue Helvetica, for twenty-five million francs. The second was a receipt from the local branch of the Handelsbank for the disbursement of the same sum in cash, in a mixture of francs, Bismarck Cluster marks, and Lancastrian Commonwealth credits. The last was another receipt, this one for the issuing of one-kilogram gold bars by the Barjah Mint to the value of seventy-five million francs.

"The cash and gold are waiting for you aboard your ship, Captain," Hsu informed him. "We sent them up earlier this morning. If you wish to verify the amounts, please feel free to do so."

"That won't be necessary. I know you're trustworthy. I'll look forward to receiving the balance of my share in a few weeks' time, once you've refined the asteroids. Please deposit it to my account with the Handelsbank."

"We shall," Huang promised. "Where are you bound now?"

"I've got to be in ten places at once, according to my calendar," he replied with a wry grin. The other two laughed. "I need to find out what's been happening in my absence. I have competent, trustworthy subordinates, but they're spread thin at present.

There needs to be central coordination and control, and in my absence, that's lacking."

"Of course. A safe and successful voyage to you, Captain. We shall look forward to seeing you, or your representative, in three months' time."

7

HOPSCOTCH

CONSTANTA

"I'm glad you're back, sir," Commander Cousins said with a weary smile as he shook hands. "How did it go?"

In answer Cochrane took out an envelope from his pocket and handed it over. Cousins opened it, took out the bearer bank draft, and beamed with satisfaction. "Oh, yeah! I'd say that's successful all right! This isn't all of it, is it?"

"No, there'll be a lot more. We've agreed on a fifty-fifty split of the proceeds."

Cousins' face fell. "Only half? I'd hoped we could get more."

"Be realistic, David. You can't push the Dragon Tong too far without risking them pushing back – and they could roll right over us, anytime they wanted to. I'd far rather establish good relationships with them from the start. Look at this." He reached into his pocket and took out a white disk. "They call this stone 'mutton-fat' jade." He handed it over.

Cousins examined it curiously. It bore a silver dragon's claw insignia on one side, with a number beneath it. Both were inlaid in silver. On the reverse side, an ornate Chinese character was inscribed, also inlaid in silver. "What is it?" he asked, handing it back.

"It's a token awarded by the Dragon Tong to those whose business they value. Black jade is the lowest level; white is the second. Basically, it says that I'm an honored friend of the Tong. If I need to approach them anywhere in the galaxy about anything at all, this guarantees that they'll listen, and help if they can – although I'll probably still have to pay for their assistance."

The Commander whistled. "That's really something. Why, I bet you could even ask them to kill somebody."

"I could ask, but I don't know if they'd agree. Fortunately, I don't intend to use their services to do that."

"I'm glad to hear it. So, when do we send them the rest of the asteroids?"

Cochrane explained the deal he'd made at Barjah. "I want to string out the deliveries. That way, they won't get tempted to stiff us out of our share of any one shipment, because they know there'll be more coming if they treat us right. Also, when we send the last shipment of asteroids, we won't tell them that right away. We'll wait until they've paid our final share into our bank account, then explain that our access to more asteroids has unfortunately been cut off.

"By the way, I know we've discussed this before, but let me re-emphasize: don't talk about the Dragon Tong *at all*, not even to our colleagues. Too many people are afraid of them – with good reason, let's face it. The only reason I've told you is that you're my second-in-command. If anything happens to me, you need to know how to pick up the pieces. I'll add the details to my confidential file for you."

"Thanks, sir. I won't mention the Tong. Are you going to try to get any more asteroids?"

"It's a tempting thought, but it might be risky. We were fortunate to spot those three fields of prospector robots, and clean up everything they'd already identified for recovery. I'm sure whoever put them there will be furious when they find out. I expect them to try to learn who did it, and go after them. Fortunately, they can't be sure it was us – but if we go back, they might figure it out."

Cousins sniggered. "By sending me in that newly leased ship, which has no traceable connection to us, and using one of Jock Murray's frequency modulators on the gravitic drive, they wouldn't have been able to identify it for sure, much less figure out that we were using it. With luck, the people behind those bot fields will blame each other instead."

"I hope so. If we can get them chasing each other's tails, so much the better! Problem is, we've no idea who that third group is, or whether they pose a threat. Don't forget, I promised NOE we'd be ready for operations six months after they signed the contract. That deadline's only seven weeks away now."

"And we're still not quite ready. All right, sir, what do you want me to do next?"

"Let me read through the signals and reports waiting for me. I'll work out a timetable for the next few weeks, then we'll go over it together. We're going to be playing the next best thing to an interplanetary game of hopscotch as things come to a head."

Cousins shook his head ruefully. "I never could figure out that game, sir."

"Well, there's no time like the present to start learning!"

It took Cochrane a full day to wade through all the material that had piled up in his absence. He read, thought, ate, slept, read some more, and began to rough out a timeline. It was the following afternoon before he summoned Cousins.

"Let's start with what others are doing, because that's going to govern our actions," he began. "You recall that *Colomb*, that repair ship from Callanish, was undergoing refurbishment?"

"Yes, sir."

"She's scheduled to be back in commission by the first of next month. What's interesting is that her crew was not dispersed to other vessels while she was in the shipyard. They were kept intact. They're under orders to be ready for departure by not later than the tenth of next month. They've been warned they'll be gone for seven to eight weeks. What does that suggest to you?"

"That they're going to make another run at Mycenae, sir. Last time, near as we can figure, they hyper-jumped to a point three or four light-days outside the system, then accelerated to cruising speed before shutting off their drive. They coasted in making no emissions at all. That let them get right up to Mycenae Primus Four without being detected. If they're going to be gone that long, it sounds like they're planning another lengthy approach, just like last time."

Cochrane nodded. "We're thinking alike. Their ship's got more than enough capacity in her cargo holds to load all the stores they'll need for so long a period in space. What's more, NOE's new satellites are scheduled to go live on the thirtieth of next month. That'll be about the same time *Colomb* arrives, assuming we've understood her intentions correctly. I reckon she'll wait until the ship deploying the satellites has left the system, then move in, just like before, to steal the new birds."

Cousins sat bolt upright, face suddenly eager. "Are we going to stop her, sir?"

"Let me explain what I want you to do."

He spoke for half an hour, referring occasionally to a three-dimensional display of the Mycenae system, highlighting features and laying out a timeline. Cousins took notes and asked questions, and sometimes contributed suggestions of his own that were incorporated into the plan.

"Got it?" Cochrane asked at last.

"Yes, sir. We deal with the situation around Mycenae Primus Four, then head for the robotic prospectors to take care of business there, then come back here to Constanta, leaving two patrol craft to look after things in Mycenae."

"That's it. I'm going to be busier than a one-legged man in an ass-kicking contest while you're gone. When you get back, we'll put our heads together and figure out what's next. Remember, keep all this under your hat!"

"Yes, sir. Compartmentalization. I get it." They grinned at each other. "I'll get the order in right away for that inflatable habitat. If we order standard modules and link them, we should be able to buy them from existing stocks, rather than wait to have them manufactured to special order."

"Do that. We can't afford to wait."

The Captain's next meeting was with Sue McBride. "How are the missiles and warheads coming along?" he demanded without preamble, voice rasping with fatigue.

She shook her head. "More important, sir, how are *you* coming along? You look worn to a frazzle!"

"That's probably a pretty fair description right now, but you don't look much better. We're all going to be that way for a while longer. About the missiles?"

"Och, it's basically as I said before, sir. We've discarded more than half as worthless. There are simply too many things wrong with them. It's not that they're worn out – they weren't fired, after all. It's just that they weren't maintained properly, if at all. Good machinery and electronics can only take so much neglect. On the other hand, we've salvaged every single piece of them that we could get working, and started running the parts through an extended test cycle. Those that survive it go into our spares bin. We're building up a useful stash."

"Will you have two pods ready for the first two patrol craft?"

"Yes, sir, and one for the Commander's ship. We've also overhauled the laser cannon that'll be fitted to each ship. They're in good working order."

Cochrane heaved a sigh of relief. "That's really good news!

Well done – and please tell your techs I said so. I think I'll have to give you all a bonus."

"That'd be appreciated, sir. In fact, if you could leave it here with me, I'd like to give it to the team as soon as Commander Cousins gets underway. We've had no liberty to speak of since we got here. I'd like to give everyone a few days on Constanta, with plenty of good food, beer, and some solid ground under their feet."

"Good idea."

At last he was able to make time to visit the owner of the shipyard. He thanked Grigorescu profusely for the hard work his employees had put in to get the first two patrol craft ready so fast.

"It's been a pleasure," the businessman assured him. "No, really, it has. These are the first ships of their type that we've worked on. By refurbishing and reinstalling or replacing every system, we've learned a lot, particularly from the spacers and technicians you sent to work alongside us. I'll be able to bid on similar projects in future with a much better knowledge of what's needed."

"I'm glad to hear it. Some of those projects may be ours. Things are beginning to come together, and our cash flow is improving, too. I'll be able to pay you to refurbish the fifth patrol craft, over and above the bank loan. I can even pay you in gold, if you prefer."

"Gold?" Grigorescu' eyes gleamed. "You must have been doing some profitable business."

"It's been good so far. Are you absolutely sure you can't get a sixth patrol craft operational?"

The other man shrugged. "I could, if absolutely necessary, but frankly I don't think it'll be cost-effective. Most of her systems will have to be replaced, including her reactor and gravitic drive. It would cost as much to refurbish her as to buy a new ship."

That's a pity. I could have used another one, Cochrane thought. He said aloud, "I suppose you're right. Keep the three derelict hulls in reserve, in parking orbits, in case we find a use for them, even if it's only spare parts for the five refurbished ships. Also, from now on, charge me at normal rates for your work. You've been very generous in working at cost-plus-five, and I'm very grateful; but now that I have more money coming in, it's time you earned a normal profit."

"All right. Thank you, Captain."

"Speaking of parking ships, I've got that other freighter that Commander Cousins brought here, too. She'll have an anchor watch aboard." *They'll be guarding the asteroids in her holds, rather than the ship herself, but Grigorescu doesn't need to know about them,* he thought with an inward smile. "Three or four more vessels may arrive over the next few months. Will you please store them in parking orbits around Constanta, along with all our other ships? Log them in Orbital Control's records as waiting for repair at your shipyard. I know I can trust you to look after them, and the small crews I'll leave aboard them."

"Certainly, Captain. There'll be a monthly fee to cover OrbCon's charges and the use of one of my shuttles for routine traffic, of course. You can arrange with one of the spaceship chandlers to supply them with everything they'll need."

"Thank you. Would you please deal with the chandler on my behalf? I won't have time – I'm heading out tomorrow. I'll leave enough with you to cover all those expenses for the next six months."

～

ROUSAY

As Cochrane took his leave of Grigorescu, voices were raised in the New Orkney Enterprise boardroom.

"*Thirty-seven!* Thirty-seven of the richest, most lucrative asteroids in the whole Mycenae system – and they've vanished without trace!" Marwick fumed.

"How do we know how many there were, if they're all gone?" another director asked, his face white with anger.

"We know how many beacons were emplaced. Our ship queried each prospector robot as to how many they had left, and subtracted that from the total with which they started. Q.E.D."

"What about the ship that stole them?"

"We have a monitoring satellite in the asteroid belt nearby. It can't use active sensors, of course, or else it'd be detected; but it recorded the ship's gravitic drive signature with its passive sensors. It wasn't one of ours."

"Was it one of those we made available to Captain Cochrane?" a third director demanded, dire suspicion in his voice.

"It didn't match their drive signatures. I asked Rousay's System Patrol Service to trace it, but they couldn't come up with a match. They'll inquire through the United Planets, but they tell me that if a frequency modulator was used on the drive, it'll be almost impossible to pin it down."

"Could Cochrane have used a frequency modulator on one of our ships, so we wouldn't recognize its drive signature?"

"Our ships aren't fitted with them, and such devices are very tightly controlled. They're military hardware, and subject to all the usual restrictions on such gear. I don't see how he could have gotten hold of one."

"Even though he's a former Captain?"

"He might have contacts that would get him one, but from where? If it was local, it would be logged in the System Patrol Service's records – but none of those units are missing."

"Could he have made his own?"

"They're very intricate pieces of electronics. They have to be, to deal with gravitic as well as electromagnetic radiation. It would take a very highly trained specialist to make one. I suppose the

Captain might know someone like that, but again, he'd have to have access to all the parts, some of which are tightly restricted."

"On balance, I'm inclined to think the Captain wasn't involved, or the ships we lent him," Marissa Stone commented. "For a start, he didn't know about our prospector robot activity. We didn't tell him, and it's not the sort of thing a routine sensor scan would detect. If he didn't know where to look, it would be very difficult for him to find it."

"There is that," the other director admitted. "What are we going to do about the theft?"

"I think we're going to have to tell Captain Cochrane about the existence of our prospector robots," Marwick said with a sigh. "I know we wanted to keep that confidential, but I daresay he won't be too surprised. If he's aware of them, his patrols can keep an eye on them."

"When does he take over security duties at Mycenae?"

"He asked for six months to get organized before he started work. That'll be over at about the same time that our new satellites are installed. I sent him a message a couple of weeks ago, asking him to meet with myself and Ms. Stone as soon as possible to give us a progress report. He should get here within the next few weeks. We'll report back to the Board about his plans as soon as we know what they are."

"And what are we going to do now to raise funds for our initial projects in Mycenae, once we've got United Planets approval?"

"I'm afraid we must write off the missing asteroids. By now they'll have been refined, and the metals and minerals they yielded will have been sold on the black market. All we can do is have our robots continue their work, this time with protection from Captain Cochrane's security force."

"Can he – will he – deal with any future thieves as they deserve? I don't mean arrest them; I mean blow them out of space!"

The others looked at the speaker, tight-lipped. Marissa Stone answered at last, choosing her words very carefully, "Please don't use such language in an *official* board meeting. I can only presume that was a joke in bad taste." Her emphasis made her meaning clear. If it could be proved that directors knew about and approved of such acts in advance, they might in due course be called to account for them in a court of law.

"Ah... yes. Yes, of course. I was only joking. My apologies for not making that clearer."

The speaker's eyes suggested otherwise. Marwick looked at him and gave a slight nod of his head. The other director leaned back in his chair, mollified.

HENRY MARTIN NURSED his tankard of beer as he looked across the table. "You drive a hard bargain. I don't know if I can raise that much so quickly."

"Oh, come off it!" Frank scoffed. "You're talking about two brand-new ships worth easily a hundred and fifty million apiece. I'm charging you only twenty percent of their combined value. What could be fairer?"

"That's their value to an *honest* buyer from an *honest* seller. Once they're stolen, you'll be lucky to get a third of that from a broker on Medusa or somewhere like that."

"Yes, but that's not my fault. Come *on*, Henry. You know I'm the best there is in this business. I deliver value for money. Your sixty million will buy you everything you need, not just the ships themselves. This is a risky job, you know – much riskier than the last one you hired me for. Security at New Westray was pathetic. It'll be a lot stricter at Goheung. These are brand-new fast freighters, being delivered to a customer by a commercial ship-yard. They'll be careful, making sure all the documentation is correct and that we're competent before they'll let us take the ships. We're going to have to disguise ourselves *real* well, to avoid being identified and arrested later. There's also the job of dealing with the passage crews, which is a whole new problem, plus three different sets of laws and regulations. If anything goes wrong, me and my boys will spend the rest of our lives rotting on a prison planet. Besides, you know you can trust me. Others might just sell the ships for their own account. They'd make more money that way. I won't. I'm an honest crook. I stay bought."

The not-so-reformed criminal heaved a sigh. "I guess you are, at that. I'll check on whether I can come up with that much, that quickly. I'll meet you for lunch tomorrow. If it's a go, I'll pay you the first half of the money. The rest will be paid when you deliver our ships."

"I reckon that'll do. You'll trust me with the ships, and I'll trust you with the rest of my money."

Later that evening, Henry briefed the Captain on the details. "He's charging high, but he's right. Not many people in his line of work can be trusted to deliver the goods, when they could make more by selling them for their own benefit. He's built his reputation by never cheating his customers. It'll cost us a lot, but I reckon he's worth it – that is, if you want those ships."

"We're going to need those we get in exchange for them. Besides, it'll put a crimp in the Callanish consortium's operations until they can replace them, and they'll have to use their own money to do so, because they paid for those new freighters using NOE's stolen satellites. What's more, they'll shortly discover that they've lost a lot more money somewhere else, which will put them in an even more difficult position."

"Oh? What have you been up to, Captain?"

"I'd better not say. Remember, we're operating on a need-to-know basis. If you don't know about it, no-one can force you to talk about it."

"I guess not. Can you afford to pay Frank the first half of his fee?"

"It'll clean out the rest of the gold I have on board my courier ship, and a chunk of my cash reserve as well, but yes, we can pay him. I'll draw an interplanetary bearer bank draft for the balance of his fee, when the ships are delivered."

"That should work; but the second payment will be just over thirty-one and a half million francs if you do it that way. There's a five percent fee to cash those drafts, and Frank won't be willing to pay it out of his end."

"Dammit, I'd forgotten about that! All right. If I can't free up that much cash or gold, I'll adjust the amount of the draft. Did Lachlan give you enough information about the itinerary of the passage crews for Frank to set up everything he needs to do?"

"Yes, he did. Frank says it'll be a scramble, but he can get there on time."

As he undressed for bed, later that night, Cochrane was devoutly grateful that he'd managed to make a deal for the asteroids with the Dragon Tong, and that they'd trusted him with an advance payment. Without it, he wouldn't have been able to pay for the current operation, not on top of all the other demands on his bank balance that were shortly to fall due.

I knew I was taking a hell of a chance when I set up this company, he reminded himself. *Fortunately, so far, it's paying off; but anything could still go wrong. We're balanced on a knife-edge until we can cash in a couple more loads of asteroids, and order the right kind of ships to stop others pushing us around. The next couple of years are going to be critical – and we've barely begun them yet.*

He went to sleep with that thought running around and around in his mind. His dreams were not restful.

"I CAME AS SOON as possible after I got your message, sir," Cochrane began as he sat down in the conference room. "I'm sorry about the delay."

"It was unfortunate," Marwick harrumphed. "How are your preparations progressing?"

"Very well, sir. I've obtained several suitable vessels. The first of them should be ready by the deadline, with more to follow. I've also armed one of the freighters you lent me. She now has her own missile pod, along with laser cannon and the systems to guide their fire."

The two directors sat bolt upright. "You *armed* our ship?" Stone expostulated. "What about when you're finished with her? Will we be able to return her to her original condition?"

"That's easily done, ma'am. It'll just be a matter of taking the missile pod out of her hold, plating over the aperture we cut for it, dismounting the laser cannon barbettes and plating over their ports, and removing the sensor panels we applied to the outside of the hull."

"I see. You should have told us ahead of time, though. People might assume we're arming our ships, when we're not."

"If you let it be known that three of your vessels have been dry-leased to Eufala Corporation for three years, people won't worry too much, ma'am. If they notice the weapons, it won't reflect on the New Orkney Enterprise, because Rousay has licensed Eufala to operate armed ships."

"I suppose so."

"Will you be ready to commence operations by our agreed deadline?" Marwick demanded.

"Yes, sir, I will. When are your new satellites going to be deployed?"

"At the end of the month."

"Good. I'll have a ship there to keep an eye on them. Don't tell your people about her, though, sir. She'll be keeping out of sight, making no emissions that your ship will detect. I want to be able to surprise anyone who tries to steal the new satellites."

Privately, Marwick wondered whether the Captain was saying that to cover up the fact that he wouldn't have a ship there at all.

Oh, stop it! he scolded himself. *If he wanted to cheat us, he could have taken the billion-odd kronor we've paid him so far, and disappeared. He hasn't, so he's probably on the level.*

"There's something else we need you to keep an eye on," the senior director told him. "We've got a field of prospector robots looking at part of one of Mycenae's asteroid belts."

Cochrane sat upright in feigned surprise. "You didn't tell me about that when you gave me the data about what was going on in the system, sir," he said in a half-accusatory tone.

"No, we didn't, and that's backfired on us," Marwick admitted. "We've just learned that all the asteroids our robots had flagged for priority attention have been collected by someone else."

"Who, sir?"

"I'm afraid we don't know."

Cochrane shook his head in pretended exasperation. "With respect, Mr. Marwick, you should have told me about the robots right away. If I'd known about them, I could have emplaced sensors to keep an eye on them, and note anyone who came calling."

"We have sensors of our own, Captain. They recorded the gravitic drive signature of the ship that stole the asteroids, but we think it was disguised. For what it's worth, here are the records." He slid a data chip across the highly polished surface of the table to their visitor.

"I'll have them analyzed in depth, sir," Cochrane assured him.

Marwick nodded impatiently. "That brings up a new consideration, Captain. We need to prevent any further theft of our asteroids. A single high-value asteroid can fetch billions, even tens of billions of kronor. Our robots are picking out such asteroids for priority attention, so to have them stolen them like this represents an enormous financial loss to the New Orkney Enterprise. Therefore, we need you to arrange that anyone trying to steal them in future is... let us say, permanently discouraged from doing so."

Cochrane stared at him, his eyes narrowing. He was silent for a moment, then said quietly, "Mr. Marwick, if pirates or smugglers attack our ships or resist arrest, we're entitled to defend ourselves, even if that means using lethal force. This is different. Depending on the circumstances, it might verge on cold-blooded murder. Now, I don't necessarily object to killing in the normal course of events – I've proved that more than once against criminals during my career, as you know – but I'm not prepared to put myself or my people in legal jeopardy."

He noted Marissa Stone's expression change as he spoke of killing, a *frisson* of atavistic anticipation running through her body. Marwick wasn't looking at her, so he didn't notice it; but Cochrane had been expecting something like that.

"Let's look at practical issues first, sir," he continued. "I can't assign a ship to permanently guard your robotic prospectors. While she's doing that, she can't patrol the rest of the system, and I can't afford to buy an extra ship to take her place – not on what you're paying me. What's more, any intruder is bound to notice the guard ship's gravitic drive emissions. She'll simply wait for the patrol to move past her, then sneak in behind it. If you want to catch her in the act, you've got to use methods she can't detect until it's too late. Furthermore, if we 'permanently discourage' her, we can't be sure that some of those who do it won't talk about it, or that sensor records won't be made available to law enforcement in future, incriminating us. Are you with me so far, sir?"

"Yes. You're saying you can't do what we want."

"Not necessarily, sir. I'm saying we need to find a better, smarter way to do it. Are you aware of this planet's defenses against attack from space?"

Marwick blinked. "Well, we have them, I know, but... no, I can't say I'm familiar with them."

"The outer defense is Rousay's System Patrol Service with its patrol craft, sir. The inner defense is orbital missile pods and nuclear space mines. The inner defenses are usually switched off, activated only if a threat is detected. After that, anything coming within range of them will be automatically destroyed, unless they've been programmed to ignore its drive signature, or it's broadcasting an identification signal they recognize. If you want to protect your prospector robots and their discoveries, you're going to have to put those sorts of defenses around them."

"You mean, orbital missile pods and mines?"

"Not missile pods, sir. They need long-range guidance systems. Here on Rousay, Orbital Control or System Control provide that via datalink. Mycenae has no OrbCon or Syscon yet, so we'll have to rely on space mines to do the job. They have their own gravitic drives, so they can adjust their positions as required, albeit slowly. They're also stealthy, making them very hard to detect on radar or lidar, and they can adopt a random pattern, moving around so they're never in one place for very long. Their drives are low-powered, so their signatures are only detectable at very close range, and not at all if they aren't moving. They have their own sensors to aim their bomb-pumped laser warheads, which can take out any small to medium-sized ship, or badly damage a larger one. What's more, they have no crews, so there's no salaries to pay, no sick leave, nothing like that. They're autonomous. You program them, then go away and leave them to get on with the job."

"They sound ideal for that sort of task," Stone acknowledged.

"They are, ma'am: and what's more, they solve the moral problem, too. If only you have the right to collect your own robotic prospectors and the asteroids they identify, anyone else doing so is clearly up to no good. There's no-one else in the Mycenae system with any right to do that. Therefore, if one of your mines takes out their ship, I don't have an issue with that; and there won't be any surrenders before the fact to worry about."

"But what if there are survivors?"

He sighed. "Ms. Stone, a space mine uses a thermonuclear

bomb to activate a cone of laser rods. They'll go through a ship from one side to the other without even noticing it. Its internal atmosphere will instantly vent to vacuum. Unless the crew are already in spacesuits – and they're not very comfortable, so that's almost never the case – they'll die very quickly. If any are in spacesuits, or can get to a lifeboat, and by some miracle they aren't maimed or killed by a laser beam or flying wreckage or an explosion, they'll be left drifting in space. There are no habitable planets in the Mycenae system where they can land. If they're not rescued quickly, they'll die too."

She shivered. "I see. How many mines will you need?"

"We'll assign one mine to cover each prospector robot, or one of the asteroids it identifies for collection. We'll need enough to cover them all. How many bots are out there?"

"We deployed eighty," Marwick replied.

"Then I think a hundred mines will do, sir. We can have some of them spread out to cover multiple robotic prospectors. High-value asteroids will be more tempting targets, so we'll make sure each one your bots flag has its own protective mine. Anyone trying to steal them will trigger it."

"But they won't shoot down our own people when they go in to recover the asteroids?"

"No, sir. We'll program them with an identification code. If your mining boats broadcast it, they won't be targeted. You'll have to warn us in advance, though, so we don't assume your boats are thieves and target them with our missiles."

"What does a mine like that cost?" Stone asked.

"The sort we'll need start at about ten million kronor apiece, ma'am. They can go as high as double that for the most sophisticated versions."

Marwick's face twisted in disgust. "That's out of the question."

"With respect, sir; if a single high-value asteroid might be worth, say, a billion kronor, that justifies spending a certain amount to protect it – and you're protecting a lot more than one of them. If you want such thefts to be 'permanently discouraged', you're going to have to buy space mines. You also need to withdraw your sensors from the prospecting field, so they can't observe anything that happens there. We don't want any inconvenient records to surface later, as evidence in court."

"But if we buy space mines, there'll be a record of that," Stone objected.

"Not if I buy and deploy them for you, ma'am. It'll simply be an extension of our security contract. You can pay the necessary funds to Eufala Corporation for some innocent-sounding purpose, perhaps 'to buy fast freighters for resupplying the security mission in Mycenae', or something like that. I'll arrange for purchase documentation for such ships, and for a few visits to be logged there, to 'prove' that the money was used for that purpose. The freighters won't be armed, so we won't have to register them on Rousay in terms of our armed vessel license – not that they'll call here, in the normal course of events. I'll use our existing ships for that purpose."

"How much money are we talking about?" Marwick demanded.

"Let's work on a cost per mine of twelve million kronor apiece, sir, including an under-the-counter premium to prevent the sale being registered anywhere. A hundred mines would come to one-point-two billion kronor, or about three hundred fifty million francs."

Marissa looked thoughtful. "Compared to the value of the asteroids they'll protect, that doesn't sound too far-fetched," she said musingly.

Marwick's face twisted sourly. "That's as much as we've already spent on Captain Cochrane and his security proposals. The Board's going to find that hard to swallow."

"There may be a cheaper way, sir," Cochrane suggested artlessly. "What tax rate do you pay to Rousay on your asteroid mining in this system?"

"Thirty-three percent."

"If you could skim off gold to the value of what I need from your refinery ship, and transfer it to my courier vessel without it being recorded officially, that would save you the tax on that amount, sir. It would have to be properly refined, of course, to four nines fine purity, and cast in one-kilogram bars, with a valid mint code. I know there are inspectors and rules and regulations to get around, but if you control the ship, there are ways." Marwick nodded, unsmiling.

"I can use gold to negotiate a better discount on the price, because it's very attractive to black market arms dealers, being almost impossible to trace. That would probably mean five to ten percent less per mine, so I'll need only about three hundred million francs. That saving would be on top of the tax benefit, of course; and you wouldn't have to account for transferring the funds to Eufala. There'd be no record of them at all, so future investigators will have nothing to go on."

"Hmm... you make a compelling case, Captain. We'll discuss this informally and off the record with the rest of the Board over the next day or so. If we give you the go-ahead, how soon can you get those mines in place?"

"I'd say within two to three months after receiving the money from you, sir. It'll take that long to order and collect them, ship them to Mycenae, and sow them in the asteroid belt. You'll also have to tell me where your sensors are, of course. I'll want to remove them before I deploy a single mine. We don't want them recording this, in case anything goes wrong in future."

"Very well. I'll let you know within forty-eight hours whether we'll proceed."

~

THAT EVENING, Caitlin Ross stared at him across her desk. "Please, sir, send someone else! That creep at Marano tried every greasy, slimy trick he could think of to get into my pants. I almost had to stamp on his feet to get him out of the doorway to my hotel room, so I could slam it in his face. If I never see him again, it'll be too soon for me!"

"I'm sorry you had to go through that. Very well, I'll send someone else. I may have to go myself, because we're all so frantically busy right now. You've got more than enough on your plate, setting up our intelligence and security departments."

"Yes, sir, I have. So, with this new order, you'll have a hundred and fifty space mines?"

"With the fifty you've already bought, yes."

"What are you planning to do with them?"

"I've got a few things in mind," he said offhandedly.

Why not tell her? he wondered; then mentally shook his head. *No, I mustn't. I said right from the start that we'd compartmentalize everything. That was the right decision then, and it still is now. Should I tell her about Frank? No, I think not. Frank's too useful to us to put him at risk through loose talk. We'll almost certainly need to use him again in future; so, the fewer who know about him, the better. The same goes for the patrol craft, and the Dragon Tong, and many other things. Keep it 'need to know'. It's safer that way.*

Caitlin asked, "What about the other two robotic prospector fields? Are you going to plant mines around them, too?"

"I'm not planning to. NOE doesn't appear to know about them – at least, they didn't say anything to me about them. I'll report to NOE at some point that we've 'discovered' them, along with the information that their high-value asteroids are also missing, and suggest that it must have been one of their owners who cleaned out everyone else's asteroids along with their own. That should cover our tracks, and give NOE something else to worry about."

"I wish you'd told me about them earlier. I'd have liked to have gone along, to see what I could learn from the prospector robots."

"You were busy at Marano, remember?"

"Oh, yes, of course. Well, it can't be helped now. What if NOE tells you to put mines in those fields as well?"

"Then they'll have to buy me more mines."

She laughed. "You're going to milk them for all you can, aren't you?"

"Why shouldn't I? Listen, Caitlin, they're as much criminals as anybody else. When Rousay put in its claim to colonize the Mycenae system, the United Planets legally halted exploitation there. Until the claim is decided, anyone can *prospect* there, but no-one's allowed to *mine* anything. NOE's jumping the gun on Mycenae Primus Four. Its 'exploration' robots are already digging out mineral ores and stockpiling them on the surface, ready to ship them to a refinery as soon as that becomes legal. Our ship got photographic evidence of that from orbit on its first visit. If the piles of ore are big enough to show up from orbit, they've got to be *huge!*

"NOE also cheated by beaconing, and planning to collect, high-value asteroids. So did whoever sowed the other two prospector robot fields. All three are in violation of the law, for what it's worth. We simply beat their 'owners' to it by collecting their ill-gotten gains before they could. I have no qualms of conscience at all about making criminals pay for our anti-crime program in the Mycenae system. I've even got a contract that says I'm legally allowed to do it, although the United Planets might quibble."

She smiled. "There's a certain irony in that, isn't there?"

"I think so."

"D'you think NOE will accept your proposal?"

"They can't afford not to. If they let others steal their high-value asteroids, they're not going to have enough money to move quickly once the Mycenae system is officially Rousay's. If they can't show fast results, the investors they need will stay away. They've got to do something to increase their income and discourage competitors."

"What if someone gets killed, and you have to carry the can for it?"

"I've taken precautions against that."

"Yes, but *what* precautions? How will they stand up in court?"

"Let me worry about that."

NOE's internal security isn't very good, he thought as he came to his feet. *I have recordings of every meeting I've ever had with them, and more besides, including copies of some of their own records they don't know I've got. All transfers from their bank to ours are documented, and if they give me the money for the mines in gold, I'll record the transfer on audio and video, and keep a bar for mineralogical analysis to prove it came from them. If they try to hang me out to dry, they'll be hanging right beside me – and, if necessary, I'll make sure they know that.*

8

FIRST BLOOD

MYCENAE SYSTEM

"Ready to proceed, sir."

"Very well. Remember, take it *slowly!* Pretend you're a hundred and forty years old, with arthritis in every joint, so it hurts you to move!"

The bridge crew, listening to the conversation over the speaker on Commander Cousins' command console, laughed aloud as the Executive Officer replied, "I'll do just that, sir."

Cousins watched through his command console displays as Lieutenant-Commander Moffatt, seated at the cargo handling console in Hold Seven, gently used tractor and pressor beams to lift *Payara* out of her cradles. The nine-thousand-ton patrol craft seemed to hover over them for an endless moment, then began drifting slowly to starboard as pressor beams pushed her, with glacial slowness, through the open hold doors and into the boundless blackness of space.

It took almost an hour for the smaller vessel to reach a safe distance from the freighter. At last the voice of her skipper came over the tight-beam circuit. *"Payara* to *Amelia.* Ready to proceed. Over."

Cousins activated his microphone. *"Amelia* to *Payara.* Take up station as instructed. Remember, tight-beam communications only, no active sensor emissions, and do not use more than five percent drive power. Acknowledge. Over."

"Payara to *Amelia,* understand tight-beam only, no sensor emissions, five percent max drive power. Over."

"Amelia to *Payara,* carry on. Out." He adjusted a control on his console. "Well done, Exec. You can go ahead with *Trairao* now."

"Roger that, sir. On my way."

The bridge crew watched the internal security vid feed as the Executive Officer closed Hold Seven's outer doors, went through the airlock into the main passageway, and crossed it to enter Hold Eight. There, he opened the outer doors and prepared to undock the second patrol craft.

"Permission to ask a question, please, sir?" The speaker was a young Petty Officer Second Class, one of the operators at the Plot console.

"Go ahead, PO."

"Sir, what do the names of the patrol craft mean?"

"Captain Cochrane named them after predatory fish species in the Amazon River on Earth. Most of them are extinct in the wild, of course, what with centuries of pollution in the Amazon Basin. The Captain reckoned that, as predators, they were suitable names for our first warships."

"With respect, sir, they ain't real powerful warships." A chuckle ran around the bridge.

"No, they're not, but they're what we've got to work with right now, so we'll make do with them until we can afford something better. The Captain's working on that. Give us time, and you'll see this company grow into something pretty impressive."

"I 'ope so, sir. That's why I joined up." There was a rumble of approval and agreement from most of the bridge crew.

"I'm betting they will, PO. That's why I'm here, too," Cousins acknowledged as he watched *Trairao* begin to rise out of the cradles that had held her securely in place during the voyage to the Mycenae system. He couldn't help wondering silently, *Will they be ready in time? Have we rushed them into service too soon? Have their crews learned all they need to know to go into combat, if necessary?*

He cast his mind back over the past few months. The first two patrol craft had been rushed through the refurbishment process at breakneck speed. That had caused problems, because the shipyard staff hadn't been familiar with them, which had resulted in costly mistakes. More of their older, crankier systems than expected had had to be replaced – at greater expense than they'd bargained for – by commercial equivalents, because it would have taken too long to repair and modernize the military-grade originals. Still, they hadn't had any choice. Eufala Corporation *had* to be operational by the time the new satellites were deployed around Mycenae Primus Four. There was no other option. The shipyard would take more time and care over refurbishing the remaining patrol craft, after which the first two could be sent back there to rectify their haste-induced shortcomings.

Cousins smiled to himself as he thought about the patrol craft. New Westray had said nothing at all about their loss except to announce, in very low-key fashion, that they'd been 'expended as targets' by their System Patrol Service. *They must have decided to save face, rather than look like fools,* he mused. At least that meant Eufala didn't have to worry about an interplanetary hue and cry being raised over the missing ships. Master Chief Wallace, the prime enabler of their acquisition, would retire at the end of the month, and join his wife on New Sanday to enjoy his pension – and his newly acquired tourist bar – in peace. *He'll never know how much we owe him. His million-kronor bribe was cheap at the price. It made all this possible.*

A little over an hour later, *Trairao* had joined her consort in formation, trailing the much larger freighter as it cruised toward Mycenae at one-tenth of light speed. *Amelia* had emerged from her final hyper-jump one light-day from the system, accelerated to cruising speed, then shut down her gravitic drive and every other active sensor. The three ships were now closing on their objective. They'd brake at low power as they drew nearer, and would arrive within a million kilometers of Mycenae Primus Four three days before the satellites were due to get there. After that, they'd keep station on the planet, imitating holes in space, watching the satellites being deployed, waiting for someone else to arrive and do something about them once the delivery ship had departed.

Cousins waited until the Executive Officer had joined them on the bridge, then keyed his microphone once more. "*Amelia* to *Payara* and *Trairao*. You have twenty-four hours to settle down and test every system you can, except for active emissions, of course. At noon tomorrow, we'll commence formation and battle exercises. Stay sharp, stay alert, and don't make mistakes. We haven't had enough time to shake down properly. This is the last chance we'll get. Let's make the most of it!"

"Do you think they'll be ready, sir?" his second-in-command asked as he replaced the microphone.

"They'll have to be, won't they? We hand-picked their crews as best we could, just as we did *Amelia*'s complement. If all our ships' systems and weapons work, we should be able to cope with what we're expecting. If something more powerful comes to the dance, we'll just have to speed up our tempo from the waltz to the samba."

Lieutenant-Commander Moffatt chuckled. "As a ballroom dancing fan, I appreciate the idiom, sir."

"I thought you'd like it." They grinned at each other.

"The samba's a damned difficult dance to do well, though. I wish I was out there on one of those patrol craft. Despite their age and all their problems, they're the spear in our hands for the time being. It'd be nice to command one again."

Cousins lowered his voice. "If I didn't need you so badly, you *would* be out there; but I need your patrol craft experience to advise me as I figure out ways for our three ships to do what's needed."

"Thanks for your confidence in me, sir. I'll do my best."

"I know you will. We all will, but I daresay we'll make our fair share of mistakes while we're learning. That's inevitable. Let's learn from them, so we don't make them again – and let's keep them small enough that no-one gets hurt or killed while we're making them."

"From your lips to God's ears, sir!"

"Let's hope he's listening."

FOR THE NEXT WEEK, the three ships practiced together. *Amelia* sent fresh provisions and other supplies to the smaller patrol craft every third day via cutter. The ships maneuvered in formation and independently, and exercised their crews in every system on board. The spacers muttered in frustration at having to repeat the same exercises again and again, but few questioned the necessity. The senior NCO of the task force, Senior Chief Petty Officer Laker, was heard to rebuke one particularly vocal spacer, "Shut up, Harris! Only amateurs practice until they've got it right. Professionals practice *until they can't get it wrong*. We're professionals – apart from you, that is!"

They slowed to a halt, one million kilometers from Mycenae Primus Four, and hung silently in space, adjusting their position as needed using minimal drive power that wouldn't be detected by sensors unless they were only a few thousand kilometers away. Cousins knew that the Callanish repair ship, *Colomb,* was almost certainly doing the same thing at the same time. If she was headed for the same position she'd used on her previous visit, she would be only a few million kilometers from the Eufala ships right now.

Right on time, a freighter from Rousay showed up to deploy the new constellation of satellites. She spent three days in orbit around Mycenae Primus Four as her specialized small craft emplaced the satellites, checked their orbits relative to each other, and set up the network linking them to the robotic prospectors on the planet below. *Amelia* and her consorts watched silently, not betraying their presence by so much as a single stray radio transmission. They used only laser tight-beams for communication, impossible to intercept unless in line-of-sight between transmitter and receiver – and they made sure that the laser dishes were never aimed anywhere close to the planet, or where they suspected *Colomb* was waiting.

The tension ratcheted higher as the installation of the satellites approached completion. The three ships' crews watched and waited as the freighter recovered her small craft, ran a final function test on the newly installed system by remote control, and switched it from test to operational mode before heading for the system boundary, on her way back to Rousay.

As they watched the departing ship's icon in the plot display, Moffatt murmured, "Will they make their move now, sir?"

"I think not. *Colomb* will wait until she's sure the freighter has left. She'll want to see her hyper-jump signature. Last time, she crept in silently to about half a million kilometers from the planet before launching her cargo shuttle. Her own gravitic drive signature didn't show up in that spot until after the cargo shuttle returned, carrying the three satellites they stole."

"Did she suspect a trap, sir? Why did she remain in silent mode for so long?"

"That's a good question. I suppose her skipper wanted to make sure there were no active defenses. If something had clobbered his cargo shuttle, he'd have sneaked off undetected to avoid being targeted himself."

"I bet the crew of that shuttle didn't enjoy being the proverbial canaries in the coal mine."

"You can say that again! For their sakes, I hope they got danger pay for that job."

"Are we going to hit the shuttle this time, sir?"

"Not if I can help it. They can't fight back, and I don't like the thought of murdering defenseless spacers, no matter whose side they're on. We'll make our move against *Colomb* when we see the shuttle's gravitic drive signature as it leaves her docking bay. That'll confirm her position. Once she's surrendered, we'll have her recall the shuttle."

"And if she doesn't surrender?"

Cousins' voice turned ice cold. "Then the shuttle will have to rendezvous with us instead, because there'll be nothing left of *Colomb* but a cloud of radioactive molecules."

"Ah... won't that be 'murdering defenseless spacers', as you put it, sir?"

"No. *Colomb* is a military-grade repair ship. She can move as fast as our old patrol craft, and twice as fast as *Amelia*. If she manages to evade our trap, she'll head for the system boundary. We won't be able to catch her, and our old-fashioned, relatively short-ranged missiles probably won't either. That means we've got to stop her before she gets too far away. We daren't allow her to warn her bosses on Callanish that we're patrolling the Mycenae system now. No, if she shows resistance, we'll fire on her. We'll have no choice."

"Let's hope they listen to reason, sir."

Cousins did not reply. He took a last, long look at the Plot display. The departing freighter's icon was now half a billion kilometers away. The location in space, relative to the planet, from which *Colomb* had launched her cargo shuttle on the previous occasion was marked with a red flashing icon. The patrol craft were not on radar, as emissions silence was in force, but their presumed locations behind and on either side of *Amelia* were marked with green icons. Dotted lines showed where they would head after receiving their orders.

His mind raced through the operation orders one last time. They could not possibly anticipate every contingency, but they'd done their best to cater for unexpected developments, given the limitations of their ships and weapons. Now it was time to put the plan into action.

Cousins reached for his microphone and activated the tight-beam circuit. "*Amelia* to *Payara* and *Trairao*. Execute Operation Intercept. I say again, execute Operation Intercept. Acknowledge. Over."

A momentary pause, then, "*Payara* to *Amelia,* understand execute Intercept, over."

"*Trairao* to *Amelia,* understand execute Intercept, over."

"*Amelia* to *Payara* and *Trairao*. Proceed in accordance with your orders, and use your initiative if necessary. Good luck to us all. *Amelia* out."

Cousins adjusted the microphone controls, switching it from the external tight-beam network to the ship's internal communications. "Bridge to drive room. Confirm that drive limiter is set to five percent only, I say again, five percent only."

The reply came back instantly. "Drive room to bridge, I confirm limiter is at five percent."

"Good. Warn everyone on duty that if they exceed that figure, the only way they'll leave this ship is when I personally feed them through the reaction thrusters!"

A chuckle came back over the circuit. "I'll tell them, sir."

"Thank you."

Cousins set down the microphone as he looked around the bridge. "Very well. Let's go get 'em! Helm, power to five percent, go to preassigned course, shut down when we reach assigned speed."

"Helm to Command, five percent power, assume assigned course and speed, aye aye, sir."

Slowly, silently, *Amelia* began her advance to contact. In her wake, the patrol craft did the same, their courses diverging slightly from hers as they moved toward their attack positions.

ABOARD *COLOMB,* the tension was markedly lower than on *Amelia*'s bridge. Her duty watch kept an eye on the departing freighter as it headed toward the system boundary. As it reached it, its icon flared into the unmistakable pattern of a hyper-jump signature, making the Plot operator's report superfluous; but he made it anyway.

"Plot to Command, freighter has left the system, sir."

"Command to Plot, understood, thank you." Commander Lamprey clicked over to another intercom channel. "Command to cargo shuttle, the freighter's left. You can undock and proceed as ordered."

At his pilot console, Chief Petty Officer Lawson replied, "Shuttle to Command, understood, sir. On my way."

He ordered his crew to double-check that the inner airlock door was secured, then disengaged the tube joining it to the docking bay airlock in *Colomb*'s stern. The concertina tube retracted into its housing and swung clear of the shuttle.

"Crew ready?" Lawson demanded. One by one, his six spacers reported that they were strapped into their chairs and ready for departure. "All right. We're off."

Lawson applied power to the reaction thrusters. Slowly, carefully, the cargo shuttle backed out of the docking bay. As soon as it was clear of the larger ship's gravitic drive field, Lawson powered up its own, much smaller drive unit, swiveling in space onto a course that would take it to a rendezvous with the first satellite.

"GRAVITIC DRIVE SIGNATURE DETECTED, SIR!" The Plot operator's voice cut through the tension on *Amelia*'s bridge like a knife. "Bearing 005:007, classified as probable cargo shuttle. It's heading for the planet. Cross-bearings are coming in from the patrol craft on tight-beam link... cross-bearings suggest a range of two hundred thousand kilometers, sir."

"Command to Plot, understood. Start the attack clock from the time of detection."

Cousins reflected that he'd never expected to give that order on the bridge of a freighter, but then, he'd never served on a freighter armed with missiles and laser cannon before. There were a lot of firsts on this mission.

The Plot operator started a counter, visible as a series of digits in the three-dimensional display, and pressed several controls. The scrolling digits of the counter froze, jumped a little as the ship's computer adjusted it, then began ratcheting up again, counting off the seconds and minutes since the gravitic drive signature had first been detected. An icon now marked the spot where that had happened, which was almost certainly where *Colomb* would be found. Cousins knew that the patrol craft would be doing the same thing.

"We're as close to right on the button as we could be, sir!" Lieutenant-Commander Moffatt's voice was exultant as he sat behind the hastily improvised Weapons console, tucked into a corner of the bridge. "She's almost exactly where we expected her to be."

"Yes, it was nice of them to use the same approach as last time. On the other hand, why shouldn't they? As far as they know, they've nothing to fear here."

"We'll show them differently, sir!" A rumble of agreement ran around the bridge, a murmur of impending triumph. They'd worked long and hard to be ready for this day.

"All right, keep it quiet," Cousins ordered, but couldn't help the smile that played around his lips. He, too, was looking forward to this. "Command to Weapons. You may fire as planned, without waiting for orders, as soon as the counter reaches ten minutes. Weapons free."

"Weapons to Command, weapons free in ten minutes, aye aye, sir."

The tension ratcheted higher as they watched the figures rolling in the counter window.

ON *COLOMB'S* BRIDGE, her duty watch felt no tension at all as they looked at the Plot display. The cargo shuttle was almost ten minutes out, arrowing toward its rendezvous with the first satellite. They'd all shared in a handsome bonus for capturing the first three satellites, some months before. If they picked up the next three as well, plus the monitoring station that they now knew existed, they'd get the same again – something to look forward to when they got back to Callanish.

Their anticipation was rudely shattered as three traces appeared in the Plot display, the first above them, the second thirty degrees below and to starboard, and the last thirty degrees below and to port. The Plot operator froze for a disbelieving second, then almost screamed, "Vampire! *Vampire!* Three missiles launched from... they're all around us!"

Almost before he'd finished speaking, Lieutenant-Commander Macaskill's voice cut over his from the Navigation console. *"They're not aimed at us!* They're offset to one side, sir!"

Lamprey felt as if he were wading through mental molasses as he tried to cudgel his astonished brain into action. He raised his voice over the sudden hubbub of startled cries and oaths. *"Silence!* Silence on the bridge!" Every instinct screamed at him to cut in the drive and head for safety right away... but those missiles proved it would be futile.

They watched in frozen, dumbfounded silence as the three missiles arrowed closer, then detonated in three starburst icons in the Plot display. Their laser beam cones were aimed away from *Colomb,* so they did no damage, instead slashing harmlessly through the vacuum of space.

Almost as soon as the last missile had detonated, a voice crackled over the Communications speaker on the interplanetary emergency channel. It was filtered through a voice modulator, so that it came over in a flat, mechanical monotone.

"Attention! *Colomb,* you are surrounded by armed vessels. Any attempt to flee will result in your instant destruction. Your ship and crew are under arrest. Order your cargo shuttle to return to your ship immediately. Your crew is to enter *Colomb's* lifeboats, taking nothing with them, and remain there until further orders. The Commanding Officer, plus a skeleton bridge and drive room crew, are to remain at their stations. Send your Executive Officer to meet an armed boarding party in your docking bay. They will give you further orders. In the meantime, you are not to damage your ship in any way. Leave all systems and equipment in fully operational condition. Do not erase any records, files or programs. If you do, those responsible will face the most severe consequences. Acknowledge. Over."

There was a stunned silence in the control center as Lamprey reached for his microphone. He somehow managed to keep his voice steady, even though his body was trembling with the shock of his reaction to the missiles that had come out of nowhere.

"*Colomb* to unknown vessel. Who are you? Identify yourself! By what authority are you trying to arrest us? There is no System Control Service in the Mycenae system, and no laws or regulations authorizing you or anybody else to arrest anyone for anything. This is an act of piracy! Over."

"*Colomb,* we are the new security service for the Mycenae

system. That's all you need to know. We don't care whether you recognize our authority. You'd better recognize the authority of our missiles, if you value your lives! As for your arrest, what did you expect after you stole three satellites from around this planet? Your presence here was recorded, and your ship identified. You are now being brought to justice for that theft. It may be frontier justice, but it's justice nonetheless. Your ship is forfeit for your crimes. You and your crew will be placed under guard while *Colomb* is taken away for disposal. After that, plus a suitable interval to make sure you haven't sabotaged her in any way, you'll all be returned to Callanish, to explain to your bosses how you lost their ship. Over."

Lamprey wanted to spit on the deck next to his console, but restrained himself. He was filled with bitter anger and frustration. He knew they had no defense against... whoever these people were. They'd heard vague rumors that the New Orkney Enterprise was considering system security in Mycenae, but his superiors had assured him that nothing had been done about it yet. They'd claimed it would take months, if not years, for NOE to buy patrol craft, hire qualified and experienced crews for them, and set up a formal security operation. What's more, NOE didn't have the money to spare for that right now. He couldn't help thinking bitterly, *It looks like they had a lot more money than we thought. They must have hired an existing outfit, rather than taken the time to raise their own. Who the hell are these people? There aren't many space security companies out there, and I don't know any who can afford to expend nuclear-tipped missiles as a demonstration like that. They cost too much.*

Slowly, he raised his microphone. "*Colomb* to... whoever you are. We shall comply, under protest. I am recalling my cargo shuttle, and will send my crew to the lifeboats and my Executive Officer to the docking bay. We await your boarding party. Over."

"Very well. Do as you're told, and no-one will get hurt, and you'll all get home safely. Stand by."

Lamprey switched to intercom. "Drive compartment, stand fast. Bridge, stand fast. The rest of the crew is to proceed to their lifeboat stations at once, and take their places in the lifeboats, but do not launch, I say again, *Do. Not. Launch.* This is not a drill. I repeat, *This. Is. Not. A. Drill.* Lifeboat commanders, call the roll. Report to me as soon as all assigned personnel are in their places."

Faintly, echoing up and down the main passageway, he could hear shouts of astonishment from the crew. Most of them knew nothing of the drama outside the hull, he reminded himself. He'd have to broadcast to them in the lifeboats, and explain what had happened.

He nodded approvingly at Lieutenant-Commander Macaskill, who'd taken it upon himself to radio the cargo shuttle and order its immediate return. "Thank you, Exec. You'd better head for the docking bay to meet the boarding party. Be careful. They may be trigger-happy."

"I'll be careful, sir." Aidan's voice was tight with anger and concern. "I wonder where they're going to put us while they take *Colomb* to... wherever she's going?"

"I daresay we'll find out soon enough. As to where she's going, surely that's obvious? They'll take her somewhere they can sell her for a lot of money, cash on the barrelhead. A newly refurbished repair ship, with all its equipment intact, is worth hundreds of millions, even in a no-questions-asked under-the-counter sale. They'll want to recover as much as they can of the value of the satellites we took from them."

"I wish we could hand them a worthless, burned-out hulk!"

"It's a tempting thought, but what would happen to our crew if we did?" They stared at each other for a wordless moment, then Lamprey shook his head. "No. We can't risk it. Our people deserve better than that."

"I... yes, sir. You're right."

"I'll broadcast to the ship's company once they're in the

lifeboats, and make sure they understand that too. No resistance, no sabotage, no funny business at all. Our families want us back alive, not in coffins!"

A WEEK LATER, Commander Lamprey walked through every compartment of his almost deserted ship. A space-suited figure walked at his side, its helmet visor dialed to mirror brightness so that he couldn't see through it from outside. Everyone who'd boarded his ship had done the same thing, and their voices had all been passed through a modulator. There was no way he or his crew would ever be able to identify them.

At last the figure beside him said, "That's it, then. All compartments are empty, and every member of your crew has been accounted for. Thank you for your cooperation, Commander. It guarantees you good treatment until we take you home."

"How long will we be here?"

"Plan on up to three months. It may be less, but I don't think it will be more."

Lamprey sighed in frustration. "What about our families? They'll be off their heads with worry. They'll think something's happened to us."

"I'm sorry. I understand your concern, but for our own security, we want to dispose of *Colomb* before we let you go. It'll take time to do that, and for word to get back to us that it's been done. Until then, you'll just have to possess yourselves in patience. We've included books, games and a few other distractions on the computer in your habitat."

"Thanks for that," he said grudgingly. "At least you haven't dumped us in those shelters with nothing to do. After two or three weeks, that would get very boring."

"Keep good order and discipline, and you'll all come through this without a problem. When the time comes, we'll ferry you up to a freighter with a personnel pod big enough for all of you, sealed against vacuum. We'll take you to Callanish and shove the pod out of the hold doors at the system boundary, with an emergency beacon attached, and send a signal to System Control to tell them who and where you are. Your System Patrol Service will respond, and tow you to planetary orbit. By then, of course, we'll be long gone."

"I suppose that'll work."

"All right, let's get you planetside."

An hour later, the cutter landed on the airless surface of Mycenae Primus Four. A series of toroidal inflatable habitats had been set up, connected to each other by airlocks and tubes. The cutter reversed up to an airlock, which extended a concertina tube that sealed itself around the flange surrounding the rear hatch. There was a brief pause while pressures were equalized, then the light above the hatch changed from red to green. The cutter pilot pressed a switch, and the hatch hinged outward and down, forming a ramp giving access to the tube.

His captor turned to him, face still invisible behind the mirror finish of his spacesuit helmet. "You've got rations for four months. We've run a cable from your shelter to a tight-beam dish over the hill. One of our ships will be monitoring that circuit via satellite link. If you need something, ask them, but don't waste our time with idle chit-chat. Use it for emergencies only. We'll check in once a week if we don't hear from you."

"Can't you give us a radio, instead of a tight-beam? What if the beam is displaced by something, and doesn't work?"

"Sorry. We don't want you listening to our transmissions. You'll have to live with the tight-beam circuit. If we notice it's not working, we'll repair it."

With that, Lamprey had to be content. He went through the airlock, sealing it behind him, and looked at his waiting Executive Officer.

"Everything all right down here?"

"Yes, sir, as far as 'all right' can apply to a temporary inflatable shelter on an airless planet!"

"It'll have to do for now."

～

COMMANDER COUSINS WAITED while the cutter rendezvoused with *Amelia* and slid into her docking bay. At last, Lieutenant-Commander Moffatt reported, "Cutter secure, sir. Ready for departure."

"Thank you, Exec." He reached for his microphone. "*Amelia* to *Payara* and *Trairao*. We're heading out in accordance with orders. Remain in orbit around Mycenae Primus Four, and make sure you observe the restrictions on active emissions and drive power. We still don't know whether another ship might visit those asteroid prospector bots, or what type of ship it may be. If one does arrive, but it can't detect you, it won't bother you; and until we have greater force in this system, we don't want to start a fight. Meanwhile, keep an eye on *Colomb*'s crew.

"You've got six months' supplies in orbit. We should be back within two months, all being well. Give local liberty to your crews when possible in the orbital inflatable habitat we left for that purpose. It's not much, but it's a lot more spacious than the cramped quarters aboard your ships, so make the most of it. We'll bring your relief crews back with us. Over."

"*Payara* to *Amelia*, have fun, you lucky bastards! We'll keep things under wraps here. Over."

"*Trairao* to *Amelia*, have a beer or three for us. Any chance you can sneak a few cases aboard when you return? Over."

Cousins grinned. "*Amelia* to *Payara* and *Trairao*. No beer. You know the rules in space. However, we'll tell them to stock up, ready for your return. You can make up for the dry months then! *Amelia* out."

He glanced across at Moffatt. "Very well, Exec. Let's go."

"Yes, sir. I wonder how the prize crew is doing aboard *Colomb*?"

"They're probably still settling down, rattling around in her like peas in a pod. There's not many of them."

"I reckon they'll get to Constanta about a week before we do. It's a real pity we can't keep *Colomb* for ourselves. After her refurbishment, she's in great shape."

"Yes, but she's too easily identifiable. Once Callanish spreads the word about her loss, we'd risk having her confiscated as stolen property if we took her to any major planet. Better to exchange her for what we need, after stripping out everything useful on board."

"That'll keep Warrant Officer McBride busy for a while."

"It sure will! Now, let's go pull that surveillance satellite from NOE's asteroid prospecting field, then check all three fields to see whether any more asteroids have been beaconed for recovery. If so, we'll take them with us, too."

9
CHANGE OF DELIVERY

DURRES

The comm unit chimed next to Captain Faraday's bed. It kept on chiming until, groaning in frustration, he turned over and reached for it. "Who the hell d'you think you are, calling me at two in the bloody morning?" he bellowed into the mouthpiece.

"I'm sorry, Captain," came a clipped, official-sounding voice. "Some of your people have been having too much of a good time. We've had to arrest them. I thought you'd want to know."

"Who the devil is this?"

"I'm Inspector Carse, Durres Planetary Police. I'm at the reception desk. I suggest I come up to your room, so the other spacers in the bar won't interrupt us."

Faraday cudgeled his brain into action. Yes, it was Saturday morning, after all. This hotel was popular with visiting spacers, and a lot of them would still be having a good time in the bar, warming up for the weekend. No sense in letting them see uniforms, and become antagonistic.

"All right, Inspector. I'm in 319. Come on up."

"Thank you, Captain. We'll be there in two minutes."

He had time to don his shirt and trousers, but no shoes, before a firm, authoritative knock came at the door. He opened it to find two men, both wearing the black uniform of the local police force.

"Come on in," he grunted, turning his back to them as he walked away – then the world went dark. He never felt his cheek strike the carpet as he collapsed to the floor.

He woke an indeterminable time later, lying under a blanket on a thin camping pad, on a cold concrete floor in some sort of warehouse or storage building. The only light came from translucent panels set in the metal roof far above. There were no windows, and the sliding doors were closed. One of them had a smaller metal door set into it, also shut.

"Wh – where the devil am I?" he muttered to himself as he pushed himself painfully up on one elbow. He winced at the movement, and put his hand to the back of his head. He found a swelling above his right ear that hadn't been there the night before.

His confusion redoubled as he looked around. Both passage crews were lying on the floor around him, looking as if they were sleeping peacefully. Trickles of blood were visible on some of their faces and heads. Beyond them in the gloom, a pile of suitcases and kitbags was piled carelessly against a wall. Looking more closely, he recognized his own among them.

He jumped, startled, as a shrilling sound came from a comm unit lying on the floor next to him. He picked it up, and put it gingerly to his ear. "H – hello?"

"Listen up." The voice was flat, dispassionate. He recognized it as the 'Inspector' of the night before. "You and your passage crews are a hundred kilometers from Durres City, in a farming area. There's no houses within five clicks of that building, and no-one will go near it. You'll find crates of ration packs against the far wall. The taps and toilets work. There are no live guards, but we've deployed armed security drones around the barn. They'll fire on any human-sized movement outside, so don't try to leave. That would be terminally stupid. Got it?"

"Y – yes, but... why are you doing this?"

"Don't ask stupid questions that you know I won't answer. The comm unit in your hand is connected to this one on a dedicated circuit. It can't call anywhere else. If you have an emergency, press the 'call' button, and someone will answer after a while. You're going to be in that building for the next twenty-seven days, so you may as well relax and enjoy it. At the end of that time, we'll send a crew bus to take you to the spaceport. Inside it, you'll find tickets for the next monthly freighter to New Stornoway, and tickets for the ferry from there to Callanish, plus 'distressed spacer' documentation to get you all the way back home."

"But – but – where are our ID's? What about the ships we're supposed to collect at Goheung?"

The voice sounded mocking as it assured him, "Don't worry, they'll be in good hands. Just remember – *stay in the building*. If you don't believe me about the drones, send one of your crew outside. We haven't locked the small door set inside the larger sliding door. Just make sure to pick someone you don't mind losing, because he won't be coming back!"

With a sick, sinking feeling in the pit of his stomach, Faraday realized that the speaker wasn't joking. This kidnapping had been too well planned and professionally executed for that.

"All right," he gritted, struggling to contain his outrage and frustration. "Twenty-seven days, you said?"

"That's right. All your gear is in there with you, plus some entertainment on the tablets piled on the table. You'll be bored, but you'll also be alive and unharmed when you get out of there. Be grateful for small mercies. We could have put you out of the way much more permanently. You wouldn't have enjoyed that."

There was a click as the speaker cut the circuit.

GOHEUNG

Three weeks later, two brand-new million-ton fast freighters were formally handed over to their passage crews. The ceremony was impressive, featuring a band, the flags of Goheung and Callanish, and speeches by the shipyard manager and by 'Captain Faraday' on behalf of the ships' new owners.

When the formalities had been observed and the guests had dispersed, the passage crews boarded their ships and settled down for the long journey that lay ahead. Frank removed the pads from inside his cheeks, used solvent to strip off the dark eyebrows and close-cropped beard and mustache he'd adopted, and combed his hair back into its normal style. It had been a prolonged and not-very-enjoyable few weeks, imitating Captain Faraday's appearance. He was glad he could abandon the pretense at last.

He returned to the bridge, set up a tight-beam link to the other ship, and cut in the intercom circuits on both vessels so that all his people could hear his words. "Listen up!" he began. "You've done real well. There'll be a bonus for everyone when we get to Medusa. We'll have to wait a few weeks for the replacement ships, so we'll go planetside and enjoy ourselves – but remember, keep your mouths shut! As soon as the other ships are ready, we'll be off again. There'll be another bonus when we deliver them. Make sure you keep them spotlessly clean and in good order. Well-paying customers like these aren't all that common. If we deliver what we promised, in top shape, they'll be coming back to us with more business. Let's make sure of that by keeping them happy!"

He replaced the microphone and relaxed. By now, the ship-yard on Medusa would have lined up the three ships Henry had asked for, in exchange for these two brand-new fast freighters and Callanish's repair vessel. They might well have been stolen somewhere, or pirated, but that wouldn't matter by the time the shipyard finished with them. Their gravitic drives, transponder beacons, and all other components with an emissions signature would be replaced; fairings would be added, and metal cut away, to alter their outline; serial numbers and identification plates would be removed from major items of equipment, preventing their being traced; and new registration documents would be provided, certifying that the vessels had originated in a defunct shipyard on the far side of the settled galaxy. Conveniently, its records were no longer available for comparison to the ships. That wasn't surprising, since it had been set up, then shut down, by a Medusa concern as a useful fig-leaf for transactions such as these.

Once all that's done, they'll be untraceable, Frank thought contentedly to himself. *Henry's boss can take them anywhere he pleases, without fear of anyone identifying them as stolen property. Even taking our fee into account, plus whatever extra he might have had to pay to the shipyard, he'll have bought two smaller fast freighters and a repair ship for less than a third of their market value. That's a good deal in anyone's language.*

～

CONSTANTA

His sentiments were echoed by Commander Cousins as he sat down in Captain Cochrane's office. "Not only did we get you a repair ship, sir; we also brought back thirty-three more asteroids."

"*Thirty-three?* I don't understand. According to NOE, it took over a year for the prospector bots to find those we collected last time. How did they find so many more, so quickly?"

"There's a puzzle there, sir. The NOE and Callanish bot fields had found only four or five apiece. Those robot prospectors with

Cyrillic plates, though; they were moving much faster. They'd spread further, and found twice as many as the other two fields combined. I think those bots are using a different algorithm to identify asteroids worth beaconing. They're working faster because they're working smarter. They seem to be programmed to abandon any asteroid that doesn't meet a tight first-pass set of criteria. That may cause them to discard some otherwise worthwhile rocks, but it also means they won't waste time on anything but the really good ones – the cream of the cream."

"You may be right. I think we need to analyze some of those bots down to binary zeroes and ones, to understand their algorithms and their artificial intelligence control program."

"I figured you'd say that, boss, so I brought three of them back with me. That was more difficult than I expected. They still exploded every time we tried to get close to them. In the end, we tried having a cutter descend from directly above them, using reaction thrusters, then spear them with a tractor beam from about fifty meters up. That worked. As soon as they were lifted off the surface, they shut down. At the ship, we moved them into a hold using tractor beams, but made sure we didn't lower them to the deck until we'd disabled their power packs. Turns out they had sensors in their feet. As soon as all of them were off the surface, that disabled the self-destruct mechanism."

"That was good work, to figure that out – dangerous, though, to take them aboard your ship when they might blow up."

"They weren't big explosions, sir. I'd seen a few by then. I figured it was worth the risk, because I'm sure Jock Murray will want to investigate them."

"Yes, he's the obvious person to start checking them out. He'll probably call in some systems specialists, too. All right, you took a calculated risk, and it paid off. Well done, Dave."

"You may not say that when I tell you the next bit, sir. I did some thinking. We know about NOE's bots, and Callanish's – at least, that's where the second field's prospector bots come from.

That field with the Cyrillic-labeled bots, though; we've no idea who put them there, or when. They're more advanced than the other bots; they work faster; and they're programmed to self-destruct rather than be captured. Putting all that together, it made me wonder; are their owners the single most dangerous threat to us, and to what we're trying to do in Mycenae?"

Cousins took a deep breath. "I had a hunch, sir. I sowed those ten space mines you gave me around the leading edge of their prospector bot field. I programmed them to listen for test transmissions, as the bots locate rich asteroids and deploy beacons on them. One mine will patrol each beacon, and hit any ship trying to pick it up. I programmed them with an ID code, too, so that if our ships broadcast it as they move in, they won't be targeted."

"But you were supposed to do that in NOE's field!"

"Yes, sir, but I think the Cyrillic guys, for want of a better name for them, are more dangerous to us. You told NOE you'd mine their field as soon as you'd bought space mines. You were going to buy warheads while we were away, and I presume Sue's using them to rebuild the mines she took apart, so I'll deploy those when I go back. If I did the wrong thing, sir, I apologize. Like I said, I had a hunch, and it was strong enough that I acted on it."

Cochrane thought for a moment. "I wouldn't have done that, but it's like I've always taught my officers. The person on the spot is the one who must make the call. You can't make it from thousands or millions or billions of kilometers away. I'm not sure you made the *right* call, but it was your call to make. We'll see how it works out."

Cousins relaxed, visibly relieved. "Thank you, sir."

"As for the mines, I had an interesting visit to Marano. I went to the same brokerage we'd used before, but refused to deal with the man who'd given Caitlin a hard time – and I told them why. He had a fatal car accident within twenty-four hours. I think, when it comes to multi-million-franc repeat orders, they don't like people who don't stay focused on the money."

Cousins whistled softly. "Looks that way. Did they do anything else to apologize?"

"Yes, they did. They gave me a hundred and fifty warheads for the price of a hundred. That'll allow Sue to rebuild the mines she dismantled, and upgrade the rest of the missiles she's restored to working order. I also bought another fifty mines, since they offered them at a very good price to 'rebuild trust', as they put it. Fortunately, the second payment from Barjah had come through, to add to NOE's three hundred million, so I could afford them. You'll be able to deploy some around Mycenae Primus Four, as well as in the asteroid belt."

"That's great, sir! When are you delivering the next shipment of asteroids?"

"Within the week. We badly need the money to refill our bank account. I think I'll take one of those prospector robots with me. The people at Barjah may be able to identify it. Asteroid mining is their business, after all."

"Good idea, sir."

"I'll leave you in charge here, to load the next two patrol craft as soon as they're refurbished, and help Sue transfer equipment and supplies from *Colomb* to the New Westray depot ship. The sooner that's finished, the better, because we need to send *Colomb* to Medusa in part trade for our own repair ship."

"I'm surprised you haven't scrapped the depot ship yet, sir."

"We don't have enough storage space here yet, so we're using her as an orbital warehouse until our new freighters get here. I transferred most of the asteroids to her as well, so that I could take the leased freighter to Marano, and now to Barjah. Once our new freighters are up and running, we'll return the leased one and scrap the depot ship."

Cochrane stretched wearily. "Sue's in transports of delight over *Colomb*'s equipment. Apparently there are very high-end tool sets for space mechanics and electronics techs, with every conceivable piece of equipment they could need, all of it manufactured to the highest possible standards. They sell for well into six figures apiece. *Colomb* had ten of each, installed as part of her refurbishment. Sue's ripped them all out, and a bunch of other gear besides, and plans to put them on our own repair ship when it gets here. It'll be empty, of course, and almost twice the size of *Colomb,* so it'll have room for all the depot ship's equipment as well as *Colomb's.* She reckons it'll take her six months to a year to set it up properly, even with the shipyard's help."

"I bet she's enjoying every moment of it, sir, even while she's bitching like mad at all the work you're loading on her back."

"I see you know her."

"Not that well, sir, but I know gearheads!" They grinned at each other. "If I may, sir, I have another suggestion."

"Of course you may. You're my second-in-command, after all. What is it?"

"Well, sir, you've mentioned that a lot of planets that really need space security, can't afford to pay for it. If we get bigger and better warships, as you hope to do in due course, we're going to have to charge a very high fee to pay for them and cover their operating expenses. On the other hand, if we offer some low-end patrol craft as well, which may be all a lot of planets can afford to hire, we won't be able to charge enough for their services to cover our overall costs.

"It occurred to me, sir; what if we charge mostly in asteroids, rather than in cash? We can ask for enough money to cover our immediate expenses. On top of that, in return for a lower up-front fee, clients must give us the right to cherry-pick some asteroids out of their asteroid belt. If we can figure out the algorithm those Cyrillic bots are using, we can program our own prospector robots to pick out high-grade asteroids very quickly, assuming they're there. In time, we might even be able to afford our own refinery ship to process them, so we can keep all the proceeds instead of sharing them. We'll make enough money to more than compensate for lower cash fees."

"That's an almost indecently brilliant suggestion," Cochrane said slowly. "I can see a number of potential problems, but none that can't be dealt with. The biggest will be existing contracts. A lot of planets have sold exclusive rights to one or more companies to exploit their asteroid belts. They won't like it if we take some of the best asteroids out from under their noses. On the other hand, they need security to operate, so they'll understand the need to pay for it. Let's bounce this idea around some more, just between the two of us. If we can refine it, and make it workable, you might just have given us a business model for the long term. Well done, Dave!"

Cousins flushed slightly. "Thank you, sir."

"All right. Let's go and see Sue. You two need to coordinate your movements and activities over the next few weeks. I'll be leaving for Barjah by the weekend. By the time I get back, I guess you'll have headed for Mycenae, to deliver the next two patrol craft and relief crews for the first two, and take the prisoners back to Callanish."

"When do you think we'll have a chance to sit down and discuss where we are, sir? I mean, all the leadership team together?"

"I don't know, but I hope it's soon. We're coping at present, but it's not good that I'm the only person who knows everything that's going on, with you as my backup – and not fully informed, at that. We need to start pulling together, rather than separately. Trouble is, I don't see how we're going to do that with so much happening in so many places at once. We don't have enough trustworthy deputies to delegate a lot of the workload."

"You're right, sir. We need more officers. Most of those we're hiring are spacers and senior NCO's. They're good, but they're not command material. The few officers we've managed to hire show promise, but there aren't enough of them."

"You're right, but how do we find more of the kind we need? There are lots of applicants, but some of them couldn't pour piss out of a boot even if the instructions were written on the heel. We need trained military officers, and leaders whom our spacers will follow, and people we can trust with our secrets. Right now, most candidates meet one or two of those criteria, but hardly ever all three."

Cousins grinned tiredly. "I guess it's like the old construction quandary, sir. Speed, high quality, and low cost. Pick any two."

"The engineers never did find a way around that, did they?"

"No, sir, but don't tell Sue McBride that!"

∿

CALLANISH

"But who the hell *were* they?" Scott's voice was shrill with outrage as he glared around the boardroom. Outside the twentieth-floor windows, offering a panoramic view of downtown Achmore, capital city of Callanish, gray clouds spread a gloom to match that inside the boardroom.

"I can only think of one possibility," Dunsinane growled. "Who else but those bastards at Rousay? They must have figured out somehow that we took their satellites. This must be their way of retaliating."

"But how could they possibly get away with it, Mr. Chairman? In fact, how do we know they did? Their people may have been arrested when they tried to take delivery of our ships!"

For a moment, several of the members of the board brightened at the thought, but Dunsinane shot down their hopes. "Don't bet on it. Whoever they hired did a very professional job, removing our passage crews from their hotel on Durres with no-one the wiser, and hiding them out in the country while they took their place at Goheung. We've sent an urgent inquiry there, but it'll take weeks for a reply to reach us. I daresay our new ships will be long gone by the time we get it."

"We may as well be back on Earth in the sailing ship era," Pentland observed bitterly. "Back then, a signal from a distant colony or naval base would take weeks or even months to reach the mother country, and just as long for a reply to get back. Dammit, battles were sometimes fought because those involved hadn't got word in time that the war was already over!"

"You'd better brace yourselves for another problem," Dunsinane said quietly. Every head turned to look at him. "The System Patrol Service told me this morning that *Colomb*'s expected window of arrival was between the twenty-third and the thirtieth. She hasn't shown up. If the New Orkney Enterprise arranged to steal our new freighters, might they also have arranged for something to happen to her in the Mycenae system?"

There was a frozen silence for a moment, then an outburst of angry shouts and bitter curses. The Chairman let it continue for a few moments, then held up his hand, and waited for the hubbub to die down. It took a while.

"We don't know for sure, but I put it to you that it's at least a possibility. If *Colomb* isn't back by the end of another week, I fear it'll approach certainty. That means we'll have lost our two new freighters – although we paid for those with NOE's satellites, so it won't come out of our pocket – and *Colomb* too. That *will* hit us in the wallet. We just paid a quarter of a billion francs to have her refurbished. Our contract with the SPS specifies we have to repair or replace her, at our expense, if anything goes wrong while she's working for us. She's covered by insurance, but not to her full refurbished value, and not against acts of war. Even if we can convince the insurers to pay out, another repair ship, even a used one, will cost at least half a billion francs, fully equipped. We'll have to finance whatever share of that the insurers won't cover."

"The banks are going to eat us alive on the interest rate," Scott grumped.

"Of course they are. If our positions were reversed, we'd do the same. That's business."

"Can we get the Defense Minister to lean on them? We're buying him a ship, after all, so he owes us – and we paid him enough under the counter to let us use *Colomb!*"

"We can try, but the banks can get the Finance Minister to have a word with him. They pay her under the counter, too, remember? If push comes to shove, they can afford more and bigger bribes than we can."

Pentland asked, "What about tracing the ships? If NOE's behind their loss, surely they'll want to use them? If we have someone check the Rousay system periodically, looking for their names in the system log or their gravitic drive signatures, we can have them seized as stolen vessels."

Dunsinane looked at him pityingly. "You've never dealt much with the interplanetary freight market, have you?"

"No."

"Look up what happens to stolen or pirated ships. There's maybe half a dozen planets where you can sell them to crooked dealers for a quarter to a third of their value, in cash, no questions asked, or trade them for other ships at half their value. The dealers will put them through a shipyard, to disguise every emission they make and change their appearance. They'll bribe a local government official to issue false registration papers, then they'll resell the ships under different names to buyers on the far side of the settled galaxy. Even if you see them again, you'll never recognize them."

"And you think that's happened to our ships, and *Colomb?*"

"If it hasn't already, I daresay it will before long."

"So... what are we going to do? We can't just sit back and let them get away with it!"

"What do you suggest?" Dunsinane's voice was biting. "We thought it would be easy to steal their satellites and plant our robotic prospectors in Mycenae's asteroid belt; but the ship that did both for us has vanished. If NOE didn't know what we were doing before, I'll bet they know now. If they took *Colomb* intact, they'll have interrogated her crew and examined her navigation records. They'll figure out what she's been up to, and find our robots in the asteroid belt. That's what makes me most angry – the fact that they'll get the benefit of all the asteroids our bots had beaconed for *Colomb* to collect on this trip. For all we know, they may have been worth billions!"

"But you said they didn't have any armed ships. How could they have captured *Colomb?*"

"We *thought* they didn't have armed ships. If *Colomb* doesn't turn up soon, we'd better revise that opinion."

"What if they destroyed her?"

"They might have; but if I'd been in their shoes, I'd have wanted her intact, for the information her crew could give me, and the money I could get for her. Repair ships cost a lot, so their used value is much higher than a freighter, even at stolen ship prices. Remember, NOE has just paid out over three hundred million for new satellites. They'll want to recover that, any way they can."

"And you're saying that *Colomb,* and our two freighters, have let them do that?"

"Can you think of any other explanation?"

The directors stared gloomily at one another. Their silence spoke volumes.

10

A NEW THREAT

BARJAH

Cochrane was once again expected. This time the *maître d'hôtel* escorted him personally to the private suite of the Royal Golden Dragon restaurant, bowing and scraping profusely. He reflected, grinning inwardly, that while he wasn't used to all this fawning attention, it had its points.

Huang and Hsu rose to greet him as he was shown into the private dining room. With them was a third person, a woman of about Cochrane's age, slim and trim, dressed in a plain, almost severely cut business suit. "This is Lu Hui," Huang introduced him. "She is a weapons specialist. She will address the questions you raised during your first visit."

"I'm honored to meet you, Ms. Lu," Cochrane said, shaking the woman's hand.

"Actually, it's Captain Lu," she said in a low, musical voice, surprising him with the strength of her grip. "I'm an officer of the same rank as yourself, in the fleet of the planet you carefully didn't name during your first visit." He knew that would be Qian-

jin, the almost fabled and very secretive planet that was widely
whispered to be the headquarters of the Dragon Tong.

"Then I'm doubly honored, Captain. You're the first officer
from that planet that I've had the privilege to meet."

"Actually, I'm not the first, Captain. Mr. Hsu is a Reserve
officer in our forces. He chose to pursue a civilian career, but he
rendered excellent service to our Fleet, and remains a valued
colleague." Hsu had the grace to look abashed at her compli-
ments as they sat down.

"I invited Captain Lu to join us tonight, so she could hear
more about our overall activities," Huang noted. "She will meet
with you privately tomorrow to discuss your questions."

"Thank you."

"Should I order for you once again?"

"Please do, thank you. I'm afraid my knowledge of your
cuisine hasn't improved since my last visit."

After they'd settled down to the first course, Hsu remarked,
"Captain, you've presented us with a unique problem, in my
experience. Those asteroids you've brought are so valuable that
we don't have enough in the way of local resources to pay you
your quarter share in advance, as agreed. I have two possible
solutions. One is that you stay a few days, enough for us to refine
some of them and pay you with the gold we'll get from them. The
other is that you take some of them with you when you leave,
along with the quarter-payment for those we can afford, and
bring them back with your next shipment."

"I can stay a few days, Mr. Hsu, particularly if I'm going to be
allowed to pick Captain Lu's brains over some other issues."

"That's good news. I can see we'll have to retain our share of
this shipment here, rather than forward it to... to its destination,
so that we'll have enough to pay you when you bring the next
shipment. You don't mind payment primarily in gold?"

Lu interjected, "You should know, Captain, that in the market
for warships, particularly where discretion is required, payment

in gold is highly prized, because it's virtually untraceable. You'll get better prices if you offer it."

Cochrane inclined his head to her in thanks. "In that case, Mr. Hsu, let's deal in gold. I'd prefer to have a reasonable sum in cash, too, in the various major currencies, because not all vendors deal in gold; but I daresay you won't have any trouble accommodating that."

"Not at all, provided it's within reason. I meant what I said about us retaining our share of this shipment locally. I'm sure our superiors will understand, once they see the sums involved. Once we've built up adequate reserves to be able to pay you as agreed, the rest of the funds will flow through our channels in the normal way."

Cochrane smiled. "On that subject, I'm pleased to be able to tell you that we recovered more asteroids. Our security agreement allows us to keep recovered stolen property like that to fund our operations, so there'll be at least half a dozen more shipments, and possibly more than that. I have a question for you, though. We've run into an intruder in the Mycenae system, a rogue operator who's deployed prospector robots in part of the asteroid belt. I know that's hardly surprising – there are smugglers and claim-jumpers throughout the galaxy – but these robots explode if we get too close."

Hsu and Huang jerked upright in their chairs. They glanced at each other, then back at him as he continued, "Their computers and memories seem to have been deliberately slagged down, rather than allow them to be captured intact. The manufacturer's plates on the robots are in Cyrillic script. We recovered a few plates from their remains, but there are no serial numbers. Have you run into anything of the kind before?"

"We certainly have!" Huang's voice was terse, clipped, angry. "They've been deployed in a couple of asteroid belts where we have... let's say, ties to the companies that mine them. They've tried to collect some for analysis, but they've always self-destructed in the same way that you report. Other clues make us think we know who's behind it – an offshoot of an Albanian Mafia family from Earth, the Bregijas. They have operations on several planets. In some ways they're not unlike the Dragon Tong, but they're much smaller, much quicker to resort to violence if crossed, and less discreet about their operations. Basically, they're thugs.

"About ten years ago – at least, that's when this started – some members of the family apparently decided to steal from asteroid mining operations. We're still trying to identify those involved. We've contacted the Bregija family elders, but they deny all responsibility. They say the group stealing asteroids is a rogue arm of the family, not under their control. However, they won't name them. We've pointed out that if the whole family isn't running this operation, and we act against those that are, the others will have no legitimate reason to interfere. They aren't happy about that, because even with dissident members, blood is thicker than water as far as they're concerned. So far, they haven't gone further than to voice their concerns."

Cochrane frowned. "If they're Albanian, where are the robots coming from? The Albanian language doesn't use Cyrillic script."

"The Bregijas have a long-standing alliance with a crime family from Serbia on Earth. The Vukovics also emigrated to the stars during the Scramble for Space. They have fingers in a lot of industrial and commercial pies on many worlds. One is an asteroid mining supply operation. It contracts with factories to build prospector robots to its specifications, including space inside for them to install additional components. When they do, they include the self-destruct mechanism and software. The Bregijas buy the robots from the Vukovics, then program their own algorithms, which we think impose a rigid set of first-pass conditions. If an asteroid doesn't meet them, it's discarded, no matter how promising it might otherwise be. They look for high concentrations of precious metals above all else, because they're easiest to dispose of."

Hsu added, "Regrettably, we haven't found any of their prospector bots in our own asteroid belts – only in associated systems, where we have an interest, but not control. We've asked all those enterprises to contact us the next time they find any, rather than try to disarm them themselves, but so far that hasn't happened. They've been too impatient, and the bots have destroyed themselves before they could be shut down and examined."

Cochrane smiled, picked up his wine glass, and sipped its delicious contents. "Then it's a good thing I asked, because we found out how to disarm them. We've captured three, intact."

Hsu and Huang stared at him, then at each other, while Captain Lu cocked her head slightly to one side, looking at him with careful consideration. He thought, amused, that her gaze was as if he were a child who'd just done something surpassingly clever for his age.

Huang took a deep breath. "Captain, may I buy one or two of those prospector robots from you? Name your own price."

"You can't buy one, but I have one aboard my ship. I'll give it to you, subject to one condition."

"Name it."

"That you share your findings with me, in full, without holding anything back. I have one of my own electronics specialists, plus a team of assistants, examining the others right now. I'll share their findings with you in the same way. That way, we'll both know more about what we're up against."

"I... I don't know whether the Tong will allow that, Captain. I would have to ask permission. It'll take several weeks for a message to reach my superiors, and their reply to reach me."

Captain Lu said, "I can't speak for Mr. Huang's operation, Captain, but I can agree to that on behalf of Fleet Intelligence. We've also been looking for more information about these people, because dealing with them may become our responsibility. From a military perspective, you're making an offer we can't refuse, particularly if your own analysis is included. How good is your specialist?"

"He just built half a dozen gravitic drive frequency modulators from scratch, to his own design, and making his own parts down to chip and circuit level."

Her eyebrows shot up. "He did? Then he's probably among the best in the galaxy. Those modulators are fiendishly complex. If he's looking at the robots from your side, he might learn even more than our own people, and they're pretty good too. All right, I'll accept your terms."

Cochrane extended his hand across the table. "It's a deal. You can collect the prospector robot from my ship tomorrow."

She returned his handshake. He was suddenly very aware that she was not only a Fleet officer of equal rank to his own, but also an attractive woman. Sternly he suppressed that reaction as he released her hand. This was neither the time nor the place for it.

CAPTAIN LU ACCOMPANIED him up to orbit the following morning. "We may as well take the opportunity to start our discussions while my people collect that prospector robot," she pointed out. He agreed with alacrity, and met her at the asteroid company's compound on Barjah. A senior officer's gig was waiting, comfortably upholstered. "I'll have a crew from my communications frigate meet us at your ship," she explained. "They can take back the robot in their cutter."

"That'll work. I'll radio ahead to have the freighter give them access to the docking bay."

"You're in a freighter?" She sounded surprised. "That's a very slow ship, given everything you need to accomplish."

"You're right. Most times I travel aboard a leased courier ship. Unfortunately, I don't have the resources of a fleet at my disposal. I had to bring asteroids this trip, and a courier vessel doesn't have enough freight capacity for them. I shouldn't even have brought them myself, because there are a dozen other things crying out for my attention, but my subordinates all have that problem, too. I was the only person who could be spared."

She nodded understandingly. "You're a relatively new operation, so I suppose you're having trouble finding the right sort of officers."

"Exactly."

"Even fleets have that problem. I wish you luck in finding them."

He sighed. "They're there. We have an outstanding pool of spacers available in the New Orkney Cluster and a couple of nearby groups of stars, all distant descendants of the Vikings and fishermen from those parts on Earth. However, as you say, we're a new operation. Most of the good people will wait to see how we shake down before they're willing to take us seriously."

"I suppose part of that is getting more combat-capable ships?"

"Very much so – hence my interest in finding a supplier who can provide what I need. I've got my hands on several old patrol craft. The first two have been refurbished and are operational, and more will follow soon, but they're barely adequate. I need more and larger warships in the short to medium term if I'm to secure the Mycenae system, and be able to make a serious pitch to other prospective customers about what we can offer." He smiled. "I hadn't planned on such rapid growth at all, but the money to pay for it fell into our laps, and in terms of our Mycenae agreement, we can use it; so, I'm striking while the iron is hot. I'll find crews for the ships while they're building. If I can get what I want, I'll have spacers lining up to serve on them. They'll likely be more powerful than anything in the New Orkney Cluster."

She looked surprised. "You're not talking about major

warships, surely? Private companies aren't allowed to operate them, according to United Planets regulations."

"That's not quite the letter of the law, but let's table it for now. I know I can't buy destroyers, but I want capabilities as close to theirs as I can manage in a smaller vessel. I've been mulling it over for three months."

She nodded, glancing out of the window as the planet fell away beneath them and the pilot switched from reaction thrusters to gravitic drive. The gig's velocity jumped as the more powerful drive boosted them toward the powered orbital bands, where Cochrane's ship waited.

"You asked for the names of suppliers that met a list of criteria," she said. "There's one company in particular I can recommend to you. We have a division of four older light cruisers, built about sixty years ago. I served as Executive Officer aboard one of them before being promoted to my present rank. Their hulls were in good shape, but their systems and missiles were outdated. Kang Industries at Goheung offered to design new missile pods for them, holding almost thirty percent more weapons than the originals, and upgrade their electronics as well. The total expense was less than a third of what new cruisers would cost. The division was so improved that it was reinstated as the core of our home system defenses."

Cochrane nodded, intrigued. "If they could redesign a missile pod to be that much more powerful, they're certainly innovative. I'd like to know more about it."

"My ship's database has more information about them. Kang did very impressive work, so much so that we've gone back to them for a squadron of their corvettes for system patrol."

"Some corvettes would be very useful right now in the Mycenae system, although we need bigger ships too. You said you were Exec aboard one of those cruisers. What's your current job?"

She glanced sideways at him. "My primary function is head of the weapons and warships desk in Fleet Intelligence. That's one reason I was asked to talk to you about your needs, as well as being the same rank as yourself. We'd like to know more about your company and your plans, because we hire outside security for some of our commercial operations in other systems from time to time. I've also been tasked to investigate the Albanian intrusion into asteroid mining. It's becoming more and more of a problem, so your information about those robotic prospectors couldn't have come at a better time."

Cochrane was struck with a sudden inspiration. "Why don't you come with me for a few weeks? We can visit Kang Industries and see what they have to offer, then you can discuss the robot prospectors with my specialist at Constanta. After that, if you like, you can come to the Mycenae system with me and see them at work for yourself. You might be able to learn a lot more, a lot faster, if you're on the spot, than if you were back at Qianjin."

She smiled. "You named my planet at last! I'm glad we've got past circumlocutions. That's a very good idea. I can send a message to my superiors through Mr. Huang, reporting what I'm doing. Under the circumstances, I'm sure they'll approve, even though I won't wait for permission. If you'd care to be my guest aboard my communications frigate, we can travel much faster than your freighter. We can visit Goheung for a few days, and still reach Constanta at about the same time as your ship."

"Thank you very much. Her crew can take her back without me. It'll also be helpful to have you introduce me to Kang Industries. That'll be better than approaching them as a stranger. May I bring the payment I'm about to receive? That'll help if I decide to leave a deposit with Kang."

She smiled. "Of course, although my crew may start wearing eyepatches and pirate hats, to celebrate all the loot we'll be carrying!" She hesitated. "There's something you should know, in all fairness. Kang pays a commission to us for any ships ordered by buyers we introduce to them. It's a standard arrangement. I wouldn't want you to think we're trying to take advantage of you."

Cochrane shrugged. "Introduction fees, commissions, incentives, bribes, call it what you will; most of the galaxy functions along those lines. I suppose it's like oil in the gears of a machine. It keeps things functioning smoothly for everybody. I can't say I like it, but there's no use farting against thunder."

She stared, then laughed aloud. "I've never heard that saying before. It's so expressive! I may have to use it during a Fleet Intelligence meeting, to see my superiors' faces when they hear it."

"Just choose the superiors carefully. It's been my experience that some of them have no sense of humor at all."

THE SIZE of the payment surprised even Cochrane, even though he'd been aware it would be a big one. The asteroids he'd brought proved to be even richer than their initial assay had estimated, due to a few that had hidden internal veins of almost pure precious metals.

As the last crate of gold bars was stowed in the communications frigate's hold, Captain Lu signed to accept custody of them from the mining consortium on behalf of the Qianjin Fleet, for delivery to Eufala Corporation. She gazed at the tablet for a moment before scrawling her signature on the screen with an electronic stylus. "I've accepted delivery of a destroyer for the Fleet before," she mused, "but even that wasn't as valuable as this shipment. How many gold bars are there? We'd better not have any accidents on the way to Constanta, or we'll be one of the richest shipwrecks in spacefaring history!"

"There's a lot of them. I've had to accept mostly full-size bars, because that many one-kilogram mini-bars would have been unmanageable. At least, if anything happens to us, we'll have every space salvage outfit in the galaxy looking for us."

"There is that, I suppose." She grinned impishly at him, then looked curious. "Just how much do you expect to make out of all the asteroids you've recovered?"

He shrugged. "If our initial assays are correct – and so far, they seem to be – we're looking at a total value of just over seventy billion francs. We'll get half of that; call it thirty-five to thirty-six billion."

She gasped audibly as she stared at him. After a moment she said, her voice shaky, "No wonder Qianjin saw fit to send the head of a Fleet Intelligence department to brief you! Money like that represents real power. There are *planets* with annual budgets less than that! What on earth are you going to do with it all?"

"Use it to break free," he said frankly. "The First Families in the New Orkney Cluster make sure that everybody else is locked into second-class status, no matter how good they are in their field. They ride roughshod over us whenever it suits them. That happened to me, and it destroyed my marriage and my career. Never again! I'm building this security company to give a way out to as many good spacers as possible, a chance to build a better future somewhere else."

"But where? Are you saying you won't be based in the Cluster?"

"No. I'm not sure where we'll end up, but I'll find a place where anyone can grow as high as their abilities let them, without being kept down by a privileged few."

"I see. You're something of an idealist, then?"

"No; a realist. When you've been screwed over, and found out the hard way how painful it is, you don't have many illusions left. I'd like to get away from those who did that to me, and make them pay for it into the bargain. Mycenae came along at just the right time, and NOE's greed to save money – which would go into their own pockets, of course – played right into my hands."

"I don't think I want you as an enemy," she said slowly. "You know how to nurse a grudge."

"Aye. That, and worse, has been said of Orkney men down the centuries."

AS HE WATCHED the communications frigate's commanding officer, a young Lieutenant-Commander, get the ship under way, Cochrane thought to himself that he'd better be very careful what he said to Kang Industries. The company had just handed over two one-million-ton fast freighters to what they thought were authorized passage crews, for delivery to the Callanish consortium. Those freighters were now being altered beyond easy recognition in a Medusa shipyard, along with the repair ship *Colomb*, while two used half-million-ton fast freighters, plus an equally large repair ship, should have already left Medusa for Constanta. By the time he got back, Sue McBride would be hard at work setting up her new repair ship. If she had her way, it'd soon be one of the best equipped of its kind in the galaxy.

That's good, he thought, *because we're likely to need it. We don't have a shipyard at Mycenae, so we'll need her to repair breakdowns or damage on the scene. I can't give Sue too long to fine-tune her. Meanwhile, I'd better make sure Kang Industries never gets a whiff of our involvement in the loss of those two freighters. Fortunately, none of our people were there, and the ships never went near the New Orkney Cluster. There's nothing to tie us to them.*

He watched with interest as the Lieutenant-Commander set course for the system boundary. Goheung lay five days' fast travel ahead. He and Captain Lu – or Hui, as he was already beginning to think of her – would use the time in intensive discussions about warships. So far, she'd given no outward sign that she saw him as anything but another officer and professional spacer... but perhaps they'd find time for more personal discussions, too. He hoped so.

11

INNOVATION

GOHEUNG

Captain Lu's presence, and the substantial orders Qianjin had placed with Kang Industries in the past, ensured that Cochrane received high-level attention when he arrived without notice, and asked to speak to someone senior about a prospective order for warships. His assurance – and her confirmation – that he had funds, and could supply a valid end user certificate, brought swift results. The two Captains were invited to be Kang's guests at an upmarket hotel in Goheung's capital city, and meet with the company's Vice-President for Sales the following morning.

Kim Do-Yun proved to be a rotund, affable-seeming man, with the sharpest, most penetrating eyes Cochrane had ever seen. He reminded himself sternly that nobody got to be a Vice-President of a major interstellar corporation without a great deal of ability and intelligence. It would not do to underestimate this man.

Cochrane explained the security needs of the Mycenae system, but was careful to point out that his long-term interests were far larger than that. "Patrol craft and corvettes are all very well for simple system patrol, but they're light forces. If we want to be a real presence in the space security market, we've got to offer ships of much greater power. They've got to not only defend an installation or system with whom we're under contract, but also be proactive in dealing with a potential threat – in military terms, take the fight to the enemy."

Kim pursed his lips. "But that's precisely why the United Planets regulates private armed vessels so strictly. They can't have more than two missile pods, which effectively means the biggest ships companies like yours can operate are corvettes or armed merchant vessels. Frigates usually carry four pods, and destroyers six, which rules them out."

Cochrane shook his head. "Corvettes' electronics and missiles have limited performance compared to larger warships. What's more, they're usually cramped, which is uncomfortable for their crews, and have lower combat endurance. I don't deny they're useful, and I plan to buy at least a squadron of them for patrol duties, but they're second-tier. Ideally, for our first-tier ships, I want as much as possible of a destroyer's capability, while observing the UP's two-missile-pod restriction."

Kim frowned. "On the face of it, that sounds like a contradiction in terms."

"I thought so, too, until I looked at the eight *Desroches* class destroyers you built for the Anse Cluster a few years ago. They're shorter and more compact than a regular destroyer. Why did you design them like that?"

Kim shrugged. "The Cluster has an old orbital dockyard, with shorter maintenance ways than a modern unit. Its Fleet decided that their new destroyers had to fit the existing ways, because it would cost too much to replace or upgrade the dockyard to accommodate them."

Cochrane's eyes lit up. "So that's it! I couldn't figure out why you used some design features, but now they make sense. Would you please call up a schematic of the *Desroches* class?"

"Certainly." Kim reached for a control unit and pressed a sequence of keys. A three-dimensional holographic display lit up above the desktop, and the sleek form of a warship appeared, its sides cut away to expose its interior design.

"Thank you." Cochrane reached into the display and traced features with his finger as he spoke. "I noted that they're deeper from top to bottom than most destroyers. That's because you put the midships nuclear reactor below the missile pods, rather than in front of or behind them."

"Yes. A warship hull is usually hexagonal or octagonal in overall cross section, flattened top and bottom to accommodate missile pods. We simply deepened the vertical sides, which made room for the reactor and some storage compartments to be moved beneath the missiles. By careful shaping, we preserved the ship's stealth characteristics, but shaved almost fifteen meters off her length."

"It was a good idea. I realized your *Desroches* design might serve as the foundation for what I want. If we take out the midships reactor, that leaves two others, one forward and one aft. They can't supply enough power for all a destroyer's systems, and its hundred-plus main battery missiles, and the same number of defensive missiles, all at once. However, if the number of missiles is reduced, two reactors – larger than usual, if necessary – could meet the power demand.

"Removing that midships reactor leaves a fair amount of space below the missile pods. Captain Lu told me about the pods you designed for Qianjin's cruisers. They're deeper from top to bottom than destroyer pods, because they hold larger and more powerful missiles. By the way, how did you squeeze so much firepower into such a compact unit? With thirty offensive missiles and thirty-five defensive, plus ten penetration aids, as far as I know, there's nothing else quite like it."

Kim seemed almost embarrassed at Cochrane's praise. "Qian-jin's older ships had limited space for upgrades, so we designed the most powerful pod that would fit their existing bays. The trade-off is that techs can't work on individual weapons when the pod's installed, because it's too tightly packed. If a missile develops a defect, it must either be jettisoned, or flagged as unavailable until the pod can be removed, when it can be repaired."

"That's a trade-off I'm willing to accept, particularly because it means you don't have to carry a full team of missile techs on board. That reduces the size of the crew. Anyway, if the center reactor and storage compartments are removed, a *Desroches* hull is deep enough to accommodate those cruiser pods. What if you replace the six destroyer missile pods with two of them? One cruiser pod would replace a transverse row of two destroyer pods. The third row would be left out, reducing the ship's length even more."

Kim nodded thoughtfully. "What about the main fore-and-aft passageway? It runs between the present missile pods, but it couldn't pass through the center of a cruiser pod."

"Couldn't it be re-routed around the pod?"

"I... I don't see why not. A cruiser pod is about nine-tenths as wide as two destroyer pods next to each other. That, plus deleting the current center passage, would provide space to run passages on either side of a pod, one for forward movement and the other rearward."

"Yes. What's more, you could build extra tanks for potable, gray and black water, reaction mass and lubricants below the passages on either side, and use the space above them for general storage. If you left a small gap between the front and rear missile pods, that would provide access to the storage and tanks without blocking the passage. With the extra storage around the missile cells, plus the reduced requirements of a smaller crew, you should be able to give the ship an operational endurance of thirty to forty-five days, or perhaps even longer."

"What crew size do you anticipate?"

"I'm not sure. I'd like to automate as much as possible of the ship's operation, provided that can be done reliably. In conventional terms, the *Desroches* class has up to a hundred and eighty crew. I think our changes will reduce that to about a hundred and twenty, plus some extra berthing space for boarding parties, or to accommodate rescued survivors. That means you can eliminate berths for thirty to forty people, which will shorten the ship even further. However, please leave all the existing officer's cabins in place. She may embark flotilla or detachment commanders, along with a small staff, or carry VIP passengers. They'll use those cabins. I'm sure you can configure a spare berthing compartment for dual use as a staff office area."

"Yes, of course." Kim sat back, rubbing his chin. "Our new automation technology might reduce her complement to a hundred or so, and we might be able to reduce her length by up to twenty meters. That would make her look short compared to the *Desroches* class ships, and rather stubby alongside a conventional destroyer. Longitudinal stability and balance may be a problem – we'll have to pay attention to that.

"Cruisers' missiles are more expensive than smaller, shorter-ranged versions, but you'll save money by carrying fewer of them. You won't need a third reactor, and we can upgrade the reactors fore and aft if necessary. Her environmental systems won't need to be as extensive, given her smaller crew and reduced hull volume. All her standard electronic systems will remain, as well as eight laser cannon barbettes, four each around the bow and stern, giving her destroyer-level capability in those areas."

He thought for a moment. "We could shorten her even more by cutting down the docking bay in the stern. The *Desroches* class carries four small craft, three general-purpose cutters and a gig for the captain, but a frigate usually carries only three."

Cochrane shook his head. "No, I'd like to retain the full-size docking bay. We might carry one or two assault shuttles for boarding parties, instead of cutters."

"I see. You know, this won't be a frigate in the conventional sense of that term. You could call her a super-frigate without exaggeration. She'll dominate any warship smaller than a destroyer, and give even a destroyer a very hard time, because her missiles, while fewer, will be more powerful and longer-ranged than theirs. What's more, she technically adheres to UP restrictions on armed civilian ships, even though she stretches them farther than their drafters could have anticipated."

Captain Lu grinned. "She doesn't just stretch them – she twists them into a regulatory pretzel!"

"*Ha!* Yes. This is a remarkable conception. I congratulate you for thinking of it, Captain Cochrane."

"Thank you. I got the idea while reading about the so-called 'pocket battleships' of the Second Global War on Earth. They carried bigger, more powerful guns than smaller, faster warships, but were faster than bigger ones carrying heavier guns. They were designed to destroy anything that could catch them, but escape from anything that could destroy them. It sounded like an intriguing proposition."

Kim pursed his lips. "It certainly does. You realize she'll be very fast indeed? She'll mass only about eighty percent of a conventional destroyer, but have the same gravitic drive power as the bigger ship. Most destroyers can reach one-third Cee, but I expect she'll improve on that, and accelerate faster than them, too. We'll have to increase the strength of her gravitic deflector shield, to protect her against space debris at such high velocities."

Cochrane grinned. "She sounds like a real sports model. I'm eager to let her have her head, and see what she can do."

Lu chimed in, "So am I! This ship is scary, from the point of view of an officer who might have to defend against her. She'll have longer-range weapons than anything except cruisers and battleships, and there aren't many planets operating those, because they're complex and costly. She'll have the speed to run rings around most other warships; and with her stealth features, if she crept in silently, it'd be the devil of a job to detect her before she got within range. I think she's going to pose a real headache for a lot of fleets."

Kim nodded briskly. "I agree. Captain Cochrane, in what currency do you prefer to deal?"

"I'm flexible, but I deal most often in Neue Helvetica francs, or in gold."

"As a non-binding guess, I think we could build her, fully equipped, for one-point-two to one-point-three billion francs, three to four hundred million less than a destroyer. Our architects will have to work up a formal design, of course, and we'll have to cost the materials. Even so, I think my estimate is accurate to within plus-or-minus ten percent. If you pay in gold, we might be able to shave the price a little further. How many ships are you planning to order?"

"Our orders will be spread out – we'll have to discuss the timing. We want a squadron of nine frigates; two combat-ready divisions of three, and a third division for ships undergoing long-term maintenance or repair, or working up their crews. I'll need a squadron of nine corvettes as well, to replace our present obsolete patrol craft. I want four depot ships, two for frigates and two for corvettes, armed with laser cannon and one pod of defensive missiles. They should be equipped to exchange and reload missile pods. They'll need the usual complement of cutters and cargo shuttles, plus two asteroid mining tenders equipped to handle prospector robots. I also want at least two fast communications vessels right away, with more to follow. Your standard courier ship design will meet our needs. We'll buy at least two full missile reloads per warship, plus sufficient spares for extended operations."

Kim shook his head ruefully. "Captain, never before have I

run across a private security company that could afford so many and such costly ships. If you hadn't been introduced to us by Captain Lu, I'd find it hard to believe – no offense meant, of course."

"None taken. We've been fortunate in recovering a great deal of stolen material. Our contract allows us to retain it, so we're using the proceeds to fund our expansion."

"I see. Even so, you're talking about plus-or-minus eighteen billion francs to buy that many ships. If you pay in gold, the price may drop by up to five percent."

"In that case, I'll do my best to pay in gold. There's another important point, Mr. Kim. Since this frigate design is our idea, albeit based on one of your designs, we want a binding agreement with you not to sell them to anyone else without our approval. It won't be automatic. Is that acceptable?"

Kim grimaced. "I don't like it on principle, but I can see why that would be important to you. You don't want competitors or potential opponents to be as well armed as yourselves."

"Precisely. There's also the question of automating these ships' operations. How far can we increase that, and reduce their crew requirements, without risking their operational effectiveness?"

"Perhaps Captain Lu could tell you something about the modifications we made to Qianjin's cruisers, and the squadron of corvettes we sold them recently."

"I can," she confirmed, sitting forward. "The cruisers' complement was reduced by a quarter, which was very useful. Corvettes usually have a crew of up to eighty, but Kang's new design needs only forty-five. Of course, that means battle damage is harder to repair, because there aren't enough warm bodies to form repair parties while still fighting the enemy; but robotic emergency equipment and triple-redundant systems can compensate for part of that. In sum, you've got to be prepared to lose more ships to otherwise survivable damage, in return for lower operating costs and fewer casualties in battle. For a security company such as Eufala, I don't know that there'll be much battle damage to worry about, because your opponents are more likely to be smugglers and pirates. They mostly use converted freighters or mining boats, not warships."

"A point," Cochrane admitted, "but they can still get lucky."

"You mentioned you need a squadron of corvettes, Captain," Kim said. "We converted one of our earlier models into a prototype for the new design we sold to Qianjin. She has all the automation of the latest version, which we can also put into your frigates. You'll also find that her reduced complement allowed us to give her much more spacious and comfortable crew quarters, which was one of your objections to older-style corvettes. We've used her as a demonstration ship since then. If you buy her, you'd be able to get first-hand experience of how such automation works. You'd also have one modern combat vessel available immediately, with modern weapons and systems. We've given the corvettes a miniaturized suite of electronics that almost matches the capabilities of our destroyer systems – and your frigates, of course, which will use destroyer systems. They can exchange fire control data with the larger ships, and each can direct the other's missiles via datalink."

"I'm certainly interested," Cochrane said slowly, mind racing as he made mental calculations. "Is she fully armed? Can you deliver her to our temporary base at Constanta, and if so, how soon? How long will her crew need to be trained, and what materials do you offer? How much are you asking for her?"

"She's fully armed, with two pods of our latest-generation corvette missiles, each with twenty-five offensive and twenty-five defensive weapons, plus four laser cannon. She's just come out of routine maintenance. We can deliver her within six weeks, although of course there'll be an extra charge for that, plus return fares for our passage crew. She has a full suite of training materials, including hypno-study modules, and a fully integrated artificial intelligence system at every operator's station. I daresay trained, experienced spacers could learn to handle her within a month. We can lend you her passage crew for a few weeks, to help with that. We're asking four hundred million francs for her."

"That's three-quarters of a new corvette's price. It seems high for an older-model hull that's been used hard for many years before conversion."

"Her hull is still in very good condition – that's why we selected her to be the prototype – and with a completely modernized interior and all-new systems and weapons, she's as good as new. We might be able to drop the price a little, given the size of the order you're discussing. As to that, there's another point. Following Qianjin's order, which launched our new corvette design, we've sold twelve more to two other customers. The last two are under construction right now. If you order your corvettes at once, we can use the existing production line. That'll save you about a hundred million francs in setup costs, plus six months lead time. You could have eight more corvettes over the next two to two-and-a-half years."

"May I say something?" Lu interjected.

"Of course," Cochrane replied, looking at her

"When we introduced the corvettes and refurbished light cruisers, it took time to retrain their crews, who were used to older ways of doing things. If you begin with corvettes to replace your obsolete patrol craft, you'll need fewer qualified spacers at first for their smaller crews, and you'll be able to train those you have more thoroughly. By the time your frigates begin arriving, you'll have experienced people ready to operate them, with much less time needed to work them up."

"That's a very important point," he conceded, "particularly given our problems in finding good officers. We can test them in the corvettes, and promote those that do best into the frigates. All right, Mr. Kim, you make a good case. What are the next steps?"

"I'll have our architects start work on your frigate design.

Ah... that's for the customer's account, of course."

"What's the normal fee?"

"We usually charge twenty-five million francs to adapt a destroyer-type design, but for so large an order, we can offer a discount. Shall we say twenty million?"

"Agreed, but only on condition we first come to an agreement about the corvettes, and another giving us the right of veto over future sales of the frigate."

"I'll make both my top priority. How long can you spend with us?"

"A few days, no longer. I can come back in a few months, but I'd rather get things moving right away. Time presses."

"Then let's see whether we can conclude those agreements while you're here. You'll also need to meet with our design team, to go over every feature you want and that we can offer, and make sure we're agreed on all the important points."

"Very well. When can you start construction of the frigates?"

"We'll have to finalize the design first. I expect that to take at least six months, what with communications back and forth. As soon as it's mutually agreed, we can begin ordering systems, weapons and fittings for the prototype. You understand, with a brand-new design like this, it would be unwise to proceed with full production until a prototype has been tested and approved."

"I understand."

"Good. Robotic construction is relatively speedy. We should be ready to run trials late next year, make any necessary modifications, and prepare for regular production to start about two years from now. The prototype will be upgraded to full production standard, to become the first of your nine frigates. If there are no corvette orders to follow your ships, we can use that production line with minimal setup delay. The depot ships and communications vessels will be our standard models, customized where necessary to suit your requirements. Our usual terms are a quarter of the price on placing the order, one-quarter when construction starts, one-quarter on completion, and the final payment when you take delivery from our shipyard."

Cochrane's mind raced, comparing expected income from asteroid sales with the construction timeline. "That seems fair. I can pay you for the design work right away, and for the corvette, too, if we buy her. What about more corvettes?"

"We can start the first pair of your remaining eight in three months, and have two ready for handover every five to six months after that. The depot ships will be built on another line, and take about a year each. Even robotic, modular construction can only move so fast, and we still have to finalize their special design features for you."

"That's acceptable. If we can agree on price while I'm here, I can pay the deposit for the first two corvettes at once. I'll also send you a half-million-ton fast freighter as soon as mutually convenient. Build pods to fit into a couple of her holds, containing classrooms and training materials for all the systems aboard our new ships, plus spacious, comfortable accommodation and upgraded support systems to accommodate up to two hundred spacers, over and above her crew. We'll use her as a training ship. When you've had a chance to inspect her, give me a quote to arm her with up to four laser cannon, and a frigate missile pod and fire control system. I may use her to help patrol the Mycenae system while she trains our spacers. There's no reason she can't do both jobs at once."

Kim nodded. "There should be no problem with any of that. We'll need four to six months for the freighter conversion, but it's relatively simple work from an engineering perspective. We can do it in space using a repair ship, without tying up a construction berth."

"Very well. When can we inspect the corvette?"

Kim reached for his desktop comm unit. "I'll arrange that for tomorrow morning, and have our Head of Design pull a team together. You can start work with them tomorrow afternoon."

12

INTERLUDE

CONSTANTA

Cochrane and Lu watched through the viewports as the Qianjin communications frigate settled into orbit. "It looks very lovely," she said, indicating the deep blue seas that surrounded the planet's three continents. "They must have some wonderful beach resorts."

"I'm told they do. In fact, I could use a short break. I've been flat out at work since I started this project, almost a year ago. Would you care to join me for a week at one of them, once I've taken care of what's piled up in my absence? No strings attached, of course," he hastened to add as she cocked her head, looking at him quizzically. "Separate rooms."

"I'm on duty, remember? I can't just take time off whenever I feel like it!"

"You said yourself you need to check on security companies like ours, because you use them for some commercial operations. This could fall under that heading."

She grinned at him. "You're reaching awfully hard, you know."

"Yes, I am, but I'd like your company."

"Well... let me think about it. What do you have to do first?"

"I'll have to check what's waiting for me. I've got to meet with the shipyard owner, to see how the refurbishment of our last patrol craft is coming along. I also want him to introduce me to a suitable contact in Constanta's government. If we're going to have an influx of ships, I want to use this planet as an alternate center – perhaps even the primary center – for our operations. I'll ask for a local license to operate armed ships, and use the shipyard as our maintenance and repair base. It'll probably be expensive, but we can afford it now, and it'll be good to have a fallback location if anything happens at Rousay."

"Do you think it might?"

"It's possible. We've done things that are sure to ruffle the feathers of the powers that be, if they ever find out about them. I'd rather not say more about that right now." Mentally, he was smiling. *If NOE figures out that their illegal asteroid prospecting has helped pay for our new ships, they'll blow several fuses – and then there's the Callanish consortium, and those Albanian gangsters. There are a lot of people who won't be happy with us, if they figure out all we've been doing.*

"While you're doing that, may I discuss those robot prospectors with your electronics specialist?"

"Certainly. I'll introduce you. You can also go over our last patrol craft at the shipyard, if you like. It's so old it qualifies as an antique, though, so it may not interest you."

She smiled. "You forget my job. Warships always interest me, even old ones."

SHE WASN'T SO SANGUINE when they met for supper the following evening, at a restaurant on the orbital space station. As soon as they'd entered their selections into the menu screen at their booth, she exploded, "I can't believe you're risking your life, and the lives of your spacers, in deathtraps like those patrol craft! I've never seen anything so decrepit in my life – at least, not in space!"

"I presume you've been looking at the one being refurbished?" he asked, and she nodded. "Well, you're seeing it at its worst. The shipyard's done a good job of fixing up their old systems, and replacing those that are past it with modern commercial equivalents. The four that were in the best condition were the first to go through the process, so you're seeing the poorest-condition ship that can still be refurbished."

"Whoever owned them before did a *terrible* job of looking after them! Where did you buy them?"

"Ah... that's a story for another time. I agree, they're far from ideal, but they're all we could get at very short notice for a sum we could afford. We hadn't recovered any asteroids at that time."

"I see; and I also see why you went ahead and ordered those corvettes right away. The sooner you can put your spacers into better, more modern ships, the better the odds that they'll survive if they run into enemies. I don't fancy their chances – not to mention *your* chance! – in those old rattletraps, even if you've refurbished them."

He smiled. "Dare I take it you care about what happens to me?"

"If you haven't figured that out by now, you aren't very good at judging women, are you?" she said tartly, then softened. "I'm sorry. You didn't deserve that. It's just that... we have a problem, Andrew."

It was the first time she'd used his given name. He felt a *frisson* of excitement, for the first time under such circumstances in several years. "What do you mean, Hui?"

She blushed as he used her given name, also for the first time. "You're setting up an independent security company, but you've no idea where you'll be based in the longer term – only that you want to break free of the New Orkney Cluster. I'm an officer in the Qianjin Fleet. My service isn't part of the Dragon Tong – it keeps its operations strictly separate from our system defense forces – but it's associated with the Tong by a common planet, if nothing else. Our loyalties are to two very different entities, based hundreds of light years apart. I'm not about to leave my job and home, and I don't think you are either."

"It would be easier for me," he corrected her, "because I don't have a home after my wife left me and took almost everything we'd built together. As for Rousay, it's where I'm currently employed, not where I live. On the other hand, I couldn't live on Qianjin. Quite apart from considerations about the Tong, you don't encourage immigration."

"No, we don't. It's bad for security, and with our history, that would never do. You see my problem, don't you? I don't give my affections lightly. In fact, you've already crossed barriers I swore I'd never let anyone through again. I also was... I suppose the word is 'betrayed'... by a previous lover, so I understand how your wife must have hurt you. I don't want to go through that again, and neither do you; yet, if we get involved, but one of us can't bring ourselves to join the other, won't that be a betrayal too? We'll leave each other dangling, desperately unhappy, but unable to do anything to avoid that."

"Won't we be unhappy if we leave things as they are? I know I will."

"Yes, but at least we haven't committed ourselves yet. If we become lovers... I think that will cross a line for me. I don't know whether I could pull back after that."

"I'm not sure, either," he admitted slowly, and sighed. "Maybe it's a bit premature to think about that beach holiday together."

"I think it is. In fact, I think I'd better take a break from... us... while the going's good, to give us both time to think." She took a deep breath. "Let's change the subject.

"I've read through Warrant Officer Murray's report on those prospector robots. He's amazing! He figured out more from their chip architecture than I would have believed possible, and the analysis of their programming by his tech team was superb. I'd like to get it back to our specialists as fast as possible, along with the robot you gave us. They'll be falling over themselves with interest when they see it all."

He sighed again. "I can see the sense in what you're saying – but I don't want you to leave!"

She smiled wryly at him. "That makes two of us. However, I'll make you this promise. I still want to visit the Mycenae system, and see those things in operation. If my superiors permit, which I think they will, I'll return as soon as our technicians have started their own analysis of the bots, and I've caught up with the work that's accumulated for me back at Qianjin. I can be back here in about six or seven weeks, by which time your new corvette will have been delivered and you'll be well advanced with training her crew. Are you going to take her to Mycenae?"

"That was my plan, yes. My courier ship will follow her there, to bring me back here."

"Then why don't I go with you? I can sell that to my bosses as a chance to see our corvette design in operation in another system, and perhaps even in combat. I'm sure that will interest them."

"Sounds good to me. I'll miss you until then, though." He reached over the table and covered her hand with his own.

She turned her hand up beneath his, and stroked his palm with her fingertips. "And I'll miss you," she whispered.

"Thank you for saying that. We'll let matters between us lie where they are for now, and see what develops."

Next morning, as Hui boarded her communications frigate and headed for the system boundary, Cochrane met with Constanta's Defense Minister and Foreign Minister.

"We've considered your request for a license to operate armed vessels from Constanta," the Defense Minister began. "You already have one from Rousay, and you're a former officer in the New Orkney Cluster's Fleet, so technically there shouldn't be a problem. However, there are our costs to consider."

"What are they, Mr. Balan?"

Before the Defense Minister could reply, the Finance Minister said, "They're administrative in nature, plus the costs of registering your ships with the United Planets as legitimately armed. We do have to pay our civil servants for such things, you understand."

I understand very well, Cochrane thought to himself. *You're looking for a rake-off to give me what I want. Well, I'm used to that.* "Do you have a sum in mind, Mr. Lungu?"

"We understand you're paying Mr. Grigorescu in gold or Neue Helvetica francs for the work he's doing on your ships. We were thinking a million francs per year, or the equivalent in gold, would cover it."

Cochrane restrained himself from laughing outright. They were asking a lot more than the market would bear.

"You surely realize I'm paying less than a tenth of that sum on Rousay?" he queried mildly. "If I were to approach another planet in the New Orkney Cluster, I daresay I'd pay about the same."

"Ah... well, we understood that you'd prefer to have a base outside the Cluster," Balan muttered. "Surely that's worth something to you?"

Cochrane kept his face impassive. "There is that. However, it's not worth a million a year."

After brisk bargaining, Cochrane promised to personally deliver two hundred thousand francs, in cash, to the Foreign Minister's office the following morning, and another two hundred thousand, this time in gold, to the Defense Minister's office, in exchange for the armed vessel permit.

"It's been a pleasure doing business with you, gentlemen," he said genially as he got to his feet. "I hope our future dealings will be as smooth."

"Provided we get our fees every year, I'm sure they will," Balan promised.

Unless you get greedy, or get a better offer to betray us, you mean, Cochrane added silently. *Well, that's only to be expected from politicians like you. I've recorded this meeting, and I'll record tomorrow's exchanges as well. If you try to betray us, I'll make sure you go down before we do.*

He made a mental note to identify the major figures in Constanta's underworld. It would be worthwhile to make certain arrangements with one of them, as an insurance policy against betrayal by the politicians. In his experience, such precautions had often proved useful. What's more, if the targets learned about the arrangement – which would not happen unless they made it necessary – they usually took them seriously enough that they seldom needed to be activated.

HIS MEETING with Mr. Grigorescu was extremely cordial. The shipyard owner was delighted to see him again.

"I must admit, Captain, your business has transformed my shipyard," he acknowledged, raising his coffee cup in salute. "My turnover is twice what it was a year ago, and it looks set fair to double again in the next year, what with maintaining your patrol craft, two regular freighters, two fast freighters, your new repair ship, and your courier vessel. If you buy any more ships, I may have to expand!"

In answer, Cochrane laid his new armed vessel permit on the desk. "I'm planning to make Constanta my main base of operations for at least the next year or two. That won't last, because we'll move on in due course, but while we're here, I'd like to use your shipyard as our maintenance base. I've got a squadron of corvettes coming, plus their depot ships, and we'll be hiring hundreds more spacers and officers to crew them. You're an essential part of my plans."

"I'm very glad to hear it."

"You earned it by giving us a break on refurbishing our first patrol craft," Cochrane assured him. "That helped us enormously, at a time when we couldn't afford to do everything we wanted. Our expansion is being funded by the proceeds of action against criminals in another system, which by contract we can retain for our own needs. You'll get a goodly share of them. For example, I want Sue McBride to speed up refitting that repair ship and getting her operational. I need her in the Mycenae system in six months, if possible."

Grigorescu pursed his lips. "That's a very tight schedule, Captain. Even if she puts her in the shipyard and lets my techs work alongside her, it'll be hard to meet."

"Do your best. We don't have a shipyard in Mycenae, so we need her there as our mobile maintenance unit. She'll be shuttling back and forth beween Mycenae and Constanta for the next few years. What d'you think it'll cost to get her up and running?"

"You've got all the equipment you need from the old depot ship that came with your patrol craft, and from that other repair ship McBride stripped before she went off again. It's just a matter of figuring out where to put everything, installing it, and connecting everything to the ship's systems. McBride's own techs are doing a lot of that. I can lend her a dozen more – all that aren't busy with your last patrol craft – and all the robotic construction gear I can spare. I reckon... oh, twenty million should cover that, plus the use of a slipway, plus six months' hard work. Parts and materials will be extra, of course."

"Done. I'll pay you that right away, plus five million in advance to cover anything you need to buy. I want to keep your shipyard in good financial health, considering how badly we'll need your services over the next few years. I hope we aren't monopolizing you, and driving your other customers away. I wouldn't like your relationship with them to suffer because of us."

"No, that's not a problem at present. To be frank, business had been tough for a year or two before you came along. You've changed all that. I've even had a couple of queries from other planets, asking about refurbishing older vessels. It seems visiting freighters noticed what we've been doing with your ships, and spread the word. That makes me happy. Competition among smaller shipyards like mine is cutthroat. I'll take every advantage I can get!"

DAVE COUSINS RETURNED from Mycenae with his freighter, and reported growing confidence and competence among the crews of the four old vessels now patrolling the system. "They're settling into their jobs well, sir. The ships aren't great, and the mish-mash of older and newer systems among them is a problem, but we'll make do until we can afford something better."

"That's coming fast," Cochrane assured him, and told him about the corvettes that would be arriving over the next two years. Cousins' eyes shone as he listened. "Our bigger warships are being designed right now. The prototype will be ready and tested in two years, then they'll start building a squadron of them. Give us five years, and we'll be stronger and better equipped than most minor planets."

"That's great, sir! What about crews? We have enough spacers and NCO's for now, but officers are still a real headache. I've had to fire a couple already, while we were working up the third and fourth patrol craft. They were all about their commissioned status, and less about getting their hands dirty, getting the job done, and leading by example."

"I'm glad you got rid of them. I know we're going to have

problems there. I've been thinking about something like the Lancastrian Commonwealth Fleet's Warrant Officer and Limited Duty Officer programs. If we can find enough good NCO's who are ready for more responsibility, we can give some of them warrant rank and make them department heads. On smaller warships like patrol craft and corvettes, that would work. That way, we might get away with only two commissioned officers on a patrol craft, and four on a corvette. The best warrant officers could be offered Limited Duty commissions on our bigger warships as they arrive."

"We've got nothing to lose by trying, sir. Have you talked to Sue McBride and Jock Murray about it?"

"I have, but both say they aren't qualified to comment. They got their warrant rank as technical specialists, rather than senior NCO's."

"That's true, I suppose. We really need one or two Lancastrian warrant officers to help us set up our own program."

"I've thought about that. There are brokers on Lancaster that offer the services of retired warrant and commissioned officers to those who can afford to hire them. They're expensive, but if we want to do this right, I think we've no choice but to hire a couple. We'll offer them a year's contract, renewable for another year, and pick those with the right personalities and skills to help us select, train and form our own warrant and Limited Duty cadre. Effectively, we want them to work themselves out of a job."

"I understand, sir, but don't tell them that!"

"The right people will understand that at once," Cochrane assured him. "How's the makeshift depot ship settling down?"

"She's in orbit around Mycenae Primus Four, sir. Dr. Masters has got the hospital up and running, but she and her staff are complaining about being bored. There's nothing for them to do. I've told them to lend a hand in other departments, as far as they can, but I don't know about a long-term solution for that."

"Neither do I. We've got to have them out there – it'll take far too long to get medical emergency cases to another system for treatment – but I can see their problem. I'll talk to Elizabeth when I get there next month. Are you and she still an item?"

"We are, sir, although it's difficult at present, with her there and me here. With your permission, I'd like to see what I can do about that in due course."

"Do I hear wedding bells in your future?"

"I reckon so, sir, if all goes well."

"I'm glad for you both. You can expect to move out to Mycenae in about four months, as soon as our last patrol craft is ready. You'll command the five-ship squadron, with Lieutenant-Commander Moffatt as your second-in-command. I'm going to leave it to you to set up patrol schedules and make sure we're covering everything important. What's the current resupply and crew relief position?"

"Once a month, a freighter delivers supplies to the depot ship, and relief crews for two of the patrol craft, sir. She brings back two crews for extended liberty here, as well as part of the crew of the depot ship."

"That's the same freighter you've been using to collect asteroids, right?"

"Yes, sir."

"All right. I'll leave her on that run, but find another skipper for her. I'm going to give you my courier ship as your personal transport, so you can travel faster in an emergency. I've already chartered a replacement for myself from a Neue Helvetica company. It'll be here next month. Initially, I've wet-leased it with its own crew, because we're so short-staffed. As soon as we have enough personnel, I'll change to a dry-lease and put our own people aboard."

"Thank you, sir. Your ship's a good one. I'll be glad to have her."

"You may need a fast ship like that to make a quick getaway. Say I have to send you to Rousay, and NOE suspects we've funded our operations using their illegally beaconed asteroids. They may try to have you arrested and questioned. If you get wind of anything like that, your ship's faster than any of Rousay's patrol craft, so you should be able to get out of the system if you have to."

"I see, sir. Uh... didn't your contract with NOE specify that if Eufala Corporation returns their money, plus ten percent interest per year, NOE's investment relationship with Eufala is terminated, and reverts to just a contract for security services?"

"Yes, it does."

"Well, sir, we've got more than enough money coming in now. Why not refund their money, and go to a straight contract? That way, all our ships will be our own, with no lien on them, and NOE will no longer have any ownership interest in them. That also means they can't complain you've taken their money under false pretenses, or anything like that, because you won't *have* any of their money anymore. It makes it less likely for friction to develop between them and us."

Cochrane nodded, slowly at first, then more quickly. "Dave, you came up with an absolutely brilliant idea for our long-term business plan, and now you've done it again. That's a real brainwave! If I return NOE's money, and tell them they can have our security services for the rest of our five-year contract free of charge, with no further payment of even operating costs, they're bound to jump at it. In fact, I'll head for Rousay right away, before anything else happens that might complicate matters."

"If they ever find out what we've really been doing, sir, things may get sticky."

"We'll cross that bridge if and when we come to it. If that happens, I intend to blame everything on either the Callanish consortium, or those Albanian intruders, or both. After all, how is NOE going to prove that's not what happened?"

"And if they want to know where we got the money for our new ships, sir?"

Cochrane shrugged. "Our contract specifically says we can keep any stolen materials we recapture, and use them for our support. They don't have to know that most of them were illegally beaconed asteroids."

Laughing, they went their separate ways.

ROUSAY

Marwick stared at Cochrane in utter astonishment when he laid on his desk a bank draft for three hundred and seventy-five million francs, in full and final repayment of NOE's 'investment' in Eufala Corporation, including interest, plus the first year's operating expenses.

"But – how – where did you get the money for this?"

"Remember I told you we'd captured the ship that stole your satellites, sir, and tried to steal their replacements? She turned out to be *Colomb,* a repair ship from Callanish. She was worth a lot, being newly refurbished and modernized. What's more, the consortium on Callanish used the money they got for your first satellites to buy other ships. We took the liberty of... ah... relieving them of their ill-gotten gains."

Marwick started to smile. "You did *what?* Are you serious?"

"I won't go into details, sir, for obvious reasons, but yes, I'm serious. You'll recall our contract authorizes Eufala to use what we recover from criminals to support our work. We're applying the proceeds from those ships for that purpose. There's more than enough to refund your money, and still pay for our operations for the rest of this year. This way, we now own our ships and our company free and clear, and NOE gets its money back to use for more important things. I'm refunding your first year's operating expenses as well, and I won't ask for more for the next year. That seems a fair way to handle this."

"Dammit, it's more than fair! The Board will be very happy to hear this. We're facing a lot of expenses in pushing colonization through the United Planets, so this money will be very welcome indeed. In fact, I daresay it'll be more than enough to get the process finalized within the next few months – then we can start making money properly!" He looked at Cochrane with an almost paternal affection. "I suppose you'll want to retain the two freighters, the courier ship, and the other gear we lent you, for the full term of the contract?"

"Yes, Mr. Marwick. I presume that won't be a problem?"

"Not at all, particularly now we can afford to lease other ships to replace them, if necessary. I don't mind telling you, Captain, this will do me personally a power of good with the Board. Several of my fellow directors questioned whether it was wise to hire your services, and whether we could afford them." He picked up the bank draft and waved it in the air. "This will set their minds at rest, and no mistake! I think they'll pay a lot more attention to my advice in future."

Marwick signed the documents to terminate NOE's lien over Eufala's assets, and handed them over with a smile. Cochrane took his leave with the director's congratulations and expressions of goodwill ringing in his ears, accompanied by the firmest handshake he'd experienced in years. He couldn't help wondering what his reception would have been if Marwick had suspected the truth. Grinning, he decided it would be better not to find out.

13

A MINER, MINED

CONSTANTA

Hui returned from Qianjin a few weeks later. Their reunion was bittersweet.

"I just don't know how to cope with intimacy without a future," she told him frankly. "I've had time to think about us a lot on the journey from here to Qianjin and back again. Yes, I'm attracted to you, and I know you feel the same way about me; but I don't see how we can build a future together. You can't move to my planet, even if you wanted to. I'm honor-bound to serve my Fleet, and therefore can't move to wherever you are."

He sighed, in both frustration and sadness. "I see where you're coming from. I'd say let's go ahead and see where things go from here, and make our decisions based on that; but I suppose part of that's the difference between men and women. For all the talk about equality, we still approach relationships differently, at gut level."

"I'm afraid you're right. Can we shelve things for now, and work together professionally? Will that be too difficult for you?"

"All I can promise is that I'll do my best. If that doesn't work, I suppose we'll have to limit how much time we spend together. One thing, though – no recriminations. Neither of us have done anything unprofessional, or anything we need to be ashamed of, so there's no point in blaming each other. We'll just have to learn to live with this."

Her face softened. "You're right. This isn't your fault, and it isn't mine. It's just... life."

The new corvette was well into her working-up period. Cochrane had appointed Lieutenant-Commander Angus Darroch as her commanding officer. He'd served under Cochrane as an Ensign and Sub-Lieutenant. Since then he'd commanded a patrol craft as a Lieutenant, and served as Executive Officer of a fleet transport as a Lieutenant-Commander. He'd jumped at the chance to join Eufala when Cochrane had approached him.

Darroch helped to come up with names for the new corvettes. "Sir, you named the patrol craft after carnivorous fish," he pointed out. "Continuing the theme of names from Earth, why not name the corvettes after poisonous plants? We hope they'll give opponents indigestion, after all!"

Laughing, Cochrane agreed, and he and Darroch spent an enjoyable hour researching the subject. They came up with a dozen names, listing them in alphabetical order. Amanita was the first, and the new corvette was christened accordingly. Her ship's crest, painted by an enthusiastic local artist on the bulkhead of her docking bay, copied an illustration of the poisonous death cap mushroom from an ancient encyclopedia. Obtaining an actual specimen had, of course, been out of the question, so far away from Earth.

Hui laughed when Cochrane told her how the names of the corvettes had been selected. "You're certainly picking the more dangerous aspects of life on Earth. What are you going to name the frigates?"

"When the time comes, we're thinking of smaller cat predators – wildcat, bobcat and so on. Earth had lots of them. We should be able to come up with enough names."

Cochrane warned Darroch, "You'll have to put up with not just one, but two Captains as passengers aboard *Amanita* for her maiden patrol." He explained about Hui's presence.

Darroch looked worried. "What about cabins, sir? We only have one spare in Officers Row, because we're carrying two extra junior officers under training."

"Give it to Captain Lu. There's an empty berth in the NCO's quarters. I'll use that."

Horrified, Darroch refused point-blank. A luckless Ensign was swiftly banished to NCO territory, and Cochrane was invited to use his cabin for the trip. Grinning, he accepted. "Sorry, Ensign," he apologized. "It'll only be for a few weeks."

"That's all right, sir," the young man retorted with an impudent grin. "If I can survive a few weeks in the company of senior NCO's, I reckon I'll be able to survive anything!"

"Be careful how you conduct yourself, then. At this stage of your career, you'll learn a hell of a lot more from NCO's than you will from textbooks or training aids. Take advantage of your time among them to ask lots of questions. You'll be glad you did."

Before leaving, Cochrane took the time to assess the company's ships, and streamline their operations. One of the freighters 'borrowed' from NOE was now serving as depot ship in the Mycenae system. The other was making monthly supply runs on the triangular route between Constanta, Rousay and Mycenae. The leased freighter was still on hand, not in regular use except for the shipments of asteroids to Barjah. He would have preferred to end her lease and hand her back, but if even one of the other freighters were unavailable for some reason, he would have to delay an asteroid shipment. With payments to Kang Industries rising steeply over the next few years, a delay might be unacceptable. Sighing, he kept her on the books for now.

He appointed a passage crew for one of the two fast freighters for which he'd swapped at Medusa, and sent it to Goheung for Kang Industries to convert into a training ship. There weren't sufficient spacers available to form a crew for the second, so he designated it as a temporary local warehouse ship. The New Westray depot ship still held its own machinery, the equipment taken off *Colomb,* and the asteroids gathered in the Mycenae system. Cochrane ordered everything transferred to the new warehouse ship, and the unserviceable depot ship scrapped, to get it out of the way. Sue McBride protested the delay this imposed on refitting her new repair ship, but he was unrepentant.

"I'm sorry, Sue, but we've got to avoid getting bogged down in unproductive work. Useless ships are part of that. They take time and attention – not to mention crews – that we can't afford."

"Och, I suppose you're right, sir. What about the three derelict patrol craft?"

"They're our only source of spare parts. We'll keep them for now."

Dave Cousins came up with another good idea. "NOE had a lien on our patrol craft, sir," he pointed out. "That's been lifted now that you've repaid their loan, but what if questions are raised in future? What if they come after us alleging we stole 'their' asteroids? What if they try to seize our ships as compensation?"

Cochrane shrugged. "We'll have to deal with that if it happens."

"But what if we can deal with it now, sir? The only ships registered in Eufala Corporation's name, so far, are the patrol craft at Mycenae. You haven't yet registered any of our other vessels – you've been too busy. Why not register them in the name of a different company, independent of both NOE and Eufala? That way, if there are any legal complications, they'll never have been Eufala assets as far as the law is concerned. NOE won't be able to touch them."

Cochrane began to smile. "That's a good idea. What's more,

I'll change our Constanta operating license to reflect the name of the new company. If Rousay pulls our license in the Cluster, we'll still be able to operate legally here. What do you think of 'Hawkwood Corporation'?"

"Hawkwood, sir?"

"Yes. Sir John Hawkwood was a mercenary captain in Italy on Earth during the fourteenth century. He was a ruthless, cunning son-of-a-bitch, by all accounts, but one of the most successful of his kind."

"I guess we're mercenaries too, sir, at least of a sort, so I don't see why not. Where will you register it?"

"I think Neue Helvetica again. If it's set up there, we can easily transfer funds between Eufala and Hawkwood via a cut-out account. It makes administration easier, and it's not subject to the authority of Constanta or New Orkney Cluster courts. That gives us another layer of protection."

"That ought to do it. What about the patrol craft at Mycenae, sir? Will you leave them in Eufala's name?"

"Yes. We only need them for the next couple of years, until enough of our corvettes are operational. As soon as they are, I'll retire the patrol craft. Even refurbished, they're so old that they're poor excuses for warships."

"You haven't thought of sending them to Goheung, to be modernized from the hull outward?"

"I decided against it, at least for now. Patrol craft can't hyper-jump. They have to be ferried aboard another vessel for interstellar travel. That's all very well when you aren't in a hurry, but what if an urgent need arises somewhere? We may not have time to get a transport to wherever they are, load them up, take them where they're needed, and unload them there. What's more, any fighting will make it too risky to load or unload them – they'll be too vulnerable. On the other hand, corvettes are interstellar ships. They carry at least twice as many missiles as a patrol craft, and they have longer endurance on patrol. We need that flexibility and speed of deployment right now."

"Hard to argue with that, even if corvettes are more expensive."

"Yes. Now, I've got a critical job for you before you transfer to the Mycenae system. We need crews for the fast freighter at Kang Industries, for the next two corvettes, for my Neue Helvetica courier ship, and as relief crews for the patrol craft and depot ship in Mycenae. We still don't have enough personnel for all those commitments. I want you to ask our existing crews to recommend us to their spacer friends. Offer cash bonuses for everyone they refer whom we hire. Make it clear we want quality over quantity. If they bring us people who don't work out, they won't get a bonus. Tell them it'll be paid after six months' satisfactory service by the new hires, or something like that."

"Got it, sir. What about officers?"

"Keep looking for good ones. I've sent to Lancaster to hire two or three former Commonwealth Fleet Warrant and Limited Duty officers, people who can help us select and train candidates for those slots from within our ranks. If we're lucky, they'll start work within the next few months. I'm going to push those avenues of promotion as hard as I can. There are plenty of spacers in the New Orkney Cluster who couldn't get ahead because they weren't First Families, or they'd pissed off someone in the First Families. If we can offer them a path upward and outward, at least some of them will take it – particularly now that we can show them a modern corvette, not just an outdated, obsolete patrol craft."

"Yes, sir. By the way, I think you'll be amazed by *Amanita*'s level of automation. I've been out on a couple of her training runs. Her artificial intelligence systems take a big load off her operators. I don't know how well they'll work in combat, but for routine operations, they do better than I'd ever have believed possible. That also means she can cope with fewer officers, because the AI substitutes for them to some extent."

"I'll look forward to seeing that for myself soon."

THE VOYAGE to the Mycenae system aboard HCS *Amanita* – the brand-new initials standing for 'Hawkwood Corporation Ship', as Lieutenant-Commander Darroch proudly informed them – was as interesting as Cousins had promised. The automation of the ship's systems had progressed far beyond anything Cochrane had experienced during his previous fleet service.

"It certainly means we'll have an easier time finding crews for our ships," he said to Hui during an evening conversation with Darroch. "She needs a lot fewer spacers than the older corvettes I'm used to. Trouble is, that imposes limits on what she can do. We've already discussed the damage control issue; then, there are boarding parties and prize crews. She can spare at most half a dozen spacers to board a ship to inspect it, or take its crew into custody. That may not be enough if its crew resists, but a corvette doesn't have spare berths to carry extra personnel for that role. As for prize crews, to get a spaceship from where she was captured to our base, that's out of the question. A corvette like this can't spare that many of her crew for an extended period."

Darroch observed, "That's true, sir, but then, it's also true of our patrol craft."

"You're right. We're probably going to have to operate mixed task forces to patrol a system, if we want to cover it properly. Four corvettes and one or two frigates should be able to cope with most threats, provided we can deploy system surveillance satellites – and that's going to be another big expense, I can see that already! The frigates have enough accommodation for boarding parties and prize crews. We've designed it into them. A corvette can stop a ship, then call a frigate to put a prize crew aboard if necessary."

"That ought to work," Hui agreed. "It may take a while for the frigate to get there, of course."

"Hmm. Yes. If there's more enemy action going on, it might take too long."

Darroch excused himself to answer a call from the OpCen as Cochrane went on, "If worse comes to worst, the corvette can put a laser beam through part of the ship's gravitic drive. That'll stop her going anywhere. She'll have to be towed back to our base after all the shouting and tumult has died down. It'll take time and money to repair her, of course. If she's not worth that, the corvette will just have to destroy her in place, after telling the crew to abandon ship."

She frowned, and lowered her voice. "That's a very ruthless attitude, isn't it?"

"Surely it's no more ruthless than any Fleet officer's, when faced with a decision like that?"

"No, it isn't, but you're *aren't* a Fleet officer any longer. Despite that, you haven't changed your approach. If you act like a military officer, but without that authority backing you up, and if a court thinks you went too far, you might face years in prison. The same goes for your crews."

He pondered that for a while. "I don't want to admit you may be right, but I guess you are," he said at last, his voice chagrined. "I doubt it'll be a factor in Mycenae, at least until it's colonized, but it probably will in other systems as we expand our operations. We may need to change our operational doctrine and training, and perhaps our customer contracts, to give us more legal protection in those situations."

"Amending contracts and doctrines is all very well, but look at your own attitudes too," she said quietly. "I think you've become callous when it comes to criminals. I know you've had to deal with a lot of very bad characters, including killing some of them. Don't let that harden your soul. I like the person you are, but if you go too far down that road, you won't be that person any longer."

"How did you deal with the problem?" he asked. "After all, you're a professional officer too."

"I've never had to deal with it. I haven't been in combat."

"Well, I'm here to tell you, combat *does* change you, and dealing with hardened criminals even more so. Put the two together, and I suppose one can grow a hard shell around oneself without being aware of it. I... I'll try to think about that. Trouble is, I may need help to deal with it; but I can't turn to you for that, because it would be... difficult... for both of us."

She nodded helplessly. "I'm sorry."

"Don't worry. You were right to raise the issue. I'll work on it as best I can."

~

MYCENAE SYSTEM

Amanita's arrival in Mycenae Primus Four orbit aroused intense interest among the patrol craft crews, all of whom wanted to tour her. Cochrane made sure they got the opportunity. "We've got more of them coming," he assured them. "Within a couple of years, the old patrol craft will be retired. You'll all be aboard one of these instead."

"Can't happen too soon for me, sir," a grizzled Senior Chief Petty Officer informed him with a grin. "Our ships are just too small and cramped. It's a good thing they can only carry enough stores for a week's patrol at a time. Any longer, and the crew would mutiny!"

Cochrane recognized him as one of the NCO's who'd served under him in the past. "What do you think of the corvette's berthing spaces?"

"They're the lap of luxury compared to our old tub. I reckon they're comfortable enough that we won't need berths aboard the depot ship."

The monthly freighter arrived shortly afterwards. Two relief crews took over *Arapaima* and *Bicuda,* and their former crews assembled aboard the depot ship. Stores for the next month were transferred, and accumulated garbage and waste products loaded aboard the freighter for disposal at Constanta.

Meanwhile, Commander Cousins took the opportunity for a brief reunion with Dr. Masters. Cochrane gave them a night of peace and quiet before summoning his second-in-command. He arrived with his fiancée on his arm. She was now wearing an engagement ring, and looked very happy, if exhausted. Grinning to himself, Cochrane refrained from heavy-handed comments about the couple's obvious lack of sleep.

"How's the recruiting coming?" he asked.

"It's improving, sir. I interviewed seven officers at Rousay, and my team spoke to about three dozen NCO's and spacers. More of them are approaching us, now that they're getting word from their friends that we're a good outfit to work for, and we pay double what the System Patrol Service does. I've told those that looked most likely to come to Constanta for final interviews and initial training, and given them travel funds."

"Good. I think –"

He was cut short by the blare of an alarm, followed by a crisp announcement over the speakers. *"Captain Cochrane to the OpCen on the double!"*

He sprinted down the corridor to the depot ship's bridge. Lunging through the door, he found the duty watch staring into the three-dimensional Plot display. More than two billion kilometers away, in the asteroid belt of Mycenae Secundus, a red flashing icon denoted an incident.

"What's up?" he demanded.

"Sir, we detected a nuclear explosion in the second asteroid belt," the Officer of the Watch informed him. "There were no gravitic drive signatures or other emissions beforehand."

Cochrane instantly knew what must have happened. One of the mines Cousins had sown, in the part of the asteroid belt being prospected by the Albanian robots, had found a target.

"Signal *Amanita* to come to departure stations and stand by for me to board her. Anyone aboard her from other ships is to disembark at once. Signal the duty patrol craft to head for the explosion at full speed. We'll overtake her on the way."

"Aye aye, sir!"

As Cochrane ran toward the docking bay, Hui came out from a side passage. "What is it?" she asked as she joined him.

"Explosion in the second asteroid belt. We're going to investigate. Want to come?"

"Of course!"

The duty cutter took them across to *Amanita,* where they found Lieutenant-Commander Darroch already in the Operations Center. "Head for the explosion," Cochrane told him tersely. "Use all your sensors as we get closer, and be careful. There may be another ship out there."

"Aye aye, sir!"

Darroch got the corvette under way, then ran some quick calculations on the command console. "It'll take us about twelve hours to get there, sir, including deceleration."

Cochrane nodded, knowing that *Amanita*'s maximum speed was one-third Cee. She couldn't go faster than that without over-stressing the gravitic shield protecting her from the impact of minor space debris. In the background he could hear the rising whine of the inertial compensator, absorbing the brutal acceleration imparted by the gravitic drive and dumping it safely into the gravity well of space's dark matter. Without it, *Amanita*'s crew would long since have been smeared to bloody paste against the bulkheads under the massive g-forces unleashed by the drive.

They passed the much slower *Trairao* before long, plugging

along at her maximum safe speed of one-fifth Cee. She'd arrive at
the scene much later than *Amanita,* but no-one complained. She
was doing her best.

As they drew closer, the tension aboard *Amanita* rose ever
higher. Darroch recalled the crew to general quarters, and set the
radar and lidar systems, and the ship's defenses, to automatic
mode. They had demonstrated their reliability and effectiveness
as the ship worked up. This would be an excellent opportunity to
test them under real-world conditions.

"Remember to broadcast our identification code," Cochrane
reminded him. "There are still mines out there, waiting for
snoopers. Also, please confirm that we're using gravitic drive
frequency modulation, and that all our other ships in the system
are doing the same."

"Aye aye, sir. Command to Navigation, confirm that our
beacon is active."

"Navigation to Command, beacon active, correct code
confirmed, sir."

"Command to Navigation, thank you." He turned to
Cochrane. "Before we arrived, I set our electronic warfare systems
to monitor every gravitic drive signature in the Mycenae system,
sir. I wanted to build up a database for comparison. Every ship
we've recorded so far has been modulated, so they can't be identified from the signature alone. It's too heavily disguised. The
system will warn us if it encounters a non-modulated signature,
but so far it hasn't, sir."

"Good. We'll have to watch that like hawks. If our enemies
can identify ships here from their signatures, they can use that to
identify them in other systems as well. Sooner or later, one way
or another, that's going to happen, but we want to delay it for as
long as possible."

A chime sounded, and an icon appeared in the Plot display.
"Contact bearing 003:007, range one zero two thousand kilometers," the operator announced. "No emissions."

"That's odd," Hui said from her place next to Cochrane. "Radar should have picked up a ship-sized target much further away than that, unless it was stealthy, like this ship; but then it wouldn't pick it up until it was much closer than that."

"Then this probably isn't a normal ship-sized target," he replied, his eyes on the Plot. He noticed a speckle of tiny echoes around the icon. "I think that's a piece of a ship destroyed by a mine. Those speckles are smaller pieces of wreckage, reflecting radar energy. I've seen that before."

"I think you're right, sir," Darroch confirmed. "Command to Helm, steer for the echo. Gravitic shield to full power. Reverse drive to halt one thousand kilometers from it."

"Helm to Command, head for the echo, max shield, halt one thousand clicks away, aye aye, sir."

Darroch turned to Cochrane. "Sir, with your permission, I'll send out an interrogative signal on the standard emergency frequency. If there are any survivors in spacesuits or lifeboats, that should trigger their beacons, so we can locate and recover them."

"Make it so."

Almost as soon as the signal went out, three icons flashed to life in the short-range Plot display. "I make that two lifeboats and one spacesuit, sir," the Plot operator said as he gave their bearings and ranges.

Darroch activated the intercom. "Cutter pilot, report to the cutter. Chief of the Ship, assign two spacers to help him. They're to get into spacesuits and prepare to recover survivors."

As footsteps began to run along the corridor ouside the OpCen, Cochrane leaned over. "Issue weapons to the cutter crew, and tell them to be on their guard. If this ship belonged to that Albanian crime syndicate, the survivors may not come quietly."

Darroch looked surprised, but nodded, and sent his Executive Officer to the ship's small armory to issue carbines to the cutter crew.

The pilot took the cutter out toward the first icon, the smallest. As they drew nearer, he called the ship. "It's a spacesuit, sir. There's someone inside, but he's not moving. I think he may be hurt, or even dead."

"Get him aboard, and bring him back here before you go to the next icon," Darroch ordered. "We'll see if the medic can do anything for him."

The space-suited figure was brought through the airlock into the docking bay foyer. The monitoring panel on the front of the suit was green, indicating that he was still alive. Willing hands stripped off the spacesuit and carried him on a stretcher to the sick bay, where the Petty Officer medic examined him carefully.

"I don't know, sir," he confessed, turning to Cochrane where he stood in the doorway. "I can't see any visible signs of wounds, but there may be internal injuries. I can put him in the Medicomp and have it check him out, but we only have one of them, sir. If anyone else is out there, they may need it more than he does."

"Let's wait and see what the cutter finds," Cochrane advised.

It found an empty lifeboat, drifting in space, and then another, this one with a light on its airlock door indicating that someone was inside. The cutter turned around and backed up to the airlock, mating its rear ramp with the entrance aperture. As soon as pressures were equalized, the pilot lowered the ramp.

Those listening on board *Amanita* heard a sudden, confused babble of voices. The transmission was cut off for a moment. When the pilot came back on the circuit, he was breathing heavily, as if either frightened or very angry. "The bastards rushed us! There were three of them. One had a knife, another had a big wrench. When the airlock door opened, they charged into the cutter and went for us. We shot the two with the weapons. One's dead, the other's badly hurt. The third one, in the rear, gave up when he saw our carbines. We're securing him now."

"Understood," Darroch said crisply. "Well done for stopping

them. Load all three aboard the cutter, then get clear of the lifeboats. We'll destroy them while you return to the ship."

A couple of shots from one of *Amanita's* laser cannon took care of the drifting lifeboats. The massive energy release at what was, in space combat terms, point blank range, reduced them to molecular particles, removing any hazard they posed to space traffic. More carbines were issued to spacers, who met the survivors in the docking bay.

The uninjured man refused to answer questions – in fact, he wouldn't say a word. He was searched, then his ankles and wrists were secured with flex-ties, and he was placed on a bunk in a berthing unit. His wounded comrade was hurried to the sick bay, where he was inserted into the Medicomp unit.

"How long before it gives us a prognosis?" Cochrane asked as he watched the man's body vanish inside the robotic treatment center.

"It shouldn't be more than half an hour, sir."

"Very well. I'll be with Commander Darroch. Keep us informed."

"Aye aye, sir."

Captain Hu came back to the OpCen just after he reached it. "I checked out that spacesuit," she told them. "All its labels are in Albanian. The one who won't talk may not understand Galactic Standard English. Do you have a translation unit aboard?"

"I'm sure there's one built into the AI, ma'am," Darroch said, and turned to his console to investigate. Sure enough, interpreter programs in most of the languages in the settled galaxy had been included in the software.

"With your permission, I'll use the berthing compartment terminal to try to communicate with him," Hui proposed.

"Go ahead, ma'am," Darroch assented.

As she hurried out, Cochrane said, "We've learned some lessons today, to add to my earlier concerns. I'm going to specify four modifications to our new corvettes. I want an extra berthing

unit or two, to house survivors, and to carry extra spacers for a
boarding party or prize crew. They can form a damage control
party until they're needed for that. I want a jail cell, where we can
secure uncooperative prisoners. I want a second Medicomp in the
sick bay, and I want a supply of damage control materials and
equipment."

"What about this ship, sir?"

"We'll wait until we have enough of our new ships on hand;
then they can either modify this ship to match them, or take her
back for what we paid for her, and build us another corvette to
our specifications."

Darroch whistled admiringly. "You don't do things by half
measures, do you, sir?"

"No point in it. If it's necessary, do it, and be damned to
anything that gets in the way."

Even as he spoke, he recalled Hui's words about his attitude.
He shrugged. She might have a point, but so did he. He'd just
have to find a happy medium between them, over time.

"Commander, send a boarding party to the drifting spaceship
hulk. Include an electronics tech. I want to know whether any of
her computer systems survived, particularly memory units. If
they did, recover them all and bring them back aboard for
analysis."

"Aye aye, sir."

∿

NEXT DAY, aboard the depot ship, Cochrane briefed Cousins and
Darroch about what they'd learned.

"We recovered her main computer intact. Its data is
encrypted, but I reckon Jock Murray and his people can deal with
that for us. With luck, we'll be able to find out where she came
from. That may lead us to some of the people behind this." He
looked at Hui. "Any luck with your interrogation?"

"No. The uninjured survivor understands the Albanian translation provided by the ship's AI, but he just curses me when I press him for answers. He doesn't seem to like women very much."

"More fool him, I'd say! The man shot by the cutter crew died last night, and the other, unconscious survivor is still out of it. He's in the hospital now. Dr. Masters reports he has internal injuries and severe concussion. She can't say if or when he may wake up."

"Can he be moved, sir?" Cousins asked.

"Dr. Masters says, if he survives the next forty-eight hours, it's possible, but she isn't sure yet. If she approves, please bring him back to Constanta with you aboard the freighter. I'll take the uninjured survivor aboard my courier ship, under guard."

"What are we going to do about interrogating him, sir?"

"I've got a few ideas, but I won't say more just yet. Let's try to keep the other one alive, in case they don't work out. Dave, I want you to collect every beaconed asteroid in the prospector bot fields sowed by those Albanians, and by the Callanish consortium; then confiscate every robot prospector in them. Make sure there are none left. If you can't pick some up, use laser cannon to destroy them. Retrieve the mines you laid in the Albanian field, and redeploy them here to defend our installation and the satellites. Bring the asteroids and the bots back to Constanta with you."

"Yes, sir, but... wouldn't it be better to leave the bots out there, along with a patrol craft to intercept any more ships trying to collect asteroids?"

Cochrane shook his head. "With its outdated sensors, a patrol craft probably wouldn't detect them until they got close enough to hit her, assuming they're armed. You'd need multiple ships, to cover each other, and we don't have that many to spare in this system yet. Let's concentrate them around this planet for the time being, where they can provide overlapping coverage."

"Aye aye, sir. What about the NOE bot field?"

"Leave that in place, along with any asteroids it's identified since our last visit. NOE is sure to send a ship soon to collect them, so let's give them something to find. I'll explain to them that we've removed the other two fields."

"I get it, sir."

"I'll leave *Amanita* here for now. Her sensors are several times better than anything else we have in this system. Make sure local commanders keep them active at all times, along with her automated defenses. If any ship launches missiles at you out of nowhere, that'll be your best defense. Remind all our people how easily *Colomb* snuck up on this planet. Other ships might do the same."

"Aye aye, sir."

"Captain Lu and myself will depart for Constanta tomorrow aboard my courier ship, along with our prisoner. I'll see you back there, Dave. Lieutenant-Commander Darroch, you'll be the senior officer of the patrol craft division until Dave gets back. Keep your eyes and sensors peeled for intruders, and stay alert."

"Aye aye, sir."

14

TRACING THE ENEMY

CONSTANTA

As the courier ship sped toward its orbital rendezvous with the planet, Cochrane asked Hui, "D'you mind if I try something with our prisoner? I'll need your help."

"What do you have in mind?"

"We've got to break his resistance somehow. If he's part of an Albanian Mafia offshoot, I presume he'll know about the Dragon Tong, and where it's based."

"I'll be very surprised if he doesn't."

"Then, if you'll please put on your best uniform, we'll see if we can get him into a more cooperative frame of mind."

As the ship slowed, Cochrane entered the cabin where the prisoner was confined under guard. He glanced at the terminal in the corner. The interpreter software was running, and would automatically translate his words into Albanian.

He turned to the guard, who'd been briefed beforehand. "All right, pack his gear." The prisoner had been issued basic underwear, utility clothing and toiletries, since all his own possessions had been lost. "We're transferring him to the Qianjin communications frigate."

As the software translated his words, and spoke them aloud through the terminal's speaker, the prisoner suddenly sat bolt upright, his eyes widening.

"Will do, sir. Is Captain Lu taking him with her?"

"Yes, she is. He won't talk to us, so we'll let the Dragon Tong loosen his tongue."

The guard laughed. "A Tong for his tongue. Dang, sir, that's almost poetic!"

The prisoner suddenly burst into a torrent of speech. The translation software interpreted, "You cannot do this! You *cannot* send me to Qianjin!"

"I can, and I will," Cochrane told him coldly. "You've given me no reason to keep you here."

"But they will torture me! They use drugs on me, then kill me!"

"So? That's not my problem. You won't tell us what we need to know. They'll make you tell them, then they'll tell us. That's good enough."

As he finished speaking, Hui entered the cabin, wearing her uniform. Her face was stiff, formal. "Is he ready?" she asked coldly.

"He is. Let's get him aboard your gig."

"Thank you, Captain."

The prisoner pushed himself back into a corner of his bunk, huddling there with real fear on his face. "You cannot do this! If... if I talk, will you keep me here?"

"You wouldn't talk before. Why should we trust you now?"

"You can truth-test me! Ask me anything! I promise I'll tell you everything!"

Cochrane exulted inwardly, but kept his face stern and impassive. "Captain Lu, what do you think?"

"I can delay my departure for twenty-four hours. If he tells you everything in that time, all well and good. You can give me a copy of his interrogation. If he doesn't, I'll take him to Qianjin, where he *will* tell us everything. I guarantee it." The cold formality of her tone was almost sinister.

"I can work with that. Did you understand?" Cochrane looked at the prisoner, raising his eyebrows inquiringly.

"Yes, but – what if I talk? What will you do with me?"

"That depends on how much you tell us. If we're sure you've given us everything you know, I'm willing to let you go. If you belong to the Albanian Mafia, you might not want to go back to them. They're said to dislike traitors."

The prisoner shook his head vigorously. "If I don't talk, the Dragons kill me. If I talk, the brotherhood kills me. All I can do is talk, then run and hide where brotherhood won't find me. You give me money to make fresh start? Maybe ticket off-planet?"

"You'll have to earn it."

"I will! I promise – but you must also promise! You not send me to Qianjin!"

Cochrane considered, then said slowly, "I promise that if you tell us everything you know, *and* the truth-tester confirms you're not lying, *and* the computer data we recovered agrees with what you say, then I'll put you aboard the next freighter leaving here. It won't go to Qianjin, or anywhere near it. When it arrives at its destination, you'll be given ten thousand francs, in cash, and your identity documents, and be taken to the planet's orbital space station. Where you go after that, and what you do, and what happens to you, are none of my concern."

"Is good! I accept deal!"

"All right. Wait here. I'll get a truth-tester team on board, then we'll talk."

As they walked back up the main corridor, Cochrane grinned at Hui. "That was very well done. Thank you very much."

"It was your idea." She relaxed, smiling as she took off her uniform cap and pulled a couple of clips from her hair, letting it fall. "Let's see what he has to say."

The man, who identified himself as Enver Asllani, had a lot to tell them. His ship, the *Puka*, had left her home planet of Patos more than a month ago to collect asteroids beaconed for collection by the Albanian Mafia's prospector robots. She had emplaced the bots a year before. She'd made one voyage to collect asteroids about four months after that, but had since been sidelined with drive problems. Repaired at last, she had crept into the Mycenae system without being detected, but had been destroyed – by what, he didn't know – as she drew near to the first asteroid beacon.

"What was that?" he demanded. "All your ships were at Mycenae Primus. We knew. We watch on sensors, and our satellite told us no other ships nearby."

Cochrane cursed inwardly. If the Albanians had a satellite watching the area, they would have recorded Cousins' ship collecting the final asteroids, then capturing or destroying all of the bots. "I'm not sure what it was. What's the contact frequency and code for your satellite?"

Asllani shrugged. "I am spacehand, not bridge crew. I do not know codes. First Mate Selimaj, he knows codes, and much more." They had shown him a picture of the man they'd left in a coma aboard the depot ship at Mycenae Primus Four, and Asllani had identified him. The truth-tester operator glanced at Cochrane, and nodded. The Albanian wasn't lying.

Let's hope the First Mate wakes up, and can tell us, Cochrane thought. *If not, perhaps we can read them off the ship's computer.* "All right, go on."

The spacer couldn't tell them much more about the events that had led to his capture. Cochrane handed over to Hui, who put him through a tough five-hour interrogation on the activities of the Albanian Mafia as a whole, his own branch of it, their interest in asteroid mining throughout the galaxy, other planets where they'd sown their prospector robots, where they took the asteroids for processing – anything and everything she could think of that had a bearing on the problem of stolen asteroids.

Cochrane left her to it, and delivered the computer to Jock Murray. He explained where it had come from. "Can you dig through it as quickly as possible, and get us any information at all that you can salvage? We're interrogating a survivor right now, and we'd like to compare what he tells us with what's on this thing."

"Sure thing, sir. I'll get to work with a couple of my system techs. We'll pull an all-nighter if necessary. We should have something for you by early tomorrow."

~

JOCK WAS as good as his word. He met with Cochrane and Captain Lu for a late breakfast next morning.

"The memory module was intact," he assured them through a mouthful of scrambled eggs on toast. "We've been working on it all night. The ship was homeported at Patos. Over the past three years, she's made seven round trips from there to systems that have active asteroid mining projects. They've all been extended journeys, because she sneaked into the systems from a long way out, coasting slowly to avoid detection, and left the same way. Mycenae was the most recent, followed by a long period out of service with a defective gravitic drive. She'd just been repaired before making her last run. She'd just collected their surveillance satellite here before she was destroyed."

"Can you identify all her movements during those three years?" Hui asked eagerly.

"Not all, ma'am. Some of them seem to have delivered the asteroids she collected to a refinery ship. The voyage tracks and coordinates for those legs of her journeys, and from the refinery ship back to Patos, are quantum-encrypted. I can't crack them."

"That's a pity. What about the codes for their surveillance satellite, that she just collected?"

"They're not in the public data on this system, ma'am. They're probably also quantum-encrypted. We'll have to ask Lieutenant-Commander Ross to look at it. That's her area."

"Even without that, you've done an outstanding job. I must get this back to Fleet Intelligence at once. If we hurry, we might find their robotic prospectors in all those systems, and be able to get our own samples, now that you've shown us how." She inclined her head to Cochrane gratefully. "Can I take a bit-level copy of the memory with me? I'll have our specialists tackle the encryption, too."

"Certainly," Cochrane agreed.

Jock nodded. "I'll already made a bit-level copy, so I'll run off a duplicate for you, ma'am. I reckon the robots will still be in those systems, too. After all, the Albanians don't know what happened to their ship. They may not even have missed her yet."

"Yes, but they will, and soon. We'll have to hurry to reach those systems before they can clean them up." She glanced apologetically at Cochrane. "I'm sorry. I know you wanted to talk, but..."

"I understand. You have your duty to your Fleet to consider."

"Yes." She shrugged helplessly.

She departed within the hour, her communications frigate scorching away from the planet toward the system boundary. They had time for only the most perfunctory of farewells. He felt an emptiness in his heart as he watched the icon of her ship receding in the Plot. *Maybe, one day...* he told himself, but he knew that might be no more than wishful thinking.

To break that train of thought, he threw himself into his work. The second courier ship had arrived from Neue Helvetica, and was standing by. He wrote a long message to Mr. Kim, then sent for her captain.

"I need you to deliver this to Kang Industries at Goheung with all dispatch. As soon as you've done that, head for Barjah and wait for me there. I'll arrive a couple of days after you, aboard a slower freighter. I'll have some business there for a few days, then we'll head for Goheung again before coming back here. The freighter will make its own way back."

"Understood, sir."

"Thank you. On your way."

It took a couple of days to deal with all the work that had piled up in his absence. While he tackled it, he had Sue McBride load thirty more asteroids into the freighter. He also ordered that the Albanian prisoner should be closely confined aboard it, taking his meals in his cabin, seeing only his guards. Finally, he left instructions for the continued confinement and medical care of the second Albanian prisoner when he arrived.

Satisfied at last that he'd put out as many administrative fires as possible, Cochrane boarded the freighter and told the commanding officer to head for Barjah. He withdrew to the owner's suite, which he'd appropriated for himself, and collapsed into bed to sleep the clock around. When he woke, he'd have more than enough work to occupy himself until they arrived.

BARJAH

As the freighter braked to enter orbit, Cochrane braced himself, already feeling mentally and morally stained in anticipation of what was about to happen. He picked up his cabin's comm unit, obtained a link via the Communications desk to the orbital telephone network, and placed a call to a private number.

It was answered within a few seconds. "Mr. Hsu's office."

"This is Captain Cochrane. I need to speak to Mr. Hsu at once. It's urgent."

"Yes, Captain. Please wait a moment."

Within a minute, there came a click on the line. "Hsu."

"Mr. Hsu, this is Captain Cochrane."

"Ah, Captain! How good to hear your voice again! You have brought more asteroids?"

"Yes, but there's something else – a potentially serious problem. Can you meet me at the space station as quickly as possible? It would be... helpful... if you could bring some assistants from your parent organization." He knew Hsu would understand he was referring to the Dragon Tong, rather than the asteroid mining operation.

"I see. I can be there in two to three hours from now."

"I'll meet you in the docking bay foyer. Is there somewhere private we can talk?"

"I will make arrangements."

"Thank you. I look forward to seeing you."

Cochrane replaced the comm unit in its cradle, went to the safe, and counted out ten thousand francs. He put it into an envelope, sealed it, and went down the corridor to the cabin where their captive was being held. Nodding to the guard on duty, he knocked and went in.

Asllani was sitting on the sofa, watching a vid. He jumped to his feet. "Captain! Where are we? You let me go now?"

"Soon, Mr. Asllani. We're at a planet named Barjah. I'll be able to send you to the space station in about four hours, as soon as arrival formalities have been completed. In the meanwhile, I wanted to give you this." He handed him the envelope.

Asllani tore it open, smiled eagerly as he saw the cash inside, and counted the notes quickly. "Is ten thousand, like you promised."

"Yes, it is. Here are your identity documents." He handed the man his passport and merchant spacer's card, both issued by Patos. "You'll need those to be admitted to the space station. There are freighters leaving here almost every day, going to several other planets. You should be able to get passage on one of them, or even join their crews if they're hiring."

"Thank you! Thank you!" The man was almost overcome with emotion at the prospect of freedom at last.

Cochrane could hardly restrain his self-loathing at the spacer's reaction, but he forced it down. "You must stay in this cabin for a few hours more. You'll be taken to the cutter when it's time to leave."

"I pack now, to be ready! *Thank you!*"

Cochrane headed for the docking bay, where the captain's gig was waiting. He climbed aboard, and was whisked away to the space station. He endured the arrival formalities, then took a seat at one side of the docking bay foyer, waiting patiently.

Half an hour later, he saw Hsu enter the foyer, accompanied by four men wearing dark suits. Their fluid, limber gait marked them as well-muscled and very fit, probably martial arts specialists among other things. He stood, and waited as Hsu noticed him and came over.

"Captain." They shook hands briefly. "I have arranged a private room."

"Please lead the way."

They walked in silence down a passage until they came to an administrative suite. One of the men led the way inside, and opened the door to a small conference room. They stood against the walls in silence while another of the four scanned the room with a small handheld instrument. At last he nodded. "Clear."

"What seems to be the problem, Captain?" Hsu asked without preamble.

Cochrane explained what had occurred at Mycenae, and what they'd learned from their captive. "Captain Lu had to leave at once, to take word of what we'd discovered to her superiors at Qianjin. I was left to deal with the prisoner."

"I see."

"I promised him that in return for his cooperation, I'd give him ten thousand francs and deliver him to this space station, after which he'd be on his own. I'll do that when I return to my ship." He took a deep breath. "It would not be good if the Albanians learned what he's told us." He took a picture of the prisoner from his pocket, and handed it over.

"I see. Thank you, Captain. You have acted very responsibly, and we are grateful. Please do not trouble yourself any further. Send your prisoner here as agreed. After that, your promises to him will have been fulfilled to the letter, and your obligations satisfied."

"Yes, they will. I have more asteroids to deliver. Can we discuss them tomorrow morning?"

"That will be in order."

"Thank you again, Mr. Hsu."

The executive and his four companions watched impassively as he let himself out. He walked back to the docking bay, cursing under his breath. He truly had no choice in the matter, if security was to be preserved – but in that case, why did he feel like such a treacherous, slimy son-of-a-bitch? It was as he'd told Hui some weeks before. You did what you had to do... but that statement no longer felt or sounded as convincing as it had in the past.

He still had no answers as the cutter carrying the Albanian departed for the space station. It returned to the freighter an hour later, empty.

GOHEUNG

Cochrane's mood was still somber as his courier ship, laden with the latest quarter-share payment from Barjah, slid into orbit. He signaled his arrival, and was invited to stay at the same hotel he'd used during his previous visit.

He was shown into Kim's office at ten the following morning.

The executive greeted him warmly. After the usual introductory formalities, they got straight down to business.

"We've studied the modifications you requested to our corvette design," Kim said. "It's good that you let us know about them when you did, as we were about to begin construction of the first two ships of your order. We'll add four frames to her length. By rearranging some of her compartments, we can insert two more six-berth accommodation units and a prison cell of the same size. We've expanded the sick bay to provide a second Medicomp unit, and enlarged her storage for damage control gear and materials, plus more supplies for her larger crew. We also increased her environmental system capacity. All those modifications will increase her mass by about two thousand tons. However, we can tweak her existing reactors and gravitic drive to give up to five percent more power, so her performance should remain the same.

"Our designers pointed out an interesting side-effect of lengthening the corvette. She already has a miniaturized version of our destroyer fire control system, using shortened active scanning arrays along her hull. The additional length means we can fit full-length destroyer arrays, if you wish. That will make her fully as capable as her larger counterparts, including your frigates, when it comes to long-range control of multiple weapons. The two classes of ship can then also control and direct each other's missiles without difficulty. It will also improve the corvette's electronic reconnaissance and countermeasures abilities. Finally, corvette weapons system operators will be able to use frigate weapons systems without additional training. Would that be of interest to you?"

"It certainly would, depending on the cost."

"We estimate we can include all you requested for an additional charge of twenty million francs per vessel. The extended array panels, top and bottom and on both sides, would add a further eight million. The bow and stern array panels would remain the same, of course."

Cochrane pondered. It was a lot more to spend, but compatibility with frigate systems would be extremely valuable, particularly if his ships operated in mixed detachments. He nodded. "Let's do that. Please include the full-size arrays as well. Will this hold up construction?"

"Only by a week or two. Our robotic constructors can slot in extra frames without difficulty, and the berthing compartments and cells are uncomplicated structures. The second Medicomp will require additional cabling to connect it to the sick bay computer facilities, but the arrays are again straightforward, needing only to be applied to the hull and wired into the battle computers. Their software can easily be updated to handle the extended capacity of the arrays."

"That's good news. Very well, I'll authorize an additional charge of twenty-eight million francs per corvette. I can pay you the extra deposit for the first two orders right away. There's one thing, though. What about the corvette we already have, your prototype? Can she be modified to the same standard?"

"That may present problems, because her hull is an older design. However, if you wish, we can buy her back from you for a reasonable sum, to be mutually agreed, and you can order another new-build corvette to replace her."

"That might work. Let's discuss that once we've taken delivery of the first four ships. There's one more thing I wanted to ask about. Do you make deep space surveillance satellites?"

"We don't, but another Goheung company does. We've referred our customers to them from time to time, and they do the same for us with theirs. Our ships' datalinks can interface with their satellites, making tactical control easier."

"That's a very useful feature. I'd appreciate an introduction, please. I have an urgent need for one, with more to follow." Cochrane tried to hide his sour displeasure at the price he knew he'd have to pay. Such satellites offered features that no ship-board sensor suite could match, but they were priced accordingly.

"I'll be glad to arrange that. You will be able to provide an end-user certificate, of course?"

"Of course."

I'd better check how many of those fill-in-the-blank Rousay certificates I have left, he thought to himself with a mental grin. *I should probably ask NOE to get me some more, before they find out what I've really been up to and don't want to help me anymore, or bribe Constanta to give me some of theirs. I reckon their Defense Minister is greedy enough that it shouldn't be a problem.*

∾

CONSTANTA

Dave Cousins was waiting when he returned. "We brought back another eighteen asteroids," he said cheerfully. "I reckon that takes our total to over a hundred and fifty."

"It does – one hundred and sixty-seven, in fact. Well done, Dave! That's all our new ships paid for, plus enough money in the bank to pay all our operating expenses for a few years, even with all of them in commission. It'll be up to us to bring in enough through security contracts, and asteroid prospecting of our own, to build on that foundation. I'm going to increase the leadership team's guaranteed profit share at the end of our startup period. I'll make it twenty-five million francs each."

Cousins blinked. "Well, *that's* better than a poke in the eye with a sharp stick!" They laughed. "How many do you think will take the money and leave, and how many stay on?"

"I don't know right now. That's OK. Everyone's earned the right to make their own decisions. I think Elizabeth won't want to stay, because she's finding life at Mycenae boring and frustrating.

Of course, if you two get married, she can settle down somewhere you both like and set herself up in practice there, while you commute to wherever we're based."

"We've talked about that. I think it'll work for a few years at least. She wants me around to help raise our kids, though, at least often enough that they're not strangers to me."

"I can understand that. What about the Albanian First Mate? Did he make it?"

Cousins sighed. "Yes and no. Elizabeth stabilized him, and we brought him back in our freighter's sick bay; but he's still in a coma. She told me to find a long-term care facility for him. Your contact on Constanta, Nicolae Albrescu, arranged that for us. He's in a private ward, and watched around the clock. He may come out of it, or he may not. Elizabeth says there's no telling, and no way to predict a timetable."

Cochrane grimaced. "That's like a sort of living death. I'd hate it to happen to me."

"That makes two of us!"

"All right. Let me take care of everything that's piled up in my absence, then we'll sit down and plan the next few months."

15

DISCOVERY

CALLANISH

The burly spacer slammed his tankard down on the bar. "I don't care what the damned Patrol Service says! They can offer all the re-up bonuses they like. It ain't worth it! We had to wait for *months* in that bloody inflatable cell until they let us go. By then, my woman was pregnant – an' she had the gall t' try t' persuade me it was *mine,* an' was just' gonna arrive a bit late! To hell with that, and with her! I got a better one now, an' I'll not risk that happenin' again! I ain't goin' back!"

The senior NCO sitting at the bar beside him shook his head. "I think you're a fool, Gray. You'd get your third stripe in another year, and be set fair for Chief a few years after that. Why throw all that away?"

"Because the damned Patrol Service darn near threw all of *us* away! Did they send anyone to look for us? *Like hell they did!* They just left us to rot!"

"Be reasonable, man! *Colomb* was the only interstellar ship in the System Patrol Service. Our patrol craft can't hyper-jump. They didn't *have* anything else to send in search of you!"

"No, but that damn company that hired her could've used one of their ships. They didn't. Shows what we're worth, doesn't it? There's a word they used in an old movie I saw. 'Expendable'. That's what we are."

The NCO pushed himself away from the bar and got to his feet. "I reckon you're wrong, and I'm sorry you feel that way. What're you going to do next?"

"I'll figure out something." Gray waved half-drunkenly at the bartender. "Hey! Another one!"

He nursed his next beer for almost half an hour, making it last rather than deplete the thin wad of banknotes in his pocket. He was about to get up and leave when the bartender placed another tankard in front of him – this one a full-size literstein, brimming with foam.

"Huh? I didn't order this!"

"That guy down the bar bought it for you." He indicated a tall man wearing a set of clean utility coveralls, with patches down both arms suggesting that he was, or had been, both a merchant spacer and an asteroid miner.

"I heard what you said to that NCO," the man called. "You're right about seniors not giving a damn. Us spacers have to stick together, you know." His voice was oddly accented, placing an emphasis on certain syllables as if he were trying very hard to speak fluent Galactic Standard English, but wasn't completely at home in it.

"Thanks." Gray raised the tankard in salute. "You new here?"

"Just passing through. I had some leave coming, and I've never seen Callanish, so I reckoned I'd spend a few days enjoying some real, honest-to-goodness *weather* again!"

Gray laughed, and moved down the bar toward the spacer. "Ain't that the truth? Funny how we hate bad weather down here, but after a few months in space with no weather at all, we'll gladly let it rain an' hail an' thunder all over us, just to feel normal again!"

Several drinks later, his new-found friend suggested they get a meal. "We need something to line our stomachs for an evening's drinking, after all."

"You got tha' right!" Gray slurred. "I know a goo' plaishe jus' downa alley. Lesh go!"

~

HE WOKE AN INDETERMINABLE TIME LATER, head aching savagely. He tried to move, but couldn't. Lifting his head, bleary-eyed, he discovered he was on some sort of gurney. His legs were strapped down, and his torso raised at a forty-five-degree angle. A strap around his chest prevented him from sliding off. His arms rested on support trays running out from the side of the backrest. His left arm hurt slightly. Craning his neck, he saw a needle had been inserted inside his elbow. A plastic tube ran from it up to a bag of clear liquid. Straps around his upper and lower arm prevented him moving it. His right arm was similarly restrained.

He struggled futilely for a moment, but could not budge from his position. He tried throwing himself from side to side, but although the gurney creaked, it did not move. He raised his voice. "*Hey!* What is this? Someone lemme loose!" There was no response. He repeated his call a few times, voice growing louder in anger and frustration.

Without warning, a bright circle of lights came on above his head, pointed directly at his face. He cried out, turning his suddenly tear-filled eyes away. As he did so, a door opened, and he heard two sets of footsteps approaching.

"Who the hell are you?" he called, still blinded. "What am I doin' here?"

"You're going to answer some questions," the voice of his erstwhile friend answered. Turning his head back, blinking away tears, he saw a hand come out of the darkness holding a medical syringe. It pushed the needle into a connector on the plastic tube running down to his arm, then depressed the plunger. He felt something cold running up the inside of his arm, and there was suddenly a musty, unpleasant taste at the back of his mouth.

"What – I – what is that?"

"Just something to relax you. Don't worry. This won't hurt."

His head began to feel heavier and heavier, as if his neck muscles could no longer support it. He let it sag back against the gurney. Dimly he realized that someone was running a pair of clippers over his head, removing almost all his hair. He tried to protest, but the words would not come. Hands rubbed gel onto his newly exposed scalp, then pulled a net of some sort over his cranium. He felt the tug of wires running from it down his right side, leading off into the darkness outside the circle of intensely bright light.

"Now, Mr. Gray, let's talk. You were a spacer on board the *Colomb*, were you not?"

"Y – yeah, I was." His voice was slow, dreamy. He felt like he was floating in a warm, soothing pool. Nothing worried him anymore. He was safe here, secure. The nice man wouldn't let anything happen to him. He could trust him. He could tell him anything at all.

"What happened to her?"

"Well... it was like this..."

The questions and answers went on for hours. Periodically, his interrogator would inject more liquid into the drip line. When he grew tired, another took over.

Finally, the two men conferred.

"Do you think he knows anything more?"

"I doubt it."

"Do we need to get anyone else?"

"No. He was aboard *Colomb* for all three of her trips to Mycenae. We won't learn more from another spacer. The officers might know more, but not enough to interest us."

"All right. What next?"

"Let's find out where *Colomb* was taken. There are only so many places to discreetly dispose of a stolen repair ship, and we know them all. Once we've traced her, we can ask more questions there."

"Very well."

Another syringe was produced, this one empty, and much larger than the first. The first speaker drew back the plunger, then injected twenty cubic centimeters of air into the drip tube. It bubbled downward and disappeared into Gray's arm. His chest heaved, and he gargled in his drugged stupor. After a few moments' struggle, his breathing and heartbeat ceased.

"There's an industrial-strength garbage disposal unit down the hall, and I bought several liters of strong cleaning bleach. Let's get rid of the evidence, then catch the next shuttle to orbit."

~

MEDUSA

Several weeks later, the prime interrogator was seated in a bar on one of the planet's orbital space stations. It was filled with ship-yard workers, celebrating payday and the end of another week's labor. He listened carefully to their conversation, exchanging cheerful remarks with other drinkers, buying an occasional round for those nearby. His generosity was greatly appreciated, and the snacks he kept ordering were eagerly consumed. Nobody minded his questions. They weren't very intrusive, and besides, no-one wanted to interrupt the flow of free food and drink. In another bar, a little further down Entertainment Alley, the inter-rogator's colleague did the same.

They rendezvoused for lunch the following day. Both were nursing headaches, and postponed conversation until they'd got some food into their stomachs. At last, they pushed back their empty plates.

"What news?" the first asked.

"I showed *Colomb*'s picture to several shipyard workers. They all recognized her. She came in several months ago, and was modified to look different before she was sold."

"Who brought her in?"

"They don't know. They're never told that, and they never meet the passage crews. One of them said she came from Constanta, but that's ridiculous. Why would she be taken to an out-of-the-way system like that? There are no pirates there that we know about."

"Not that we know about, but I learned something that may confirm it. Two new fast freighters came in ahead of *Colomb*. When I say new, I mean brand-new – straight out of a construction yard at Goheung. They modified them for resale, too. In exchange for all three, they shipped out two smaller fast freighters and another repair ship, bigger and newer than *Colomb*, but not yet equipped with tools and machinery. Guess where they went?"

"Constanta?"

"You're learning."

"Who took the ships?"

"Passage crews took the two freighters – the same ones that delivered the new ships in exchange for them. The repair ship was picked up by the crew that delivered *Colomb*."

The men looked at each other expressionlessly. The junior said, carefully, "There's been no official announcement of any fast freighters being stolen on their delivery voyage. If a company lost them, you'd expect them to be screaming about it. *Colomb* was under charter to a Callanish consortium that's opposing Rousay's application to colonize Mycenae, but the consortium hasn't said a single word about her loss. Did they also order the freighters?

Were their ships deliberately targeted, presumably by Rousay or the New Orkney Enterprise?"

"Possibly. Their silence is certainly deafening. It's the same with *Colomb*. Callanish's System Patrol Service announced she was missing, but very discreetly, as if it didn't matter. Their news media downplayed it, which can only mean the government there leaned on them to keep it quiet. Her crew didn't get back until almost four months after she left, but their families weren't told anything was wrong. When they finally arrived, they were told to tell their families that *Colomb* had had an accident, and been abandoned in space."

"If we'd done the job, the crew wouldn't have got back at all. That was stupid, to release them. Bad security. As for the consortium, and the System Patrol Service... why keep the losses quiet?"

"That, my friend, is a very good question. To help answer it, I want to learn more about the people who brought the ships here, and took the others away. I think they were professionals, who do that sort of thing for a living. There are not many like that, and the crews they hire are never told who they are ultimately working for. Only the boss will know, and maybe a few of his top people. We need to learn his name, and where we can find him; then talk to him, if the brotherhood allows."

"And if he doesn't want to talk to us?"

"Then we'll have to encourage him."

"And visit Constanta."

"Agreed. Let's get to work."

PATOS

The old man behind the desk listened patiently as his two visitors explained their movements and inquiries over the past half-year.

He sipped at a glass of clear liquid from time to time. The bottle of plum *rakia* next to it, slightly dusty with age, showed its source.

At last the two men finished their report. He nodded approvingly. "You have done well. Get yourselves glasses from the sideboard." He pushed the bottle toward them. "I must think."

They glowed with pride. To be offered vintage *rakia* from this man's private cellar was a signal honor. They filled their glasses, sipped in silence, and waited.

The man sat quietly for almost a quarter of an hour, fingers steepled together beneath his nose, deep in thought. His eyes were far away, as if he were staring at something only he could see. At last he straightened, and leaned forward, putting his elbows on the desk.

"So. We found our asteroids missing, and our satellite informed us that a ship with a disguised gravitic drive signature had taken them. We also learned that this Callanish consortium had emplaced its own robotic prospectors, using a ship with a disguised gravitic drive signature. We therefore assumed, at first, that their ship had stolen our asteroids. Correct?"

"Yes, Patriarch."

"You went to Callanish to confirm that suspicion, but instead found more questions than answers. You decided to pursue them, and after several false starts, ended up at Medusa. Correct?"

"Yes, Patriarch."

"You learned at Medusa that the Callanish repair ship, *Colomb*, which we know the consortium there used in the Mycenae system on at least three occasions, had been sold to a local shipyard. You also learned that two brand-new fast freighters had been taken to Medusa shortly before, and sold to the same shipyard. Those freighters had been bought from Kang Industries at Goheung by the Callanish consortium. Correct?"

"Yes, Patriarch."

"You therefore assumed that the same person or organization

was behind the theft of all three ships. You further assumed that the same person or organization exchanged them, plus possibly a sum in cash, for two smaller fast freighters and a larger repair ship. You also assumed that the same passage crews both delivered the stolen ships, and ferried those exchanged for them to their destination. Correct?"

"Yes, Patriarch."

"You have identified the person who commanded the passage and ferry crews as Frank Haldane, who is said to be based on Skraill and Rousay. Correct?"

"Yes, Patriarch."

"You have confirmed that at least one of the smaller fast freighters, and the repair ship, are in the Constanta system. They are owned by a Neue Helvetica security company, Hawkwood Corporation. It may be associated in some way with another Neue Helvetica security company, Eufala Corporation, which is under contract to the New Orkney Enterprise to provide unspecified 'security services' in the Mycenae system. Correct?"

"Yes, Patriarch."

"Eufala Corporation has come into possession of several old patrol craft, source unknown, that are being modernized in a shipyard at Constanta. It is sending them to Mycenae as they become available, presumably to patrol the system, and replenishing their supplies through monthly ferry runs using at least one, perhaps two freighters. Correct?"

"Yes, Patriarch."

"Very well. Events have not stood still while we waited for your findings. A second batch of asteroids was stolen, again by a ship using a frequency modulator to disguise its gravitic drive. Since our satellite could not use active sensors for fear of being located, it could not determine any other characteristics of the thieves' ship. Our next mission to Mycenae did not return. We sent another ship to investigate. It reported finding scattered wreckage and debris among the asteroids where our prospector robots used to be. They have all been either removed, or destroyed by laser cannon. In the light of what you learned, the cannon were probably aboard one of Eufala Corporation's patrol craft. The same happened to the prospector robots sown by the Callanish consortium, but not to NOE's. Our ship reported that the patrol craft are concentrated around Mycenae Primus Four, where NOE has focused its exploration and prospecting activities. They are not – or were not then – patrolling the asteroid belt of Mycenae Secundus, or protecting NOE's robot prospectors."

His two listeners sat immobile as they absorbed the news. Their leader said, carefully, "Does this mean we are at war with a rival organization?"

"Probably – but who? It is not necessarily only this security company, or even the New Orkney Enterprise. They may have been motivated to act against us by a rival organization. This is a very complex situation. There is also the question of how much our unknown enemy knows about us. I shall discuss these questions with Agim Nushi. You are to wait until we have reached a decision; then we shall have more work for you."

"We hear and obey, sir."

THEY WERE SUMMONED BACK to the office three days later.

"Kostandin," the older man began, "Vasil speaks well of you. He says you have matured, and are now old enough to control your previous youthful impatience. He has recommended that you be given your own team, and allowed to operate independently. We have decided to accept his recommendation."

The younger of the two visitors flushed, glancing sideways at his mentor. "Thank you, Vasil – and thank you, Patriarch."

"You are to select a team to assist you. Find this Frank Haldane, and question him. We want to know everything he can tell us about the ships he stole, those he ferried, and the people who paid him. Also, see whether he knows anything about either Eufala Corporation or Hawkwood Corporation, and the people behind them. In particular, find out whether any other organization like ours is associated with them, or whether they are acting alone."

"I hear and obey, Patriarch."

"Make sure Haldane does not learn anything about us in the process, and ensure he is not able to provide information to anyone else when you finish with him."

"I hear and obey, Patriarch."

"Vasil, you will select a new team and go to Constanta. Find out everything you can about Eufala Corporation and Hawkwood Corporation. Do they have the same principals? Are they allied, working together, or are they in fact the same organization? What is their relationship to the New Orkney Enterprise? Are they associated with any organization like ours? Where did they get their patrol craft? How many do they have, and how well are they armed and equipped? How many other vessels do they have? Where, and of what type? Did they destroy our ship in the Mycenae system, and did they recover any survivors or clues that might lead them to us? All these things you must learn. Move slowly and carefully. They must not learn that we know about them."

"I hear and obey, Patriarch."

"I am sending a third team to Callanish, and a fourth to Rousay. They will concentrate on the two consortia operating in Mycenae. When we have gathered all the information we can from all four missions, we shall decide what to do next." He paused. "You had a question, Vasil?"

"Yes, Patriarch. What if I find that there were survivors from our ship? Should I leave them in Eufala's or Hawkwood's custody, or silence them?"

"Rescue them if you can, silence them if rescue is impossible, but do not expose yourself to detection in doing so. Also, find out how much they knew. Ordinary spacers could not tell our enemies much. Officers could tell them a lot more. We must know."

"I hear and obey, Patriarch."

16

ON THE RUN

SKRAILL

F rank picked up the shrilling comm unit, frowning as he checked the call display. He hesitated for a moment, then shrugged. It cost nothing to be courteous, even though Jamshi wasn't among his most trusted contacts. He clicked the 'Accept' button.

"Hello, Jamshi."

"Frank!" The other man's voice was hearty, but with an undercurrent of relief. "I've been trying to pin you down for days!"

"I don't normally let people pin me down. What's up?"

"Ah... there's a contract come up. I know you and I haven't worked together, but the guy I usually use isn't available, and the job's urgent. It pays well. I need you, Frank."

"How well?"

"Ah... this is an open line."

"And I've got an open schedule, but only if the money's right. How well?"

"Ah... let's just say it's seven figures."

"I don't normally take low-paying jobs like that. Last one cleared me a lot more." Frank grinned as he said it. He'd been able to stash several million francs in his off-planet 'retirement fund' out of the sixty million Eufala had paid him for the freighter job. He and his core people were now enjoying the relative luxury of not having to look for another job in a hurry. They could afford to pick and choose, and live well while they waited.

"Ah... this one might, too, but it depends how fast we can move. The faster you can get there, the more money there is to be made."

Frank frowned. That made no sense, unless there was a time- and cost-critical cargo on the ship or ships Jamshi was after. Even that was unlikely, since the theft or disappearance of such cargoes tended to attract a whole lot of attention, making their quick disposal very difficult.

"I don't know. You're talking big numbers, but without details. What's going on, Jamshi? You wouldn't be trying to get me in dutch, so that I attract all the attention while you get away with something else?"

Jamshi's laughter sounded almost as if he were relieved to hear such suspicions. "Aw, come on, Frank! If I did business like that, no-one would ever trust me again. I know you and I do things differently, and you don't like some of my methods, but this is quick, easy money. I need your help to get it. In return, I'll split it with you, straight down the middle. I can't talk about it on an open circuit. I can tell you more face to face. Can I come around to your place?"

"Hold on a moment."

Frank muted the conversation and paced back and forth, frowning. He normally didn't allow outsiders to know where he lived. In fact, come to think of it, how had Jamshi learned his direct comm code? Only his most trusted insiders were supposed to know it.

He lifted the comm unit once more. "I can meet you tomorrow morning. Be at the Café Bosna at nine, and I'll buy you breakfast." They'd be out in the open, in a very public place. Jamshi wouldn't be able to try anything stupid at such a venue.

"Ah... can't we meet tonight? That would be much more convenient for me – and I'd like to meet somewhere private. Better for security, you know. If your place isn't convenient, how about my warehouse?"

Frank's suspicions intensified. He glanced at the time display on the phone. It was thirteen. "I'll have to check whether I can cancel something else. I'll call you back in an hour to let you know."

"All right, but try hard! This is big money, Frank. If you take the job, I'll even give you the first half-million in cash, tonight, to sweeten the pot."

Frank knew at once, for sure, that something was wrong. Jamshi had never been known to throw money around like that. He only paid for results. He was notorious for it.

"Wait for my call."

He cut the circuit, then hurried over to a terminal against the wall. He spoke rapidly, recording a warning message, then dispatched it to everyone in his core team. Those on Skraill would receive it within seconds, and it would reach the others via normal channels in due course. He could only hope that by then, the situation – whatever it was – would have been resolved. If they did not receive a second, stand-down message within twenty-four hours, those on this planet would vanish from their normal haunts, to make for a prearranged rendezvous.

He thought a moment, then checked the contents of the safe concealed in his bedroom. It held identification documents from several planets in different names, a couple of weapons, and a dozen fat wads of high-denomination banknotes in the major interplanetary currencies. Four leather drawstring purses each contained a hundred gold *taels,* round, oval and square, weighing about thirty-seven and a half grams each. He grinned as he hefted one of the purses, blessing the Chinese who'd migrated to the stars and brought their distrust of paper money with them. Gold was good everywhere. That's why he kept it on hand.

He walked back to the living-room and picked up the comm unit once more. He was going to need help tonight. Time to call in a favor... a big one.

"THERE ARE four of Jamshi's people stationed along the street. One's behind that tree; a second is pretending to be drunk, lying in front of that advertising hoarding; a third is in the yard of this warehouse, standing between the perimeter wall and the gate-house; and the fourth is inside the cab of that truck parked at the far end of the road. They're all armed. Three people went into the warehouse two hours ago, a tall man and two shorter guys. They were all wearing spacer's coveralls, and all armed. None of their faces is on file in our database, so they're probably from off-planet."

Frank snorted. "Sounds like they're looking for trouble. What were the three who went inside carrying?"

"The leader had a shoulder holster, the second had a gun behind his left hip – probably a southpaw – and the third had one in his right cargo pocket, and another in an ankle holster on his left leg. The leader was carrying a briefcase. We don't know what's inside it."

"All right. Are your toys ready?"

"They sure are. You gave us just enough notice to get every-thing set up before Jamshi got here and unlocked the place. He's already inside, with two more of his boys, also all armed."

"I expected that."

The man beside him, and six more lounging in the dirty,

dusty room in the office section of the derelict warehouse, were wearing plain black coveralls with police flashes on the shoulder. The pistols at their hips, and the carbines carefully leaned against the walls, were far from merely decorative in purpose. Frank looked at them one by one as he raised a quizzical eyebrow.

"I'm putting my life in your hands tonight. Please take good care of it!"

"We will." The leader of the team spoke with quiet confidence. "These toys you got for us will help make sure of that." He patted the control console on the table. "Once the situation's stable, what next?"

"Depends on who these people are. I've got to learn everything they know, and why Jamshi's helping them. I may have to find out the hard way."

"We're here to help. After all, we're cops. We can do anything."

Frank had to suppress a frown at the man's words. Here on Skraill, that was no more than the truth. The police *could* get away with anything, because the powers that be gave them almost unfettered authority – and asked no questions about confiscated loot – in return for their unquestioning obedience, particularly when dealing with political opponents, agitators and troublemakers. Of course, that's why people like Frank used Skraill as a base in the first place. Once law enforcement came to equate loyalty with payoffs, those who could afford – and were generous with – the biggest payoffs, earned the most loyalty, irrespective of their official status.

"I may have to take you up on that. If it comes to that, there'll be a nice bonus for all of you, on top of what we already agreed."

The seven men grinned broadly. "Mister Haldane, don't take this wrong, but I really like the sound of your voice," one said with a wink. The others laughed.

Frank took his personal comm unit from his pocket and dialed a code. "Jamshi? I'll be there in five. Have the gates open."

He could hear the relief in the man's voice. "Great! Drive straight into the warehouse. The gates and doors will close automatically behind you. I'll come out to meet you."

"All right."

"And our toys will come out to meet them," commented the team leader, drawing more hard laughter from his people.

"Just make sure they don't get too enthusiastic," Frank warned. "I'll be in there too."

"Here." The policeman tossed him two small flat black boxes, strung on a cord. A red light in the corner of each box glowed faintly. "Put that around your neck, beneath your clothes, one box in front and one behind. As long as it's there, they won't hurt you."

"I hope you tested it."

"I did. It works."

Frank hurried out the back of the old, dilapidated warehouse, exiting onto the street on its far side. His runabout was waiting in the rapidly fading light. He slid into the driver's seat, activated the power pack, and drove slowly around the block. As he passed the truck parked at the end of the road, he could see a shadowy figure in the cab raise something to his face. He knew he'd be warning Jamshi that Frank was on his way.

The gates were open, as promised. He turned slowly into them, then spun the wheel in the opposite direction to make the tight turn into the long, dimly lit warehouse. As the sliding doors began to close behind him, he drove forward slowly, stopping in the center of the building. Jamshi appeared at the door of a row of offices, set against the rear of the building, and waved him forward.

Frank started forward at a crawl, flicking on the vehicle's headlights as he did so. He'd already set them to high beam. Jamshi put a hand to his eyes, blinded by the sudden glare, and turned his head away – then he staggered suddenly, slapping at the back of his neck as if he'd been bitten by one of Skraill's notorious stingers. He rubbed the place for a moment, then staggered again, and crumpled to the ground.

Frank pulled up by the offices and waited. After about three minutes, there came a tapping at the window of his door. He looked out, to see a small, winged, insect-like machine hovering there. Two short, stubby tubes protruded from its base, like the tiny barrels of a diminutive gun. The needle tip of a dart protruded from one of them. The flitterbug bobbed up and down, three times, then rose and flew away. Exhaling in relief, he got out of the runabout.

Jamshi was unconscious. Frank relieved him of his weapon and wallet, and searched his pockets, putting everything in his vehicle; then he went into the offices. He found two more of Jamshi's men and the three strangers there, also unconscious. He searched them, too, taking everything he found to the car. He removed the local currency from the wallets and formed it into a thick wad, dropping it into a trouser pocket.

To his surprise and pleasure, Jamshi's safe in his office was unlocked. He rifled through its contents, discarding most of the documents as irrelevant to his needs, but whistled sharply as he opened an envelope containing more than a dozen interplanetary bearer bank drafts in negotiable currencies. Jamshi had clearly been making a lot of money recently. They were all in five or six figures, with one in the low seven figures. He took them out to his vehicle, along with all the hard currency in the safe. He added the local money to the wad in his pocket.

He heard the warehouse doors slide open again, and the whine of power packs as two heavier vehicles entered. He walked out of the office in time to see two police transporters pull up next to his runabout. The seven cops got out, pulling four limp bodies from the back and carrying them into the offices. The leader joined him.

"See? No trouble at all."

"You were very good. I'm glad I gave you that shipment of flitterbugs I lucked into a year ago. I never thought I'd need them myself!"

"We're glad, too. The boss won't buy any for us. He reckons they're 'not cost-effective', but we all know he pocketed the money that was budgeted to buy them. These have saved us some real headaches over the past year, letting us stay out of range rather than risk getting hurt. I'm glad we could return the favor."

"So am I. Here." He took out the accumulated wad of Skraill banknotes and handed them over. "There should be enough to buy all of you a real good time."

"I'll say!" The policeman counted swiftly, then slid them into his pocket. "This is enough for a long weekend at Maddy's for all of us, with everything thrown in."

Frank grinned at the mention of Skraill's most luxurious and infamous brothel. "Enjoy it."

"I will!"

One of the other policemen came out, carrying a briefcase. He opened it. "Thought you'd want to see this, boss."

"What the hell is all this?" The team leader stared in bewilderment at the saline solution, drip tubes, narcotic ampoules, hypodermic needles, syringes, hair clippers, conductive gel and neural scalp net.

Frank felt his blood turn to ice in his veins. "I know what it's for. I've run into kits like this on other planets. That drug makes someone talk, and you can verify he's not lying by connecting that net to a portable truth-tester." He lifted a tray in the briefcase to show the small electronic device hidden beneath it. "Trouble is, some interrogation drugs also fry your brains. If this is one of them, after about five or six hours, the victim will start to talk nonsense, then go into a coma. He won't come out of it. It's irreversible."

"*Bastards!* You mean they were going to do that to you?"

"If this is one of those drugs, it sure looks like it, doesn't it?"

"Uh-huh. Want us to help you do it to them instead, when they wake up?"

"Funny you should say that. I think it would be only fair, don't you?"

"It sure would – and we'll learn whether this drug is the bad kind or not, at their expense. You know how to use all this stuff?"

"I've never used it myself, but I've heard about it, and I reckon I know enough to get started. We'll begin with Jamshi's people, then him, then the three strangers. The hired men won't know as much as their boss, so if I make any mistakes, that won't matter. By the time we get to the big shots, I'll have figured out how to use this. D'you mind helping with cleanup afterwards?"

"Hell, no! This bunch would have ended up in the garbage, anyway. Their kind always does. We'll just lend nature a helping hand by speeding things up."

FRANK WASHED his hands as he watched the policemen put the last corpse into a body-bag. The half-light of dawn was showing through the windows as they loaded it into the back of one of their transporters. He felt unclean after working his way through no less than ten criminals, but he'd had to learn who was after him, and why. Now he knew that he and his core team were in mortal danger. The Albanian Mafia didn't play games. They wouldn't stop after one failure, and they'd want revenge for their dead brothers. They'd be coming after them all again.

Jamshi was a damned fool, he thought savagely. *If he hadn't been so damned greedy, he would never have offered that shipment of stolen drugs off-planet, and the Albanians would never have heard of him. He was greedy then, and he got greedier when they waved money at him to help them catch me. Well, he'll never learn now.*

He picked up his comm unit from the table, and terminated

its recording function. It had stored everything said by the prisoners during their interrogation. He dropped the unit into his pocket as the team leader came up, face wan with fatigue after their all-night session. His eyes were somber. He'd heard what the Albanians had revealed.

"I'd say you're in big trouble, Frank."

"Maybe... but there may be a way to turn the tables on them. I need one more thing from you and your team. It's a big favor, but if you'll do it for me, you'll all be rich by tonight."

The cop was suddenly alert, all business. "What do you need?"

"Call your people together and let me explain."

He looked around at the seven. "I need the courier ship these guys used to get here. I know you're not System Patrol Service, but you must have friends in that crowd. I need them to take you to that ship, and help you arrest every member of her crew. They're not Albanian Mafia, just spacers that came with the chartered ship, so I don't want anything to happen to them. Wear facemasks so they can't recognize you, and don't identify yourselves. Cover their heads so they can't see what's happening, bring them all planetside, then let them go somewhere outside town. Have a few of your friends standing by to arrest them for illegal immigration – no papers, no entry stamps, that sort of thing. Make sure they can't reach any officials for a day or two. By the time the mess is sorted out, we'll be long gone. There's half a million kronor in it for each of you, in gold and hard currency."

They stared at him for a long, wordless moment. The Sergeant said carefully, "Frank, you've always been straight up with us, but... half a million apiece? Do you have that kind of money on hand?"

"I tell you what. While your crew dumps these bodies, you come back with me to my place. I'll show you the money – in fact, we'll lock it in my apartment, and code the lock to your DNA instead of mine. I won't need to go back there, so you can have it, too. I'll give you the title deed. You can keep it for a squad hang-out, or sell it and split its price among you. I'll send some messages to get my people together while you organize things with the SPS. As soon as you leave the ship with your prisoners, we'll take her out of the system. We won't be coming back, so no-one will cause trouble by asking awkward questions about us. You'll be able to enjoy your loot in peace. How about it?"

One of the cops said eagerly, "If he's good for the money, boss, I got a brother-in-law in the SPS. He runs one of the customs boats inspecting arriving ships. For a decent cut of the money, enough to keep his crew sweet as well, I reckon he'll take us all to the courier boat, and bring us back to the orbital terminal. We can bring the spacers planetside in one of our official shuttles, with no-one the wiser."

"If Frank's got the money, we can give him a quarter of a million in cash or gold, and get that back when we sell the apart-ment," the Sergeant agreed. "Are you all in this with me?"

Six voices chorused their assent.

"Right. Go drop this lot in the city dump. Have the workers unload a couple of garbage trucks over them, then roll everything nice and flat. By the time you've done that, Frank and I will have taken care of our business downtown. How long will your people need, Frank?"

"We can meet you at the spaceport by noon. There'll be eight of us, each with one or two suitcases and bags."

"All right, noon it is, at the police dock. Let's go."

Frank grinned as he steered his vehicle out of the warehouse. The foreign currency and interplanetary bearer bank drafts he'd taken from Jamshi and the others would more than cover the loss of the money in his safe, and the value of his apartment. The spaceship would be a bonus.

~

FRANK and his men lined the rear bulkhead of the courier ship's diminutive docking bay. They stood in silence, watching, as the protesting crew were bundled aboard the customs boat, hands cuffed behind their backs, heads obscured by thick black cloth bags pulled tight – but not too tight – around their necks with pull-cords. The cops and SPS spacers followed them. Last to board was the Sergeant. He paused in the airlock doorway, looked at Frank, and gave him a thumbs-up sign. "Good luck to you all."

Frank didn't reply, just made the same sign in return. He didn't want the spacers to be able to recognize his voice, if they heard it again in future. The Sergeant grinned, went through the airlock, and sealed the inner door behind him.

They waited until the customs boat had pulled clear of the ship, then Frank spoke. "All right, there are nine of us to handle the duties of a thirty-strong crew. We're not going to get much sleep until we get where we're going. Pick berths for yourselves, drop your gear there, and divide the various duty stations among yourselves. Captain's cabin is mine. While you do that, I'm going to make a departure signal to System Control. I want to be under way within half an hour."

The others nodded somberly. They'd all had to rush like men possessed to get ready in time, and they'd all had to abandon most of their goods and property planetside. That was regrettable, but they all had assets safely stashed elsewhere. They wouldn't starve. Besides, Frank had made it clear that they faced a mortal threat. Getting off-planet alive and unhurt made up for a lot of losses.

"Where are we heading, boss?" one asked.

"Ever heard an old proverb that says, 'The enemy of my enemy is my friend'? That's where we're at right now. We need to link up with someone who has as much cause to worry about the Albanians as we do, and who's strong enough that it's worth our while to join forces with them to protect ourselves. I reckon there's only one option."

"You mean..."

"Yeah. Let's go by Rousay, send warnings to the others, and ask Henry for an introduction to his boss. He can also warn him to watch out for the Albanians, which should put him in a receptive frame of mind to talk to us. Before we go see him, we'll take this courier ship to Medusa and sell her. That'll make up for what we lost on Skraill. After that, we'll adopt new identities, split up, and head for Henry's boss using different routes. The Albanians know me, but not you – at least, that's what their investigator said last night. If we aren't seen together on Medusa, they won't identify you, or associate you with me, for a while longer. By the time they do, we'll be in a safer place."

"Can't we just drop out of sight?" one of them wondered.

"This is the Albanian Mafia. They're not the biggest crime syndicate out there, but they're one of the most ruthless. They keep people scared of them because they never stop coming until either you or they are dead. They can't let us go without risking that reputation. This bunch seems to be an offshoot of the main body; but in some ways, that's worse, because without the backing of the rest of their people, they've got to be even more ruthless if they want to be convincing. No, they won't let us alone. They'll keep looking, and one day they'll find us. When they do, I want us to be ready to fight back and win – and that means we need allies."

"What if their boss expects us to be loyal to him, rather than to you?"

"I'm sure he will. Henry told me he's former military, and they're big on that. Thing is, we've been useful to him in the past, and I reckon he'll need people like us again. We've all got military and merchant spacer backgrounds. We can all serve as officers aboard his ships, and three of us are qualified commanding officers. If he's as good as Henry says he is, I won't object to taking his orders, at least for a while. As for the longer term, who knows? Let's take care of problem number one. We can worry about the rest later."

"Works for me."

"All right. Let's go!"

17

ENEMIES AND ALLIES

CONSTANTA

The nurse slid a picture across the table. "That's him."

Vasil's heart leapt with mingled triumph and sorrow as he gazed at the image. He'd traveled on Pavli's ship before, and recognized his face instantly. It hurt to realize that he'd have to give his comrade the final mercy, but he knew Pavli would understand – if he'd been able to, that is.

He ground his teeth as he realized Pavli's comatose condition might be the result of drug-assisted interrogation. After all, what else could have caused it? Why hadn't they killed him when they were finished? It would have been a lot cheaper than keeping him alive in a nursing home. Did they think they could use him, even in a vegetative state, to put pressure on the brotherhood? If not that, then perhaps their opponents were weak. Did they find it difficult to kill in cold blood, rather than in the heat of battle? If so, they would be easier to deal with. People with scruples stood little chance against those who had none. However, Pavli's fate was also a warning. He could never allow these people to take him alive. He would have to make sure his team realized that, too.

"Thank you," he managed to say in a neutral tone, masking his feelings. "It may be him. I'll have to see him to be sure. When are visiting hours?"

"By appointment only, and restricted to family or legal guardians unless special permission is given. You'll have to prove your relationship to him. Security is strict."

"But if he's in a coma, he can't confirm I'm his relative, can he? How did my brother – if it's him – end up in a place like that?"

The nurse shrugged. "Maybe he did someone a favor sometime, and they felt sorry enough for him to pay his monthly bill. Must have been a big favor, though. That place is expensive."

"Could you help me get in?"

Her eyes narrowed. "Listen, mister, didn't you hear what I said about security?"

"Yes, but..." He rubbed his fingers together suggestively.

"I don't know... When did you want to come?"

"How about in the evening, when there'll be fewer staff to notice me?"

"Maybe I can swap duties with another nurse, and let you in. It'll take me a couple of days to sort that out, and I'll need to pay someone to exchange."

"Of course." He reached into his pocket, took out his wallet, and counted out a thousand leitra. Her eyes brightened as he slid it across the table.

"That'll do it – but what's in it for me?"

"Ten times that, if everything works."

"How about half up front? I got expenses too, you know."

"I don't have that much with me right now. I can give it to you tomorrow night, if you'll meet me here at nineteen."

"All right. I should be able to tell you by then when I'll be able to let you in."

As Vasil walked away, he thought, *I'll have to bring the team with me. I'll silence Pavli and kill the nurse, while they make sure I get in and out without anyone else interfering. This is going to take some careful planning.*

THE LOCAL SECRETARY called through the door, "Boss, Nicolae Albescu is calling."

Cochrane looked up, suddenly alert. He'd turned to Albescu, a high-level criminal in Constanta's underworld, to prepare an 'insurance policy' in case the Finance and Defense Ministers tried to welsh on their deal with him. He'd had occasional dealings with him since then, often enough to realize Albescu would not call in person unless it was important.

"Thanks, Otilia. Put him through."

He picked up the desk comm unit as it shrilled. "Hello, Nicolae."

"Hello, Andrei. Are you well?"

They exchanged pleasantries for a couple of minutes, then his caller got to the point. "Andrei, remember that spacer in a coma?"

"Yes. You helped us find a nursing-home for him."

It had been just what they needed. Some of Nicolae's elderly family members lived there. He didn't want them used as a bargaining counter by his rivals, so he made sure the place was secure, and kept it under close and careful scrutiny. As part of that, he charged Eufala a hefty monthly premium to keep an eye on their prisoner.

"Someone has been asking questions about him. A nurse reported this morning that a man wants to get in to see him, claiming he might be his brother. He gave her a thousand leitra to arrange a shift swap with another nurse, so she can let him in, and promised her ten thousand for her help."

Cochrane felt suddenly cold as he glanced at the printout on the desk. Frank's warning, sent via Henry, had reached him only two days before. He said carefully, "Do you think she can go ahead and set that up, so we can be waiting for him? There are questions I need to ask him."

"I think we can arrange that. Will you use your people, or should I provide you with some of mine?"

"I'll use mine, thank you, provided you can arrange access for them. It would be helpful if you could have someone liaise with them, to avoid complications."

"That is easily arranged. There will be no danger to my family?"

"I doubt it. If you're worried, you can have some of your people stand guard over them. It might be best to move my patient to a different room, further away from your family. Also, I'd like to hire a team of your very best people to follow this stranger, find out where he's staying, and note anyone else he's working with. He mustn't suspect anything, of course. After we've dealt with him, I want everything he and his men brought to Constanta. Let me know what I'll owe you."

"I will set up all that at once. As for the money, let us see what our expenses amount to when this is over. We'll settle our accounts then."

"All right. Please thank the nurse for her help. Tell her I'll pay her twice what he offered her if we catch him and anyone with him."

"You are generous, Andrei. I shall get that information to her. She will appreciate it."

He thought fast as he replaced the comm unit on the desk. Based on what Frank had told Henry, there might be real danger in tackling the 'visitor' and anyone he brought along. It would be better to be over- rather than under-gunned for such an encounter. Fortunately, Tom Argyll had more than a little experience in security matters. He'd put together an experienced team to protect company headquarters at Constanta, both in orbit and here on the planet. They would do nicely for this job. It would be a good real-world test of their abilities.

THE EXTERNAL LIGHTS surrounding the nursing home came to life, banishing the encroaching twilight, brightly illuminating the lawns and gardens. Vasil tensed. That was the signal he'd been waiting for. The nurse would be at the side door in precisely two minutes, to let him in.

He reached for the pen-like comm unit in his chest pocket, and pressed once on the clip. The hidden, miniaturized bud in his left ear brought the sound of two clicks in response. Besnik was in position in front of the nursing home, ready to block the street with his rented van if necessary. A few seconds later, three clicks sounded. That meant Gentius was similarly positioned on the left of the building, where a side road led up to the brow of the hill on which it stood. Shpresa, several blocks away and out of sight of the nursing home, sent four clicks, signaling she was ready to relay communications if necessary.

He reached inside his jacket and loosened his pulser in its shoulder holster, then pulled three hypodermic syringes out of his pocket, glancing at them in a final check. Their pressure chambers were charged with a clear liquid, and their spring-loaded needles safely retracted into their protective housings. When a release catch was pressed, they would flash out into flesh and disgorge their contents automatically. Satisfied, he replaced them before moving out from behind the bushes. Walking slowly, casually, as if he had every right to be there, he sauntered across the grass toward the side door.

The nurse appeared at the glass-paneled door, and waved casually at him as she reached for the handle. Before she could touch it, a voice boomed from a loudspeaker concealed beneath a bush next to the entrance. In perfectly accented Albanian, followed by the same phrase in Galactic Standard English, it commanded, "*Mos lëviz!* Don't move!"

In the instant that the words sounded, the nurse threw herself away from the door, and Vasil's hand swept into his jacket. He drew his pulser in a blindingly fast movement, pumping three rounds through the corridor wall as he spun around. He reacted so quickly that those rising from their places of concealment in the garden were caught off-balance, giving him a chance to lunge toward the small gate leading out to the lane. One of the ambush team paid the price for his hesitation as Vasil put two rounds into his chest, the rapid *bap-bap* of the suppressed pulser sounding loud in the enclosed garden.

The weapons that fired back were not suppressed, and therefore much louder. The last sound Vasil heard was a drumroll of rapid shots. He was hit by eleven projectiles as he fell sideways, including two that went through his skull. He died without hearing two other teams, outside the walls, take down Besnik and Gentius. They, too, did not go quietly; and they, too, died hard. None of the three knew that the shots with which they hit several of their attackers were wasted on their body armor.

The ambushers hastily gathered up their victims and their weapons, stuffed them into their vehicles, and steered all three away at a sedate pace, so as not to alarm passersby with wild driving. Other vehicles collected the rest of the ambush parties, including four who were cursing volubly at the pain of bead strikes that had broken up against their body armor. They'd be bruised for days, perhaps weeks... but they were grateful to still be alive, and able to feel the bruises.

By the time the first police vehicles arrived to investigate the shooting, there was no sign that anything untoward had occurred in the garden. Even the blood on the grass had been hastily watered into the soil. The only casualty still on hand was the nurse. She was tucked away out of sight in a dressing station, swearing in pain and sweating with fear as a colleague applied a dressing to a line scored across her skin below her left ribcage. Vasil had come terrifyingly close to punishing her 'treachery' by taking her with him.

LATER THAT NIGHT, Albescu met with Cochrane at Eufala's offices. Some of his men carried in suitcases and holdalls filled with clothes, equipment and paraphernalia. "We recovered these things from their rooms, and their bodies. As agreed, we will turn it all over to you." Albescu handed over three syringes that he'd carried in a transparent bag. "The leader had those in his pocket. I think you should handle them very, very carefully."

"That's for sure!" Cochrane agreed fervently. "I'll send them for analysis. I bet that clear liquid is a fast-acting poison. There was no reason for him to take anything else in there with him."

"I agree. Also, I think you'll find the leader's briefcase particularly interesting."

Cochrane opened it, to find similar contents to those Frank had discovered at Skraill some weeks before. He mentally compared Frank's list to the case in front of him as he rifled through it.

"I know what this is. We've heard of something similar. Thank you very much."

"Each man had three sets of identity documents. I presume they are all false."

"Probably." Cochrane didn't enlighten the gangster that he already knew the real names of the three men. During interrogation, Kostandin had revealed them, and Frank had included them in his warning message to Henry Martin. *I'm going to have to do something nice for Frank and his people,* Cochrane mentally decided. *Without their warning, we would have been caught off-guard.*

Something was nagging him. He suddenly realized what it was, and looked inquiringly at Albescu. "Didn't they have any money or convertible assets with them?"

"They did, but I have retained it. I thought I should not ask you to repay my expenses when they were able to cover them instead."

"Oh. That's... that's good of you. Thank you."

He knew Albescu's uncharacteristic generosity must mean he'd recovered more money from the three Albanians than he'd expected to get from Hawkwood. However, he would never admit that, and there was nothing Cochrane could do about it. Besides, the intruders' equipment and documentation were far more important than their funds.

"What will you do with the bodies?"

"They are being disposed of as we speak. My people will also see to it that the false identities they used to enter Constanta are recorded as having left the planet, as passengers aboard a freighter on the circle route. We'll see to it that they are logged as disembarking somewhere else, after which they will simply disappear."

"How unfortunate for their families." Cochrane's voice was dry as dust.

"Indeed. Most sad." Albescu actually managed to look sorrowful and sympathetic for a moment, before he spoiled it with a cackle of laughter.

As THE CRIME boss left Cochrane's office, he beckoned one of his bodyguards. In a low voice, he said, "We must ensure that such dangerous intruders have no reason to disturb my relatives again. See to it that the comatose spacer does not live until morning. Leave no traces."

"Yes, sir. A pillow over the face?"

"I leave the details in your hands."

"Yes, sir."

Albescu got into his vehicle, smiling happily. He had placed the good Captain under a further obligation to him; collected a very satisfying sum in hard currency and gold; and disposed of a potential threat to his elderly family members. It had been a productive and fruitful evening.

IN HER SMALL HOTEL ROOM, Shpresa packed her bag, shivering with tension. After all the shooting that evening, and her comrades' failure to call her afterwards, it was obvious something had gone terribly wrong. If they talked, the enemy would come looking for her, too.

She closed her bag and rose to her feet. She would find somewhere else to stay, under another name that she had not yet used on Constanta. As soon as she'd found out more what had happened, she'd leave the planet and report to her superiors. They would have to decide what to do next. She could only hope that they would allow her to be part of avenging her friends.

TOM ARGYLL ASKED to see Cochrane the following morning. He found his boss in a somber mood.

"That Albanian spacer died last night," Cochrane informed him.

"Oh! Ah... that was rather sudden, sir, wasn't it?"

"Yes. According to his latest medical report, he wasn't getting better, but he wasn't getting worse, either. Funny that he should die the same night someone tried to get to him. Oh, well." Cochrane shrugged. "Speaking of last night, we've got some lessons to learn from it, and from events on Skraill a few weeks ago." In a few succinct sentences, he described what had happened to Frank Haldane and his team.

Argyll nodded. "If Haldane ran into the same kind of professionals we did last night, he's damned lucky to be alive.

I've got to say, sir, I've never seen anybody move so fast as those three did yesterday. We recorded the whole engagement on our bodycams, and from drones overhead. I'd like to show you the main engagement in the garden, slowed down, with a timer running."

"Go ahead."

The Senior Chief called up a file on the tri-dee display and started it running at one-twentieth speed. "Here he is, walking across the garden, sir... Now the announcement starts playing." He paused the playback. "Watch how he's moving before the second word is spoken. He had hair-trigger reflexes."

They watched, almost mesmerized, as Vasil's gun emerged from his jacket while the nurse was still in mid-air in her dive for cover. He swung it into line and triggered three fast shots, aiming low, trying to hit her body through the wall.

"He was already turning, sir. He fired on the turn, then straightened and hit full stride within two steps, heading for the gate. He hit Sean in the chest as his foot landed from the first step." They watched as the pulser spat twice. "Notice how the weapon doesn't jump much at all. He's got a death grip on it, holding it as steady as if it were in a vise."

Vasil was already turning the gun to aim for a second member of the team when he jerked suddenly as the first return shot hit him in the right arm. Blood spurted from his head and torso as more shots slammed home. He was clearly dead before he hit the ground.

"Why didn't he surrender, dammit?" Cochrane raged. "He *must* have known there was no way out!"

"That's the thing, sir. He didn't want to be taken alive. He must have figured it would be better to die, rather than betray his brotherhood's secrets. He knows how interrogations are done, remember – or, at least, how *he* used to do them. He might have reckoned it was better to die quickly and cleanly, rather than have his brain fried."

"I can't say I'd argue with him about that. All right, Senior Chief, why did you want me to see that?"

"Sir, you just watched the best professional display of reflexive gun handling I've ever seen. I trained with our Marines, and worked alongside other armed forces on United Planets expeditionary missions. I've never seen anyone react so fast, shoot so well, and so nearly succeed in breaking what I would have sworn was an unbreakable ambush. Sir, we need better training. We need to hire experts as good as he was, and have them train us. The only reason we didn't lose four people last night in those three gunfights was that we wore body armor. If we run into a fight without time to prepare for it, and they're as good as that lot were last night, we'll lose people for certain, unless we get a whole lot better than we are now, right across the spectrum – marksmanship, tactics, teamwork, the lot."

Cochrane nodded thoughtfully. "I take your point, particularly because your people are responsible for headquarters security. If the Albanians or anyone else try again, we're a soft target compared to a warship. Where can we find instructors that good?"

"I don't know yet, sir, but with your permission, I'm going to find out. It'll probably cost a lot to get them out here, but I reckon it'll be worth it. We'll probably also need better equipment, but I'll wait for expert advice on what that should be."

"Do it, Senior Chief. Find those instructors, hire them, and have them advise us on better gear. You've got *carte blanche* and an open budget. Plan on recruiting more people, too, to provide security for off-planet visits as well. I'm thinking at least three twelve-person teams of guards, plus communications, support and other elements. You're free to vary that according to the advice of your experts. Oh – and another thing. It'll be good to have those skills for our own defense, but you know the old saying as well as I do."

"You mean 'The best form of defense is attack', sir?"

"That's right. If we're going to go to the trouble and expense of importing top instructors, hiring more people, and buying the best gear on the market, let's form an assault team or two. You never know. We might need to rescue some of our people who've been taken prisoner, or take out a nest of enemies who're planning to attack us, before they can make their move. Plan for that, too, and let me know what it'll cost. I'll make the funds available."

"Thank you, sir. I'd also like permission to pay big annual bonuses for every year without casualties among those we protect. That'll motivate our people to accept the risks." Argyll hesitated, and took a deep breath. "There's one more thing, sir. Those Albanians are ruthless. That interrogation drug that fries a man's brain? The poison the leader was carrying last night? Those things are typical of them. All three men last night, expecting us to be as ruthless as they are, chose to fight and die rather than surrender. That means, sir, if we want to find out what they're up to, we're going to have to knock them out somehow, tie them up, and inject them with truth drugs like their own until we've wrung them dry. After that, I guess killing them will be a merciful end. I hate having to suggest that, sir, but I don't see any other way to handle it."

Cochrane nodded, a sour expression on his face. "It's another variation on the Golden Rule. This version says, 'Do unto others what they're trying to do unto you – but do it first'. I don't like it any more than you do, but you're right. Realistically, what choice do we have?"

"Yes, sir. With your permission, I'd like to form a 'hard team', for want of a better description. It'll have three or four interrogators, willing to do whatever it takes to learn what we need to know. We'll give them the interrogation kit we captured last night, and analyze its drugs at molecular level, so we can make more if we need them. I'd like to build up another kit or two like it, if possible. The 'hard team' will have normal security duties until the need arises. When it does, they'll be issued their gear and turned loose on our prisoners."

"You do realize that people like that are likely to have at least an element of the sociopath in their makeup?"

"Yes, sir; but sometimes, a sociopath you can point in the direction of the enemy, then turn loose, isn't a bad thing to have on your side – if you can keep him under control, that is."

Cochrane stared at him for a long moment, tapping his fingers on the desk... then he nodded. "All right, Senior Chief. I'll authorize your 'hard team' – but dammit, I feel sick inside for doing so!"

"You and me both, sir. Unfortunately, we have scruples. Our enemies don't, and that gives them an edge. They won't hesitate where we will. The only way we're going to win is to overcome our hesitation reflex and do unto them first, like you said. I guess, in the process, we can't avoid becoming a little like them."

"True, perhaps... but it doesn't make me feel any better to acknowledge it."

"Nor me, sir. Nor me."

Cochrane nodded. "Very well. As of right now, we have a new Headquarters department, Security. I'm commissioning you as a Lieutenant-Commander with immediate effect, to command it. Appoint a Lieutenant under you to head up the guard detachment, and another Lieutenant to lead the assault unit. Pick whomever you please. They can have whatever subordinate officers and senior NCO's you think they need."

Tom stared, then grinned. "Me an officer, sir? Are you sure the company wardroom will be able to stand the strain?"

"I reckon so. If not, we'll use those who can't as moving targets for your teams!"

∽

FRANK HALDANE ARRIVED three weeks later, aboard a freighter

carrying miscellaneous cargo around a circular route of minor planets. He registered at the space station under a false identity as a transient merchant spacer, and booked into the spacer's barracks. He was not surprised to find five of his team members already staying there, also using assumed names. They celebrated their safe reunion in one of the space station's restaurants over *tocana de vita,* a rich beef stew served with noodles, and a passable local red wine.

He called Hawkwood Corporation next morning. The company, forewarned by Henry Martin, had been expecting their arrival. Planetary visit permits were immediately arranged for the 'visiting spacers', complete with rooms at a comfortable downtown hotel.

Cochrane met with him the following day, and shook his hand in real gratitude. "I'm very glad you made it safely. Your warning helped us deal with some Albanian investigators here. Without it, we might have been caught short."

"They won't be the last, sir. Those buggers are persistent."

"So I understand. If you're going to join us, which Henry said was your plan, you can help us be on the lookout for them. What sort of association with us did you have in mind?"

Frank explained his dilemma. "We can't face them alone, sir; but, frankly, neither can you. We need allies, people we can stand beside against the Albanians. We'll strengthen them just as they strengthen us. I may not have many people in my inner circle, but they're all qualified spacer officers. About half of us have military backgrounds, including me, and the other half come from the merchant service. We're all very, very good at what we do."

"I certainly need good officers. One question, though; where is their – and your – primary loyalty? If I take you on as part of Hawkwood Corporation, I'm going to want to know that for sure. We use compulsory truth-tester interviews as part of our hiring process. We repeat them every two years for spacers, every year for officers and senior NCO's, at random intervals. It's the only way I can think of to ensure security."

Frank's eyebrows rose. "That's very intrusive, sir. It gives the impression you don't trust anybody."

"Not many. I have few illusions. All other things being equal, most people will look to their own self-interest in the final analysis. We offer high salaries to the right people, and a share in our profits, so we can be selective in who we hire. We reject four out of five applicants. Even so, I know outsiders – the Albanians, for example – might offer a lot more than that to find out what we're doing. Therefore, in return for high rewards, we demand proof of our people's trustworthiness on a regular basis. It's like the two faces of a single coin. You can accept or reject the whole coin, as you see fit, but you can't choose just one of its faces. The only consolation I can offer is that everyone, including me, goes through the same process. There are no exceptions."

"I suppose that does make a difference. Er... what happens if someone fails the truth-tester?"

"It depends who it is and how he fails it. A low-level spacer who doesn't know much will probably be fired at once, kicked off his ship at the next stop, and left to make his own way from there. An officer who's betrayed our secrets would be different. I haven't encountered that problem yet, but if we found evidence that a betrayal had cost us a spaceship, or the lives of some of our people, I'd probably shoot the bastard myself, without the slightest compunction."

Frank's eyebrows rose. "You're a harder man than I thought you were, Captain."

"Ask the gangsters of Cubbie about that – the surviving ones, that is."

"That was you? I heard about what happened there, but the rumor mill only said it was people from off-planet. All right, Captain, I guess you can be hard enough when you need to be. It's actually a relief to know that."

"I'm glad to know you approve, because I'm going to have you meet with Lieutenant-Commander Tom Argyll, my security chief, later today. He's putting together what we call our 'hard team', to deal with people like these Albanians. We captured their interrogation kit, poisons, and other equipment, and we'll use them ourselves if necessary. Do you still have the interrogation kit you captured at Skraill?"

"Yes, I do."

"Good. Please give it to Tom Argyll, and tell him what you learned about its use."

After further discussion, Frank agreed that he and his team would go through the normal employment formalities, including truth-tester examination, and then be hired as officers aboard either warships or support vessels, depending on their background. They would serve Eufala/Hawkwood for a minimum of five years, irrespective of developments with the Albanian Mafia. At the end of that period, their contracts would be open to renegotiation.

"I know about your freighters and repair ship, Captain, but what sort of warships are you going to operate?" Frank asked. "The only ones I know about are those old patrol craft we helped you get from New Westray."

Cochrane smiled. "Wait until you've been through the truth-tester examination, and you're officially on board. I think you're going to be very pleasantly surprised."

He would say no more, to Frank's frustration and intense curiosity.

18

NEGOTIATION

ROUSAY

"Captain Cochrane is here, sir, and Ms. Stone."
Marwick looked up from the document he was studying, and pressed the intercom key. "Thank you, Marti. Send them in, please."

He laid the paperwork aside, pushed back his chair and stood as his visitors were shown in. He shook Cochrane's hand firmly. "Thank you for coming to Rousay so quickly, Captain. Things are moving fast, and generally well, but a problem has arisen that we need to resolve."

"I'm at your service, Mr. Marwick."

"You certainly proved that, by refunding our investment in Eufala Corporation so early. That impressed a lot of Directors. It's why they agreed to meet with you to discuss their concerns, before acting on them."

Cochrane's eyebrows rose. "That sounds almost like a threat, sir."

"Not from me it isn't, but some of them were pretty angry

until I calmed them down. Let me explain. Next week, the United Planets will officially announce the grant of exclusive colonization rights for the Mycenae system to Rousay."

"Congratulations, Mr. Marwick. That's been a long time coming."

"Yes, it has, largely due to complaints and protests from rivals; but we were able to prove our case in the end."

Cochrane couldn't help smiling as he thought, *You mean you were able to afford more and larger bribes than they could. Oh, well. UP bureaucrats have to eat, too.*

"We're going to ramp up our activities there immediately. That'll include sending a refinery ship to Mycenae Primus Four to exploit the minerals we've found there. We'll take them up to orbit in cargo shuttles for processing. As soon as we can afford it, we'll build a refinery on the planet's surface. Meanwhile, we'll also collect asteroids from Mycenae Secundus, and tow them over to the refinery ship using tractor beams."

He sighed. "That's where the problem has arisen. Your report about discovering two unauthorized fields of prospector bots, and destroying a ship trying to harvest what they'd found, caused a lot of heartburn. It's bad enough that others are trying to poach on our preserves, but on previous visits, they stole asteroids *our* robots had beaconed. You see, we expected our bots to have beaconed scores of high-grade asteroids by now. Instead, there are only a few. We're sure someone's been stealing them. I'm afraid some of my fellow directors even wondered whether you might be involved in that."

Marissa Stone hastened to add, "We took care of that. We pointed out that someone who'd returned our investment, without having to be asked, was hardly likely to steal from us. After all, you could have kept the money, and we'd never have been the wiser. The two actions – stealing asteroids, and giving us the money – just didn't add up. After they thought about it, they were forced to agree."

One up to you, Dave, Cochrane thought warmly, although he didn't allow any expression to appear on his face. *If you hadn't suggested that, we might have had a lot more explaining to do.*

"I'm glad you were able to clear up any misunderstanding, sir" he said politely.

"We have, to a point," Marwick assured him. "However, there's a lot of pressure for NOE to take a more active role in securing our investment. Marissa and I wanted to discuss that with you before the board meeting tomorrow, to see if we can work out a solution that's fair to all concerned. After all, right now we simply can't afford to spend what it'll take to provide our own comprehensive security force, so we'll need to rely on your services for some time to come."

"I'm at your service, Mr. Marwick. If you could explain what the other directors are considering, I'll see whether Eufala Corporation can accommodate their wishes."

THE BOARD MEETING had been in progress for almost an hour before Cochrane was finally summoned. He passed the time sipping coffee provided by the Managing Director's secretary, reading the news headlines on a tablet provided for visitors, and running through in his mind the arguments he'd need to use to persuade the board.

When he was admitted to the big, luxuriously finished boardroom, it was clear that discussion had been heated. Some directors glowered at him, eyebrows lowered, while others were flushed with annoyance. He ignored them, and took the seat indicated at the foot of the table.

The Managing Director, a florid, overweight man named MacLellan, said, "Captain Cochrane, there's been a good deal of friction over how to protect our interests, now that our exploitation of the Mycenae system is assured. Some of our members want to exclude outside interests from access to them, in order to maintain the tightest possible control. That would, of course, include your company. What do you think of that?"

"The board is, of course, entirely within its rights to make any decisions it sees fit about its commercial operations, sir," he replied politely. "However, for the record, I'd like to point out that the New Orkney Enterprise entered into a binding contract with my company to provide security services in the Mycenae system. Therefore, whatever NOE decides to do will need to take that into account." There were a few mutters of discontent around the table at his words, but they weren't clearly audible, so Cochrane ignored them.

"But we're not actually paying you anything for that contract any more, are we? You returned our initial investment, saying you'd earned enough from other clauses in your contract that you no longer needed it."

"Yes, Mr. MacLennan. That seemed the honest thing to do."

There was a murmur of approval from almost half the directors. Marissa Stone pointed out, from her seat near Cochrane's, "That money is what helped us finalize UP approval for Rousay's colonization of Mycenae. Without it, we might still be waiting."

"A good point," MacLennan admitted. "We're not ungrateful to you, Captain. I'm aware of how you... recovered... certain assets from a rival consortium. Within these four walls, I'll admit we thought it was no more than poetic justice. However, did you recover enough to fund your operations for the balance of your contract? It still has several years to run, even if we don't extend it."

"Yes, we did, sir. Those weren't the only recoveries we've made in the Mycenae system. For example, there were those two fields of prospector robots I reported to you. Are you aware of the cost of autonomous, self-propelled units like that?"

"I'm not. Anyone?"

"The most sophisticated can cost fifty to sixty million kronor each," one of the other directors put in.

"That's correct, sir," Cochrane agreed. "We confiscated over two hundred of them, plus beacons and other gear. We were able to sell them for about three-quarters of their new value. That'll fund our needs, both capital and operational, for some time to come."

He kept his face expressionless, but grinned mentally as he recalled the rows of robotic prospectors stored at Constanta. Jock was already reprogramming them with new algorithms, based on those gleaned from the Albanian bots. In due course, they'd be redeployed to find asteroids for Hawkwood. However, the board didn't need to know that.

The directors' faces showed astonishment as they mentally calculated. "But that's seven or eight billion kronor!" one protested. "Why haven't we received any of it?"

"Because we're the only ones entitled to it, sir," Cochrane pointed out calmly. He held up a hand to still the sudden hubbub of protest. "Our contract explicitly authorizes us to use the proceeds of anything we recover from Mycenae to fund our operations. Eight billion kronor won't go all that far. For example, a single new patrol craft costs approximately one billion kronor. What we recovered has to buy new ships, to allow us to expand our activities, and cover our operating costs as well. We've already put down deposits on a squadron of modern vessels. The rest of the money will fund our continuing operations. I daresay we'll encounter more intruders before long, and seize their ships and equipment too, and dispose of them for our benefit. That way, you won't have to fund our expansion."

"There's a great deal to be said for that," Marissa Stone observed, and several directors nodded thoughtfully. "We need all our resources to begin exploiting the Mycenae system. We can't afford to divert them to other needs right now."

"I take your point, Marissa," MacLellan agreed. "Nevertheless,

Captain, a number of us would like to see NOE exercise more direct control over the security of our operations. I'm looking for ways to do that without spending too much money, and without breaching our contract with your company. Do you have any suggestions?"

"I do, sir. Let me clarify one thing, please. You're talking about supervision of your actual operations, not the entire Mycenae system, right?"

"Yes. If we base a refinery ship at Mycenae Primus Four, or build a refinery on its surface and send the refinery ship to the asteroid belt, we'd like to control those locations specifically, and a reasonable volume of space around them. However, we certainly can't afford to patrol the entire system, not yet at any rate. We'll need to fund that sort of expansion of our security force by the profits from our operations there. That will take several years, I think."

"Yes, sir. I'm willing to offer a modification to our contract with NOE that I think will satisfy both parties. I'm prepared to withdraw our ships and people from areas designated by you as NOE operations. You can patrol them in your own vessels, and provide your own security. Hawkwood will patrol the Mycenae system outside those areas. It'll provide its own depot ship, orbiting another planet in the system, and continue to have the right to exploit any captured material to fund its operations. I daresay we'll still run into enough intruders to make that worthwhile. Obviously, there'll have to be ongoing liaison between your people and ours, to avoid interfering with each other's operations. Each party will also have the right of passage through areas controlled by the other, given prior arrangement."

There was a buzz of approval. "I think that meets our needs very satisfactorily," another director observed.

"There's one problem, though." A director raised his hand, looking down the table at Cochrane. "I'm Tom Nicolson, Captain. I like your proposal, but it means we'll have to buy our own security vessels, and raise crews for them, and put our own depot ship in place. That means spending money we can't spare right now."

Cochrane pretended to think for a moment. He'd foreseen this question. "I think we can resolve this without any cash changing hands, Mr. Nicholson. You need patrol craft and a depot ship. I need two large freighters, each of two to three million tons capacity, to serve as orbital warehouses and long-term storage ships. Why don't we swap? You give me two big freighters from your member companies' cargo operations. They must be well maintained and in good condition. You'll sign over ownership of both vessels, free and clear. In exchange, I'll make over to you the four reconditioned patrol craft we're currently using in Mycenae, plus their missiles, spares, and so on. I'll also return one of the freighters we borrowed from you. She's currently serving as our depot ship at Mycenae Primus Four. We've armed her for self-defense, and installed a hospital pod and personnel pods. You can use her as your security headquarters in the system."

"That sounds feasible, but what about crews for the patrol craft?" Nicolson asked.

"Why don't you approach Rousay's government, sir, to lend you spacers from its System Patrol Service? They should be able to supply a core crew for each vessel. You can hire more from among retired SPS spacers, or transfer some of your merchant ship crews to the patrol craft. It won't take long to get them up and running. We'll help by providing some of our people to train yours. We'll need them back soon, to crew our new vessels as they come out of the shipyard, but I'm sure we'll be able to work that out over time. I daresay the handover will take six months to a year."

There was a short silence as the directors pondered. Marissa Stone asked, "What about the second freighter and the courier ship we lent to you for three years? Would they also be returned, along with the depot ship in the Mycenae system?"

"I can return the freighter, three months after we receive the two larger vessels we're getting in exchange for the patrol craft. I'll need the courier ship for the full agreed term, though."

"What about paying for the two freighters?" another director asked. "We can't just take them away from our cargo lines. They're major assets."

Marwick shook his head. "That's mere bookkeeping. A creative accountant can always find ways to write them off as a loss for tax purposes. We might even make a paper profit on the deal!" A rustle of amusement ran around the table.

"All right," MacLellan said firmly. "I think what we've discussed offers a way forward that satisfies everyone's concerns. I propose that the Board approve Captain Cochrane's proposals in general terms, and delegate responsibility for finalizing them to Mr. Marwick and Ms. Stone, who are also authorized to conclude contracts and agreements as necessary. All those in favor?"

Hands went up all around the table.

THAT NIGHT, Cochrane dined with Caitlin Ross, Lachlan McLachlan and Henry Martin, the only three members of Eufala's leadership team still based on Rousay. He briefed them on the morning's discussion.

"You've all done great work here, but it's time to consolidate," he concluded. "We need to draw all our operations together, partly for administrative convenience, partly for security reasons." He told them about the unhealthy interest being shown by the Albanian Mafia. "We've managed to deal with the threat so far, but it's likely to get worse. I can secure one location, but not two. We don't have enough people or ships for that."

"But why Constanta?" Caitlin asked. "It's a minor planet, not on any major interplanetary trade routes. It's a backwater."

"That's why I'm using it. We can do things there, like assemble a small fleet of warships and train our crews, that would raise too many eyebrows in a busier system. Also, there's a small shipyard there whose owner I trust. He's handling all our routine maintenance needs at present. We have contacts on the planet who've come in handy from time to time, and we have a license to operate armed vessels there. All those things make Constanta perfect for us right now. In the longer term, yes, we'll need a better base; but let's cross that bridge when we come to it."

"But what about NOE? Won't it take too long to communicate via spacecraft, shuttling back and forth between Constanta and Rousay?"

"We won't have to. We'll both be operating in the Mycenae system. After all, our contract is for security there, not here on Rousay. That'll be our communications hub with NOE."

She frowned. "I suppose you've answered all my questions, but... I can't help thinking I'll be bored there. There won't be much to do outside of work."

He shrugged. "You can bring with you all the resources you need to keep yourself entertained. As for outside interests, sure, there won't be many; but then, we're going to be very busy. I've got a major project waiting for you that'll take up most of your time."

"Oh? That's good news. I've grown bored with supervising personnel security and hiring procedures. I'd like more variety."

"You'll get it. You're going to learn everything you can about the Albanian Mafia in general, and one offshoot branch of it in particular. I'll tell you more at Constanta."

"What about me, Captain?" Lachlan asked. "What will I be doing there that I can't do here?"

"You're going to be our logistics director and fleet coordinator. We're going to take dozens of ships into service over the next four to five years. You'll set up routine maintenance, crew rotation and resupply schedules for them all, and help plan their deployments. You'll also make sure we keep in stock enough spare parts, weapon reloads and other necessities to keep them all in operation. As we get more customers, we'll make up detachments comprising two or three different types of ships to meet their requirements, send them out to where they're needed, and rotate them back and forth to our base as required. You'll help with that, too. I'm also going to ask you to find more ships for us from time to time, some bought, some leased. Several support functions will report to you."

Lachlan beamed. "Great! Sounds like a challenge."

"It will be. Oh – right away, even before you leave for Constanta, start looking for two or three reasonably-priced communications vessels. We're going to need them soon. Try to keep the prices affordable, but I know they're more expensive than freighters. We'll just have to live with that."

"And what about me?" Henry asked.

"Caitlin will be trying to learn all we can about the Albanian Mafia and other potential threats to us, on top of her other duties. I need her at Constanta. You'll be her and my off-planet hands and feet, eyes and ears. One of the new communications ships will be assigned to you. There'll be a lot of investigating to be done, and a lot of discreet contact with others who might be able to tell us what we need to know. You already know the criminal circles in this part of the galaxy, and you probably have good enough contacts to figure out who to talk to elsewhere. Am I right?"

"I suppose you are, Captain. It'll take time, though. I'll need to make detours to identify new sources, and get introductions to them from people they'll trust. Without that, they won't talk to me. They might even think I'm a cop, and get rid of me on general principles as a precaution."

"That's what I mean. None of us know how to do all that except you. I want you to build up a network of sources and informers for us. I'm sure it'll be difficult work, and sometimes dangerous. I'll provide a security team for you, or let you hire your own at our expense. Just make sure you hire good people. I need you alive!"

"I'm biased toward staying that way myself." Everyone laughed.

Cochrane looked around the table. "All right. Wrap up your work here, and pack everything you want to take with you. If you want to retain any property here, or store belongings, that's up to you, but I daresay it'll be a long while before you get back this way. I think you'll be better advised to sell anything you can't bring with you. Be ready to catch our monthly supply run. The freighter will be here in about three weeks. She'll take you to Constanta via Mycenae. It'll be a slow journey, but there's no direct commercial service, so it's the best I can do."

"Where will you be going next, sir?" Caitlin asked.

"I'm heading for a shipyard. There are some things I need to arrange. I'll see you all back at Constanta."

∼

GOHEUNG

Kim shook his head in disapproval. "Captain, I don't see why you want to spend so much money stripping derelict old patrol craft down to the bare hull, then replacing every one of their systems with modern ones. That'll cost up to two hundred million francs each, perhaps a little more. We can sell you brand-new, larger, more capable patrol craft for only three hundred million each."

Cochrane shook his head. "It's a question of confidentiality, Mr. Kim. I can't go into details, but believe me, this way is better for us."

He couldn't explain that Eufala's last four patrol craft, one currently undergoing limited refurbishment in Grigorescu's shipyard at Constanta and three derelicts in parking orbits nearby, were still unnamed and unregistered. There was no record that the company owned them – only the four already serving in Mycenae. Once those were signed over to NOE, Eufala would officially have no patrol craft at all. Neither would Hawkwood, its successor corporation. It might be convenient if potential enemies believed that to be true.

He continued, "I've provided you with blueprints. Your designers will have to figure out how to shoehorn most of a corvette's critical systems into her, along with a single pod containing defensive missiles only. Based on what you achieved with those cruiser pods, I'm hoping you can fit forty to fifty of them into the space where she used to carry fifteen main battery and fifteen defensive missiles, all old and outdated. I want as much automation as possible, so she can operate with not more than ten to twelve crew. If you can figure out a way to have her operate under remote control, with no crew at all, I'll be seriously interested in that option. It might also let you cram more missiles into her hull, since she won't need crew quarters at all for remote operation."

"This is most unusual. I've never heard of a similar design."

"Perhaps, but you hadn't heard of anything like our superfrigate, either."

Kim smiled. "That is true. With defensive missiles only, what will be her function?"

"She'll provide point defense to specific targets on an as-needed basis. In between those times, she'll be stored aboard a freighter, unmanned, but ready for immediate action. Her systems will have to cater for that duty cycle."

"I see. I'll have our designers consider the problem. We'll probably convert one as a prototype, then, if both parties are satisfied, we can convert the remaining two hulls. Can you stay for a day or two, so the designers can ask questions if necessary?"

"I think so, but not longer than that."

"Very well. You can also inspect progress on your first two

corvettes and the first depot ship, if you wish. Their construction is well advanced."

"I'd appreciate that, thank you."

Sitting in his hotel room that night, Cochrane nursed a headache as he calculated crew requirements, delivery dates and operational commitments for his ships, existing and forthcoming. *The sooner Lachlan gets to Constanta, the better,* he thought as he scanned columns of figures. *I need to dump all this on his desk, to free myself for operations.*

He smiled as he thought of Kim's confusion regarding the patrol craft. He planned to put one aboard each of the large freighters he was acquiring as orbital warehouses and store ships. They might have to visit or operate from planets that would not permit them to be armed. Under normal circumstances, he'd have other ships providing security for them, but that might not always be possible. If he couldn't mount missiles and laser cannon on them, he had to find another way.

The big freighters could list a patrol craft, carried in one of their holds, as cargo in transit from one planet to another. It wouldn't be regarded as the ship's own armament. Nevertheless, they could launch it if necessary. With its defensive missiles and two laser cannon barbettes, it would provide almost as much protection against incoming missiles as a corvette. What's more, modern defensive missiles, even the smaller models carried by corvettes and patrol craft, had a powered range of up to three million kilometers. Their guidance units, aided by shipboard weapon control systems, were more than capable of locating, tracking and hitting an attacking vessel, not just a missile.

The big freighters might never need such defenses; but if they did, and didn't have them available right there and then, it would be too late to buy and install them. He couldn't afford to lose billions of francs worth of asteroids, nor all the stockpiled stores and materials it took to operate a squadron of modern warships. Such defenses would be cheap at the price by comparison. As for

keeping their existence secret, he was sure Mr. Kim could arrange
to record false names and owners for the patrol craft – for a small
fee, of course – while they were being refurbished. Their secret
would be preserved, until an assailant found out about them the
hard way.

He went to bed still smiling at that thought.

19

RETALIATION

PATOS

The restaurant shut its doors after lunch, and a notice was placed at the entrance: CLOSED TONIGHT FOR PRIVATE FUNCTION. Callers asking for reservations that evening were politely turned away, and the few who'd already made them received calls apologizing for having to cancel their booking. To compensate them for their trouble, they were offered free meals on any subsequent night of their choice. Given the well-deserved reputation of the restaurant's food, and its prices to match, all accepted the offer with alacrity.

Beads of sweat on his forehead, which were not entirely due to the late summer temperatures, the head chef had visited the markets early that morning to personally select meat, vegetables and fruit. All afternoon, his assistants labored to chop, grate, slice and dice everything according to his exacting standards. Clouds of aromatic steam and fragrant smoke filled the kitchen as its finest dishes were prepared. The sommelier chilled five cases of wine, and ordered his assistants to polish the glasses to gleaming perfection.

When the dining-room staff had finished cleaning up after lunch and changing the tablecloths, they were ushered out. The doors were closed, and guards posted at each one. A two-man team entered the room, carrying heavy suitcases. They took out several delicate instruments and proceeded to scan every square centimeter of floor, walls and ceiling, including around and beneath every table and chair, and the curtains and their valances. Even the serving table's hot trays were lifted out of their sockets, and the cavities beneath checked.

Satisfied at last, the two men reported to the Chief of Security that all was well. He ordered his guards to ensure that no-one, repeat, *no-one* was allowed to enter the dining-room without an escort, who was to closely supervise everything he did inside. If there was even the slightest suspicion that all was not well, he was to be called. More guards took up their stations in the kitchen, randomly searching waiters as they went in and out of the dining-room. The staff wanted to roll their eyes in rebellious resentment at this imposition, but they knew better than to be caught doing so.

More guards surrounded the premises, walking slowly through the gardens, peering suspiciously into bushes and behind trees, looking for anything out of place. They didn't find anything... at least, not below head height. They either didn't notice, or didn't think twice about, what looked like several large moths that flew over the walls, and settled into the tops of the bushes growing in such profusion around the windows. With their wings folded, clutching the stems and branches with their tiny feet, they blended in so well as to be effectively invisible.

A few of the 'moths' carefully positioned themselves so that their wings, when unfolded and bent into a shape curiously like a small dish, were 'aimed' at the tops of trees just visible over the wall. Others crawled along the branches until they could 'see' the vent bricks set at intervals in the upper part of the restaurant's walls. Those ventilating the dining-room appeared to gather the most interest. The insects' 'antennae' vibrated slightly as they were adjusted to the right angle.

Four of the 'moths' crept along branches until they were positioned just outside the dining-room windows. Two remained motionless, while two others flitted across to the windows and seemed to 'defecate' on them, leaving brown streaks running down the glass. Their work done, the polluters flew away.

It didn't take long for one of the waiters, laying silverware at the tables, to notice the marks. He brought them to the attention of the head waiter, who was unamused. "Why are you telling me about them, instead of cleaning them? *Get to work!* There isn't much time!"

Muttering to himself, the waiter went over to the windows. He realized at once he could not reach the stains from outside. The vegetation was too thick, and too close to the walls. He would have to open them, and clean the glass from inside the room. Sighing, he fetched water, rags and cleaning fluid, and endured the searching hands at the door. Carrying his gear over to the window, he opened the first and set to work. In his concentration on the job at hand, neither he nor his guard noticed as first one, then another 'moth' flew on silent wings over their heads and into the room. Each flew to a valance adjacent to a vent brick, hid inside it, then froze, immobile.

IN A HOUSE A COUPLE of hundred meters up the hill from the restaurant, three men watched the display screens on their consoles, looking through the 'eyes' of the 'insects' in the dining-room. They were on tenterhooks in case something went wrong, and breathed sighs of relief as first one, then the second flitterbug reported that they were safely inside. Their signals traveled through the vent bricks to the listening 'moths' outside. They, in turn, relayed them to the 'insects' that were in line-of-sight to the treetops over the wall. They passed on the signal through the 'dishes' formed by their wings, to other 'moths' who relayed it through more of their kind up the hill. There were eleven links in the chain before it reached the house, each with multiple redundant elements in case a flitterbug should malfunction or be detected.

"All right," the leader said with a sigh. "We're in. They've already swept the place, so they've no reason to do so again. If there's any sign that they're going to, shut down the flitterbugs at once so they don't detect their microphones. They'll stay down until they get a signal from the bugs outside."

One of his team objected, "But what if they draw the curtains? The bugs outside won't be able to look inside, to show us when it's safe to resume listening."

"Then we won't resume listening. It'll be too dangerous. If they get even the faintest idea people like us are on the planet, we may not leave here alive."

"And if they find a bug that's shut down?"

"By then we'll have withdrawn all those in the chain leading here. We can dump everything where it'll never be found, and go back to pretending to be businessmen. You can bet your boots they'll search every visitor to the city, and maybe have the cops interrogate us too – they own the law here, after all. Still, if there's no evidence to connect us to the bugs, we should be OK."

"I wish you'd said 'will' instead of 'should', boss," the other team member commented.

"Why would I lie to you like that? Have I ever?"

"No – but now would be a comforting time to start!"

A DOZEN COUPLES and a few single men, most elderly, a few only middle-aged, came to the restaurant that night. They arrived in private vehicles, which were whisked away to a secure parking lot by men smartly dressed in black suits. Each new arrival brought one or two men with them, dressed similarly, with bulges at their hips or beneath their shoulders. Inside, their guards peeled off to a room set aside for them, offering the same excellent food that their employers would receive – but no alcoholic beverages. Guards needed to be sober on duty, no matter what.

The couples were ushered ceremoniously into the dining-room, and seated at six tables placed in a circle. A sumptuous five-course meal was served, waiters flitting back and forth between the kitchen and the diners, watched with unblinking eyes by the guards on duty. A different wine accompanied each course. Some of the ladies imbibed freely, but none of the men. They sipped abstemiously at their glasses.

The meal over, and the chef congratulated (to his relief) on the excellence of his cooking, the couples adjourned to an adjacent lounge for coffee and liqueurs while the dining-room was cleared. A large round table was brought in, covered with a cloth, and a dozen chairs were set around it. Coffee cups and glasses of water were set at each place. When all was ready, the men filtered back into the room, while their wives settled down to talk among themselves. The galaxy might have evolved toward equality of the sexes, but that did not apply here.

When everyone was seated, the oldest man present rose to his feet. "I thank you all for coming here this night. We have sad news to hear, and options to consider. I declare this meeting of the Brotherhood Council open, and I call upon Agim Sushi to take the chair."

Hidden inside the valances, the two flitterbugs faithfully transmitted every word.

A middle-aged man, thick-set and muscular stood as the older sat down. He began without preamble, "Brothers, Kostandin and his team reached Skraill. Their initial reports indicated that they had identified Frank Haldane. A local man, with whom we had contact some years ago, agreed to help them kidnap him for interrogation. Since that report, we have heard nothing from the team at all. Their next scheduled report is now sixty days overdue. I fear we must consider them lost."

A rustle of disquiet ran around the table, but he held up his hand for silence. "That is not all. We sent Vasil to Constanta to investigate several issues. In his first three reports, he told us that Eufala Corporation and Hawkwood Corporation are effectively one and the same. Eufala has a contract with the New Orkney Enterprise to provide security in the Mycenae system. We already knew that Eufala was probably responsible for the theft of the Callanish repair ship *Colomb,* used by the consortium there, and of two fast freighters ordered by that consortium from a shipyard in Goheung. All three ships were exchanged for others at Medusa, which are now in the possession of Eufala. The company has four patrol craft and a depot ship at Mycenae. We presume one of those patrol craft destroyed our ship some months ago.

"Vasil informed us that a certain Captain Cochrane, from the New Orkney Cluster, is the driving force behind Eufala and Hawkwood. Of greater concern is that he appears to have found powerful allies. A Captain Lu of the Qianjin Fleet visited him at Constanta some months ago, and spent time aboard his ships in orbit. We checked her name against Qianjin's published Fleet Register. She is listed as a senior officer in their Intelligence Department."

"*Qianjin?*" one of his audience exploded. "But that –"

"Yes, Skender. We all know who is based on Qianjin. Nominally, the planet's military forces are distinct from the Dragon Tong, but in practice, we cannot be sure how distinct they truly are. Captain Lu was not there by accident. We know Cochrane captured some of our robotic prospectors, and Vasil reported that he took at least one prisoner from our missing ship." Another rustle of dismay ran around the table. "If there was one, there may well have been more. Cochrane was probably able to give Lu information that the Dragon Tong would value. We must presume they reciprocated by telling him at least some of what they know about us."

"How do we know he took a prisoner?" another demanded angrily.

"Because of this." The speaker pulled a printed picture from his pocket and passed it down the table to the questioner. "Please pass it around. That is a picture of a terminal displaying an official death report for a patient at a Constanta long-term care facility. Vasil had been able to persuade a nurse to provide a picture of him. He reported that it was, unmistakably, Pavli Selimaj, the First Mate of our missing ship *Puka*. As you see, he was not listed under that name on the facility's list of occupants. He was reported to be in a vegetative state, very similar to that caused by our interrogation drugs. Vasil was going to try to give him the final mercy, assisted by Besnik and Gentius. It appears that they failed, and were captured or killed."

"How do we know that?"

"Because Vasil took with him a fourth team member, a young woman who was still under training. All four were staying at separate hotels, of course, for greater security. Shpresa waited in a nearby street to serve as a relay point for communications. She heard shots from around the nursing home, but was not close enough to see what happened. When Vasil failed to make contact, she checked his hotel. His room had been let to someone else. The same had occurred with Besnik and Gentius. She was intelligent enough to search for recent deaths at the long-term care facility, and found that record. She then left Constanta and made her way back here. That means either none of the three was taken alive, or, if they were, Eufala's interrogators did not suspect that there was a fourth member. If they had asked about her, they would have identified her, and made sure she did not escape. She was extremely fortunate."

"She was," another man said. "We owe her much for bringing

us this information. Without it, we might have been left in the dark for several months yet – months in which our enemies might damage us even more than they have already. May I suggest that she be commended?"

"Thank you for suggesting that, Perparim. I have already seen to it. We shall need more like her, now that two of our best teams have been eliminated." He looked around the table. "I fear that is not the worst news I have for you tonight, brothers. Some months ago – the news has only just reached us – it seems that a delegation from Qianjin approached the leadership of our parent family, asking about our activities in several asteroid belts." There was a hiss of indrawn air. "Yes, brothers; *they went to those who disdained us.* The Bregija clan told the delegation enough to identify some of us, and stated that we were acting on our own, without their approval and outside their aegis. I therefore presume Qianjin will feel free to act against us, if they think it necessary, because they will assume that our parent family will not help us."

There was a stunned silence in the room.

"*Will* they help us, if it comes to that?" an older man asked at last.

The speaker shrugged. "I think there will be voices raised in our support. Blood calls to blood, after all. Whether there will be enough voices to bring the Bregijas in on our side, I cannot say."

"We should not count on it." The speaker was the old man who'd opened proceedings. His hands and arms trembled as he pushed himself erect. "I request the floor, Agim."

The younger man bowed. "The floor is yours, Patriarch." He sat down.

The old man looked around at his colleagues. Every eye was fixed on him in rapt attention. He began, "When I conceived the Fatherland Project, forty years ago, I pointed out that all three of the great criminal enterprises in the galaxy – the Dragon Tong, the Nuevo Cartel, and the Cosa Nostra – had their own planetary bases. These provided them with security and an extradition-proof sanctuary, from which they could plan, launch and guide their enterprises. All of them also have allied governments and planets, which offer them bases from which to operate in different regions. All have achieved greatness by taking great care to ensure that these foundations of their interplanetary operations are always secure.

"I told the Bregija Clan that we needed to do the same; that unless and until we did, we could not hope to be as prosperous and respected – yes, and as feared – as the Three. I pointed out that our forefathers had grown to be giants on Earth, operating in almost every nation on the planet. I said how disappointed they would be that we, their descendants, had failed to live up to their example; but they would not listen. They laughed at me. They *laughed!*" His voice trembled with fury. "They said I was a hopeless romantic, longing for greatness that had long since passed us by."

He breathed heavily for a moment. "That was when I led some of you, and some who are no longer with us, to break away. We dedicated our lives and our fortunes to the Fatherland Project. We determined that we would make a home for ourselves where we could be secure, in control of our own destinies, and defy the rest of the galaxy if need be. From that base, we would expand our interests and our influence until we, too, achieved greatness, and honored our forefathers with our success.

"We have worked hard, these past forty years. It took many years of scrimping and saving to build our war chest, to learn the ways of asteroid prospecting, to develop the technology that is built into our robots, and to learn how best to deploy them and gather their harvest. We had to seek out the most productive fields, and sneak past the defenses of those who guard them, to steal away with the best they had to offer. Building our own refinery ship and learning how to operate it were very great challenges, and very expensive. It is only in the past few years that all these strands have come together at last, and we have begun to achieve success.

"Now our success is threatened. We need much more money than we have already raised, if our Fatherland is to become a reality. You all know the need, and how we plan to meet it – but if our enemies unite against us, that may become impossible. Even if it does not, it may be so long delayed that it will not happen in our lifetimes."

He drew himself up. "I know I do not have long left to live, but I have dared to hope that you, my sons in flesh and spirit, will take the reins from my hands and drive the Fatherland Project onward to fulfilment. Now, I see fear in you. I see hesitation. I see doubts. To your fear, to your hesitation, to your doubts, I say simply this: *remember our forefathers!* They rose to greatness on Earth. They were feared by nations around the globe. They were respected by other criminals. They are all looking down at us now, and they command us: *Do not take counsel of your fears! Remember us, and all we achieved! Do thou likewise!*"

His audience applauded, their faces flushed with renewed enthusiasm. The old man looked around, nodding. The spirit was still there. It had merely burned down to embers for a while, needing only to be fanned into flame again and given new fuel – fuel that would burn hot enough to warm their hearts with pride, and sear their enemies' hearts with terror.

He held up his hand, waited for silence, then said softly, "That is why I gathered you. That is why I led you for so many years. That is why I selected Agim to take over when I grew too old. He now directs all our efforts toward our goal." He looked toward his chosen successor. "Agim, do not dishonor my life, or my death, by wavering. Redouble your efforts! Do not let your enemies strike fear into you. Instead, *strike fear into them!* Hit back at them! Show them that for every blow they direct against us, we shall return it ten times harder!"

Agim sprang to his feet. "Patriarch, again you inspire us with your example! Again, you show us the way with your wise counsel. Where do you suggest we strike?"

"Where they have hurt us most – in the Mycenae system. We have lost a ship there, and its crew; so, in answer, destroy *all* their ships, and *all* their crews! Make them pay so high a price for daring to challenge us that they will never dare do so again!"

Agim nodded slowly, looking around the table. "Brothers, only a few of you have seen our forces, and our refinery ship that they protect. That is because we base them at a deserted star with no inhabitable planets, to keep them secret. Nevertheless, those of you who have visited them know we have come far." Four heads nodded around the table.

"Among other ships, we now have a division of four destroyers, all older vessels modernized with new systems and weapons. Even one of them has more missiles than all Eufala's patrol craft put together! Two of them should be more than enough to wipe out their flotilla to the last vessel and the last man. What say you, brothers?"

Every man around the table raised his hand in assent.

"Very well. We shall send word to our forces to prepare. It will probably take a month to six weeks to prepare; then, we strike! I shall go with them."

The old man raised his voice. "Agim, you are brave. It is one of the reasons I selected you to succeed me. Even so, I counsel against your going. You are our leader now. You must manage all our activities, not just one. Your absence for so long may cause disruption. If one of us should be there to represent the Brotherhood, let another be selected for that task."

Agim hesitated, then nodded slowly. "I yield to your wisdom, Patriarch." He looked around the table. "Does any other Brother wish to represent us, and lead our forces into combat with our enemies?"

"Let me go," the old man said. An instant chorus of opposition burst out, but he held up his hand. "I am old, and I am dying. Give me one last chance to strike a blow for our cause!"

"But what if your health fails you, Patriarch? It is a long journey."

A shrug. "I will die soon, no matter what happens. I would rather die as a man, fighting for our Fatherland, than in bed, surrounded by the wailing of women!"

Agim bowed his head. "So be it, Patriarch. We could not ask for a finer representative."

IN THE HOUSE on the hill, the three men watched and listened with growing concern. One glanced at their leader. "We've got to get word back to Qianjin right away! What if Captain Lu is visiting Mycenae again when they attack? She might be killed!"

"We can't. From this backwater planet, we need at least two or three connecting spacecraft to reach Qianjin. That'll take five or six weeks. By then, these bastards will be ready to hit Mycenae. We *can't* warn them in time."

"So, what are we going to do?"

"We're going to record the rest of this meeting, then pack up everything and get out of here. I'll have lunch at that restaurant tomorrow, and find a way to pick up those flitterbugs from the valances. That'll make sure no-one finds them, and wonders how long they've been there and how much they heard. We'll keep things low-key, as if we're the businessmen we claim to be. We won't do anything that might arouse suspicion. In two days' time, you'll catch the weekly ferry to Capida, from where you can get scheduled service to bigger planets *en route* to Qianjin. The most important thing is to get this recording back to base. Even if the Captain doesn't make it, the Admiral will want to know who killed her, so we can hit back."

"And what are you and David going to do?"

"We're going to go into business here, just like our cover story suggests. We'll keep an eye on things. Tell the Admiral where to find our dead drop. If anything happens to us, his people will know where to look for our reports up to that time. Tell him we'll need a lot more people and resources to watch these people properly – probably a complete second team, to operate independently of us. This is turning into a bigger job than anyone figured."

"It sure is! Have you ever heard about this 'Fatherland Project'? It's new to me."

"Me too. The Bregijas certainly didn't mention it. I reckon we'll have to put it at the top of our list of things to investigate."

"Where the hell did they get hold of destroyers?" the third man wondered.

"They probably bid through a front company to buy old warships listed for the scrapheap. Instead, they sent the hulks to this fleet they've got hidden somewhere. A repair vessel would take much longer than a shipyard to modernize them, but given time, it could do the job. As for their systems and weapons, they're operating their own refinery ship, so they have access to precious metals. You can buy a lot if you've got enough of that, no matter how illegal the sale might be."

His colleague frowned. "So now Eufala's got to face modernized warships. I wouldn't like to be in one of their ancient patrol craft when that happens. From what the Captain reported, they've also been modernized, but not by much, and they're still using real old missiles that aren't all that reliable."

The team's leader nodded. "I'm glad I'm not working for them at Mycenae. Things are about to get real interesting there."

20

PREPARATION

CONSTANTA

Cochrane was buried in administrative issues when Jock Murray was announced. He pushed them aside with relief, clearing his terminal screen as he called, "Come in!"

"It's good to be back, sir," Jock said as he walked through the door. "Got any coffee?"

"In the pot." He motioned to the carafe on the sideboard.

Jock filled a mug, sipped, and scowled. "You've been letting these damned planetary coffee shops get to you, sir. This isn't Fleet coffee!"

"No, it's not, but have mercy on my regular visitors. If they drank what we're used to aboard ship, it'd strip the lining from their stomachs – not to mention keeping them awake for a week! Is the surveillance satellite up and running?"

"It is, sir. It's actually a constellation of four satellites, deployed in a tetrahedon formation, ten thousand kilometers apart, in Mycenae Primus Four's L1 orbital position. It took Sue's techs two weeks to iron out all the kinks. It's not that there were any real problems, you understand; it's just a complicated thing to install. Each satellite has six arms, five hundred meters long, with passive sensors spaced along them, set at ninety degrees to each other. There's also the datalink to the constellation's special Plot display on the depot ship. My techs had a hard time getting that up and running, but we got it right in the end."

"It sounds like a complicated job all round."

"It was, sir, even with robots to help. Still, it was worth it. Once we got the sensors dialed in, we could monitor a radius of four billion kilometers in every direction. It's an amazingly sensitive system, even though it's not real accurate at bearing and range over longer distances."

"Yes. It takes a system surveillance array to be more accurate, with multiple satellites millions of kilometers apart, for better cross-bearings and much longer range – out to three or four light-days. Those things cost anywhere from five to ten billion, though. They're way outside our budget."

"How much did our system cost, sir?"

Cochrane grimaced. "Nine hundred million francs."

Jock whistled in surprise. "Is it worth that much to us, sir?"

"I think it will be. Up to now, everyone sneaking into Mycenae has coasted in silently, using their drives at the lowest possible power only when they needed to brake or maneuver. Shipboard sensors simply can't pick that up, except at relatively close range. We need to know about them long before they reach us."

"Well, this'll do that, sir. We sent *Amanita* out to five billion clicks, then had her come back using only five percent power. She's got a very quiet, modern drive unit, but it picked her up and tracked her all the way in, no matter how she tried to evade. Ah... if you spent this much on it, sir, you must be expecting trouble?"

"I am. Our mines killed an Albanian ship, and we confiscated that Callanish repair vessel. Both groups might want to get even. I would, if I were in their shoes. If they try, we need to know they're coming before they reach us. As soon as we can afford it, I'm going to buy another of those satellite constellations to deploy in this system, too." He stretched. "How's Sue enjoying HCS *Vulcan*?"

"She's putting her new repair ship to good use, sir. She's already run checks on *Payara* and *Trairao,* to make sure their old systems are holding up. So far, they seem to be. When I left, she was planning to do the same for *Arapaima* and *Bicuda*."

"I presume Commander Cousins is temporarily using their crews aboard *Piranha,* while they wait to get their own ships back?"

"Yes, sir. *Vulcan* unloaded the fifth patrol craft as soon as she arrived, even before the satellites. Commander Cousins says he wants to wring her out thoroughly, because she was the worst deteriorated of all of them before being modernized. He wants more spacers out there, so he can crew all five ships at once."

"All in good time."

Jock grinned. "Sue's still getting used to the stripes on her sleeve. She's thought of herself as a Warrant Officer for so long, it's a shock to find herself a Limited Duty engineer officer, especially a full Commander."

"She's earned the rank if anyone has. You have, too, so why did you turn it down?"

Jock shrugged. "I just don't feel comfortable at the thought of being an officer, sir."

"Well, anytime you change your mind, let me know. Sue needed to be a Commander, because *Vulcan's* skipper holds that rank too. He's not her boss, after all – he just takes the ship to where she's needed, and keeps her running. Sue's responsible for all the work she does."

"Yes, sir. She and Commander Frith seem to be getting on well together."

"I thought they would. That's why I appointed him to *Vulcan.* He's got enough experience and common sense to know when he needs to exercise authority, and when to back off and let Sue have control. She'll learn a lot from him about being a good officer. I'm glad Frank brought him to us."

"Ah... as a matter of interest, sir, how are you sorting out ranks and authority levels?"

"Commander Cousins and I have been working that out for several months. Briefly, command levels will be Lieutenants in command of patrol craft, Lieutenant-Commanders of corvettes, and Commanders of frigates. A division of two to four patrol craft will be under a Lieutenant-Commander, two to four corvettes under a Commander, and two to four frigates under a Captain. Major auxiliaries like our depot ships, *Vulcan,* and the big store ships, will be skippered by Commanders, while the smaller freighters and courier vessels will have Lieutenant-Commanders."

"And you, sir?"

"I'm going to promote Commander Cousins to Captain next month, because he'll be in command of our Mycenae station and all the ships assigned there. As we expand, all major station commanders will be Captains. He suggested I promote myself to Commodore, as the commander of our whole fleet. For the sake of a clear chain of command, we'll probably do that."

"Works for me, sir. You can have a salute from me anytime, no matter what your rank."

THE FIRST OF the large freighters NOE was swapping for the patrol craft arrived at Constanta the following week. Cochrane immediately went out to look her over.

As his gig approached the two-and-a-half-million-ton ship, he noticed a raised, elongated fairing on her spine, about two-thirds of the way toward her stern. It looked like a flattened hump. He asked the skipper of her passage crew about it as soon as he stepped aboard.

"Oh, that's her engineering spaces," she told him. "Instead of having the reactor and gravitic drive compartments hanging down from the ship's spine, protruding into the cargo holds, this ship's designers put them above the spine, taking up no cargo space at all. It looks odd, I'll admit, but it functions perfectly well."

"I see. Well, it makes naming this ship a lot easier." She gave him an inquiring look. "We're naming all our freighters after whale species on Earth. They're the largest animals on that planet. This one practically begs to be christened *Humpback!*" She couldn't help laughing.

He had Grigorescu' engineers and technicians go over *Humpback* from stem to stern, making sure she was in good order and condition. As soon as they gave her a clean bill of health, he ordered the long-term cargo stored aboard their second, hitherto unused fast freighter, now named *Minke*, to be transferred to the new arrival.

While that was in progress, Frank returned with the leased freighter from a trip to Barjah and Goheung. He entered Cochrane's office looking more than a little frustrated. Cochrane recognized the signs, and smiled inwardly. He'd been expecting this visit, and was prepared for it.

"How did it go?" he asked cheerfully, leading his guest to a group of chairs in the corner.

"It went fine, sir. We delivered the asteroid shipment, got the quarter payment for them in gold – it's in our strongroom – and then took the patrol craft hulk to Goheung. Kang Industries promised to have it ready for delivery with our first two corvettes." His face grew animated as he mentioned the warships. "I must admit, sir, I was impressed by their plans for that patrol craft. *Fifty* defensive missiles! That's as many as a corvette carries. That's really something, to shoehorn that many into so small a space, along with a modern weapon control system and sensors."

"Yes. To fit them in, they had to chop out most of her crew

quarters; but they gave her a lot more automation to compensate. She'll need only a dozen spacers for normal operations. She can be handled and fought by as few as four if necessary, although that's obviously for emergencies only."

"I get it, sir. At first, I thought the idea was crazy, but now I've had a chance to think about it, it makes a lot of sense. If you can't fit missiles to your ship, fit a smaller ship that can carry the missiles on its behalf. Are all our freighters going to have them?"

"No, just the two big ones. Their cargoes will be very valuable, because of all the essential gear we'll store aboard them – missile reloads, engineering and electronic spares, ration stockpiles, uniforms, you name it. That'll justify the cost of protecting them. I'll have the other two patrol craft hulks converted as well in due course. They'll need shipyard maintenance from time to time, so we'll rotate the three of them between the two freighters."

"Makes sense, sir." He hesitated. "Sir, when are you going to get me out of that freighter and into something with teeth? I know I said I'd do anything you needed, but carrying cargo around the galaxy isn't very exciting."

"You needn't worry. I put you aboard her because I needed a trustworthy skipper to handle the asteroid shipments. You proved your discretion and ability during our early operations, so you were a natural choice. Let me tell you what I have in mind for you.

"I want to use your experience to prepare the whole company for the expansion that's about to hit us. Therefore, I'm going to give you command of our new armed fast freighter. Kang is making good progress with the conversion. She'll have a frigate missile pod, plus a full fire control system, plus accommodation for up to two hundred entry-level and senior spacers under training, with classrooms and other facilities. She'll patrol the Mycenae system from time to time, and handle sensitive shipments like taking our asteroids to Barjah and bringing back the payment for them. The trainees can carry on with their work during those voyages. She'll be fully combat capable, with fewer missiles than a corvette, but they're much more powerful and longer-ranged weapons."

"Laser cannon, too?"

"Yes, four of them, the same as a corvette."

Frank began to smile. "Well, she's not as nimble as a corvette, but she'll be much more comfortable, given that she's fifteen times their size."

"True. While you train our first batch of entry-level spacers, and teach our fire control teams how to use a frigate's weapons and combat systems, I want you to start developing operational doctrine and tactics for the frigates. I'll work on that with you from time to time. You'll also deploy our robotic prospectors to stars that nobody's claimed. We can leave some to explore their asteroid belts for a year or more, then go back to collect whatever they've found. You'll deploy some space mines along with them, to protect them against intruders trying to steal them."

"But, sir, the reason a lot of those stars haven't been claimed is that they don't have resources worth exploiting. They've been checked out by survey ships, and found wanting."

Cochrane shook his head. "That's not the whole picture. Survey ships go there for at most a year or two, including time out to return to base for crew rest and maintenance. They leave robotic explorers to carry on until they get back. They can't possibly sample all the planets and asteroids in a system; only a few. If those come back negative, they give up and try somewhere else. There are enough stars out there that it makes sense to do it that way – cherry-pick the best of them, and ignore the others. However, that doesn't mean there may not be some really good asteroids among the thousands in a typical system. It just means they weren't identified by the survey.

"I reckon, if we're willing to let our prospector bots have their heads and range through the system on their own, they might find one in a hundred, even one in a thousand asteroids that's worth recovering. We can sow the bots, then come back a year later to pick them up, along with whatever they've found. We might even do a quick survey from a mining boat, to identify potentially richer concentrations of asteroids, and sow the bots there. If we recover even, say, ten asteroids worth a few hundred million apiece, that'll more than repay our investment."

Frank nodded thoughtfully. "That makes sense, sir. OK, you'll have me train our spacers in the frigates' weapons and systems, patrol Mycenae from time to time, ferry asteroids and gold around, and maybe deploy a few bots here and there. That's still a lot of routine, mundane stuff. When do I get to do more exciting things?"

Cochrane smiled. "In less than two years, our frigate prototype will be ready for testing. You'll already have more experience with her systems than anyone else in our fleet. Who better to command her, and wring her out thoroughly? The lessons you learn will lead to improvements in their final design. They'll be built into the rest of the ships on the production line, while yours will be modified to include them. A couple of years after that, when enough frigates are in service, I'll promote you to Captain, to command our first frigate division."

Frank's eyes shone. "Now you're talking, sir!"

"I think you're the right man for the job. Prove it to me. The Good Book says, he who is faithful in smaller tasks will be trusted with greater. You've been faithful in all I've asked you to do so far; so, every year or two, I'll be giving you bigger jobs with greater responsibility." He hesitated for a moment. "I think we're going to have more trouble with those Albanians. If they keep coming at us, we're going to have to do something about them; and the best form of defense is attack. I want us to be able to take the fight to them, rather than wait for them to attack us. That'll be a big part of the doctrine and tactics you'll help to develop for our frigates. The corvettes are patrol and defensive ships. The frigates will pack our big punch. If we have to deliver it, and if you've proved

yourself, you'll command it. After all, you have a personal stake in
the outcome."

"I sure do! Thanks for trusting me, sir. I'll be ready when the
time comes, and I'll make damned sure our ships are, too. Oh –
that armed fast freighter. What's her name?"

Cochrane explained about the new policy of naming
freighters for whale species from Earth. "Since yours will be our
only armed freighter, at least for now, her name was a no-brainer.
I've christened her *Orca*."

"The killer whale? I like it!"

"I thought you would. Now, let's get down to brass tacks. I'm
transferring you and your crew to *Minke,* our other fast freighter.
As soon as you've offloaded her cargo, send your old command
under a passage crew back to the broker from whom we leased
her. Take *Minke* as well, to bring back the passage crew. That'll be
a good shakedown cruise for her. After that, you'll do a resupply
run to Mycenae, then take another shipment of asteroids to
Barjah, then head to Goheung to take delivery of *Orca*."

"Can I take my crew across to *Orca* with me, sir?"

"I'll try to let you do that, but I have to have a crew for *Minke,*
too, so some of them may have to stay aboard her, at least
temporarily. We're hiring more spacers as fast as we can find
trustworthy candidates and put them through screening. I'll do
my best for you."

To Cochrane's surprise and pleasure, he received a call the
following week announcing the arrival at Constanta's system
boundary of a communications frigate from Qianjin. Captain Lu
was aboard. He hastened to clear his desk of the rest of the day's
tasks, to free up time to spend with her once she arrived, then
headed to the space station to be there when she arrived.

She wore her full uniform to meet him in the docking bay

foyer, looking very smart but depressingly official. He felt a surge of attraction and desire as she halted a meter away, holding herself stiffly upright. "It's good to see you again, Captain," she said formally.

"It's *very* good to see *you* again," he said warmly. Her lower lip trembled suspiciously before she caught herself. "Do you plan to stay in orbit, or may I escort you planetside? I can offer you a choice of accommodation. Eufala has bought a twenty-four-unit apartment block, in the interests of security. It's well protected. I live there when I'm planetside, as do most of our senior people. It has two very comfortable guest apartments. Alternatively, we'll gladly put you up at Constanta's finest hotel, in a private suite."

"I'd like some time planetside," she admitted. "I've been hard at work since we last saw each other, so I'll be glad to relax for a few days. May I use one of your guest apartments?"

"With pleasure." He turned to his aide. "Contact the building manager. Tell him to make sure a guest apartment is ready by the time we arrive."

"I'm on it, sir." His aide was already reaching for his comm unit.

She would not talk on the way down from orbit, casting a sideways glance at his aide and the pilot before shaking her head slightly. He got the message, and refrained from asking any questions until they were alone over supper at a good restaurant downtown. She watched, frowning slightly, as his security team discreetly but carefully checked out the private room he'd reserved, then disposed themselves in and around the facility to ensure their privacy and safety while they ate.

"That's new," she said when they were seated at last. "You never used to have such heavy security. Is that because of...?"

"Yes. Those Albanians had quite a long list of interests. Eufala and Hawkwood were on it, and so was I. What really got my security people going was the quality of their training. We got all three of those who attacked the nursing home – well, one who tried to penetrate it, and two that backed him up – but they were much, much better than we expected. They were so much better than our own people that we've hired a team of top instructors to completely overhaul our training. We're going to expand our security force as well."

"Who did you hire?"

"We went to Sicherheit Zuerst in the Bismarck Cluster. They employ a lot of former secret service and diplomatic security personnel, plus some former Grenzschutzgruppe operators – that's the Cluster's anti-terrorist outfit. Sicherheit's very expensive, but they're top quality at what they do. Their team is on Constanta now, training several groups of our people. Our security detail tonight is among the first to graduate from their basic course. They'll go on to advanced training once we have more basic graduates to replace them. Sicherheit will also help us set up an offensive element, to deal proactively with enemy threats when we find them."

"I see. I'd like to know more about what they're teaching your people."

"Would you like to come out to our training camp with me tomorrow, and see for yourself?"

"I'd like that very much."

Over their meal, she told him more about what she'd been doing. "Your captured data plates from those Albanian bots caused quite a scurry. We compared them to serial numbers taken from other destroyed bots in other systems. If the numbers show sequential production, they indicate that over three thousand of those bots have been made by now."

"Three *thousand?* But that means..."

"Yes, it means they must be active in many more systems than the few where we've detected them. We're mounting a big effort to survey every rich asteroid mining field we know of, to see whether they've been clandestinely spread there. We've already identified three more where they have. It looks like the

Albanians are deliberately choosing only the best and most productive asteroid fields, because that way they don't have to do any preliminary surveying. They're also using more sophisticated beacons in the better defended fields, remotely activated ones that use infrared lights rather than radio to identify themselves. Unless a patrol is close enough, and looking in the right direction to see the light, and using infrared sensors, they'll miss it."

He thought for a moment, putting down his knife and fork. "That means they can't have been doing this – at least, not on this scale – for very long. If they had, their bots would have been noticed a lot more often than they have."

"That's what our people think. They reckon this is a recent expansion of their activity, probably after years of preparing for it, perfecting the bots and their algorithms, and training their spacers to sneak in and out of asteroid fields without being detected. That also fits what you discovered in Mycenae, of course. That ship you destroyed had been in several asteroid belts over the past three years. Prior to that, she had no record of visiting one at all – just normal commercial freight runs. It's as if she only recently began asteroid work."

"Uh-huh. That might also explain why they responded to her destruction by sending a team here, and another to Skraill. They were trying to find out who was interfering, and why. I think they probably planned – are still planning, for that matter – to take direct action against us once they learn all they need to know. Fortunately, we interrupted them on both planets. They'll have to regroup, which gives us time to improve our defenses."

"Yes. Thank you for forwarding reports on those actions. Our Intelligence Department found them very useful. In fact..." She hesitated. "I probably shouldn't tell you this, but I think our people are mounting some sort of intelligence operation against the Albanians. It's not in my department, but... some people... asked me so many questions about what I'd seen and heard that it had to have been more than just curiosity. Forget I said that, all right?"

"Said what?" They smiled at each other as he picked up his utensils again. "I have to ask, though: I've shared everything I've learned with you. Will your Fleet share anything it learns with me? If it's not going to be a two-way street, I'm going to have to spend a lot more money trying to find out for myself what those bastards are up to."

"I don't know. As I said, whatever they're doing is outside my department. I'll ask, if you like – in fact, I'll officially recommend it – but I don't know how they'll respond."

"If it'll help, put it as an official question from me, coming from someone who's helped them in the past. You might also mention that the Dragon Tong is making billions out of me through processing asteroids. If I'm not going to get the intelligence I need from Qianjin, I may as well invest some of the money I'm making in buying my own refinery ship. That way, I'll double what I get out of the asteroids, which will give me enough money to fund my own intelligence setup.

"Of course, if I don't need that, because Qianjin is telling me all I could learn for myself anyway, then I may as well go on refining my asteroids through the Tong. Just between you and I, I'd actually prefer not to have to manage another department, not to mention tying up billions of francs and several hundred people in refining activities not related to our main purpose – but don't tell that to your superiors."

She smiled, her eyes twinkling. "It'll be our secret. I know you understand the Fleet isn't linked to the Tong in any way, at least officially; but I'm sure that at higher levels, there's a certain amount of liaison. If you say that to your contacts on Barjah, they'll tell their bosses how much money they're going to lose if we don't cooperate. If I also mention it to my Fleet superiors, someone, somewhere is bound to connect the dots and take notice."

"All right. We'll try both avenues, and see what happens."

NEXT MORNING, an instructor showed them the shooting ranges and 'fun house', the classrooms, driving course, and other aspects of the training camp. Hui's eyes flickered everywhere, noticing everything, watching in awe as the instructors showed the trainees how a house-clearing problem should be tackled.

At one point she asked their instructor escort, "How many rounds do you people shoot every year, to keep your standards this high?"

"Our goal is five thousand rounds every month, ma'am, through all of our weapons. We don't often achieve it, because it takes a while to shoot that many – shoot them purposefully, I mean, not just spray the landscape – and we have many other demands on our time. Still, we average three thousand rounds a month. Captain Cochrane has told us to get his people up to our level, and that means they'll have to shoot that much themselves."

Cochrane sighed. "I can see I'm going to have to triple or quadruple the ammo budget."

"Yes, sir, you are, but that's what you hired us for."

"Oh, don't worry. I'm not complaining!"

"When are you coming out for your next session, sir?"

"I'm leaving for Mycenae in a few days, but I'll try to free up a week when I get back."

The instructor tut-tutted in disapproval. "You need to spend more time here, sir. Your guards can do a lot, but if you're caught by surprise when they aren't around, you have to be able to defend yourself until they can reach you."

"You're right. I'll do my best."

As they drove back to town, she asked him, "How much training have you already had with them?"

"Only one week so far. I fired about two thousand rounds, and got a lot better with a carbine and a pulser than I had been, but they reckon I've only just begun."

"And you're going to keep that up?"

"The instructor was right. If I'm caught without my guards, or we're pinned down somewhere, I'm going to have to fight too. The better I'm trained, the more likely I am to survive if that happens. I'm going to have all our Headquarters personnel go through at least basic personal defense and firearms training. It's not a normal spacer activity, but we're not exactly normal spacers, are we? We won't reach the level of professionals, or be as good as our security people, but we'll be a lot better than average by the time the instructors finish with us."

"How did you get permission to set up such an elaborate training camp, and get weapons permits for all your security people and yourself?"

He laughed. "Simple. We offered the same training, free of charge, to a select team from Constanta's Presidential Security Corps. They look after cabinet ministers, too. Given that incentive, the Defense Minister couldn't sign the paperwork fast enough!"

She joined him in his apartment that evening for a private supper. He surprised her by preparing a simple but flavorful meal of pasta, sauce and salad, accompanied by a bottle of red wine.

"I didn't know you could cook," she said half-accusingly as she sipped from her glass.

"I'm not very good at it, but I have a few favorite recipes. This is one of them. My mother used to make it."

"It's very tasty. Savory."

"Yes. She liked to use herbs and spices. I used to have her spice set, until my former wife took everything in the divorce. She was First Families, you see, and I wasn't, so the court was bound to rule in her favor." His face grew distant for a moment. "She took great pleasure in telling me she'd donated everything I valued to a local thrift store as soon as I went off-planet. By the time I got back, it had all been sold."

Hui put her hand across his and squeezed gently. "I'm sorry."

"So am I." He heaved a sigh. "Oh, well. That's in the past now. Let's leave it there."

They took their wine glasses out onto the sixth-floor balcony of his two-bedroom apartment, looking out over the city. They did not bother to turn on the light, preferring the darkness of the evening, and the silence, and the intimacy of being close to each other.

He said softly, "Hui... I promised I'd keep my distance, but... I really want to kiss you."

She trembled. "Andrew... I... I do, too."

She put down her glass as she turned to him. He took her gently into his arms, and she leaned into him as she turned up her face. Their lips met in a long, indescribably tender melting moment.

"Andrew... I..."

"Shhh." His hand crept up to gently caress her breast. She shivered, gasping, but did not pull away. Instead, she leaned closer, pressing tightly against him, molding herself to his body.

He drew her gently inside, and closed the balcony door behind them.

SHE WOKE next morning to find him beside her, his body wonderfully, intimately warm against hers. He was already awake, looking at her with smiling, loving eyes. She stretched, luxuriating in the sensation of lying next to him, very aware of his eyes as the sheet fell away to expose her breasts. She laughed deep in her throat as he pulled her to him, and came willingly.

"Should I apologize?" he asked her later, teasingly, as he made coffee in the apartment's small but well-equipped kitchen.

"You should. You shamefully took advantage of me."

"Huh! Seems to me I recall a certain amount of cooperation going on."

"Nonsense! That was all a figment of your imagination."

"So that's what they call this on Qianjin. May I have another figment soon, please?"

She giggled. "Silly! No, Andrew. You don't need to apologize. I've fought this for months, but I think I always knew it was a losing battle. I still don't know how we're going to work this out, but I couldn't hold back any longer. I didn't just want you – I *needed* you."

He leaned over and kissed her gently. "That makes two of us. I needed you very badly."

They spent the morning relaxing in each other's company, oblivious to the world outside. As they cooked lunch together, he said, "I daresay my staff are sending all sorts of worried looks in this direction by now. I sent a message that I wouldn't be in today."

She blushed. "They probably think I've stolen you away."

"In a very real sense, you have, you wicked thing, you."

She laughed, then sobered. "How long do we have? You mentioned you had to leave for Mycenae soon."

"Yes. I want to see for myself how that surveillance satellite constellation is performing, and speak with Dave Cousins about our plans to shift operations to Mycenae Secundus Two orbit, once NOE takes over our depot ship and patrol craft."

"What will you use in their place?"

"Our first proper depot ship will be ready in three months, along with the next two corvettes. We'll send them straight to Mycenae to work up there, rather than do that in the Constanta system. Dave will be in local command, and he'll put them through their paces. Until they're operational, the first corvette and our armed freighter will handle patrols, along with NOE's patrol craft. They'll share our old depot ship until our new one is ready."

"I'm glad the handover seems to be going smoothly. You'll move the surveillance satellites to your new location, won't you?"

"Yes, of course. I'm not leaving a billion-franc present behind for NOE! Would you like to come with me? It would give us a couple more weeks together. If you travel aboard my ship, your communications frigate can stay here and give her crew liberty planetside."

She nodded, almost shyly. "I'd like that very much. I can use the excuse of wanting to see the surveillance satellite. We have a full-system surveillance network, much bigger and more capable than yours – it can reach out four or five light-days from Qianjin – but nothing this small and compact. I think my superiors will be interested to hear a first-hand report of how it helps secure Mycenae."

"It's a deal. We'll leave in two days."

CONFRONTATION

MYCENAE SYSTEM – BROTHERHOOD DESTROYER SKENDERBEG

"Any sign of enemy movement?" the destroyer's captain demanded.

"No, sir," the Plot operator replied. "There's just the patrol craft over near Secundus' asteroid belt, two billion kilometers from their depot ship, and another about three hundred million kilometers beyond the target group, almost on our course, sir."

"We'll take care of that one on our way out of the system," the captain grunted in satisfaction. "Weapons, make sure you reserve ten missiles for her, but don't worry about a firing solution yet. We'll develop one after we've dealt with the main group."

"Aye aye, sir," came from the Weapons console. "What about the one over at Mycenae Secundus?"

"We'll leave her. We want her to be able to tell others what happens when they challenge us."

The captain gazed in satisfaction at the Plot. An enlarged section in one corner showed icons representing the gravitic drive signatures of six ships in the target group. He presumed they were the other two patrol craft he'd been warned to expect, their depot ship, and three others – probably mining vessels, visiting freighters, or couriers. At such extreme range his systems couldn't classify them with any accuracy, or pinpoint their positions except to recognize that they were orbiting Mycenae Primus Four. Every ship would be targeted by ten missiles from each destroyer. They were still blissfully unaware of the death and destruction streaking toward them.

The captain turned to the old man, sitting in a wheelchair beside the Command console. "We're on course, on speed and on time, Patriarch. They're only three billion kilometers ahead. We'll begin braking now, very slowly, at low drive power, to reduce speed before our firing pass."

"Why reduce speed, captain?" came the labored reply. The old man was clearly not in the best of health. "Why not go at them full speed ahead?"

"It's our sensors, Patriarch. They aren't the most up-to-date. At one-quarter of light speed, the distortion is so great that they can't direct our missiles as well as we'd like. If we slow to one-tenth of light speed, they'll be much more accurate."

"I understand. I shall mention this to the Brotherhood Council. We must see about getting you better sensors."

"Thank you, Patriarch." He turned to the Helm console. "Drive to braking mode, power five percent."

Almost imperceptibly, the destroyer began to slow her headlong rush. To one side and a little behind, only ten thousand kilometers away, her sister ship detected her diminutive drive signature, and matched her actions.

～

HCS AMELIA

Cochrane ran into the depot ship's Operations Center still buttoning his shirt, its brand-new epaulettes, bearing the single thick gold stripe of Commodore's rank, bouncing heavily on his shoulders. His fly gaped open, and his feet were thrust into half-fastened shoes. "What is it?"

"The surveillance satellite has just detected two high-speed bogeys, three billion kilometers out, sir, plus-or-minus two percent," the Officer of the Deck replied crisply. "They started up their drives at very low power – or, rather, they started them two-point-seven-eight hours ago, sir. That's the estimated light speed delay between the plotted position and our own. They're headed for us, in close formation."

Cochrane finished adjusting his clothing as he listened, staring into the Plot display at the red warning icons. "How fast are they moving?"

"Initial analysis indicates one-quarter Cee, sir."

His blood ran cold. Those had to be warships at that speed, or perhaps fast freighters. If the latter, they'd surely be armed. They hadn't emerged from a hyper-jump at the system boundary, like normal traffic. Instead, they'd come out far beyond the Mycenae system, then accelerated toward it and cut their drives to avoid detection. They were clearly looking for trouble, or they would have arrived in the usual way. They'd almost certainly just begun decelerating, to make it easier to target Hawkwood's ships as they drew nearer.

Dave Cousins, now wearing the four stripes of Captain's rank on his epaulettes, ran into the OpCen, followed closely by Hui. In a few short phrases, the Officer of the Deck brought them up to speed.

Dave glanced at his boss. "Looks like they want a piece of us, sir. Only warships could be coming in at that sort of speed, and they're not signaling their arrival. If it hadn't been for the surveillance satellite, they'd have taken us unawares."

"Yes. I'm suddenly very glad we spent so much money on it!" A strained chuckle ran around the OpCen. "I agree, they're most likely warships, or perhaps armed fast freighters like *Orca*. The question is, who are they?"

"I don't know, sir, but I don't plan to wait until they get into range to find out. If they continue to come straight for us, without any arrival signal, I request permission to treat them as hostile."

"Permission granted. You're the local commander, Dave. You're in charge. I'll backstop you if you want advice."

Cochrane itched to take control himself, but that was one of the cardinal principles of delegating authority. If you did, it had to *stay* delegated, unless and until the person wielding it proved incapable of handling it. As the old farming metaphor had it, if you kept taking back the reins, a new driver would never learn to control the team.

"Please hang around, sir," Cousins requested. "I'd like to bounce ideas off you. Meanwhile, let me get our people ready."

"Go ahead."

Cousins turned to the Communications console. "Command to Communications. Send to all ships, flash priority, tight-beam transmission only to prevent interception. Unidentified vessels approaching at high speed from outside the system, intentions unknown. All ships are to remain in their present positions relative to each other. Keep drives at current power levels. Do not use active sensors, or make any transmission that might indicate we're aware of our guests. Come to general quarters, and stand by for orders."

"Communications to Command, recorded, aye aye, sir."

Hui came to Cochrane's side. In a low voice, she asked, "Can I do anything to help?"

"Stick around. You can help Dave and I. Three senior heads should be better than two."

"Don't you remember the old saying about too many cooks?"
Dave snorted. "Yes, but we're not cooking."
She laughed.

BROTHERHOOD DESTROYER SKENDERBEG

"Any change?"

"Nothing visible in the Plot, sir," the operator responded, trying to keep irritation out of his voice. Did the captain think he wouldn't speak up if he noticed anything? Why did he keep asking the same question every five minutes?

The old man next to the command console reached up and plucked at the captain's sleeve. As the commanding officer bent down to him, he said softly, "You are nervous, my son, and your constant questions are making your people nervous. Be calm. We are hours away yet. Set them an example of unperturbed leadership. Silence is your friend."

The captain flushed. "I apologize, Patriarch. This is the first time I, or any of us, have led our warships into battle. It is a momentous occasion."

"It is indeed. That is why I am here, too. Come. Let us enjoy a cup of coffee in the wardroom. Send your crew to eat and drink, half at a time, rather than let them sit and stew in their action stations. They will be better for the break."

The captain wanted to protest, but stifled his words. The Patriarch had commanded half a dozen vessels during his younger days, before he conceived of the Fatherland Project and led the breakaway. He knew whereof he spoke.

"I hear and obey, Patriarch."

"Good. Please push this wheelchair for me, my son. My arms grow too weak. Curse the frailty of age!"

"It will be my honor, Patriarch."

HCS AMELIA

Cousins straightened, drew in a deep breath, and nodded to himself. He turned to Cochrane. "Here's what I propose, sir."

He marked courses and movements in the Plot display with colored lines and icons as he spoke. "They're still coming in, but slowing down. They'll be in range in about eight hours. I want to be able to deal with a worst-case scenario, so I'm going to assume they're destroyers, or have equivalent firepower. If we plan to deal with that, we should be able to handle anything less."

"I agree," Cochrane encouraged him.

"I propose to have *Amanita* deploy a decoy in her present position, broadcasting her gravitic drive signature at its present power level. Whoever's out there should assume she's still in orbit. I'll have her creep out toward them at low power, using all her stealth systems. She should be able to reach a good firing position before they get into range of us. She can take them under fire while they're still at extreme range, forcing them to respond to her rather than shoot at the rest of our ships. If they survive her fire, they'll probably scoot past the planet before they can gather their wits, recalculate their firing solution and take us under fire. If any missiles come our way, the patrol craft can deal with them using their defensive weapons. After that, they can go after those ships, if necessary."

Cochrane scratched his chin thoughtfully as he gazed at the Plot. "That's not bad, Dave, but I'd like to suggest a couple of changes, if I may."

"Go ahead, sir. You know more about this than I do."

"If I were the enemy commander, I'd want to engage at less than maximum range, to be as sure as possible of hitting my targets. That's doubly true because he has to aim at six ships, not just one. That's a big test for any fire control system, getting the missiles close enough to their targets to be able to discriminate between them. If he's got modern destroyer missiles, they'll have a maximum powered range of about eight million kilometers; but they'll take several minutes to cover that range, giving us time to activate our defenses and take evasive action. Therefore, I'd say he's likely to close in to half, or even a quarter of that range before he fires, particularly if he figures we don't know he's coming. What do you think?"

Cousins sucked in his breath. "We'd be taking a big chance to rely on that, sir. What if he fires at longer range?"

"We'll have to face his weapons, no matter what. If they're destroyers, those two ships will be carrying more missiles between them than our corvette and three old patrol craft. We can't match their throw weight, so we've got to outsmart them. I think his crews will be so busy perfecting their firing solution, and getting so close that we can't properly defend ourselves, that they'll be oblivious to anything else. If *Amanita* lets them get close enough to develop target fixation, she may catch them completely unawares. They'll take precious seconds to break their focus on us, realize what's going on, and defend themselves against her missiles – much less fire back at her. It'll throw them into confusion."

"I see, sir." Dave's voice was doubtful. "I still think it's taking a hell of a chance, though."

"Let's come back to that in a moment. The other suggestion is, why not use the patrol craft main battery missiles for defense, as well as their defensive missiles? They only have fifteen of each. Given the age and unreliability of their old weapons, let's use them all for the most important task; stopping those incoming missiles."

"And what if those ships survive *Amanita*'s fire, sir? What if they turn around and come back? If all our warships have emptied their pods, we'll have no defense left against them except the pod aboard this ship, and we don't have a modern fire control system."

"No, we don't. I'd advise reserving this ship's missile pod for use in emergency. If they go past us, it'll take them up to an hour to brake to zero velocity relative to the planet, then accelerate back toward us. During that time, all our undamaged ships can leave orbit, head out at full blast in the opposite direction, get up to maximum speed, then kill their drives and change trajectories using their reaction thrusters. Since they'll no longer be emitting any radiation for passive sensors to find, the enemy will have to look for them using active sensors – radar and lidar. Those have a maximum effective range of less than a million kilometers.

"If we scatter far enough, fast enough, they'll have a hell of a time finding any of us. The patrol craft should be able to escape into the outer reaches of the system. The hyper-jump-capable ships can head for the system boundary, to get away and call for reinforcements. I don't think the enemy will waste much time looking for us. They'll want to make their getaway before anyone else arrives."

There was a long silence as they stared into the Plot. Finally, Hui said quietly, "May I offer a suggestion?"

"Of course, ma'am," Dave assured her.

"You've laid an excellent foundation, and Commodore Cochrane has built on it. I propose..."

HCS AMANITA

Lieutenant-Commander Darroch adjusted his chair at the corvette's command console, and ran his eyes over the screens and readouts one last time. *Amanita* was in position, and the time had come.

"Command to Weapons. Commence launch procedure, as

slowly and stealthily as possible. Remember, those bastards will be listening for so much as a single peep out of a mass driver. Ease those missiles out like you were walking on eggshells!"

Amid chuckles from the rest of the OpCen team, the Weapons Officer said, "Weapons to Command, understood, sir. Here we go."

He pressed a key on his console, initiating a program that had been crafted with enormous care as *Amanita* crept out to her firing position. With almost dream-like slowness, the first two missiles slid very gently out of their firing tubes. As they tilted over toward the oncoming enemy, two more followed them, then two more, and more, and more. The missiles moved with seemingly glacial slowness as their gravitic drives kicked in at minimum power.

Forty-nine of *Amanita*'s main battery missiles crawled toward their final rendezvous. One remained in its tube, the victim of a mass driver malfunction that prevented it from being ejected. It was instantly flagged by the fire control system as unavailable, and its internal reactor was powered down. Maintenance crews would have to deal with it at some future date.

The Weapons Officer reported, "Weapons to Command. Missiles under way, sir."

"Command to Weapons, thank you. Break. Command to Electronic Warfare. Any trace of emissions from the missiles' gravitic drives?"

"EW to Command. I'm picking up minimal feedback, sir, but we're right on top of them. It's already fading as they move further away. I don't think the enemy will have noticed them, sir."

"Command to EW, good. Break. Command to Helm. Turn onto previously advised course, drive to three percent power. Let's get into position to defend the other ships as best we can."

"Helm to Command, turning onto course, drive three percent, aye aye, sir."

Slowly, silently, *Amanita* crept back toward Mycenae Primus

Four, staying a couple of hundred thousand kilometers below the enemy's predicted trajectory. As she moved, her Weapons Officer prepared her fifty defensive missiles for action.

BROTHERHOOD DESTROYER SKENDERBEG

The tension in the destroyer's OpCen ratcheted up hour by hour as they drew closer to their targets. All the training in the galaxy could not alter the fact that this was the first time any of those aboard had seen combat in space. It was very different to creeping around an asteroid belt, dropping off clandestine prospector bots or recovering their harvest. Asteroids couldn't shoot back.

The captain opened his mouth to ask, yet again, whether anything had changed, but restrained himself. Beside him, the Patriarch nodded approvingly, but said nothing.

Suddenly, out of nowhere, white traces erupted in the Plot display – *and they were only one million kilometers ahead!* The operator stared, shocked rigid, then almost screamed, "*Missiles!* Many missiles! They're at point-blank range on a closing course! Time to intercept estimated five zero seconds!"

Instantly, the captain realized what must have happened. Their enemies had somehow detected their arrival, and laid an ambush for them. His mind racing, he snapped, "*Attention!* Weapons, set defensive system to automatic fire! Begin launching main battery missiles according to previous fire plan! Let's get as many of them away as possible before the enemy's weapons reach us!"

The Weapons Officer stammered, "B – but, sir, shouldn't we fire at the attacker's position?"

"*No!* Fire at our pre-programmed targets!" As the Weapons Officer bent to his console, pressing keys, turning dials and flicking switches, the captain added, "Those missiles weren't launched a few at a time from a ship – their drives all kicked in together. That means they were already in space, waiting for us. The ship that launched them won't be there anymore."

"Understood, sir. Firing!"

Within seconds, main battery missiles began to vomit from the destroyer's five missile pods. Their older technology could only eject one missile from each pod every two seconds, but their numbers grew as the seconds passed. Meanwhile, the defensive system assessed the incoming missiles, allocated counter-missiles to each one, and tried to fire – only to find itself blocked. The Weapons Officer had instinctively given top launch priority to the main battery missiles. Until they had all been fired, no defensive missiles could be used.

Recognizing the problem, the captain shouted orders. Flustered, the Weapons Officer canceled his first order to the launch system, and entered another – but now only the defensive missiles could fire. The main battery weapons were blocked. It took him ten more precious seconds to untangle the mess, and begin to launch alternately, first a main battery weapon, then a defensive missile. All the while, the incoming missiles tore closer at the maximum acceleration their modern, powerful gravitic drives could provide.

The first defensive missiles slashed at the incoming weapons, destroying several of them; but they were too few to get all of them. Of the twenty-five missiles aimed at the first destroyer, sixteen survived. They screamed into range, rolled to line up their bomb-pumped laser warheads at the ship, and exploded in thermonuclear fireballs. The nuclear energy devoured the warheads' tightly-focused cones of laser rods. In the instant of its destruction, each rod emitted a powerful beam that streaked across the ten to twelve thousand kilometers separating the warhead from its target. More than half hit the ship, smashing through hull plating and frames, cutting through internal compartments, equipment, and the bodies of the crew as if they did not exist.

The destroyer shuddered under their blows. Within seconds, two of her fusion reactors went into emergency shutdown. The third reactor was not so fortunate. A laser pierced its compartment, scoring a direct hit on the magnetic field generator that kept its reaction within bounds. The dying reactor instantly vented its fusion-fueled fury upon the ship that carried it. With a blinding thermonuclear flash, the destroyer was reduced to its component atoms. Everyone aboard died instantaneously.

The second destroyer was further away, and did not suffer the problems caused by her compatriot's hapless Weapons Officer. However, she was much slower to react. Her defensive missiles took out fourteen of the incoming weapons. Ten survived, sending their laser beams slashing into her. Holes speared through her from side to side and bow to stern, destroying the divisions between her airtight compartments, venting her entire internal atmosphere to vacuum. None of her crew were wearing spacesuits. They died at their stations as her reactors and gravitic drive shut down.

Her captain's last desperate act, as he gasped for air that was no longer there, was to hit the 'Abandon Ship' button on his command console. It not only broadcast that message to all compartments – inaudibly, now, because there was no longer any atmosphere to carry the sound – but it also automatically activated the ship's emergency beacon. Powered by a capacitor, it did not rely on the now-defunct reactors. The destroyer's lifeless hulk sped onward at one-tenth of light speed, its passage marked by the doleful wailing of the beacon, summoning aid that could no longer avail the corpses of her crew.

~

HCS AMANITA

The corvette had no time to celebrate the destruction caused by the missiles she had so carefully laid in ambush. In fact, her OpCen crew did not even notice their triumph at first. They were too busy targeting the main battery missiles launched at the ships in orbit around Mycenae Primus Four.

At the first sign of enemy reaction, Lieutenant-Commander Darroch snapped, "Command to Weapons. *Weapons free!* Hit them!"

The Weapons Officer did not bother to reply. The frigate's fire control system was already analyzing the flight of the enemy missiles. Her radar and lidar emitters sprang to life, providing more accurate targeting information. As the first enemy missiles streaked overhead, accelerating toward her compatriots, her defensive missiles rose to meet them.

Of the forty-seven main battery missiles that the two destroyers managed to fire before they were silenced, twenty-nine were blown out of space by *Amanita's* counter-fire. Only eighteen survived, to speed toward the five ships still in orbit around Mycenae Primus Four.

The corvette could do nothing more to help. She could only hang in space, all her missiles expended. Her crew waited on tenterhooks to see what would happen. It was up to the patrol craft now.

FROM OUT OF the welter of thermonuclear explosions, missile traces arrowed toward the Hawkwood ships. The patrol craft did not bother to get under way to meet them. There was no time for that. Instead, they launched everything they had from their orbital positions; main battery missiles first, then defensive units. Seventeen of their aged, less reliable weapons malfunctioned.

The remaining seventy-three missiles, all the weapons they had except for their laser cannon, streamed out toward their targets in a ragged volley.

The longer-ranged main battery missiles reached the incoming weapons first. Bomb-pumped lasers fired, but their cones had been designed to spread across the length and breadth of a spaceship. The gaps between their laser beams were too wide to be fully effective against the much smaller missiles. Despite this handicap, six of the incoming weapons exploded under their impact. The remaining twelve missiles bored in.

The defensive missiles reached them while they were still half a million kilometers from their targets. The interceptors carried thermonuclear blast warheads rather than lasers, designed to both kill nearby weapons and overload the sensors of those further from the explosion, so they could not home on their targets, or know when they had reached the most effective range to fire their laser cones. In a series of rolling fireballs, more of the incoming weapons were destroyed or blinded.

The survivors streaked through the blast front. Two, their electronic brains scrambled, zoomed aimlessly past the ships to smash into the airless, desolate planet beyond them, diving into its surface at almost a quarter of the speed of light, digging deep craters, raising towering clouds of pulverized rock and dirt and dust. Two more swerved from side to side as their ruined sensors searched in vain for a target, then blew themselves up as their self-destruct mechanisms were automatically activated.

The last three incoming weapons closed in on their targets.

One missile selected HCS *Amelia*. Its bomb-pumped laser beams ripped into one of the depot ship's forward holds, damaging and destroying many of the supplies stored there for use by the patrol craft; but there were no spacers in the compartment to be injured or killed, and no critical systems to be put out of action. The ship rocked under the impact, alarms clanging their cacophonous summons to the damage control team, but she was otherwise unharmed.

Another missile selected HCS *Trairao* as its prey. It zoomed in closer, but the patrol craft's laser cannon were firing as fast as they could cycle. In the split-second before the missile triggered its warhead, a laser beam shattered its nosecone and penetrated right down its body. The shattered fragments of the missile erupted in all directions as they sped past, to collide with the planet like a giant pattern from a shotgun, raising plumes and spurts of dust and dirt over a wide area.

The last missile was just too fast for the defensive cannon fire. It slipped past all the beams tearing through space around it, rolled to align its bomb-pumped laser cone on its target, and exploded at a range of just nine thousand kilometers.

HCS *Piranha,* the most recently arrived patrol craft, still working up to full operational readiness, turned into a glowing, expanding cloud of radioactive particles as her fusion reactor let go under the impact of a laser beam. All thirty-one of her crew died with her.

HCS AMELIA

There was an agonized, collective groan in the depot ship's OpCen as they watched *Piranha*'s icon in the Plot display flare into the starburst signature of a nuclear explosion, then slowly shrink. Dead silence fell as they watched it fade away.

At last Cousins cleared his throat. There were tears in his eyes. Lieutenant-Commander Moffatt, until recently his Executive Officer aboard HCS *Amelia,* had been on board *Piranha,* supervising her working-up period prior to taking command of the entire patrol craft division.

"May... may God have mercy on *Piranha*'s crew. The rest of

us... well, we're still alive. Now we've got to clean up. Communications, signal to *Amanita*. Tell her 'Well done' from all of us. She's to go after the second enemy ship. It appears to have no power, so the only way to track it is by its emergency beacon. She is to board, arrest any survivors, then use her tractor beam to tow the hulk back here."

"Communications to Command, recorded, transmitting now, aye aye, sir."

He looked at Cochrane and Hui. "Thank you both very much," he said simply. "I couldn't have figured out as good a plan on my own."

"Neither could I," Cochrane admitted. "It took all three of us." He glanced at Hui. "Your suggestion for a stealthy missile launch, putting them in position to ambush the enemy, was the deciding factor. They might have spotted *Amanita* at that range, but the missiles on their own were too small a target. They were caught completely off guard."

"Not completely," she said sadly. "They were still good enough to get some of their weapons away. They hurt us, and killed *Piranha*."

"Yes, but they might have killed a lot more of us. Let's give thanks that they didn't!"

"What now, sir?" Cousins asked.

"I want to examine that hulk. Let's find out who they were, and what their ships were, and where they came from. We can learn a lot from the wreck. When we've finished with it, we'll drop it into Mycenae Primus or Secundus, to be fuel for the star."

"Please, wait until I can report back before you do!" Hui asked urgently. "I'm sure my superiors will want to send their own investigators to look at it."

"All right," Cochrane agreed, "but we'll have to tow it to another planet in the system, so NOE doesn't see it when their spacers arrive to take over. If it doesn't emit any electromagnetic or gravitic signature, they won't notice it. We'll keep it out of sight in a parking orbit until your people get here. It'll probably be best for them to travel aboard one of our ships, to avoid complications."

"I think I can arrange that."

"Very well." Cochrane rose to his feet, forcing down a wave of sorrow for his dead people. "We've got a lot to do, including sending *Amanita* and two patrol craft back to Constanta to load fresh missile pods. The sooner we get a real depot ship out here to handle that, the better!

"Oh, yes. Another thing, Dave. Don't mention this fight to *anybody*, particularly not to NOE when they arrive to take over. Pass the word to all our people to treat it as top secret. I presume those ships were sent by the Albanians – at least, I don't know any other enemy that might have that ability. If they can't find out what happened, it might make them think twice before trying again, at least for a while."

GIRDING LOINS

PATOS

"We simply do not know, brothers." Agim's voice was hoarse with sorrow. "We are doing all in our power to find out, but we dare not send another ship into that system until we know what happened to our destroyers. In the absence of that information, the Patriarch's fate is unknown. However, I fear he must be dead. It has been two full months since the attack was scheduled to go in. He would surely have contacted us by now, if that was possible, but we have heard nothing."

"Then that means our ships must have died with him," Perparim said softly.

"I fear so."

"That can only have been through enemy action."

"That is not the only possibility. What if they collided while on their approach to the system, or ran into some obstacle in space – an asteroid, or wreckage, or other debris? At space travel velocities, that would destroy them as surely and completely as a missile strike. I admit, it is unlikely, but what is the likelihood that four outdated patrol craft, mounting in total fewer and shorter-range missiles than even *one* of our destroyers, could destroy both of our ships? I should have said any of those outcomes was so unrealistic as to be impossible – but here we are."

"There has been no word in the news media of the planets concerned?" Skender asked.

"Not a word. The New Orkney Enterprise trumpeted its entry into the Mycenae system, and taking over local security from Eufala, but nothing was said about any recent combat. Eufala handed over four patrol craft and a depot ship, the same number of vessels they had before. NOE will now patrol its own operations, while Eufala will cover the rest of the system."

"What will Eufala use for ships, if NOE has their patrol craft?" another asked.

"We do not know. The press release spoke of new vessels, but gave no details."

"Could some of those new vessels be more capable? Did they, perhaps, fight our destroyers?"

"Again, we do not know. I fail to see how any spaceship's sensors could detect incoming vessels that were first coasting, then braking under minimum drive power. Only a system surveillance satellite could do that at any meaningful distance. There is no record that Eufala or NOE has deployed anything of the kind, and we saw no sign of it during earlier visits. They are so expensive that I have to think it doubtful they could afford one."

"So, what are we going to do?" Skender demanded. "Sit back and let them have the initiative?"

Agim met his glare full-on. "For the moment, they *do* have the initiative, in the Mycenae system at least. However, we shall not be idle. To do that would be to dishonor our Patriarch. If Eufala has killed him, we shall avenge him. Bear in mind, too, that if they learn we are behind many of their troubles in the Mycenae system, it is likely they will seek revenge on us, or at least try to dissuade us from interfering with them again. We shall need to defend ourselves, as well as attack them."

He ticked off points on his fingers as he continued, "We dare not risk our remaining two destroyers until we know what befell their compatriots. We shall send more spies to Constanta, to see what ships show up there. If Eufala or Hawkwood obtain new vessels, they will surely visit that system in due course. We shall also see about attacking their leaders there, although they are bound to be on their guard against such attempts.

"We shall ensure that the Callanish consortium learns of Eufala's involvement in the loss of their three vessels. If they seek revenge – which we shall discreetly encourage – we shall watch their efforts, see what Eufala does to protect themselves, and learn from that. We may even be able to use their efforts to disguise or mask our own attacks, so that they will be blamed for everything.

"Finally, it is likely that Eufala has, or soon will have, ships that are at least as capable as our own. We spent years refurbishing those old destroyers, and a few smaller craft, but they may no longer be adequate. I propose that we use as much as necessary of the funds accumulated for the Fatherhood Project, to buy modern warships."

There was an instant uproar of protest. Voices clashed and climbed over each other as the delegates tried to make themselves heard. Agim waited a few moments, then raised his own voice in a bellow. "*SILENCE, brothers!* Let me finish!"

He waited for the hubbub to subside. "I know many of you think we should reserve the Project's funds solely for its ultimate purpose. However, let me remind you that spending on our own defense is part and parcel of the Project. If we are threatened, so is the Project. If we are defeated, the Project will go down into the dust of history alongside us. Therefore, to spend money for our own defense *is* to spend it on the Project. The two are indivisible."

Slowly, reluctantly, heads began to nod. One man raised a

hand. "Where shall we obtain such ships, Agim? We have not been able to in the past."

"You are right, Dardan, but that is because we put security above all other concerns. If we had made a major effort to obtain warships, violating interplanetary laws and regulations by doing so, we would have risked exposing ourselves. The Patriarch advised, and we all agreed, that the risk was too great. Now, I submit, the situation has changed. We risk more by not being well armed than we do by arming ourselves."

Dardan scowled. "I agree, but where shall we look for them? How long will it take to get them? We cannot afford to delay, if Eufala offers that much of a threat."

"That is true. Warships will be very hard to obtain, but we shall seek them. As an interim measure, let us buy fast freighters and equip them with modern weapons. You all know of the struggle of the Laredo Resistance, and how, with an ally's help, they converted old fleet assault transports into very powerful armed merchant cruisers."

There was a general murmur of understanding. The Laredo War had captured popular imagination throughout the galaxy, as its Resistance successfully fought back against the Bactrian invaders of their planet.

"We can follow their example while we look for warships. Modern weapons and fire control systems are strictly controlled, and hard to buy clandestinely, but they are much cheaper than warships, and we have gold enough to pay a premium for them. There are always those who will be greedy enough to put profit over principle."

All around the table, heads nodded grimly.

"All those in favor, brothers?"

The vote was unanimous.

∿

GOHEUNG

Kang Industries wanted to set up a major news conference in their auditorium to cover the delivery of four brand-new vessels to Hawkwood Corporation. Cochrane had to insist very firmly on the need for confidentiality before Mr. Kim reluctantly agreed to cancel the publicity arrangements.

A select group gathered in Kang's boardroom. Cochrane himself was there, of course, along with Hui, who had arrived at Goheung from Qianjin that very morning. The newly-promoted Commander Darroch glowed with pride, still unaccustomed to the three stripes on his jacket sleeves, a promotion awarded in recognition of his success at what they were already calling, among themselves, the Battle of Mycenae. Commander Frank Haldane had brought the passage crews for the new ships aboard *Orca*. One of his core team, the also newly-promoted Commander Theo Bale, stood alongside him. Three newly minted Lieutenant-Commanders completed the Hawkwood delegation. Mr. Kim represented Kang Industries, flanked by the leaders of the design teams that had modified the ships to Hawkwood's requirements, plus the lead engineers of the building ways that had constructed them.

After several remarks complimenting Hawkwood and Cochrane on their wisdom in choosing Kang Industries to build their ships, more on the quality of the vessels, and a few congratulations to those who had built them, Kim formally handed over the builder's certificates for each ship. Cochrane accepted them on behalf of Hawkwood, and made several congratulatory remarks of his own, referring to the many vessels still to come off Kang's ways for his company. Those listening applauded politely at the right moments.

The handover complete, Kim excused himself and his delegation, leaving the highlight of the day to Cochrane. He turned to the assembled officers.

"Lieutenant-Commander Aiton, you are appointed in command of the corvette HCS *Banewort*. Lieutenant-Commander Maclean, you are appointed in command of the corvette HCS *Belladonna*. Lieutenant-Commander Mahaddie, you are appointed in command of the communications vessel HCS *Agni*. Commander Bale, you are appointed in command of the depot ship HCS *Anson*. Finally, Commander Darroch, in addition to your present command of HCS *Amanita*, you are appointed as Officer in Command of Hawkwood Corporation's First Corvette Division, comprising all three ships of that class currently on our books. I congratulate all of you, and wish you the very best of success in your future endeavors."

Everyone shared congratulations and handshakes. Frank broke out a magnum of champagne he'd smuggled past Kang's security guards, popped the cork, and poured it into disposable cups. They ignored the less-than-formal drinking vessels as they toasted the new commanding officers.

Hui moved to Cochrane's side as the others chatted among themselves. She pressed her arm lightly against his before assuming a more suitably formal distance. "Where did you get the names for the communications and depot ships?"

"We're naming communications vessels for ancient mythological messenger gods, or messengers of the gods. Our depot ships will be named for famous admirals. All the names come from the history of Earth, of course."

"What about the patrol craft hulk you were converting for point defense? I thought she was going to be delivered today, too?"

"She is. She'll be loaded aboard *Orca*, for delivery to *Humpback* in Constanta. Grigorescu's shipyard will adapt one of her holds to accommodate her. Frank brought the other two hulks with him, to be converted in their turn."

"What will you call her?"

"We won't name her. After all, the three of them won't operate as independent warships, but as local tenders to large freighters like *Humpback*."

"I can understand that. You're only going to have three of them?"

"At present, that's the plan; but our encounter in Mycenae started me thinking. Our point defense was stretched to the limit. If we hadn't had three patrol craft on hand, things might've gone much worse for us. It'd be good if we could strengthen the point defense capability of all our cargo vessels and depot ships, not just the very large freighters.

"If you think about it, a cargo shuttle can carry up to ten thousand tons. That's more than the mass of those old patrol craft. I'm wondering whether cargo shuttles might be converted to carry defensive missiles, too. They don't have very powerful reactors, of course, and they have no fire control systems at all. They'd have to be simple missile trucks, with all the guidance and control provided by their parent ship; and they'd need auxiliary reactors to fire up the missiles, and provide power to mass drivers to launch them. Dave Cousins and I are knocking the idea around. If we can figure out something, we'll build a prototype and see if we can make it work."

"You two never stop thinking! What are you going to come up with next?"

"I don't know, but it'll be interesting to find out."

"I'll say!" She sobered. "My recommendation, that you be kept in the loop for everything we learn about the Albanians, has been approved. I've been officially relieved of my former responsibilities, and appointed as our Fleet's liaison officer to Hawkwood Corporation. Do you think you can stand to have me around that much?"

He beamed with pleasure. "Just try me! As a matter of fact, I have several exciting liaison positions in mind."

She blushed. "Oh, *you!* I'll brief you on recent developments when we're in private. Also, you're going to get a visit soon from the boss or the second-in-command of our corvette squadron, and maybe a couple of its commanding officers too. They want to learn more about *Amanita's* performance in combat at Mycenae."

"They'll be welcome. Will they come to Constanta, or Mycenae?"

"Where will *Amanita* be? They want to talk to Commander Darroch, of course, since he commanded her during the fight."

"He'll be in Mycenae, helping the two new corvettes work up, as well as the depot ship. Along with *Orca*, they'll patrol the system until the next two corvettes are ready. *Vulcan* will shuttle back and forth to look after any maintenance requirements, and the monthly resupply freighter will exchange part of their crews on every visit, bringing them back to Constanta for rest and recreation. Once we have more ships out there, we'll start cycling corvettes through Constanta for crew rest and routine maintenance."

"All right." Her face turned pensive. "I wonder what the Albanians are up to?"

"I'm willing to bet it won't be anything to make us happy. I expect more shenanigans at Constanta, and I'm sure they're doing everything they can to find out what happened to their ships. Our people have all been warned not to talk, but sooner or later something's bound to leak. What did your experts find out about that destroyer hulk?"

"She was one of seven sold as scrap by Anshun, about a decade ago. Anshun swears the scrap dealer cut through their spines, in front of witnesses from its Fleet, before they were taken away on a ferry. Our experts looked closely at the hulk. They say they can see where she was welded together again, with reinforcing material added. It looks like the Albanians diverted them from the scrapheap, and modernized them. The hulk was equipped with electronic systems that were two or three generations old, sourced from several planets. She carried ninety main battery missiles, eighteen in each of five pods, and the same number of defensive weapons. The missiles were bought from several sources, and the pods modified so they could fit into the cells. She was a real mish-mash."

"She may have been, but if we hadn't had *Amanita* there, she and her sister ship would have run right over us. I wonder how many more destroyers they renovated?"

"Anshun told us that a couple of the destroyers were beyond repair. They'd been in service for over fifty years, and then rotted in their Reserve Fleet for thirty years or more. Our experts think the Albanians might have gotten four or five working, but no more than that."

"Well, they'll be looking for something better now, that's for sure."

"Yes. I'm glad you've got something better coming, in the medium term, to deal with that."

"So am I. I just hope we can get the frigates into service in time to deal with whatever the Albanians throw at us next."

"You've done pretty well so far."

"And with your help, we'll go on doing well. I think you and I will make a great team, in more ways than one."

"I'd drink to that, but..." She glanced mournfully into her cup. "It's empty."

"We can fix that. The champagne's over there."

"Is there still some left?"

"There'd better be. If there isn't, I'll send Frank to smuggle another bottle past security, on pain of immediate demotion if he fails!"

Laughing, they turned to join the others.

EXCERPT FROM "AN AIRLESS STORM"

Here's the opening of Book 2 of the "Cochrane's Company" trilogy.
"An Airless Storm" will be published in June 2018.

T he prisoner was trembling as the jailers unlocked his cell door, cuffed his hands behind his back, and led him out into the corridor. The escort commander, a stone-faced major, inspected him from head to foot, and grimaced in distaste. The fear-stench added a sour, bitter overtone to the already rank odor of the man's grimy clothes and unwashed body. *Then again, why bother letting inmates here wash?* he thought to himself. *None of those in this corridor will stink much longer.*

He led the prisoner and his guards down the passage to a heavy double door. It opened onto an enclosed courtyard, its green grass contrasting with the dark, damp stone of the crenellated walls around it. Several observers looked down in silence from atop them, dressed warmly against the damp chill. They watched as the major signed a form, accepting custody of the prisoner. The guards went back inside, and the doors closed behind them.

The waiting escort snapped to attention at the command of their sergeant. He marched them behind the officer as he escorted the stumbling, shivering prisoner down the graveled path, then turned ninety degrees towards the rear wall. He led the prisoner towards a thick head-high wooden stake planted firmly in the ground, two meters before the wall. Behind it, a thick pile of sandbags had been erected against the stone. A few pockmarks in the wall at its edges showed where it had sometimes failed to provide an adequate backstop against poor marksmanship.

The sergeant halted the escort, formed them into a single line and dressed the rank, while a corporal went forward to assist the officer. The two of them briskly, impersonally turned the man to face the line of soldiers. The corporal went down on one knee and tied his feet together, then tethered them to the base of the stake. The officer waited until the prisoner's feet had been secured, then took from his inside jacket pocket a formal decree. He unfolded it and read it aloud.

"For the crime of selling advanced military weapons to unknown enemies of the state, in dereliction of his duty and responsibilities, and to the grave detriment of the security of Keda and its star system, Lieutenant-Commander Wira bin Osman is hereby sentenced to death by firing squad. The sentence is to be carried out within one week from this date."

He folded the document and returned it to his pocket. "Do you have any last words, prisoner?"

"I – you can't do this! I have the right to appeal the sentence of a military court-martial to the Supreme Court of Keda! My – my lawyer is –"

"Your lawyer has already filed your appeal, prisoner. By edict of the President of the Supreme Court, it has been rejected without a hearing. The sentence of your court-martial stands."

"B-but... I..." Tears came to the prisoner's eyes, and his knees wobbled, as if he were about to fall.

"*Control yourself, damn you!*" Revulsion curled the major's lip. "Your execution will be televised. At least try to die like a man, even if you could not live like one!"

"I..." The condemned man seemed to find a last reserve of courage. He drew himself up. "Major, I... I am being murdered to cover up the crimes of my superior officers." His voice was hopeless. "Who will bring *them* to justice?"

The officer did not answer. He nodded to his corporal, who produced a length of black cloth and briskly, impersonally, tied it over the prisoner's eyes; then he pulled a small white card from his pocket, and pinned it to the convict's shirt over his heart. Snapping to attention, the two soldiers turned their backs on the doomed man and marched back to the firing squad. The major took up his position at one side, while the corporal retrieved his rifle and joined the line.

The sergeant bellowed, "Ready!" The eight-man squad snapped to attention.

"Load!" There was a rattle of metal on metal as beads were chambered.

"Aim!" The firing party took a half-step back with their right legs and lined their weapons at the prisoner. The trembling man against the post tried to stand straighter, as if that would somehow control his shivering. It did not.

"*Fire!*"

The shots crashed out as one. The electromagnetic mechanism of the rifles in the soldiers' hands accelerated their projectiles to hypersonic velocity as they left the muzzles. The impact of the rounds raised puffs of dust from the card and the prisoner's grimy white shirt beneath it, before both were stained with red as blood gushed out. The man slammed back against the post, crying out once, short and sharp; then he toppled slowly, stiffly, to his left. The card came loose as he fell, fluttering downward through the air. He bounced once on the grass, rolled halfway onto his back, and lay still.

The major marched briskly forward from his position at the side of the firing squad, unbuckling the flap of his holster and drawing his pulser. He stood over the prone figure, aimed down at the black band around its eyes, and fired once – then skipped back with an exclamation of disgust as a few drops of blood splattered on his gleaming, immaculately polished boots. The sergeant bellowed a command that sent the corporal scurrying forward, pulling out his handkerchief to wipe the footwear clean.

The firing squad formed up in two ranks, and the sergeant marched them down the path towards the portal. The major returned his pulser to its holster, then followed his men, walking briskly. Others, menials, would clean up the mess. He had more important duties to attend to.

Of course you died to protect your superiors, he thought disdainfully as he closed the door behind him and turned down the corridor towards his office. *What else did you expect? You didn't seriously think they were going to take the blame, did you? In your shoes, I'd have been sorrier for my wife and children than I was for myself. Their punishment is only just beginning!*

ABOUT THE AUTHOR

Peter Grant was born and raised in Cape Town, South Africa. Between military service, the IT industry and humanitarian involvement, he traveled throughout sub-Saharan Africa before being ordained as a pastor. He later immigrated to the USA, where he worked as a pastor and prison chaplain until an injury forced his retirement. He is now a full-time writer, and married to a pilot from Alaska. They currently live in Texas.

See all of Peter's books at <u>his Amazon.com author page</u>, or visit him at his blog, <u>Bayou Renaissance Man</u>. There, you can also sign up for his mailing list, to receive a monthly newsletter and be kept informed of upcoming books.

BOOKS BY PETER GRANT

MILITARY SCIENCE FICTION:

The Maxwell Saga:

Take the Star Road

Ride the Rising Tide

Adapt and Overcome

Stand Against the Storm

Stoke the Flames Higher

Cochrane's Company:

The Stones of Silence

An Airless Storm

The Pride of the Damned (coming July 2018)

The Laredo War:

War to the Knife

Forge a New Blade

Knife to the Hilt (coming soon)

FANTASY:

King's Champion

WESTERN:

The Ames Archives:

Brings The Lightning

Rocky Mountain Retribution

Gold on the Hoof (coming soon)

MEMOIR:

Walls, Wire, Bars and Souls

Made in the USA
Middletown, DE
09 August 2022

70930844R00201